PRAISE FOR RACHEL HARTMAN

Seraphina

A *New York Times* bestseller

Winner of the William C. Morris Debut Award

Eight starred reviews

"Beautifully written, well-rounded characters, and **some of the most interesting dragons I've read in fantasy** for a long while."
—Christopher Paolini, *New York Times* bestselling author

"A book worth hoarding, as glittering and silver-bright as dragon scales."
—Naomi Novik, *New York Times* bestselling author

"Seraphina is strong, complex, talented. . . . **I love this book!**"
—Tamora Pierce, *New York Times* bestselling author

"Full of grace and gravitas."
—*The Washington Post*

Shadow Scale

Three starred reviews

★ "Blazing. Clever surprises, and lovely prose."
—*Booklist*, starred review

★ "Enough history and detail to satisfy even the most questioning of readers, doing it all so naturally that **it's hard to believe this is fiction**."
—*Kirkus Reviews*, starred review

Tess of the Road

An NPR • *Boston Globe* • Chicago Public Library • *Kirkus Reviews* Best Book of the Year

Four starred reviews

"*Tess of the Road* is **astonishing and perfect**.
It's the most compassionate book
I've read since George Eliot's *Middlemarch*."
—NPR

★ "Not to be ignored. Absolutely essential."
—*Booklist*, starred review

"The world building is gorgeous, the creatures are vivid
and **Hartman is a masterful storyteller**.
Pick up this novel, and savor every page."
—*Paste*

In the Serpent's Wake

A *New York Times* Best Science Fiction
and Fantasy Book of the Year

"**Instantly immersive and deeply affecting**. . . . Complex,
compassionate and challenging as all Hartman's novels are."
—*The New York Times*

★ "Hartman deftly reflects our own world's worries
in this adventurous fantasy, but always with
an eye toward hope and healing."
—*Booklist*, starred review

"**Conceptually rich, serious, emotionally complex**; a worthy
addition to Hartman's already considerable achievement."
—*The Horn Book*

AMONG GHOSTS

Also by Rachel Hartman

Seraphina

Shadow Scale

Tess of the Road

In the Serpent's Wake

Among Ghosts

Rachel Hartman

Random House 🏠 New York

In memoriam: Casey Davis and A. J. Birtwistle.
The world is better for having had you in it.

Random House Books for Young Readers
An imprint of Random House Children's Books
A division of Penguin Random House LLC
1745 Broadway, New York, NY 10019
penguinrandomhouse.com
GetUnderlined.com

Text copyright © 2025 by Rachel Hartman
Jacket art copyright © 2025 by Eliot Baum

Penguin Random House values and supports copyright. Copyright fuels creativity, encourages diverse voices, promotes free speech, and creates a vibrant culture. Thank you for buying an authorized edition of this book and for complying with copyright laws by not reproducing, scanning, or distributing any part of it in any form without permission. You are supporting writers and allowing Penguin Random House to continue to publish books for every reader. Please note that no part of this book may be used or reproduced in any manner for the purpose of training artificial intelligence technologies or systems.

Random House and the colophon are registered trademarks of Penguin Random House LLC.

Editors: Emily Shapiro, Mallory Loehr, and Lynne Missen
Cover Designer: Sylvia Bi
Interior Designer: Ken Crossland
Production Editor: Clare Perret
Managing Editor: Rebecca Vitkus
Production Manager: Tim Terhune

Library of Congress Cataloging-in-Publication Data is available upon request.
ISBN 978-0-593-81372-0 (trade)—ISBN 978-0-593-81375-1 (lib. bdg.)—
ISBN 978-0-593-81374-4 (ebook)

The text of this book is set in 11-point Adobe Caslon.

Manufactured in the United States of America
10 9 8 7 6 5 4 3 2 1

The authorized representative in the EU for product safety and compliance is Penguin Random House Ireland, Morrison Chambers, 32 Nassau Street, Dublin D02 YH68, Ireland, https://eu-contact.penguin.ie.

Random House Children's Books supports the First Amendment
and celebrates the right to read.

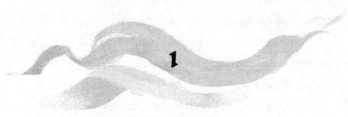

1

The Old Abbey

orth of St. Muckle's, overlooking the muddy valley of the Sowline River, the crumbling Abbey of St. Ogdo's-on-the-Mountain hulked darkly in the predawn mists. The monks had abandoned the place long ago, and the forest had moved in to reclaim it. Even if you didn't believe in ghosts—and what sensible person did?—it looked haunted. The jagged remains of broken towers poked into the eye of the sky, vines slithered over the thick stone walls, and the wind, blasting down from the craggy heights, moaned and sighed among the ruins.

Into this desolate place came three lads. Finding the front gates locked, they set about climbing the ivy-tangled walls.

The first to the top was a tall, handsome fellow, leader of this covert expedition—Rafael, called Rafe, the son of Lord and Lady Vasterich. He paused upon the battlements, rubbing ivy sap off his hands, trying to catch his breath and gauge how much time was left until sunrise. About an hour, by his reckoning, but broody, low-hanging clouds obscured the sky and made it hard to tell. The clouds spat drizzle at him. Rafe wiped his face with his fine linen sleeve and pretended he wasn't furious.

But he was. If he'd wanted to wallow in the mud, he could have stayed in St. Muckle's. He'd come here to fight a duel at dawn, and the sky was supposed to be a dramatic red.

The ruins spread below him, within the encircling arms of the wall. Dragon-fighting warrior monks had once lived in this abbey, led by the notorious Battle Bishop, back before dragon fighting had become the exclusive domain of knights. Hence the battlements. They'd built this place to last. Even so, after two hundred years most of the roofs had collapsed, as well as some of the smaller buildings. A grove of pale birch trees had pushed through the broken flagstones of the courtyard; vines and weeds choked every other available space.

Hardly anyone came here anymore. From St. Muckle's, nestled among muddy turnip fields in the armpit of the valley, it was a several-hour hike up the mountainside; from Fort Lambeth, on the north side of the mountain, it was even farther. This isolated ruin was the perfect place to kill someone, although not—Rafe had learned—ideal for hiding the body.

Rafe had selected his two comrades, Wort and Hooey, for size and strength; they were only now reaching the top of the wall. They flopped onto the battlement, gasping like fish out of water.

"You didn't tell us we were going to have to climb the blasted ivy," cried Wort when he had recovered enough to speak. He was a well-muscled lad, good for landing a punch, but apparently not so nimble on a vertical surface.

"Someone locked the gates," said Rafe disdainfully. "They weren't locked the last time I was here."

"It was probably the Busybody Brigade, trying to keep people out after that boy fell down the well," offered Hooey. He was narrower, wiry, and trying very hard to grow a goatee, which made his face look smudged from a distance. "Remember that boy who drowneded a couple years ago? John Eel-Hook?"

Rafe glared across the ruin and didn't answer. He remembered *that boy*, more vividly than either of these louts possibly could. Rafe remembered him screaming.

Without another word to his companions—they weren't *friends;* he didn't have friends—Rafe turned and strode along the battlements until he found stairs down to the courtyard. The other lads scrambled to keep up.

"*I* remember John Eel-Hook," Wort was saying. His mess of curls made him look like a sheepdog. "He'd been dead a week before they found him."

They—the people who'd found John Eel-Hook's body—had been a convoy of traveling Porphyrian merchants. Apparently, they made a habit of stopping at the Old Abbey to water their horses before the last leg to St. Muckle's. The horses had shied away from corpse water. Horses could always tell.

Those same Porphyrians were probably the ones who'd locked the gates, in fact, and not the Concerned Busybody Brigade of St. Muckle's (accursed meddlers). Rafe scanned the courtyard from the bottom of the steps and saw that the Porphyrians seemed also to have put a wooden cover over the mouth of the well, to stop anyone else from stumbling into it by accident.

Everyone had assumed John Eel-Hook had drowned. His

body had been so bloated that not even that dragon doctor (disgusting person) could make out his cuts and bruises.

And, to be fair, the boy's death had been an accident. Rafe had only meant to teach him a lesson about respecting his betters. Things had gotten out of hand.

Charl's death wasn't going to be an accident, though.

"So what's the plan?" said Hooey, strolling out from under the birches into the weedy half of the courtyard. He dropped his rucksack and rolled his shoulders.

"There's a sally door in the gate," called Wort, who had wandered that way. He meant the smaller door set into one of the larger wooden gates. That entrance wasn't padlocked, merely barred from the inside. Wort unbarred it without asking permission. "I'll leave it a bit ajar," he said, "so the kid won't have to climb the wall."

Rafe gritted his teeth at this show of unnecessary consideration. Wort had no business taking such initiative—and how dare he call Charl a *kid*? That so-called kid was not some artless innocent. He wasn't a child; he was thirteen years old, albeit short for his age. *Kid* suggested that Wort (soft-hearted imbecile) sympathized with him, and sympathy was trouble. It made people balk from doing what was necessary.

Not for the first time, Rafe questioned his decision to bring these two clowns (boneheaded peasants). They seemed as likely to be a liability as an asset. But if he did this right, they'd feel too guilty to talk. They'd be implicated in everything, and they'd be highly motivated to give him an alibi.

"What's the plan?" Hooey repeated. "Smack him around? Scare him a bit?"

"I mean to challenge Charl to a duel," said Rafe archly. "With swords."

Wort and Hooey burst out laughing. Rafe bristled like a cat.

"What swords?" asked Hooey, gesturing extravagantly at Rafe's waist, where no sword belt hung. "Did you leave them at home?"

"They're in the sanctuary." There was only one sword in the sanctuary, in fact, but these louts didn't need to know that.

"Isn't this the kid who beat you at swords once already?" said Wort, sitting on a rock that looked uncomfortably pointy. "Guess I won't feel too sorry for him, then."

"Those were just wooden swords," said Rafe through clenched teeth. "Besides, his mother was standing right there. I couldn't very well go after him with my full strength."

That wasn't quite what had happened, though. In fact, Rafe had wanted nothing more than to see Charl's mother weep—that meddlesome woman, that foreign interloper who'd turned the rightful order of things upside down. She'd been a constant thorn in his family's side. Rafe had kept an eye on her all tournament long. Whenever her precious little Charl was in a skirmish, she had covered her eyes, hardly daring to peek through her fingers. Rafe moved up the tourney ranks and did what he could to make sure Charl also advanced. It had meant sabotaging one lad's handgrip and another's pants, but none of that put the slightest crimp in Rafe's conscience. He'd had a loftier goal: to face Charl in the final and "accidentally" put out his eye.

Charl's mother, that busybody innkeeper, Eileen, would collapse screaming. She'd take her precious baby and go back to Samsam, and everything would revert to the way it was supposed to be. The Vasteriches would be on top again; the lowborn would remember their place.

Alas, it had all gone wrong. Eileen (redheaded witch) had been joined by her friend the ex-nun (obnoxious know-it-all), who'd bolstered and cajoled her into watching without her hands in front of her face. And Eileen's face—damn her to the Infernum—had proven too great a distraction for Rafe. He'd wanted to catch her eye, to smile right at her as he popped her precious son's eyeball from its socket. He'd wanted to watch her melt into agonized grief and savor every moment of her pain. So intent had Rafe been on keeping the mother in his sights that he had vastly underestimated the son, who'd slipped through his defenses and won the match.

And, of course, everyone in town took it as emblematic of the new order of things. The heir of the landed gentry (Rafe) bested by the brat of the incorrigible idealists who were turning St. Muckle's into a peasants' paradise. The rabble had taken Charl up on their shoulders and paraded him through the streets, hooting and cheering.

No matter. Let the pathetic fool keep his pathetic victory. There was one thing Charl still didn't have that he desperately wanted. Even supposing someone of his class could afford such a thing, his idealistic mother (laughable pacifist) would never let him have it.

A real sword.

That was how Rafe had lured him up here. *Meet me at the Old Abbey at dawn, and I will show you what I found. The sword of the Battle Bishop himself, lost for two hundred years.*

Rafe hadn't added, *And then I will stab you dead with it.* That part would be a surprise.

"So, what's the win condition for this duel?" Hooey was a gadfly, buzzing in his ear. "Will you use corked sword tips and fight to five touches?"

"Or uncorked tips, fighting to first blood?" Wort interjected, ghoulishly cheerful.

That was the kind of bloodthirsty enthusiasm Rafe had been hoping for. "Uncorked, until he learns some respect for his betters. Until he's in ribbons, if that's what it takes."

Wort and Hooey exchanged a sidelong glance, suddenly looking wary. Rafe did not understand why they should.

It was probably the word *betters*. Perhaps he shouldn't have said that, in front of these two. Certainly, their families were well off—almost as comfortable as his, at the moment, although that would surely change. The Potters and the Tilers were respected artisans in town, but everyone knew they came from dirt-common peasant stock. Three generations as free townsfolk (what a joke) didn't change their essential natures.

"There are plenty of ways to scare him without slicing him to ribbons," said Hooey at last. "I bet he'd poop his pants in terror if he fell down the well where John Eel-Hook died."

Again, treating Charl like a little kid. "He's not a *baby*," snapped Rafe.

"Oh, cack!" cried Wort, using a childish word of his own, a peasant's idea of cursing. He sounded relieved, though. "D'you think John's ghost is still down there?"

Three generations in town hadn't driven all the foolish peasant superstitions out of their heads, either. "There's no such thing as ghosts," said Rafe sternly.

"I know," said Wort, squirming in his clothes. "I was joking."

"We'll need a rope, to pull him out when he's had enough," said Hooey, hands on his hips, looking around for one. It was still too dark to see much. "Wort, help me with this lid."

Rafe, disgusted, left them struggling with the well cover. This was turning out worse than he could have imagined. Not only were they unexpectedly shying away from bloodshed, but they were coming up with alternative plans of their own. Rafe needed them to understand what a blight Charl was upon the natural order of things. That he needed to be put down.

"You can't just come to St. Muckle's and become anything you want," Rafe grumbled to himself. "People are born to their proper stations, and should accept that."

Rafe walked the perimeter of the courtyard until he found what he was looking for: wagon tracks leading deeper into the ruin. It had occurred to him that the Porphyrian traders who'd stopped here for water might also store things here, and since one of the things they imported to St. Muckle's was spirits—liquor, that is, not ghosts—it was worth checking to see if they'd stashed any away. Wort and Hooey (intemperate clods) were not the sort to say no to a drink. It wasn't Rafe's fault if it was stronger than they were used to.

With a little pisky in them, they'd be more biddable. They'd do things they wouldn't do under normal circumstances. They'd be ashamed, afterward, and would never tell anyone what had happened.

The tracks led to a sturdy cellar door of new construction, like the well cover. Rafe grinned joylessly. This was the place. He flung open the door and descended some wooden steps. The cellar was full of crates, and each crate held a dozen ceramic jugs, stoppered with corks. Enough pisky to pickle every liver in town twice over.

Well, not Rafe's. He would never allow himself to be impaired in such way. He didn't even like the smell of pisky.

He lifted a jug and carried it back to the lads.

They'd been busy in his absence. They'd dragged the well cover off to one side, located the bucket and draw-rope, and then—absurdly—built themselves a cheery little campfire. The courtyard looked set for a picnic, not a deadly duel.

Rafe swallowed his rage and reminded himself that everything would be back under control once these buffoons were drunk enough. He wrestled his expression into a smile—which felt wrong, and hurt a bit—raised the jug, and called out, "Look what I've found!"

Wort and Hooey were at the edge of the birch grove, trimming slender birch switches for themselves. Rafe could not imagine what they intended to do with those twigs. Trip Charl, so that he fell into the well? Whip at him futilely? Anyway, the lads looked up when Rafe called, and grins spread slowly across their faces as they realized what he had.

"There's a welcome sight!" said Wort, stepping toward Rafe.

"Toss it here," said Hooey, holding up his hands.

Rafe lobbed the jug softly to Hooey.

It was not a bad throw, but something happened as the jug arced through the air.

A pair of eyes glinted from the open sally door behind them.

And a woman stepped out of the birches, so pale she was almost transparent, wearing a mournful expression and an old-fashioned gown. She walked right through Hooey as if she hadn't noticed he was there.

Hooey froze, a horrified look on his face, and failed to close his hands around the jug.

The jug landed at his feet and exploded into a massive fireball.

It completely engulfed Hooey. Hooey was gone in a flash.

Flaming liquid spattered all over the courtyard. Some hit the nearest birches and set them on fire. Some spattered onto Wort, who started screaming. He dropped to the ground and rolled in the weeds, but that didn't extinguish the flames. It only spread them.

This wasn't the sort of fire you could put out that way, Rafe recognized dimly. The jugs weren't full of pisky after all. They were full of pyria—the sticky, highly flammable oil that knights used for killing dragons.

Wort ran toward Rafe, trailing flames and screaming. Rafe cringed, flinging his arms up around his head like a coward, but Wort wasn't coming for him. Wort, in desperation, flung himself down the well.

You couldn't extinguish pyria that way, either. Rafe, shocked and sickened, stood at the lip of the well and watched the flames rage under the water. The water boiled.

Nausea roiled in Rafe. He turned his back on these horrors and staggered off.

"I didn't know," he muttered. The flaming courtyard raged behind him. "I didn't do it. He should have *caught* it." Unseeing, he stumbled deeper into the ruins. "They were too stupid to live. They were going to ruin everything."

Ahead of him, between the hulking shadows of the ruined buildings, a little light shone. Twinkled. A welcoming light, unlike the towering inferno he'd left behind him. Rafe walked toward it, drawn like a moth.

"They were just peasants," he whispered.

Come closer, the light whispered back.

It was a candle flame, he could now see, set up in the window of the sanctuary. The whole monastery lay crumbling around him, but the sanctuary still had glass in its windows. It still had its big wooden doors. They opened soundlessly at Rafe's touch.

He'd been here before, he recalled vaguely, but it hadn't looked like this. Now every lamp and candle was lit, dazzling his eyes. The wooden trim was newly lacquered, the gold leaf restored, the cobwebs cleared away. Bishop Marcellus's cadaver tomb no longer had ivy crawling all over it but gleamed alabaster white. Rafe didn't question these changes; they seemed to make sense, the way a dream makes sense.

He entered like a sleepwalker and stepped toward the altar, where the candles burned brightest. Someone was there, a bulky, shadowy figure kneeling in prayer. Rafe's heart turned to ice, but he kept walking, because he could not stop.

"I didn't mean to kill them," said Rafe as he neared the altar.

So, who did you mean to kill? said a voice that made his insides ripple like water.

The figure rose. It was a smoke-colored blur, a smudge in the air, except for the eyes. The eyes were two dark pits that seemed to lead downward forever, down to someplace cold. Rafe felt himself teetering, as if he were standing on the edge of a precipice. As if he might fall into those bottomless pits.

"They were idiots," whispered Rafe, trying to delay the inevitable. "People get what they deserve."

I agree. But tell me: What do you deserve?

Rafe whimpered, too terrified to speak.

Two shadowy hands reached out and grasped Rafe's head. The icy fingers pressed deeply, pressed all the way into his mind, and he screamed.

And screamed.

Outside, the petulant clouds burst forth in rain.

2

The Harbinger

Charl may not have seen everything, but he saw enough. He saw too much.

He'd arrived at the Old Abbey earlier than he was supposed to because he'd known this was a trap. That unrepentant bully, Rafe, had invited Charl halfway up the mountain to see the Battle Bishop's sword at dawn. *Right.* Either the sword was a lie, and Rafe was going to show him something worse, or there really was a sword, and Rafe intended to stab him with it.

The presence of those two louts, Wort and Hooey, suggested the latter. Charl was small but nimble, stronger than he looked, and the only way he would have held still long enough to let himself get stabbed was if someone else was holding him down.

Besides, if there really was a sword, he meant to get it for himself. And if there was any stabbing to be done—well. That was surely up to the person with the sword and how merciful he was feeling.

Charl had crouched behind the open sally door, spying on the three older boys and trying to work out Rafe's exact plan. Wort and Hooey, at least, seemed more interested in scaring Charl than hurting him; Charl thought he could avoid falling down the well, unless they picked him up and threw him in. Rafe, plainly disgusted with his companions, went off in a huff. Wort and Hooey busied themselves making a campfire and cutting birch switches.

For a moment, Charl considered stepping out of his hiding spot and speaking to them. *Hey,* he might've said. *Why are we doing this? Rafe is stupid. Let's go home.*

But he didn't do it.

Rafe—four years older and more than a foot taller—had been Charl's personal bully almost the whole time Charl had lived in St. Muckle's, seven long years. Aris, an ex-knight and a dear friend of his mother, had been teaching Charl to defend himself for nearly as long. Charl had finally beaten the older boy, fair and square, in an honorable fencing contest. That should have put a stop to the bullying, according to Sister Agnes's theory of boys, but it hadn't worked out that way. Being beaten by a thirteen-year-old had only humiliated Rafe and made him angrier. Charl was going to have to beat him more decisively—unfairly and unsquarely, if necessary—or this would never be over.

And more than that, he *wanted* to beat Rafe again. Rafe had it coming. He'd terrorized and tormented not just Charl, but anyone who'd dared befriend Charl, or who came from peasant stock, or who simply got on the older boy's nerves. Rafe needed to be stopped, and only Charl seemed willing to do it.

He was itching to do it, truth be told.

It would be no simple matter, though. Charl hadn't managed to bring along any weapon of his own. Aris, who was no fool, kept his real swords locked up at night, and Charl had not quite dared to steal a knife from the inn's kitchen. (His mother would be angry enough that he'd sneaked out, and she was as intimidating as Aris, in her own way.) Anyway, didn't Aris always say the most dangerous weapon was your mind? A small-for-his-age thirteen-year-old was never going to be stronger than a taller, older boy—but he could be smarter.

The birch switches that Wort and Hooey were now swatting each other with, giggling, looked promising. A well-placed strike on some tender spot would surely sting like the devil—

He never finished that thought, because that was when he saw her.

The ghost.

Ghosts weren't real—he knew that, of course—but how else to explain why he could see the campfire right through her? She stepped out of the grove of birches, barely there, a tall woman who cast no shadow. She walked slowly, her pale hair loose, the sleeves of her gown so long that they trailed on the ground behind her. Her lips trembled as if she might weep. Rafe had returned to the courtyard and was saying something, but Charl was so transfixed by this transparent woman that he barely noticed.

She passed right through Hooey, as if he wasn't there.

And then Hooey really *wasn't* there, because a huge ball of fire obliterated him.

Charl acted without thinking; there wasn't time to think. He dashed forward to see if he could pull Hooey out of the flames, but there was nothing of Hooey left to pull. Wort was rolling in the grass, through flames so thick Charl couldn't get near him. Charl shouted at Rafe, telling him to cut Wort's clothes off him, but Rafe was staring open-mouthed and seemed not to hear him. Wort threw himself down the well, and then Rafe just kind of stumbled off, muttering to himself. Charl rushed to the lip of the well and tossed down the bucket and rope, as if he might haul Wort to safety, but the water churned and the bucket caught fire and—

And then his memory simply ended for a while. Maybe that was for the best.

The next thing he did remember was trudging across the fallow turnip fields toward home, rain pouring down and mud up to his knees, pulling Rafe along by the hand. Rafe's dark hair was plastered down over his eyes, his fine white shirt was stained and torn, and he was crying—not silent weeping, but long, loud sobs interspersed with groans. The groaning turned to braying, and the braying to screaming.

They reached the farming hamlet halfway across the flats, and then there were people all around, running out of their thatched huts. They wrapped Rafe in blankets, trying to calm him, but he would not quiet and he would not be led. The farmfolk ushered Charl inside, to a seat before the hearth, and then dispatched a runner to town to notify both boys' parents.

"You did right, lad," said someone. A bowl of broth was thrust into Charl's hands. "The grown folk have things in hand. He'll be taken care of. It's off of your shoulders now."

But it wasn't, was it? Two boys were dead, and he could have prevented it.

Charl quietly wept into his soup.

Rafe's parents, Lord and Lady Vasterich, arrived first, on horses. Charl could hear them outside, demanding answers of the peasants, exclaiming in dismay at the sight of their disheveled, crying son. Someone must have mentioned Charl to them, because Lady Vasterich began to shriek about "that harpy," "that termagant," "that uppity Eileen," who needed to "get her violent offspring under control" or the Vasteriches would be forced to take things into their own hands.

Violent offspring. She was one to talk.

If Lady Vasterich was that upset about Rafe—who was merely muddy and blubbering—how were Hooey's and Wort's parents going to react when they heard their sons were dead?

But they wouldn't know yet, would they? Charl hadn't mentioned the other boys to anyone, and Rafe was in no condition to narrate what had happened. Charl shivered in spite of the hearth fire, and didn't let the cottagers take his empty bowl. His insides were roiling, and he feared he might need it again.

The door opened, and a brown, bearded face peered around it, blinking in the dimness. It was Aris—thank Allsaints. Of all the possible adults who could have come to fetch Charl home, Aris had the softest heart, even if he used to kill dragons for a living. Right now, he looked more worried than angry.

The ex-knight said a few quiet words to Charl's hosts, and they cleared out. Aris pulled up a stool and sat opposite the boy, his crow-keen eyes glittering in the firelight. Charl looked at the big man's calloused hands, which held a shovel or a horse's reins more often than a weapon nowadays.

"We knew you'd sneaked out," said Aris at last, "because Agnes heard you. She told us at breakfast. Your mother was a wee bit cross that Agnes didn't wake the house rather than let you go, but you know how Agnes can be."

"She was testing a theory," said Charl, pressing his mouth into a shape that he hoped resembled a smile. Sister Agnes had more theories than was good for a person, his mother always claimed. Her Theory of Charl basically amounted to *Let him fall on his face, or he'll never learn.*

"Where did you go, Charl?" said Aris. "And what the devil happened to Rafael? They can't get a sensible word out of him. He's gibbering on about ghosts, like a madman."

Charl took a deep, shaky breath and told Aris everything he'd seen.

Everything but the ghost. Aris didn't seem like he would believe that part.

Aris sucked air sharply through his teeth upon hearing the fates of Wort and Hooey.

"Excuse me a moment," said Aris, standing up and going outside.

Charl couldn't make out the words, but Aris's sharp, urgent tone suggested that he was telling the villagers they needed to fetch two more sets of parents, and quickly. A rider departed with a thudding of hooves, and then Aris came back inside.

As the big man sat down again, he kissed his knuckle toward Heaven and said, "St. Eustace see them home"—referring to the Saint who leads souls up the Golden Stair after death. Charl did the same, absently, wondering whether St. Eustace ever missed anyone.

Wort and Hooey were gone; it seemed impossible. Sixteen years old, swatting at each other and laughing, and then—

boom!—no longer in the world. He could scarcely comprehend it, and he'd been there.

His description of the massive fireball seemed to particularly perplex Aris. "Only pyria explodes that violently," he muttered, tugging his beard. "How the devil did Rafael get hold of pyria? The nearest knights are in Fort Lambeth, and they guard their stores fiercely.

"But tell me," said Aris, looking Charl in the eye. "Was there a quarrel? Do you think Rafael killed the other boys on purpose?"

"No," Charl whispered, mouth dry. "He seemed shocked when it happened."

"It is far too easy to set pyria off by accident," said Aris grimly.

But something else had occurred to Charl: *Was that pyria meant for me?* Had Rafe intended to char his bones beyond recognition and leave them where no one would ever look? Mama would surely have spent years—maybe the rest of her life—searching for him in vain, wondering what had happened, whether he'd simply run off or whether his father had finally stolen him back to Uchtburg.

The thought made Charl dizzy with misery. The tears he'd been fighting broke through.

Aris saw. He pulled Charl into a bear hug that engulfed his head.

"Now you listen to me." Aris's voice was muffled by his massive arms. "You saved Rafael's life, if that makes you feel any better. Imagine how it would feel to accidentally kill your friends—or look at the state *he's* in, if you can't imagine. He might have wandered the mountain for days, completely out of his mind, might've wandered off a cliff or been eaten by wolves. You led him home. You kept him safe."

None of this made Charl feel better. In fact, it made him feel worse.

"I could have saved Wort and Hooey, but I didn't," he finally managed to sob out. He was getting snot and tears all over Aris's jerkin.

"You could only have saved them by seeing the future," said Aris. "Which is something you can't actually do."

"It's my fault they were there!"

"Ah, we come to it at last," said Aris. "What *were* you all doing up at the Old Abbey at the crack of dawn? Bearing in mind that your old sword master wasn't born yesterday and knows when duels are most commonly fought."

Aris sat back, arms folded, and listened carefully to Charl's answer—that he'd known it was a trap and he had gone anyway.

"But why, Charl?" said the big man. "You have better sense than that."

Shame welled up in Charl's heart, but he made himself tell Aris the truth: "I wanted to hurt him. The way he's hurt everyone else."

Aris looked down, collecting his thoughts, which meant he was disappointed; Charl cringed inside, awaiting judgment. Aris finally said softly, "I've told you before, and I'll tell you as many times as I must: I understand being angry, or even hating him, but this is not the way. If you want to fight him, beat him fairly in a—"

"That tournament didn't solve anything!" Charl blurted out. "It only made him worse."

"The tournament wasn't for him—it was for *you*, to get some of this rage out of your system, so you wouldn't go and do something stupid," said Aris, an edge to his voice now. "In which case, you're right, it didn't work. But what would you have done, up at the Old Abbey, if the accident hadn't happened? What had you planned?"

"I don't know," said Charl miserably. And he really didn't. His whole plan had consisted of *Get the Battle Bishop's sword before Rafe does* and then *Make Rafe beg for mercy*.

"What if you had killed him, even by accident?" said Aris, and his voice was a dagger. "Look at Rafe, as we leave, and see what violence—even committed accidentally—has done to him. I need you to understand how serious this is. It's not a joke."

Rafe's shrieks and wails had ceased at some point, but the sound still seemed to echo in Charl's ears. He pictured the look on Rafe's face as he'd led him through the mud, and his heart wrenched in sympathy.

It was an awkward and unsettling thing to feel about his longtime bully.

Aris sighed. "Your mother will be beside herself about all this, and you know who will get the champion's portion of blame." He pointed at his own dark, curly head. "She'll say I made you violent, teaching you swords."

Charl swallowed some angry words, knowing how they would've made his mother arch an eyebrow, as if they proved her point. "That's ridiculous," he managed to say. "Anyway, you would have told me not to go, but to let bygones be bygones and make peace."

"So you *do* listen to me, a bit," said Aris with a wink. "That's some consolation."

"That's why I sneaked out without asking," said Charl. "You would have stopped me."

That wrung a wry, regretful smile out of the big man.

"Maybe let the phantom Aris in your head advise you next time. Anyway, let's get you back to the Fiddle, fed and watered and cleaned up. Maybe a nap under your belt. You've witnessed real horrors, whatever else is true. I'll make sure your mother appreciates that before she lectures you."

Aris got to his feet, rummaged in his pouch, and left a piece of silver on his stool as a thank-you to the farmers. Charl rose in turn, stiff and achy as an old man. He hurried after Aris, not forgetting to look for Rafe as he went, but Rafe had apparently already been taken home. Charl followed the ex-knight along a muddy track straight across the turnip fields, toward a cluster of stone buildings huddled on the outskirts of St. Muckle's.

Toward the Fiddle, that is—the inn they called home.

The Fiddle hadn't always been an inn; certain details made that clear. It had a stone facade, instead of the brick-and-timber that characterized most of the rest of the town, and two slender turrets with conical roofs, one at each front corner. A crenellated stone wall encircled the yard and the stables, which was more fortification than one usually sees at an inn. The grand, curving staircase with its fancifully carved spindles, the secret passage down in the cellar, and especially the coat of arms depicting three finches carved in stone above the hearth—all suggested that this had been the stately home, long ago, of some forgotten noble family.

Charl's mother, when she'd arrived here from Samsam, had bought the building cheap and gently dilapidated from a man who'd aspired to make an inn of it before realizing that no one traveled to St. Muckle's, or even through it, if they could help it. It was he who'd given the inn its name, although he'd intended to call it the Fiddler. The wooden sign out front depicted the eponymous musician, ill-looking and gaunt, his lumpen instrument held on the wrong shoulder. Whoever had painted the sign had planned poorly and couldn't squeeze in the *r* at the end of *Fiddler*, but had probably also figured (correctly) that most of the townspeople wouldn't notice.

It was a tribute to Sister Agnes's literacy initiatives that most people now realized they'd been calling the place by the wrong name for years, and they had corrected themselves.

A contingent of local wiseacres would sometimes suggest that the real reason it was called the Fiddle was because it was such a *vile inn*. Of course, they'd say this after a good dinner with their feet up on the warm hearth, in merry company with friends and neighbors, and no one ever mistakenly believed that they meant it. Because, while it was true that people didn't travel in from elsewhere very often, the people of St. Muckle's had hungered for just such a place, where they could go in the evenings to eat, drink, gossip, laugh, plan, argue, and play. The Fiddle had quickly found its place at the heart of everything and everyone, and Charl's mother had made it so.

By the time Charl and Aris came through the arched gateway at the end of the stables, the rain had picked up again. Sister Agnes was waiting in the back porch. Her brown lay habit made her resemble a grouse. She had folded her plump arms and was leaning against one of the carven-stone columns, staring intently through a sheet of rainwater pouring off the porch roof. She waved at them.

Aris waved back and called, "I thought you would be down at the harbor blessing."

"I was, but now I'm back, and under strict instructions to tell *you* to get your oafish carcass cleaned up and down to the waterfront," Sister Agnes called back cheerfully. "There's been a delay, while the Vasteriches fetch their son home. All our citizens of 'quality'—the usual Malavrils, Ruddig-Fengers, and Goolidges—are now agitated on the Vasteriches' behalf, of course, and so Eileen has decided she's going to want the muscle at her side, more than the nun."

Aris made a little sound in his throat, like a growl, but he hurried up the steps and toward the door.

"Boots off!" Agnes called after him before turning her lightly amused gaze upon Charl.

Charl glanced down at himself. He was, by this point, almost all mud.

"So," said Sister Agnes, eyes twinkling. "You're going to clean up, too, and then your mother's left quite a long list of chores."

The chores weren't terrible, although Charl wished he could have shoveled out the stables *before* his bath, rather than after, for obvious reasons. Sister Agnes joined him for the indoor work—wiping down tables in the public room, sweeping floors, mopping the foyer and the boot room, taking Aris's boots back outside and holding the soles under the rainspout, polishing the handles on the big front doors. They changed bedsheets, dusted chandeliers, washed windows, and even scrubbed the hearth tiles, which hardly ever got done.

Sister Agnes wasn't working alongside him out of the goodness of her heart, Charl felt certain. She had been recruited by his mother (he suspected) to do her devious nun trick, wherein she got him to tell her everything without appearing to ask. Of course, she *did* ask—he'd figured this out over the years—but she did it so subtly you'd hardly notice unless you knew what to look for. Charl listened carefully to her chatter, determined to resist this time.

She waited until they were almost done mopping up the last loosened soot from the hearth tiles, before saying in a low voice, "I got a glimpse of Rafe, by the way, when his parents brought him back to town. I don't know what you did to that boy, but good work. He'll never bully anyone again."

That was all it took. Charl burst into tears and told her everything. Even the thing he hadn't told Aris.

He told her about the ghost.

One thing you could say for Sister Agnes and her restlessly theorizing mind: she wouldn't scoff at a story like that. As Charl spoke, her eyes seemed to gleam brighter. She might not have believed him entirely, but she was *interested*.

She handed him her handkerchief and sat back on her heels. She was not the cuddliest member of the household, despite being the softest-looking. As Charl blew his nose, Sister Agnes said, "I know you don't believe in ghosts. I've taught you better than that. But that doesn't mean you didn't see something. Do you know the word 'harbinger'?"

Charl shook his head.

"It's a sign that tells you something else is coming. This warming weather is a harbinger of spring floods in St. Muckle's." She met Charl's eye, and he nodded to show he understood. "Some people will take any strange sight as a sign—a three-legged dog, or a beetle crawling backward—and they'll kiss their knuckle toward Heaven to ward off evil. That's mostly superstition, but sometimes it's not. Sometimes people get real premonitions that frighten them."

"The way Mama used to get when she heard boots stomping around upstairs," Charl offered. Everyone had to leave their boots in the boot room off the foyer now.

Agnes opened her mouth and then closed it again. "That's... a little different," said the nun carefully. "Your mother was remembering a real thing that happened. This is more what my old prioress, Mother Trude, used to call 'crawly neck,' where you don't know why, but the little hairs on your neck rise up like they're trying to warn you of something.

"Which brings me to my point: sometimes people see a sign and feel crawly, but sometimes people feel crawly first, and then they need to explain it. My theory, Charl, is that you knew something bad was about to happen, but there was no obvious sign. Your mind then created a harbinger for itself in the form of a ghostly woman weeping."

Charl sat back on his haunches and studied Sister Agnes's round face, so calm and solid and certain; it was hard to believe in ghosts while looking at a face like that.

"It was my imagination," he said.

"The vision was," she said firmly. "But the *feeling* was real. Something terrible did happen, soon after. You got that part right."

This didn't entirely make Charl feel better. "I wish I'd had it earlier, so I could have saved Wort and Hooey."

Agnes's brows curved sadly. She reached over and squeezed his hand. "I do, too."

People were beginning to trickle into the public room,

looking for supper and ale and a lively chat before the fire. Charl and Sister Agnes hurriedly laid the fire, and soon it was roaring cheerfully.

Of course, some version of the events at the Old Abbey had already spread through the town like seeping floodwater. Charl could tell who knew, because they looked at him differently. Old Zano Cooper ignored Charl as usual, but his friend Willie Do-Naught gave him a knowing look as he limped by. Jenny Sugar, the pie maker, gave Charl's shoulder a little squeeze on her way to make a delivery in the kitchen. And Gorlich Smith, who came in with his wife, Nancy, tousled Charl's curls with one brawny hand and said, "Somebody had to stop him, Charl. That Rafe was a terror, strutting around like a rooster. I've feared for my Mellie and Gert, if they should ever catch his eye."

Nancy said nothing but slipped a honey toffee into Charl's hand. Charl smiled his thanks, but couldn't bring himself to eat it. Two other boys were dead (did they not know that?), and whatever the Smiths were thinking, he hadn't *done* anything to Rafe.

And even if he had, being rewarded for hurting someone felt wrong (now that Aris had made him think that through). It felt grotesque.

Charl felt hot, itchy, embarrassed. He couldn't stay here, where people knew—or thought they knew, which was somehow worse. He would go wait in his bedroom until his mother came home. Charl mumbled, "Excuse me," to no one in particular, then turned to quit the room.

And almost ran into the dragon.

That wasn't a metaphor. Dr. Caramus really was a dragon in human form, a so-called saarantras (to use the borrowed

Porphyrian word). Charl had never seen him in his dragon form; no one he knew had, except possibly Mama. Charl was forbidden from discussing the doctor's true nature with anyone outside their household. People tended not to trust dragons, for obvious reasons; all the human nations of the Southlands had been at war with dragonkind for generations, until Samsam had made its separate peace.

Even as an ostensible human, however, Dr. Caramus wasn't widely trusted. Slim-fingered and oddly colorless, he seemed always to appear when and where he was least expected. He had just come in from the rain, as evidenced by his oiled cloak; he had not removed it and was dripping all over the floor. In one hand, he clutched a small glass bottle.

"It's time," said the doctor ominously, shaking the bottle in Charl's face.

He could make anything ominous. The bottle merely held Charl's health elixir, administered every month.

They went into Mama's office, taking a lamp, because it was getting dark. Charl drank his medicine, which was not such bad stuff. The doctor gave him his monthly once-over, every bit of Charl measured and recorded, including his weight, the length of his hair, and the number of his teeth. (He'd gotten some new ones at twelve, which no one had warned him about, but they'd all come in now.) Caramus inquired after his appetite, the other end of the digestive process, sleep, exercise, and dreams. Charl submitted as docilely as possible, the quicker to get it over with.

"Tell me," said the doctor, leafing through the notebook where he recorded all Charl's measurements. "You haven't been feeling agitated or . . . aggressive, have you?"

"No," said Charl.

"Violent? Bent on vengeance?"

"*No,*" said Charl, realizing now what this line of questioning must be about.

"Quick to anger?" said Dr. Caramus.

In fact, Charl *was* beginning to feel a bit angry. Now was definitely the wrong time to own up to it, however. He turned the inquiry around: "Do you think your elixir might be to blame if I were?"

"No," said Dr. Caramus, snapping the book shut. "I think your mother might think so."

"I don't, Caramus," said a voice from the doorway, and then there she was, back from the harbor dedication, his mother, smiling wearily. Her red hair, gone frizzy from a day of rain, looked like a cloud spangled with shining droplets. Charl leaped from his seat, ringed his arms around her waist, and held her tightly.

She rested her hands upon his head and bent over him like a kindly tree. "Aris and Agnes have told me all," she whispered. "I'm so sorry for what has happened."

She straightened up again and said in full voice, "The Samsamese delegation will be staying here tonight. One of the women got some sort of bite on her ankle at the harbor, and it's become red and swollen. Would you look at it, Doctor? They're upstairs already."

"Of course, Eileen." Caramus inclined his head slightly, grabbed his things, and went.

Mama closed the door after him. She went behind her desk and began pulling her large, comfy chair around to the fireside; Charl poked at the sluggish hearth and fed the fire twigs until it was snapping happily again. Mama collapsed into her chair and held her arms out to her son. Thirteen was far too old to sit on a mother's lap, even if he was still technically not too large to fit—Charl had let her know this, in no uncertain terms, on his birthday. On a day such as this, however, he was willing to wedge in beside her and rest his head upon her shoulder.

He watched the fire until it began reminding him of Wort and Hooey. Then he turned his face away and buried it in his mother's hair.

She finally spoke. "How are you feeling, good heart?"

Charl was too overcome to speak, which was probably all the answer she needed.

"I hope it will ease your mind a little," his mother said, "to know that a group of townspeople went up to the Old Abbey with the boys' parents, so they didn't have to face it alone. They recovered Wort's body from the well, where you said it would be, plus whatever of Hooey's things were left behind. So that's finished. Their families are very sad, but at least they weren't left wondering."

The fire crackled in the grate.

"We have been through some things, you and I," she began again after a long pause. "I am so sorry I couldn't bring you to a place where nothing bad ever happens. I've tried, you know, to make this town nicer for everyone. The new harbor will help—we shall finally see trade from the coast and send our wares abroad. St. Muckle's will grow and prosper as it hasn't done in a century. But these Vasteriches preferred everything the way it was, when they felt superior by dint of birth and could squeeze the peasants with impunity. I did not see that by trying to help everyone, I was making enemies for you, and I'm so sorry."

"It's not your fault," mumbled Charl. He wasn't just saying

that to be nice. Rafe had been bullying people long before they'd moved here; Charl might have caught his evil eye for any number of reasons, regardless of who his mother was.

Poor Rafe.

The thought shocked him so badly that he sat up. His mother looked at him in surprise.

"Have you seen Rafe?" asked Charl, his voice straining. "Is he still . . ."

"He's not in a good way," said Mama in a low voice. "I told Lord and Lady Vasterich that Dr. Caramus would gladly look at him, but they refused. They seem to have gleaned that Caramus is a dragon, which is unfortunate."

Charl leaned back against her shoulder. "Mama, I . . . I don't know how to feel," he said. "I hate Rafe. I wanted him to suffer, and now he *is* suffering, and I . . ." Charl raised a hand and dropped it again.

"You pity him," said Mama.

"I refuse to feel sorry for that cruel, entitled—"

"Not 'sorry for,'" said Mama. "Sorrow. It makes you sad to see anyone suffer, even him."

Charl, overcome again, only nodded.

"That's good," said Mama firmly. "And hard, because the world is full of suffering. I see it, too. It never ends, and it breaks my heart every single day."

"But what do you do when that happens?" cried Charl despairingly.

Mama smoothed his hair back and kissed his forehead.

"You do what you *can*," she said.

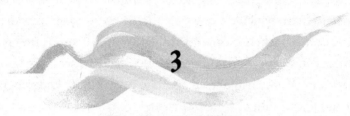

His Personal Bully

hat night, Charl felt certain that he was never going to get to sleep, that he'd be haunted by visions of burning boys. And for a while, he was, but his mind eventually turned back to the cause of it all: Rafe Vasterich.

His personal bully.

Agnes's theory (that Rafe picked on Charl because he was small) and Mama's worry (that Rafe hated her boy because she'd made enemies of the Vasteriches) may both have been correct in their own way, but they weren't the whole story.

Charl had arrived in St. Muckle's at the age of six, just as the weather was turning wintry. There had been so much to do—helping Mama, Aris, and Agnes fix up the Fiddle, learning to speak Goreddi—that Charl had hardly set foot outdoors for four months. He hadn't minded, particularly; he was used to being cooped up. Back in Uchtburg, in the Samsamese highlands, he'd never been allowed outside, for fear that one of his father's enemies—who'd seemed to increase in number with each passing year—might snatch him up and hold him for ransom. In St. Muckle's, however, there were no such considerations, and so when springtime rolled around, Sister Agnes got a theory in her head that Charl should finally be set loose upon the world. Mama had agreed, and the two of them had ganged up and tossed him outside like a cat.

The closest neighbor to the Fiddle was the smithy, and so naturally this was the first place Charl arrived in his explorations, drawn by the ringing clang of hammer against anvil. He had never seen metal being worked, and was so amazed by the roaring forge and the white-hot iron that he went no farther, settling in to watch. Gorlich Smith had let young Charl pepper him with questions for hours, until at last he grew weary of it and called for his twin daughters to take this strange boy off to bother someone else. Mellie and Gert took one look at Charl, pale and slight as he was, and decided he needed to be taken in hand. They were a few months younger and a few inches taller, with long, wheaten hair, distinguishable from each other only by the band of freckles across Gert's nose. And it was lucky they'd found him (as they never stopped reminding him), because Charl couldn't have asked for more knowledgeable, enthusiastic guides to the wonders of St. Muckle's.

Because even if St. Muckle's was more famous for mud than anything else, even if it sounded like sarcasm to claim anything more, there were still wonders to behold, small wonders, for anyone willing to look. And Charl was exactly the right person to appreciate them.

To him, every mundane thing seemed like a miracle. He was

no longer stuck inside castle walls, looking at the world from a distance; he could choose where to go and what to do, like anybody else.

He loved the mud, and the turnip fields. He loved the brickworks and the tileworks, the squat kilns and the slick clay. He loved the slender bridge over the sluggish Sowline, and the eel fishers, setting their traps and casting their sniggle hooks. He loved the Porphyrian merchants who arrived every few months to sell all sorts of interesting things out of the backs of their wagons—ribbons (Mellie's favorite), honey toffee (this was Gert's), glassware, pepper, harness bells, fancy shoes. He loved having a copper to spend, and being absolutely unable to make up his mind about what to spend it on.

But most of all, he loved the children.

There were children everywhere, always, in St. Muckle's, even on rainy, foggy days, playing Holly-hoop-thy-neighbor or tromping up and down on improvised stilts. Mellie and Gert knew where all the best fun was to be had: rolling barrels up and down alleys, leapfrogging along the river road, and playing cuckoo-ruckoo (where the new kid, blindfolded, tried to find his cuckooing, laughing friends). Charl quickly learned the rules to knucklebones, marbles, mumblety-peg, shoot-the-nut. Mellie was the town champion at climbing the statue of Pendergard Vasterich at the front of Allsaints Church; Gert was the reigning queen of hide-and-seek in the graveyard at the back (and the only person Father Donal had never grabbed by the scruff of the neck and ejected, because he'd never found her). Charl had to settle for being quickest at tag, which was no small accomplishment, because the girls always, always cheated and worked together, even if only one of them was it.

One gusty spring day, Mellie was climbing the statue and Charl was standing below with Gert, egging her on, when he noticed a group of older boys watching from across the square. Some of them he'd played street games with before: brickmakers' sons, John Eel-Hook. Maybe Wort and Hooey had been among them, although Charl hadn't known their names back then.

A dark-haired boy, tall and haughty and as narrow as an icicle, stood a bit apart from the rest. He wore a pair of well-tooled boots (in contrast to his companions' clogs), a slashed scarlet doublet, and a soft black hat perched at a precarious angle. Charl hadn't seen anyone that ostentatiously dressed since Uchtburg. The haughty boy was clearly the leader of the group; the others watched him cringingly, like a pack of whipped hounds.

The boy glared at Mellie, up the statue, with cold eyes.

Charl had never seen this fellow before but found the intensity of his stare unsettling. He nudged Gert, who immediately whistled for Mellie, who slithered down from Pendergard's shoulders in a trice and landed catlike, on her feet.

"Come on, let's go home," said Mellie, tugging one of Charl's arms; Gert had already latched on to the other and was trying to get him moving toward their father's forge.

"Are you peasants getting a good laugh, climbing up my grandfather's backside?" called the boy, beginning a slow saunter toward them. "Is that fun for you, despoiling his dignity? He used to crush people like you beneath his heel, I hope you realize. What degenerate times we live in, that your kind no longer tremble before his image. Lowborn whelps."

Mellie and Gert tugged harder, but Charl didn't like the boy's tone.

"Don't talk to my friends that way," he called back stoutly.

"*Vot* vay?" sneered the boy, mocking a Samsamese accent Charl didn't actually have.

"You don't know who that is," Mellie whispered in one of Charl's ears.

"Don't provoke him, Charl," whispered Gert in the other.

"Don't provoke him, widdle baby," the boy mimicked back. "Get out of here, Smithlings. I want to talk to this lad. Man to man."

For a moment, it looked like the twins would refuse to abandon him, but Charl squeezed their hands to reassure them that he'd be all right. The girls scampered off home, but not without anxious glances over their shoulders.

"Before they come back with their oafish father," said the haughty boy, "I want to give you a chance. You're new here, so maybe you don't realize that nothing good comes of associating with such low types."

Around him, several of his gang shuffled their feet uncertainly, as if they feared they might be considered "low types" themselves and the haughty boy simply hadn't noticed yet.

"My name is Rafael Vasterich, but you may call me Rafe," the boy said, pressing the fingertips of his right hand against his chest, over his heart. A picture of sincerity. "You've no doubt heard of my father, Lord Vasterich. We're the true ruling family of this dismal town."

Rafe couldn't have been more than eleven years old, thinking back on it, but at the time it had seemed to Charl that he'd carried himself with an adult authority.

"I've heard of your family," said Charl cautiously. He'd heard his mother complain about them, in truth. Even back then, the Vasteriches had been obstructing her plans.

"And I've heard of you," said Rafe archly. "Thus, I invite you to join my circle of friends." He gestured to the gaggle of boys. "Out of respect, and as a particular favor, you see. I'm giving you the choice because I'm told you come from good stock."

"I don't . . . think so?" said Charl. The last thing he wanted to talk about was where he came from. His mother had given him clear instructions on that point. She had changed her name; Charl had changed his. When asked, he was supposed to say he came from Blystane, down on the coast, and that his father was a common sailor who'd died at sea.

Charl was a terrible liar, though. He hoped he wouldn't have to say anything.

"Don't be so modest," said Rafe, his eyes widening ingenuously. "Isn't your father a Samsamese earl of some sort?"

A little flare of panic ignited in Charl's chest. No one was supposed to know that.

"Wh-who told you that?" said Charl.

Rafe's smile sharpened. "No one had to tell me, you dolt. Your mother comes to town with enough money to buy the old hall. She speaks with a gentle and refined accent. Her very manner of walking and being in the world—confident, arrogant—the tidiness of her dress, all say she used to be somebody just like us, even if she's pretending she isn't. We recognize our own."

Rafe put his hands on his knees, bending down so his eyes were exactly level with Charl's. "And so what I'm asking, really, is this: Are you your father's son? Or are you a sniveling little mama's boy?"

An icy hand seemed to close around Charl's throat, and he couldn't answer. Rafe had conjured up the specter of his father, and now the past and the present seemed to blur and blend. Painful memories flashed before Charl's eyes:

His father screaming *You're no son of mine!* before the entire court.

His mother pulling up her collar to hide her bruises. *I'm fine. It's nothing.*

Soldiers staggering home, bloodied and battered, from endless wars.

He stood there, trembling and haunted, while Rafe's smile sharpened cruelly.

"You should be able to answer that question right away," Rafe said. "Even the smallest hesitation suggests that you are a sniveling little mama's boy, in fact. And that simply won't do."

He punched Charl in the stomach. Charl crumpled and sank to the ground.

And then he was being kicked, in the back mostly, since he'd curled into a ball and wrapped his arms around his head. He left himself, as he used to do, and then it was as if someone else were being kicked. He only heard the blows—thud, thump, wham—until suddenly they stopped.

Charl ventured to peek between his arms. A wiry, wary Porphyrian boy, older than Rafe—an actual teenager—was standing over Charl protectively. The nephew of one of the merchants had apparently heard the fracas and come running. On the other side, John Eel-Hook was holding Rafe back. (Nothing had ever been proven, but it was impossible not to wonder, in hindsight, whether John Eel-Hook had sealed his fate in that moment.) Rafe had lost his hat and was yelling something, but Charl couldn't focus on it, because he had not quite returned to himself.

Then Gorlich Smith arrived, on the heels of Mellie and Gert, and it was all over. Rafe was chastened. The Porphyrian boy was thanked. Charl was asked, repeatedly, if he was all right, and was finally sent home. He promised Gorlich that he would tell his mother what had happened.

He did not tell his mother, or anyone else in his household. He shoved his torn clothes into the bottom of the laundry pile, plastered on a smile, and pretended he wasn't hurt, just like Mama used to do. That was what one did, after all.

It didn't take long for everyone to find out what had happened anyway, although there were several near misses first. Mama had found the clothes at the bottom of the laundry pile but assumed he'd ruined them in the usual way, tearing up and down the alleys with the Smith twins. Gorlich Smith asked Aris that very evening whether Charl was recovering, and Aris, assuming this was some reference to Charl helping out at the forge, replied inanely, "I wish I recovered half as fast as these children!" Even Dr. Caramus came near the truth when the Porphyrian merchants delivered his special order of herbs. A young man, nephew to one of the merchants, had dropped off an odd gift for Charl, a little boot knife. The good doctor had thanked the lad but put the knife with his herb-chopping tools, knowing full well that Eileen would never allow Charl to carry such a thing.

Sister Agnes, of course, was the one who figured everything out. She'd noticed that afternoon that Charl wouldn't meet his mother's eye, and then that he was easily startled. By evening (to hear her tell it later) he'd assumed the posture and expression of a kicked dog, and that was when she'd decided to get devious.

She'd plopped herself down beside him at breakfast the next

morning, and she began picking the raisins out of her oatmeal and depositing them into his bowl.

This was nothing unusual; she did this almost every morning. That day, however, raisins were piling up uneaten. Charl's stomach still hurt from being punched, and he couldn't stop turning Rafe's question—*Are you your father's son, or a sniveling mama's boy?*—over and over in his mind, which would make anyone lose their appetite.

"Do you recall the first time I met you?" said Sister Agnes, nudging him with her elbow. "You were eating oatmeal then, too. Or rather, you were eating raisins and feeding the oats to a hound under the table. What was her name—Patches?"

"Peaches," said Charl, suddenly missing that dog terribly. He blinked several times.

"Right," said Sister Agnes brightly. "Your mother, Heaven love her, was worried even then that you were small, and she pointed out this oatmeal-avoiding subterfuge as evidence that you weren't eating. But I said, 'Take heart, milady. Maybe he isn't eating the oatmeal, but he's eating the raisins, and that says something about his character. Raisins are the most difficult part of porridge. Raisins take *courage*.'"

It was the word *courage*—one thing a sniveling mama's boy surely lacked—that cracked the shell of his silence and made him confess.

"Please don't tell Mama," he'd pleaded, wiping his eyes on his sleeve.

"I won't have to," said Sister Agnes. "Because you are going to gather your considerable courage and tell her yourself. I'll stand beside you, if it helps."

It did help, a bit, but what helped even more was Sister

Agnes leading Mama off to another room afterward to help her calm down. And then Sister Agnes summoning Aris and the doctor to a meeting that evening at the office, where she nudged everyone toward making a plan.

"I know what you're hoping for," said Dr. Caramus, in response to Agnes's first query. "But my elixirs aren't magic. I can't make him suddenly sprout up taller; everything must happen in its proper time. If you want to deter bullies, a systematic regime of exercise might be more to the point."

Aris nodded vigorously. "And I've just the thing for exercise, as I've been telling you all along, Eileen. Fencing is perfect, not only for strength but for balance and—"

"No." Mama had cinched her arms around Charl, who'd been sitting in her lap. "No swords. No weapons. No violence, Aris."

"Obviously, I wouldn't start him off with a sword," said Aris, looking chastened. "He needs conditioning first. Running, jumping, dancing—I know that's not your favorite, Charl, but nothing teaches you more quickly where all your limbs are at any given moment."

"No," Mama said again, gripping Charl a little tighter. "Heaven forbid my son end up the sort who reaches for a sword before he reaches for his own good sense."

There was a long, painful silence.

"Is that how you see me?" Aris had asked, his voice strangely small and broken.

"I wasn't thinking of *you*."

"Were you not, though?"

"Do you know what's interesting?" Sister Agnes interjected in a musing tone.

Mama and Aris both looked at her like she'd just fallen out of the sky, but that didn't stop her.

"I have been considering the word 'courage' all day. Did you know the root of that word means 'heart'? And isn't that what you want for your boy in the end, Eileen? To be kind-hearted, good-hearted, advised and led by his heart in general."

"He is that already," said Mama, glancing at Charl with glittering eyes.

"Just like our Aris," said Sister Agnes, nodding at the ex-knight, whose eyes were also glittering. "And if Aris can be as big-hearted as he is, knowing what he knows, then who better to show Charl how to balance it? For this bully boy has got to be deterred somehow, Eileen. You know his parents won't lift a finger. And it's not like I—or you, or even Aris—can do much to Rafe that wouldn't cause us all more trouble in the end."

And so the very next morning, Aris was at Charl's bedside before dawn, shaking him awake. "When I was a page boy, about a thousand years ago, this is exactly what my mornings were like," the big man said to his yawning charge as they descended the stairs. Charl turned sleepily toward the kitchen, but Aris's enormous hand steered him by the scruff of his neck out across the flagstone yard and into the stables, where a pitchfork awaited him.

A wooden practice sword was eventually introduced into the mix, but Aris was good to his word and spent as much time teaching patience, perspective, and peace as any warlike skills. Only once, in Charl's recollection, had Aris shown himself the least bit interested in violence, and it was only because Charl (with a six-year-old's cunning) had provoked him.

"What if the Vasteriches attacked us?" he'd asked once

during a water break, mostly trying to delay the next set of heavy chores. "Couldn't we attack them back?"

"They won't," said Aris. "And before it got to that point, I should hope we'd tried to talk to them like reasonable people."

"What if a dragon came and burned down our town? Couldn't we fight it?"

That one made Aris laugh. "If a dragon ever comes, Heaven forbid, I want you to hide and run, in whichever order seems safest."

"What if my father came and stole Mama and me back to Uchtburg?"

Aris's hand had tightened around his water cup, and he looked like he was staring at something far away. Finally, he said, "Don't tempt me, Charl. Don't tempt me."

At some point, sleep had overtaken Charl's reminiscences, but he didn't realize until he suddenly jerked awake, feeling crawly.

He sat up in bed. Yes, the feeling was definitely real. A chill seemed to run from the back of his neck down his spine, and it wasn't going away.

The rain had stopped, and the moon sent a shaft of light through his window. Charl knew, without knowing how he knew, that he was going to have to look through that window. He put his bare feet on the cold floor and took one step, then another. The dread in his heart only grew.

Outside, in the flagstone yard of the inn, stood a dark figure, silhouetted by moonlight. The crawly feeling on Charl's neck grew almost unbearable.

It was Rafe. He was staring directly at Charl's window.

Rafe threw back his head and began to scream.

He screamed and screamed.

He screamed until someone came running out of the inn—Aris, in his nightshirt—wrapped him in a blanket, and led him away toward home.

Poor Rafe.

And yet... Charl couldn't help thinking, as he tucked himself back in bed and tried to slow his racing heart, that this crawly feeling wasn't merely about Rafe. Something else was about to happen. Something bad.

And this time, Rafe was the harbinger.

4

The Stranger

Willie Do-Naught, as his name suggested, was disinclined toward work. He was not philosophically opposed to it. Only he'd spent twenty years delving for silver down Baronet Ruthivar's mines, starting from age nine. He'd surely done a lifetime's share of labor already.

Goreddi tradition had long held that if a serf could escape their master for a year and a day, their debts were null and they were free to start over. Tradition, alas, depends upon a willingness to abide by it, and plenty of nobles did not. They might swoop down decades later to reclaim a debt, and an ex-peasant would have no recourse. The enterprising magistrates of St. Muckle's had been the first to codify the old tradition into law: if you could get your serfy self within the town walls for a year and a day (never stepping outside it), the town of St. Muckle's would defend you against your former lord in court if need be.

Even in the depths of the silver mine, rumors of this peasants' paradise reached Willie's ears. When he ran away, he ran straight for St. Muckle's. Well, first he hared off toward Trowebridge, completely the wrong direction, because he didn't actually know where St. Muckle's was. Neither did anybody else; St. Muckle wasn't even a real Saint, according to the priests. It took Willie almost the full year and a day just to go far enough southwest, along the Samsamese border, to a valley so muddy and dismal that even the dragons (with whom Goredd was constantly at war) never bothered attacking. It was surely too soggy to burn.

And once he stepped within its walls, well, Willie realized at once why they'd made the law. St. Muckle's needed people. It was as empty and hollow as an alabaster tomb. The town had been shrinking for almost two generations, and no wonder: It had no harbor and only one narrow bridge across the Sowline River. (And that was Samsam over there, so the bridge was well guarded.) The only way in and out—the way Willie had come—was to start at Fort Lambeth and take a narrow track south over an entire mountain. It took faith to believe there was a town on the other side, and that the knights weren't pulling your leg.

"It used to be called St. Michael's," a wiseacre knight had told Willie. "But the muck gets everywhere there. You'll see."

Still, a law was a law. Willie entered the protective circle of the town walls and lived a year and a day. Then he lived a second year and a second day. By this point, he'd lived about thirty years more (he'd rather lost count), and Baronet Ruthivar, if he was still alive, had surely forgotten all about one slag-hauling serf who'd disappeared. Willie hadn't pocketed any silver. His only debt was all the labor he hadn't done, and good luck wringing that out of him now.

He hadn't done a lick of work since he came to St. Muckle's. Well, until recently.

Supper at the Fiddle was part of his pay, and Willie never missed it. It could be hard to make himself leave afterward, especially if there was to be music, and double especially on a lashing-wet night like tonight. Still, Willie Do-Naught dutifully put on his boots and clapped his large leather hat onto his head, took up his lantern and the little sack the cook had packed him, and headed out into the cold.

It wasn't *that* cold, under his thick wool cloak. He was sweating by the time he reached his sturdy little booth perched atop the thick floodwall that edged the harbor.

The night watchman's booth was almost the nicest place he'd ever spent a night in. The catacombs under Allsaints Church had been the nicest, except for the cadavers and ghosts. The booth was all his, from dusk till dawn. Gorlich Smith had fitted it with a wrought-iron brazier for burning charcoal, so Willie could sit on a little stool and warm his toes. It was decadent and luxurious and more than he deserved, although his old bones were grateful for it.

The rain started coming down harder, if such a thing were possible, just as Willie reached his shelter. He didn't go inside straightaway but stepped to the edge of the floodwall, raised his lantern, and looked down upon the harbor. That was his job, after all: To watch. At night. He could hardly see anything now. The lantern lit up raindrops, mostly, and left the rest of the harbor in darkness. He could just make out the looming hulks of three big boats, one at each of the floating piers, the first river trade in a century.

Surely, nobody with any sense would be lurking and thieving in this driving rain. He'd go look around properly after he'd warmed up a bit.

Inside the booth, Willie hung up his bucket-like hat and poked at the fire to rouse it. A few petulant sparks rose up. He blew on it, and finally the embers began to glow.

From his little sack, he extracted some chunks of peeled turnip. The cook at the Fiddle always gave him something to snack on in his booth, not because she was sweet on him—he was too stenchy to love; he'd been told this more than once—but because she was under orders from Lady Eileen. Lady Eileen was always watching out for everyone.

(Lady Eileen did not like being called *Lady,* and Willie would never have called her that to her face. She was a true-born noblewoman, though, and it shone through her every word and deed, even if she'd officially renounced her title. Even if she'd come to St. Muckle's, the armpit of the world, like any base commoner, to live a year and a day apart from her husband the earl.)

Willie carefully put the chunks of turnip on top of the grating to warm up.

Out in the darkness, something groaned. Willie froze.

It didn't sound like a ghost. Willie knew what ghosts sounded like, after years of sleeping in the catacombs—to say nothing of the silver mines—although he'd learned not to admit that to anyone in town. Folks here would give you a pitying look and patiently explain that you didn't see what you saw. It was simpler to stay quiet.

The groan came again. It sent a shiver down Willie's spine.

There was no choice but to go see what it was. It was his duty as night watchman. He slapped his bucket hat back on his head, took up his stick, and hobbled out into the blowing rain. The stone steps down to the waterside were slippery, and the stone lip around the harbor's rim even more so. He dreaded to learn how slippery the gangways to the jetties were going to be.

Fortunately, he didn't have to. At the water's edge, he realized he was hearing the boats. As they bobbed and nodded in the storm, their boards creaked and groaned and mooed. The wooden jetties were groaning, too, as they rubbed against their pilings.

Willie laughed at himself for an old fool and slowly climbed back to his booth.

His turnips were getting brown on the bottom, so Willie flipped each one over with his fingers. Turnips were as hard as rocks before they were cooked. These wouldn't be ready until after midnight, but that was by design. A body needed something to look forward to.

He settled himself onto his little stool to watch and wait.

He was awakened, hours later, by a scream and a splash of moonlight in his eyes. The storm had cleared off while he slept.

The scream was just an echo now, if it had happened at all, if he hadn't dreamed it. There had been a boy who screamed like that back at the mine. He'd been trapped by a cave-in and rescued after four days, but he'd kept screaming as if he were still trapped. Like he believed he would be trapped forever, whatever his lying eyes might show him.

The Vasterich boy had been screaming the selfsame way yesterday. There was a particular tone to it that you never forgot. It gave Willie a crawly feeling.

Willie stretched and turned to his turnips. They were getting burned on the bottom, from being left so long unturned, but that was all right. Turnips were best with a little char. He turned them over again; they singed his calloused fingers.

He heard another sound. Footsteps, down on the jetty.

Somewhere out on the piers, someone was walking around. Willie stood in the doorway and peered out. At the end of the easternmost jetty, a cloaked figure was bending over the black water. Willie took a step toward the edge of the floodwall, squinting; there wasn't quite enough light to see who it was, or what they were doing. He should definitely go and scare this person off. Nobody was allowed down there this time of night.

The figure straightened, holding something at the end of a rope—a basket of some sort. It dripped all over the planks of the pier. They reached into the basket—no, the *trap*, Willie gleaned—pulled out their catch and transferred it to a mesh cage that hung from their belt loop.

What were they catching? Crayfish? Tadpoles? Could you get anything edible out of the Sowline this time of year? Willie had his doubts.

Willie also had a pang in his heart, seeing this, a sharp spark of pity. You didn't dredge cockles (snails?) out of the Sowline unless you were really hungry.

He'd been hungry. He knew.

Willie went back inside and plucked the plumpest chunks

of turnip off the fire. They were too hot to hold, so he spread the empty sack over one hand like a floppy tray and arranged them on the burlap. A little burlap never hurt anyone. Then he took up his cane and limped down to the jetty.

The person had moved to the middle pier now. To Willie's surprise, he recognized the fellow, a broad-shouldered man with a square, stubbled chin and a scar through his left eyebrow. He'd been in town a couple months, at least. Willie had seen him at the Peasants' Hostel—where newcomers to St. Muckle's often started out, and where oldcomers, like Willie, often went to have a drink and relax among people with familiar manners. Willie had wanted to ask whether that scar was from mining, but he hadn't gotten around to it.

Willie had also glimpsed the fellow sleeping rough in the porch of Allsaints and in Slough Alley, some of Willie's old haunts. The man was welcome to them, of course—Willie had a booth to sleep in now—but Willie had felt guilty for walking by without a word.

Willie thumped up to the stranger, who turned, looking mildly surprised.

Willie held out his improvised tray of turnips. Steam rose off them in the moonlight.

"Thank you?" said the stranger, taking one. He spoke with heavy Samsamese sounds, which wasn't that odd. Samsamese peasants fled to St. Muckle's almost as often as Goreddis did.

"You en't supposed to be here, this time of night," said Willie, taking a chunk of turnip for himself. "But I glean that you were hungry."

"Hungry?" said the man, his brows shooting up.

Willie's mouth was full. He gestured toward the dripping

trap in the man's hand. Had he hung one from each pier? When had he managed to do that without Willie noticing?

"Oh, *this*," said the stranger. "You assume I must be catching crabs or some such."

He spoke formally for a miner. Willie reconsidered the scar. A soldier, maybe.

The stranger gave the wicker trap a little shake and then reached one gloved hand inside it. He pulled out a beetle the size of a peach pit, gripping it firmly by its carapace so that its jagged legs flailed in the air. He shook the trap again.

"Just the one, but this middle trap never catches as many," he said pleasantly, casting the trap back into the water.

"What is that?" Willie's whole face screwed up, squinting at the bug.

The man held the beetle out so Willie could get a closer look. It had looked a fathomless black at first, but took on an oily gleam in the moonlight. It had two flat legs for paddling through the water, and a pair of sharp mandibles. Willie didn't like to guess what those were for.

On its belly, black on black, was a shape like a death's head. Willie kissed his knuckle against evil.

The stranger pulled out the wire-mesh cage on his belt, unlatched the top, and put the beetle inside. Moonlight glistened off many more carapaces within. Maybe a dozen.

"You en't gonna eat those?" asked Willie in hushed tones.

The man laughed. "Indeed, I *en't*." He looked Willie up and down. "I suppose you're some sort of night watchman?"

"I am." Willie puffed out his chest, but only for a moment, because he couldn't grip his cane properly when he stood so straight.

"What happened to your leg?" said the man. He had apparently been sizing up Willie at the same time Willie was scrutinizing him.

"Cave-in," said Willie. "I was a slag hauler in Baronet Ruthivar's silver mine."

"I see. You're one of *Eileen's* urchins."

Willie did not like the way he'd said *Eileen*.

"Watch your tone," Willie snapped. "She's why this new harbor exists, you know. She's why half of us are here. Sure, the law was on the books—stay for a year and a day!—but it weren't no peasants' paradise until she came and said, 'Let it *be* one, for true.' Then Sister Agnes started teaching folk to read, Sir Aris built the hostel, Dr. Caramus treated us for free, and Lady Eileen—"

"Lady Eileen!" scoffed the stranger. "What a scam she's running here, with her peasants' paradise. So much for giving up her title."

Willie was sorely tempted to launch into a long defense of her ladyship, to tell the story of how he himself had resisted the changes in the town, refusing to learn to read or see the doctor, sleeping rough on the streets when he didn't have to. How he'd been sleeping in this very place, back when it was merely a construction site, the night the Vasteriches had sent thugs to tear it up, and how he'd (somewhat inadvertently) scared them all away. How her ladyship had come in person to thank him and to offer him the post of night watchman if he wanted it, and how he had felt necessary and wanted for the first time in all his fifty-nine years . . .

But something stopped his tongue. An inkling. A suspicion. Why was this man here if he scorned the peasants' paradise?

That was the entire reason people came to this muddy corner of a soggy valley; they weren't all peasants, but they all believed in the idea.

So why was he here? Willie looked at the stranger with new eyes, untrusting.

The man was walking back up the jetty. "I have one more trap to clear. Won't take long," he called over his shoulder.

Willie, determined to keep an eye on him, hobbled after.

"If you en't eating them," said Willie when he caught up to the man, "why are you catching them?"

"Maybe I'm an entomologist," the man offered, but that meant nothing to Willie.

The stranger was pulling his beetle trap up out of the water, hand over hand. Halfway along, he encountered a single beetle clinging to the rope. He plucked it off like fruit, hauled his arm back, and threw it as hard as he could up and over the floodwall.

"Up in the Samsamese highlands, near where this river begins, there is a bog," the man said as he landed his last trap on the jetty. "Hafken Bog. You may not have heard of it. The highland earls send serfs up there to harvest peat. Half the serfs die of bog ague, but that's just the cost of peat, as the saying goes."

Willie hadn't heard that saying, but it horrified him. "A-and you escaped?" he asked.

The stranger looked startled. "Me? No. I'm not from Hafken, but I know about it. It's my job to know things. Knowledge is the sharpest knife, if you know how to wield it."

Willie, feeling like perhaps the not-sharpest knife, did not know what to make of this.

"My point is," said the man, "these are blood beetles. They lived undisturbed in the bog since time out of memory, snacking on creatures unfortunate enough to get stuck there. More recently, snacking on peasants. But about a century ago, the earls pressed their excavations too far north. They opened a channel from the bog into a mountain stream. The mountain stream flowed down into a rivulet, and the rivulet emptied into the muddy Sowline here."

He nudged the trap with his foot. It twitched and quivered, almost bursting with beetles.

"They're . . . dangerous?" said Willie, putting two and two together. He glanced toward the floodwall. The stranger had thrown a beetle over it, into the town, with no concern.

"They spread bog ague—also called blood fever—so, yes, they're dangerous," said the stranger. "Their bite is no joke, either. And if you drink water with their eggs in it and they hatch . . ." He gave a low whistle, shaking his head.

"How come I never heard of them?" snapped Willie. He didn't know why he felt suddenly angry.

No, he knew. This could ruin everything Lady Eileen was trying to build. That was why.

"Usually these beetles float harmlessly by, and you'd never know they were there," said the stranger. "That's because a hundred years ago, the people of this town gave up *everything* to build long levees and a floodwall that would keep your unworthy carcass safe in the future. They filled in their harbor. They tore down their wide causeway and replaced it with a spindly, single-span bridge.

"But now you've rebuilt the harbor. The beetles have pilings and planks to climb up on. You'll be seeing many more of them this spring. You can count on it."

Willie stared at the quivering trap in horror. Plague beetles were worse than anything the Vasteriches could have thought up, and they would hurt the Vasteriches as well. Maybe the infestation could still be stopped, if everyone was told right away, if everyone worked together . . .

"Wh-what can we do?" cried Willie. "Can you trap and kill them all?"

"Trap and—" The man's smile broadened. It was a wolfish smile. "Oh, no no. That's not what I'm doing, friend watchman. Quite the contrary. I've been opening the flood valves every night and letting them into the storm drains."

An iron glove of shame seemed to grab Willie's very heart. "Every night?" he squeaked. It was all he could manage with his heart in a vise grip.

"You always fall asleep eventually," said the stranger, raising one and a half eyebrows in mock sorrow.

Rage surged through Willie's old bones, rage like the spring floods. This ended now, this sabotage, this treachery! Willie raised his cane above his head and swung it hard at the shuddering trap, intending to crush the blood beetles in their basket with one mighty blow.

Alas, the blow never landed. The stranger reached out one gloved hand and grabbed the cane halfway through its arc. Willie tried to wrest it free, but the man was too strong for him. The stranger got a second hand on the stick and then used his leverage to knock Willie backward onto the boards.

That was the last thing Willie would remember.

It wasn't the last thing that happened to Willie, however.

When the harbor workers found him in the morning, his head had been badly bashed, and he'd lost a lot of blood. His face and hands were covered in red welts, like flea bites, but larger. Most of the workers mulled around uncertainly, reluctant to touch a dead body, but one—young Hamish from Ardhold—stepped up and checked Willie's pulse.

"He's alive," cried Hamish. "Fetch the doctor!"

Several of his coworkers fell over themselves, trying to be the first up the steps and away. To the ones who'd stayed, Hamish called, "Help me sit him up. You, there, start unfastening his jerkin. Help him get some air."

Willie's jerkin was bulging. If they'd thought about it, they would have recalled that he'd always been a scrawny fellow, without much of a paunch. But nobody thought about it, and they opened his jerkin right up.

A buzzing black cascade of beetles burst forth, pouring out all over the jetty.

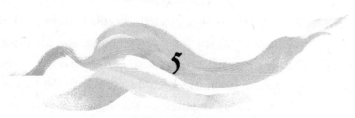

The Plague

"Beetles didn't give Willie that concussion," said Dr. Caramus that evening. "He was attacked."

It was late; the Fiddle's patrons had cleared out of the public room and gone home, except for the Samsamese merchants who went upstairs. Mama, Aris, and Sister Agnes had drawn chairs around the fire, to hear what Caramus had to say about poor Willie Do-Naught. Charl, who should have been in bed, wasn't; he was sitting on the hearth, poking the fire with a stick. None of the adults—all of whom felt perfectly free to act like extra parents at any time—seemed to mind that he was there.

Being thirteen meant having one foot in adulthood—sometimes, anyway.

"He couldn't have slipped and hit his head?" said Mama, elbows on her knees.

"Not like this."

"Or," Sister Agnes began, "what if he was swarmed by beetles and—"

Dr. Caramus gave her a withering look.

"Oh, come on now," she protested, wimple bristling. "Don't tell me the beetles aren't the most disturbing part of this story. We don't even know what they were—those foolish harbor louts didn't think to catch a single one, even after five of their own were bitten. There's an entire swarm, hundreds of bugs"—her voice lowered ominously—"still out there, Heaven knows where. They could wreak all kinds of havoc. Just *think* about it."

Sister Agnes had evidently been thinking about it. A lot. Charl didn't want to; he kept his eyes on the fire.

"I'm more disturbed that this might be murder," said Aris. "That would mean we've got a murderer on the loose."

"Well, it wasn't, and we don't," said the doctor. "Willie isn't dead—yet. He may still revive enough to be able to say who did this."

It struck Charl suddenly, and very hard, that this was two people now who couldn't say what had happened to them: Willie and Rafe. And Rafe had screamed under Charl's window that very night, maybe even right when Willie was being hit. Charl had felt crawly before and after the screams. He knew, logically, that there was no connection between these things, and yet it felt in his heart like there was. As if Wort and Hooey dying and Rafe's mind breaking had only been the start.

Something worse was still coming.

"Excuse?" said a voice from across the room. It was the Samsamese merchant, one of the three who'd arrived for the harbor's triumphant opening only the day before. He stood in the doorway, hat in hand, looking pale and drawn.

"What can we get you, Master Farmau?" asked Mama in eloquent Samsamese. "Some milk? Another blanket?"

"No, thank you," the man answered in Goreddi. "Please, my wife. She has fever, and her ankle is swellen. Would the doctor please to look at her again?"

"Of course," said Mama. Caramus was already on his feet, heading for the stairs.

Charl felt cold all over, even close to the fire. He scrutinized the firelit faces before him for any small sign of reassurance; they all looked at one another with eyes like full moons.

Agnes finally spoke: "Am I the only one thinking it? Didn't Mistress Farmau get some kind of *bite* on her ankle at the harbor ceremony?"

The silence deepened. The only sound was the fire snapping and the wind in the chimney top, which sounded an awful lot like a distant scream.

From everyone's expressions, Charl would have sworn they were all having the crawly feeling then.

On the jetties of the new harbor, up the sabotaged storm drains, into the cracks and crannies of St. Muckle's, *something* was crawling on wiry black legs. Scuttling in search of blood, darkness, and a wet place to lay their clustered, sticky eggs.

They crawled down into the catacombs under Allsaints Church, which held the silent, pristine tombs of the town's oldest families. They burrowed into piles of muck heaped in the streets, and lay in wait.

They scuttled into the vaulted dragon refuge under the town

hall—the place everyone was supposed to hide in the event of dragon attack. Dragons had never attacked St. Muckle's, that anyone could remember, but it would have been foolish not to have such a stronghold, just in case.

The beetles who found wells and troughs and other standing water dove in straightaway and got to work making more beetles, and making the water utterly undrinkable.

Rafe had been screaming for a week. The Vasteriches set guards at every door of their house, locked Rafe in his room, and slept outside his door, and somehow he always managed to slip out. He would wander around town and then scream under someone's window, like an enormous terrifying rooster, trying to wake them to what a nightmare this existence was.

Or was about to become.

He had ended up under Charl's window only the once, but Charl still woke up every night, no matter how distant the screams, and lay there shivering and clutching his pillow until they stopped.

On the seventh morning, he could take no more. He was exhausted and sorrowful and wretched. And oddly guilty, even though he knew he hadn't done anything to Rafe, and Rafe had possibly been planning to kill him. Still, he was the only living person who'd been up at the Old Abbey with Rafe, the only person who'd seen what had happened and knew it had been an accident. Surely there was something he could say to console the older boy, somehow.

He was pondering all this, half nodding off into a bowl of

oatmeal, when Sister Agnes came downstairs into the public room, wiping her hands on her apron. She smiled when she saw him and came near, and he saw that she, too, didn't seem to be getting much sleep. She had dark circles under her eyes, and a drawn and worried look.

Charl knew what was worrying her. "How is Mistress Farmau?"

"No better," said Sister Agnes, pulling up a chair. "The good news is, it seems not to be catching. Her husband is fine, and the others among the Samsamese delegation are well—if a bit impatient that they can't head off for Blystane yet. Some of the dockhands who found Willie have come down feverish, though. Caramus hypothesizes, and I think he's right, that it's the beetle bites that do it. The key, I suppose, is not to get bitten."

"How's Willie?" asked Charl.

"Worse," said Agnes, looking away. She clearly didn't want to talk about this.

"Well, I've been thinking—I want to talk to Rafe," said Charl. "If we made peace, maybe that would give him some peace. I know you're trained in ways of talking to people . . ."

"I *am*," said Agnes, looking interested now. "But what are you planning to say?"

Charl explained, all in a messy gush. Some things he hadn't realized until he said them: how he knew it had been an accident, how he couldn't bear to see anyone suffering like this, how he was also suffering, and felt responsible.

Sister Agnes, as he talked, stole his cold, neglected oatmeal and helped herself to it, since all the raisins had already been eaten. She licked off the spoon thoughtfully. "And you want to do this for his sake, or for yours?"

"Well . . . both," said Charl.

She looked at him shrewdly out of the corner of her eye. "Your scheme sounds like a good one, although there's no guarantee it will relieve his mania. Caramus thinks he needs a long rest in monastic isolation." She scraped the dregs of oatmeal out of the bowl. "And it may not make you feel much better, ultimately, if you only talk to him. The people you really ought to be talking to are Wort's and Hooey's parents."

Charl's heart seemed to fall so fast it should have landed on the floor.

"That's harder, isn't it?" said Sister Agnes, smirking gently at his dismay. "In these sorts of situations, the harder road—the one that takes courage—is often the one that needs following. The easier path leads to an empty gesture at best."

"I can't face them," Charl whispered. "Agnes, I can't."

"What if I went with you?" she said. "We might stop by Vasterich Hall first, for practice. Why not. A gesture that's empty on your end may still leave someone else feeling full." She rose, pushing her chair back. "Let me just tell your mother we're going and fetch my shawl."

It was a bright, cold day, a welcome break from the rain, although the streets were still dappled with puddles. Here and there, in the middle of the street, were clods of various sorts—rotten turnips fallen off of carts, horse apples (which were not apples at all), and other unidentifiable muck. Charl was used to avoiding these obstacles, which stuck to your boots and created stink wherever you went, but today Agnes was going after them. She rushed up to every quivering turnip-and-sewage pudding and gave it a swift kick.

She was wearing boots, too, under her brown lay habit.

"What are you doing?" asked Charl, trying to stay out of spatter range.

"Aris thinks I'm daft," she began, "but I have a theory—" She cut herself short because the pile she'd just kicked over had apparently proven her theory correct.

Three large black beetles had been hiding under a lump of horse manure. They scurried away, or tried to.

"Get them!" cried Sister Agnes, stomping one under her heavy heel.

She crushed another, and Charl got the third. Each made a satisfying crunch, like stepping on a hazelnut.

"Well, that's an opportunity missed," said Agnes, hands on her hips. "I should've thought to bring gloves and a jar, so I could catch one for Caramus. Although I suspect samples will grow easier to find with each passing day."

"Are these the same beetles they found in Willie's jerkin?" asked Charl, bending over to examine the wreckage beneath his heel.

"Maybe the very same; no one saw where they went," said Agnes. "But don't come outside without your boots on. If beetle bites cause fever, we've got to figure out where the little villains hide and exterminate them."

They continued on, prodding and kicking and observing. The beetles showed a marked preference for shade over sun, for dung and plant detritus over plain mud, and for puddles. The best habitat they found was a large puddle where several horses or cows had apparently relieved themselves. Stirring that stenchy muck with a stick revealed seven, no, twelve, no, at least fifteen beetles—and there were almost certainly more.

They'd been walking gently uphill all this time, toward the

great house built on the highest rise in town (which was not so very high, as the whole valley bottom was originally a mudflat). Vasterich Hall. It was old and quite fancy for St. Muckle's, with gables and turrets and portcullises. Part of the house had been turned into apartments and a bakery, and part of it had been let out for studio space, but it still looked imposing.

In particular, it had a big, formidable front door. When Charl and Sister Agnes reached it, a handful of people had already gathered there. Their leader, a tall man in a leather apron, was pounding on the door and shouting at the guard who'd poked his head out a high window.

"Call your lord and lady forth!" cried the leader—a brickmaker, by the look of him, although Charl did not know his name. "We demand to speak with them!"

"We will not stand idly by," a woman at his elbow cried, "while their son brings death and ruination upon us all."

"It's his fault Willie's dyin'," called a third fellow, who carried a pitchfork.

"It's his fault my Maudie's got the fever now!" shouted the fourth.

"Him and his haunted eyes," shouted the brickmaker again. "We know what a man looks like what's seen a ghost."

The others murmured agreement. The pitchfork carrier glanced around furtively, as if ghosts might be watching him right now, but he stopped and turned scarlet when he noticed Sister Agnes.

Charl had hung back, not liking to insert himself into this cluster of foul-tempered folk. Sister Agnes was scanning the group. She leaned over and whispered out the side of her mouth, "Did Rafe see the same ghost you saw?"

"I—I don't know," said Charl. "I thought you said it was my imagination."

"Of course it was." Sister Agnes shook her head as if she couldn't believe she'd entertained such a nonsensical idea, however briefly.

She straightened up, cupped her hands around her mouth, and cried, "Good people, we are reasonable individuals, are we not? Surely we left superstition behind us when we left our old lives to start anew."

The group turned toward her, looking incredulous. "You've heard him scream," said the brickmaker. "But have you seen him? Have you seen his *eyes*?"

"I've seen the eyes of our fever patients in the infirmary, even your Maudie," Agnes called to Maudie's man, who looked like he'd been up all night crying, "and this isn't some otherworldly miasma they're tainted with, I can assure you. It's the beetles. I don't know where they're coming from, but if you see them, stay away. Their bite is poisonous, probably. We're not sure yet, but Dr. Caramus is working on it."

There was a commotion up at the little window, and then Lady Vasterich stuck her head out in place of the guard. Her hair was pinned up inside a butterfly headdress; the wind threatened to blow her wispy veil away. First, she scowled, red-lipped, and then she pointed a bony finger at Charl and Sister Agnes.

"So!" she shrieked. "Egging them on, I see. I knew Eileen had to be behind this mob."

Four disgruntled townspeople hardly made a mob, although there was the one fellow with a pitchfork. He seemed to have come directly from mucking out a stable.

"We were advising them to go home," Sister Agnes called back, but even as she said the words, three more angry-looking people arrived. They were greeted heartily by their fellows at the front.

"Oh, yes, very plausible. And you had the brazen gall to bring along that devil child?" Lady Vasterich shot back, wagging her finger at Charl. "Does no one but me find it suspicious that four boys went up to the Old Abbey, but only one of them came back whole?"

Down by the great doors, someone started chanting, "Send out Rafe! Send out Rafe!"

"How dare you!" Lady Vasterich screamed back. She disappeared inside, and seconds later a projectile came sailing out the window.

It was a rotten turnip. It ricocheted off the brickmaker's head. This made the crowd angrier, and then five more people showed up to make the crowd mobbier.

Sister Agnes sighed loudly. "Charl," she said, "I hate to do this, but I'm going to have to run back to the Fiddle and fetch your mother. She's the only one who might have a chance of talking these angry people down. Even the original four wouldn't listen to me." She looked at him, her mouth flat and serious. "You know where to find the Potters and Tilers. Will you be all right going on your own?"

Charl nodded. There was no way he could get in to see Rafe anyway; even if everything outside had been tranquil, Lady Vasterich apparently held a grudge. He may as well go find the other boys' parents and say what needed to be said.

Provided they weren't among the crowd. He craned his neck to see.

"Good lad. Don't let the beetles bite," said Sister Agnes. She skirted the crowd, trotting quickly toward home.

The Potters and the Tilers lived out at the western edge of town, by the clay pit and the kilns. It didn't take long to get there; St. Muckle's wasn't large, and Charl had already crossed half of it. When he arrived, he was lucky enough to see the very people he was looking for, together beside a well, talking.

He had never considered that he might speak to both boys' parents at once. There was Wort's ma—Ilva Potter—and Hooey's parents—Martin and Jonquil Tiler—and even Hooey's uncle Ferdie. Charl had met them at various functions his mother had run over the years; they would surely recognize him the moment they saw him.

He didn't know exactly what they'd heard about how Wort and Hooey died, though, or how they'd react to his presence.

His steps slowed. They hadn't noticed him yet. He could still turn around and go home.

No, he had to speak to them. He owed those dead boys that, at the very least.

Charl came nearer, but they paid him no heed. They had their eyes on Jonquil, who looked pale and shaky. Beads of sweat ran down her face, and she clutched at her stomach.

"Jonquil, love, what is it? Ferdie, hold her up. Don't let her fall," Martin was saying.

"Can I bring you some rusks?" said Ilva. "They settle the stomach, usually."

Jonquil shook her head, whimpering. She almost collapsed backward, but Ferdie and Martin caught her.

Charl tried to come up with a way he might help. Run and fetch something? A stool, maybe? He was still considering what to say when Jonquil lurched to her feet, took three steps toward him, doubled over, and vomited all over his boots.

She vomited yellow bile, and hundreds of tiny, wriggling beetle nymphs.

"Oh, child," she said weakly, pressing a hand to her mouth. "Forgive me."

"Forgive *me*!" blurted Charl, absurdly. This was not how this conversation was supposed to happen. Not at all.

But there were more pressing concerns. The beetle nymphs were trying to climb his boots. He rubbed his feet together, scraping them off, and then got stomping. The ground was soft—even the road was wet clay here—and stomping didn't actually kill the bugs; it just pressed them into the ground.

"Oh, cack! What are those?" Ferdie shouted, also trying to crush beetles. He was having even less success than Charl, because he was barefoot.

They were all barefoot. You had to go barefoot on the clay; it ruined shoes, which usually got no traction anyway.

"Don't let them bite you!" cried Charl.

But the adults had all gathered around Jonquil again. Vomiting had not cured her—not by a long shot. Her face was growing red and hot now, and she looked like she might collapse again.

"Some water, love?" Martin was saying, and then something clicked in Charl's mind.

When he and Agnes had been searching along the road, they'd observed that the beetles loved puddles better than anything.

"Stop!" cried Charl, loud enough that they all looked at him. "Don't drink any more water until Dr. Caramus has a look at it."

"Only drink beer," said Ferdie sagely. "Got it."

"We need to get her to the infirmary," said Charl. "She's got the beetle fever. Dr. Caramus has been seeing a lot of patients just like her lately."

Not *just* like her, it turned out, when they arrived at the public sickroom. This was apparently the first instance of someone vomiting beetles. After he got Jonquil tucked in and comfortable, Dr. Caramus made Charl describe it in detail, slowly, four or five times.

"Extraordinary," said the doctor at last. "I believe you may be onto something, regarding the water. I deduce that she must have swallowed a large quantity of eggs, which the acids of her stomach somehow failed to neutralize. You and Agnes must find me some eggs, so that we might determine how best to destroy them."

Charl agreed, although he also dreaded the assignment. He turned to go, and then remembered the other thing he was dreading. He'd been about to run away from it again.

He approached the bed with Jonquil Tiler in it. The others were still gathered round.

"Excuse me," said Charl from the foot of the narrow bed. One Potter and three Tilers looked up at him. He cleared his throat, which seemed suddenly full. "You probably heard that I was there, the night Wort and Hooey died. I . . . I just wanted to tell you that I was the one Rafe meant to hurt, not them. They were trying to come up with another plan, to scare me rather than hurt me. They weren't cruel-hearted, like Rafe. They didn't . . ." He paused because he couldn't quite breathe. "They didn't deserve what happened to them. I wish I could have saved them."

There wasn't a dry eye at the other end of the bed. Only Uncle Ferdie was calm enough to walk over and clap Charl on the shoulder. "That means a lot, lad," he said grimly. Then he nodded toward the others. "And that settles it for me. I'm joining that demonstration at the Vasteriches'. You stay and comfort our Jonquil. I'll see Rafe brought to justice, if it's the last thing I do."

"He killed them by accident," Charl called after Ferdie's retreating back, belatedly realizing he hadn't said "accident" in his little speech, so maybe it hadn't been clear. But he was too late, or else it didn't matter to Ferdie. The man was gone.

Then Ilva and Martin both hugged him and thanked him, and Charl felt a bit better and also a bit worse. And he wondered, as he walked back to the Fiddle, whether it was possible to do something so unambiguously good, so unimpeachably right, as to never feel torn and worried and miserable afterward.

"So how did you settle things in the end, Eileen?" asked Aris much later, before the fire at the Fiddle. "You didn't find it necessary to call in the muscle, anyway."

"Don't be sour about it," said Mama, leaning her head against his shoulder. "Muscle is always most effective when kept in reserve."

Charl and Sister Agnes were on their knees before the hearth, looking at the fire through a glass jar full of well water. If you looked at it from just the right angle, you could see almost-invisible spheres of transparent jelly, as big as the head of a pin.

In the center of each sphere, if your eyes (or your imagination) were very good, you could see an infinitesimal black speck—an unhatched proto-beetle (Agnes's word).

"All I did," Mama continued, sitting up again, "was tell everyone that I would talk to Lord and Lady Vasterich on their behalf, and that they should go home and let me settle things. Most dispersed, although there was one very determined Tiler who wanted Rafe's head on a plate. I promised him Rafe would be dealt with justly, and that satisfied him temporarily—I hope he is still satisfied tomorrow when he learns what solution we arrived at."

"And what was that?" asked Agnes, not taking her eyes from the jar. She flicked the glass with her fingernail, and the eggs began to quiver, which made them easier to see.

"They're sending Rafe away, to an aunt in Port Marti. It's a retreat and a recovery, but it's also exile," said Mama. "It's not a perfect solution for anyone, but it's a compromise. And I'm just glad we could reach one."

"Did you hear what superstitious nonsense they were saying about him?" asked Agnes. "Ghosts, and the evil eye. People are scared, and scared people will look for someone to blame. If Rafe gets sent away, who knows where the blame will land next?"

"I'm not going to let them blame a child," said Mama curtly. "Not even the bullying, rotten offspring of my political rivals."

She looked tired and worried. Charl scooted over toward her and put his head on her knee. She tousled his hair absently.

"Did they sail?" came an incongruous question from across the room. It was Dr. Caramus, just arriving. He tossed his cloak onto a table and stomped toward them on boots he'd forgotten to remove. "They said they might, but if they haven't sailed yet, I need to—"

"They left this morning," said Aris, quickest to work out who the doctor must mean. The Samsamese delegation, impatient after a week's delay, had decided to sail back home to Blystane, even though Mistress Farmau was still sick.

Dr. Caramus pulled a chair up to the fireside and sat down heavily. "That . . . is unfortunate. If they'd delayed, I would not have let them depart. I shouldn't have given them permission this morning, had I thought it through. I hope no ill will come of it."

Everyone was silent. The fire crackled.

"Why should you not have let them go?" asked Mama slowly.

"Because I've seen seven new cases today," said Caramus. "That's twenty-six in a week. The Riverside Infirmary is full. Willie Do-Naught is dead."

Oh no. Charl felt his heart contract. His mother's hand, on his head, stilled.

"May he rest on Heaven's hearthstone," said Aris quietly, and everyone but the doctor kissed a knuckle toward Heaven.

"This is a full-blown plague," said Caramus. "And we just let a sick woman sail off to Samsam."

"But the beetles make you sick," Sister Agnes reasoned. "She won't spread the illness herself."

"How do we know their boat wasn't crawling with beetles?" said the doctor. "Did anyone check it?"

That silenced everyone a bit longer.

"We'll have to close the new harbor for now," said Mama,

staring hard at the fire. Charl could almost see the wheels turning in her head. "We must put up the quarantine flag."

"I'm going to have to requisition Sister Agnes's services," said Dr. Caramus solemnly.

"No," said Sister Agnes. "*No*. I left the convent for exactly this reason. I am not a nursemaid, by temperament or inclination. If you want help looking for a *cure*—"

"I do," said Caramus. "And, at the same time, I will also need help caring for patients."

"Bah!" cried Agnes, folding her arms.

Charl, partly to deflect this argument between them and partly to cheer Agnes up, gingerly lifted the glass jar from the hearth tiles and brought it to Caramus. The doctor held it up and stared through the water intently; he didn't even have to ask what was in it.

"Good work," he said at last. "And perhaps some good will come of the Samsamese leaving, after all. We're going to need their beds." Dr. Caramus looked at Mama, his eyes swimming behind his spectacles. "We're going to need every bed you have, before this plague is done with us."

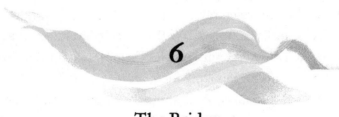

6

The Bridge

outh of the Sowline River rose the Samsamese highlands, a place of forbidding crags and sudden drop-offs, majestic wild waterfalls and perilous bogs. If you went far enough south, of course, you would reach Uchtburg, a sizeable city, ten times as large as lowly St. Muckle's. But the road between the two places was rough and winding and seldom used, except by those who lived along it, or by a highland earl or two, who had hunting lodges there.

A nun was traveling north along this road, riding a mule. That sounds like it is the start of a joke, but it is not.

She had been traveling for several days and was heartily sick of it. Her mule, which had been white at the start of the journey, was now spattered in mud. Her habit, also white, had fared a bit better, except along the hemline.

She reached the top of a rise and saw a fieldstone house with a large thatched roof, which she recognized from the description she'd been given. It was called the Last House, because it was the last place one could stop before St. Muckle's. It wasn't quite an inn—not enough travelers came this way—but rather a farmhouse that accepted lodgers for a small fee.

Only five more miles to St. Muckle's, then. She looked at the sun nearing the horizon and tried to guess how many more hours of daylight she had. One, and then an hour of twilight. Probably. The road beyond this point was famously bad, however—hairpin turns and hundred-foot drops. Her mule could do it, but it would pick its way slowly. Darkness would surely fall before they reached the Sowline River.

Her old bones ached for rest, but more than that, she was tired of the journey. If she waited until morning, it would just take that much longer to get where she was going.

She spurred her mule onward, and left the Last House behind.

She didn't get far. A hundred yards along, around the first bend, a rope had been strung across the path, blocking the way. Three yellow, triangular flags hung from the rope.

The Three Teeth, they were called. Plague ahead. No passage.

It is not a nun's usual practice to curse, and she did not, but every curse she'd ever heard was written in her face as she rode back to the Last House and tied her mule outside.

She paused in front of the door and darted her gaze around, looking for telltale signs, but there was no iron ring protruding from the corner, no mistletoe under the eaves. Not pagans, then. A faithful, Saint-abiding house, where a nun would be welcome. She knew how to talk to pagans and put them at their ease, but this was simpler, and appreciated, since she was tired.

"Allsaints save all here," she called as she stepped through the door and saw what kind of night she was in for. The Last House was a house-barn, really—spacious, and probably warm, but. Well. It was still a barn. The sheep were all at the far end, at least, behind a wooden partition. At the near end, sleeping pallets lined the walls. Two tables flanked a fire pit in the middle of the floor; the smoke was supposed to rise up through the thatch, and most of it did, but the smell certainly did not. At least it masked the smell of sheep.

No, there it was. Sharp. A needle under wool.

Sitting at the tables were about twenty people—extended family, most likely. The bristle-bearded patriarch was on his feet, coming forward to greet her. "Welcome, Sister—Prioress, that is," he amended when he got close enough to see her ring.

"Mother Trude," she said. One nice thing about being a nun was you didn't have to smile if you didn't feel like it.

"I'm Vulfi," said the man, bowing some sort of way. "And my family . . ."

He introduced every one of them. Mother Trude nodded solemn acknowledgment of each, knowing she wouldn't remember any of these names in five minutes. She did take note of a few curious descriptors, like "my brother's cousin's sister" and "my niece, who found her girlhood just this year." Finally, Vulfi introduced the person seated farthest from the door as "our other houseguest tonight, Lieutenant Miga."

The sea of family parted, revealing a slender, ageless woman with short, pale hair and dark eyes set in an elfin face. She was clad in leather, with two swords strapped across her back. She didn't look up when Vulfi said her name but kept shoveling stew into her mouth.

If Mother Trude had noticed Miga sooner, she would have left immediately. It was too late now.

It was impossible for Mother Trude to look at the so-called lieutenant without remembering their first encounter: when Miga, in her natural, draconic form, had plummeted through the sky toward the gaggle of pagan peasants cowering against the convent walls, blasting them with flame. Mother Trude had stood atop those walls, forcing herself to bear witness as the tears streamed down her cheeks.

She sometimes wished she hadn't. She'd have a lot fewer nightmares now.

Vulfi ushered Mother Trude toward the table, to a seat across from Miga, who finally looked up. A bowl of stew was placed before the prioress, and a chunk of dark bread. Mother Trude, not ready to endure Miga's stare, folded her hands in prayer and closed her eyes.

Sweet Heavenly Eminence, grant me patience, charity, and forbearance, and grant Lieutenant Miga the basic courtesy required to leave all these innocents still alive by morning....

When she opened her eyes again, her bread was missing. Miga, across the table, was chewing it with her mouth open.

Miga grinned impudently, crumbs tumbling from between her lips. "So," she said. "You decided to try for that bounty after all, did you?"

It was such an incongruous question—albeit typical of a dragon—that it took Mother Trude a moment to make sense of it. And then, because it was none of Miga's business, she ignored it. Instead, she called down the table toward anyone who might know, "I saw the plague flags, up the road. Is that for St. Muckle's, or . . . there isn't someplace between here and there, I suppose?"

"For St. Muck's, Your Grace," said a young woman, who may have been Vulfi's daughter. "It were kind of them to set the flags up this far, so no one wanders all the way down to the bridge and then has to climb back up."

"I see," said Mother Trude, carefully lifting a spoonful of stew to her lips. She'd managed to keep her habit white this far (except the hem); it wouldn't do to dribble stew on herself now.

It was mutton stew. Utterly unsurprising.

"I am skilled in the healing arts," said Mother Trude. "I don't suppose you know *which* plague they've got? Graypox? The sticky mange? The pernicious creep?"

"Man didn't say," said Vulfi.

Lieutenant Miga yawned and stretched. "Blood fever," she said. "Bog ague, technically, but it's escaped the bog. The bog no longer binds it—that's bad news for everyone."

"Thank you, Lieutenant. That was helpful," said Mother Trude tartly.

Around the tables, however, the denizens of the Last House muttered and shifted in their seats. Bog ague, they seemed to have heard of.

They were burning peat in their fire pit, Mother Trude observed. There must be a bog not far from here. Maybe they had experience with the ague themselves.

"I should like to go down and lend those poor people a hand," said Mother Trude. "But I'm not familiar with bog ague. What should I know about it? How do you treat it up here?"

That set everyone talking. The oldest woman in the household, a wrinkled crone who Vulfi had called Granny, hobbled over from the other table and stared at Mother Trude expectantly. Everyone seated to Mother Trude's left scooted down the bench, so Mother Trude realized she was expected to scoot as well. Granny sat heavily on the empty end of the bench.

"Three things ye mus' know," she said. It took some imaginative deciphering to understand her. She seemed to have only four teeth, all in the back somewhere.

"First," said Granny, "ne'er let the beetles bite ye. Second, ne'er drink bog water without ye boil it well."

"Half an hour, at least," called Vulfi.

"Third," Granny continued, "an' they start coughing gray, ye run away."

"Run away *fast*," a younger cousin added. Nervous laughter all around.

"It becomes contagious with a *gray* cough?" asked Mother Trude, trying to decipher this cryptic utterance.

No one seemed to know the word *contagious*.

"It does," Miga interjected languidly. "Normally, you can only catch it from bog beetles, but in about fifteen percent of cases, the ague invades the lungs. They start hacking up a gray dust. You'll see it, if you go down. It's easy to spot, harder to avoid."

Miga seemed to know all about this. Of course she did.

"Is there a cure?" asked Mother Trude.

"Probably," said Miga. "Brus is down there. You know, egging it along. He wouldn't have attempted something like this if he didn't have a way to avoid getting sick himself."

Of course he was. *That man*. Mother Trude pushed her stew away, no longer hungry.

Around the table, Vulfi's family seemed not to have

understood about Brus. They were chirping out treatment suggestions. "Leeches," called one.

"Eel oil—not the river eel, though, but a proper sea eel," called another.

Honey with garlic. Dead man's fingers (this was a mushroom). Pig placenta. Garlic with honey. Clearly, none of them knew anything.

"But do these remedies cure the illness," Mother Trude burst out in frustration, "or do they merely ease symptoms?"

Everyone grew silent then. Finally, Granny said in a quiet voice, "The ague takes you up the Golden Stair on St. Eustace's arm, or it don't. You have two, three weeks before you know for certain."

It was fatal, in other words. "How many survive?" asked the prioress, suddenly hoarse.

"Two in five," said Miga, drawing Mother Trude's bowl across the table and polishing off the last of her stew.

Mother Trude said a little prayer.

When Samsam had made its separate peace with dragonkind, ten years ago, everyone had been afraid that saarantrai would start showing up and no one would be able to tell who was what. There had been riots, born of fear. But over time, it had become apparent that dragons—most of them—had better things to do than walk around Samsam fooling people. Dragonkind were still at war in Ninys and Goredd, after all; every able fighter was needed elsewhere.

The dragons who took human form and came to live in

Samsam were either too old and infirm to fight or they were exiled deviants hiding from their own people. This didn't stop every earl in Samsam from trying to put one on the payroll, just so they could brag to their rivals that they kept a dragon at court.

The Earl of Pettarfon's dragon had no teeth and could only emit the tiniest burp of flame; the Earl of Bonce's dragon was a pacifist and determined seducer of women, men, and anyone in between. Only the Earl of Ucht was lucky enough to have recruited a dragon who was willing and able to take her natural shape, and credibly—nay, enthusiastically—threaten his neighbors.

His fellow earls weren't his primary focus, however. Earl Ucht, first and foremost, aspired to eradicate pagans from the highlands. He suspected, and he wasn't entirely wrong, that there were enclaves of crypto-pagans—people who pretended to follow the faith of Allsaints, but still secretly practiced foul witchcraft and sordid rites in the privacy of their own homes. People who had fooled even their closest neighbors. People who must be forced to convert at the point of a sword—or the mouth of a dragon.

What had been difficult before was now easy. He had only to parade his dragon around, and peasants would readily turn on their neighbors to save themselves. In this way, dozens of villages had been cleansed of their pagan contamination.

Except, not completely. Some of the pagans were escaping—fleeing their homes, hiding somewhere, and then coming back when the coast was clear. It took the earl's genius spymaster, Jarlbrus, more than a year to figure out what was happening.

Nuns were spiriting pagans away and hiding them at the

convent of Our Lady of the Glacier, at the direction of their prioress, Mother Trude.

Ironically, many of these rescued pagans converted to the faith out of gratitude; Mother Trude accomplished more in this way than the earl ever did with his threats. Conversion, for Earl Ucht, had always been more pretext than point, however. She was spoiling his campaign; she had to be stopped.

He sent Jarlbrus to the convent with a message for her.

"Please, Mother, call me Brus," the spymaster had said that day, sitting in her private study. He was not a large man, but wiry and taut as a drawn bowstring, with a scar through one eyebrow. He smiled as she poured him a cup of tea, and said, "This is a friendly visit, I hope you understand. We're all friends here."

She'd glared at him as only a nun can glare, pulling out all the stops of her displeasure, but this only seemed to make him smile more broadly.

"Here's how it's going to be," said Brus, pausing to take a sip of tea and smack his lips. "We are going to raze the village of Echstau. It's full of pagans, Mother. Not cowardly crypto-pagans, but priests and cornas. Antler-men. Practicing openly and corrupting the young. You know Echstau?"

She did. It stood at the other end of the narrow, curved valley that led directly to Our Lady of the Glacier.

"We are going to burn that village to the ground," he said, turning the delicate teacup on its saucer. "And the villagers are going to flee in this direction, up the valley, hoping to take shelter in your convent—as so many have before them. Oh, yes, we know all about that."

Mother Trude felt like the blood in her veins had been replaced with acid. Her heart pounded like it was trying to escape.

"Only this time," said Jarlbrus, "you're not going to let them in. They are going to cluster together at your gates, and then the dragon Miga is going to burn them all to death."

"We *will* let them in." Mother Trude's throat felt dry and prickly.

"Then you will be responsible for the death of all your sisters, as well as the pagans. Your convent walls can't stop this dragon."

"The earl wouldn't dare," she whispered. "The self-styled Protector of the Faith, killing nuns?"

"*Faithless* nuns."

"Our duty is to Heaven and the Saints. We are not afraid." She quaked and looked down at her hands as she said it. Surely she could order her sisters to get themselves to safety—

"Very well," said Brus. "If you won't protect the women in your charge, perhaps you might still be persuaded to consider the life of Sister Agnes."

Mother Trude looked up at Brus sharply. He was smirking.

"She didn't tell you where she was going when she ran away, did she?" he said. "Well, she's with us at Castle Ucht. She has become fast friends with the earlina—isn't that sweet? She's fine, for now. But you need to know we have her, and that we know what she is to you."

How? How could they possibly know? Agnes herself didn't know . . .

Brus set his cup on her desk and stood up. "I think we understand each other, Mother Trude. I believe we will have your cooperation, if not for your sisters' sake, then for your daughter's."

He did have her cooperation, and she was sick with shame, even after all these years.

She had thought that watching the massacre she'd allowed to happen—all that blood on her hands, all those souls on her conscience—would be her punishment. But, no, Heaven had not considered that to be enough. The Regent of Samsam, hearing of the heartless slaughter, did not have the guts to seize Earl Ucht. The dragon Miga was forbidden from flying over Samsam and forced to become an ordinary, stabbing sort of assassin. Jarlbrus managed to weasel out somehow, as he always did. But the Regent decided someone must be imprisoned for this crime against humanity, and the easiest person to make an example of was the prioress of Our Lady of the Glacier.

Mother Trude was sent to Bagren Prison, with the intention of letting her rot there.

The worst part was not the loss of freedom, not the gruel that froze to the tin plate if you didn't eat it fast enough, or the thin blankets that never got you warm, or the ghosts, making her relive that terrible day, over and over. The worst part was learning that Agnes hadn't been in Uchtburg at all during the massacre of Echstau. She had already given Earl Ucht the slip, along with the earl's wife. Mother Trude had betrayed everything she believed in, for nothing.

At bedtime, Vulfi's clan dragged all the straw pallets but two into the sheep enclosure and bedded down among the woolly beasts. The last two pallets were laid out one on each side of the fire. "You'll be warm here, and we'll be warm there, and we won't bother you from sleeping," Vulfi explained.

Mother Trude sighed as she nestled into the straw mattress. Being so close to Miga was going to "bother her from sleeping" more than sheep or children would. She wouldn't be able to close her eyes without seeing the pagans at the gates, and Miga charging toward them.

And yet if she didn't close her eyes, Miga was going to try to talk to her.

"Psst," said Miga from the other side of the fire. "Pssssst! Old woman . . . I always forget your name."

Never mind that Miga had been the person Earl Ucht had sent to secure Mother Trude's release from prison. How had she managed it with such a bad memory? one wondered. Maybe he'd sent her with paperwork, and she hadn't read it. The prioress clucked her tongue and said, "Mother Trude."

"Ah, right. You never answered my question."

"What question?" snapped Mother Trude.

"'You decided to try for that bounty after all, did you?'" said Miga in a singsong voice, quoting herself as if she had been a child a couple hours earlier. "It's a lot of money. Maybe even enough to tempt a churchy sort like yourself."

Saints in Heaven.

"The earl has offered me no money," said Mother Trude, rolling onto her side. "You seem to have forgotten my circumstances. I was given no choice but to help him."

Agnes was still his carrot and his stick. *Would you like to see her one more time, or would you like to go straight back to prison? Would you like to see whether you can bring my child and my ex-wife back to me before Brus gets ahold of them? To say nothing of your Agnes. Brus has very particular orders regarding her.* Mother

Trude felt instinctively that it would be a bad idea to spell this out any more clearly for Miga, though; Miga was the sort to take your vulnerabilities and make you eat them later.

"I'd planned to go take the measure of things in St. Muckle's," Mother Trude said, changing the subject. "See what seems feasible. This plague has broken the axle of that plan, though, and Brus will go out of his way to ruin my prospects if he sees me." She narrowed her eyes at Miga, who'd worn all her leathers to bed. "What about you? Why aren't you down in the thick of things if there's a bounty to be won? Clearly, you have been, since you know so much about what Brus is up to."

"I was biding my time, observing his progress. But I got bored," said Miga. She yawned enormously as if to underscore that point. "You know what he's like."

"Cruel? Merciless?"

"Excruciatingly thorough. He will subtly destroy everything the earl's ex-wife has built, making her believe it's her own fault, but he'll take six months to do it."

It had already taken Brus longer than that, in fact. The earl had lost all patience, which was why he'd roped in Mother Trude.

"So I figure," Miga continued, "let him toil. Brus is softening the earth for me—or for *you*—or for anyone prepared to snatch his victory away at the last moment."

"So you'll be back," said Mother Trude.

"When the time is right. Or when I get tired of messing about," said Miga.

Mother Trude rolled onto her back and stared at the smoke-blackened thatch. She could still go to St. Muckle's. They'd probably welcome a skilled, experienced healer. If she stayed out of Brus's way, and avoided catching the fever herself, how long would she have to carry out her (revised) plan before Miga came back and . . . did what? Something worse than plague, certainly.

Across the Sowline River, in Goredd, they were still at war with dragons. Miga might pass for an ordinary enemy combatant, set St. Muckle's ablaze, and escape safely back to Samsam, with the townspeople none the wiser.

Mother Trude shuddered.

She glanced apprehensively at Miga and found the dragon assassin staring back at her, eyes glinting like two black pearls. Miga took this as an invitation to speak: "Have you ever heard anyone refer to me as Mighiletta?"

Another incongruous question. "Wh-what?"

"It's a diminutive form of Miga, meant as a term of endearment, possibly."

"Yes, I know. I just . . . Why would you ask that? You're a killer-for-hire. You're not even human. No one has ever called you anything the slightest bit endearing within my hearing."

"*Right?*" said Miga, sounding weirdly incredulous. "Why would anyone *do* that?"

It was late; Mother Trude wanted nothing so much as for this extremely off-putting person to stop talking and let her sleep. But the question was an invitation, and she was a nun. She had a very particular set of skills, and her curiosity was starting to prickle. "You sound almost relieved," she said. "That name felt like a burden to you. Why would that be?"

Miga propped herself on her elbows and leaned in. "Can I tell you something?"

"If you must."

The lieutenant (she wasn't really, Mother Trude knew; she'd

given herself the title so no one would question her right to carry swords) darted her gaze back and forth, as if the sheep might be listening. "I don't remember most of my past. I did . . . *something,* apparently. Something bad, perhaps. My memories were stolen from me, years ago."

"You were excised?" That was the technical term dragons used for cutting memories out of the heads of so-called deviants. What had Miga done? Surely it couldn't have been even more horrifying than her current murderous career.

The dragon assassin nodded enthusiastically. "But they did a sloppy job," she said. "I still have little ragged edges of some memories left. I get intense déjà vu and can never work out why. Down in St. Muckle's, it was the strongest it has ever been. That's why I can't stay down there while Brus prepares the way. Fragmented memories are like an itch you can't scratch."

"And you remember being called Mighiletta?"

"No," said Miga sharply. "I went to the town archives and saw the name among some records. From over a century ago." She shook her head, her gaze grown distant. "If it *was* me, I was a member in good standing of the pancake makers' guild."

"That doesn't sound like you."

"Indeed, it does not."

Miga fell silent and then rolled over with her back to the fire. Within minutes, she began to snore. Mother Trude finally felt like she could close her own eyes safely.

Still, she lay awake a long while, trying to plot her course between these two terrors—Brus the clever planner, on the one hand, Miga the reckless bludgeon on the other. Surely there was some way to wriggle in between them and foil them both. She didn't mind about the earl's ex-wife so much, and she didn't see what she could do for the town itself if Brus and Miga were really determined to destroy it. But the child... She knew what it was to lose a child. She hated to admit it, even to herself, but she had some sympathy for Earl Ucht's sorrows in that regard.

And that was an uncomfortable way to feel.

7

Arrivals

harl had arrived in St. Muckle's still wrapped in blankets from his bed. He'd never so much as heard of St. Muckle's before, and Mama had seemed a bit embarrassed and apologetic about the place. But, as she'd explained to him that first night, as he was finally growing warm and drowsy before their new home's great hearth, they hadn't had much of a choice. St. Muckle's was the best they could do, under the circumstances.

And indeed, circumstances had been urgent.

Everything had happened soon after that horrible Feast of St. Auberge, held to celebrate the harvest. Charl's maternal grandmother had insisted that he attend, in proper, itchy, lace-drenched ceremonial dress. She'd curled his hair and pried his feet into tight little wobbly shoes. He remembered the dressing-up part only vaguely, as if it had happened to someone else and he'd been watching through a window. He remembered the feast not at all. His clearest memory was of afterward, lying in bed while his mother and grandmother argued in front of the fire.

Mama's silhouette was wiry and flickering; Grandmama's was like a granite wall.

"You had your chance already," Mama had said, pacing back and forth. "You shaped my whole existence. I gave up my 'notions,' as you called them, for you. I married the earl of your choosing. I did my duty. But you will not—*not*—force Charl into the same mold. I am his mother, not you. If he wants to run and explore and be free—"

"Then you will be raising the vilest, most selfish brat in Samsam, Sylvina," said Charl's grandmother. Mama had been called Sylvina in those days. "People are born into a certain station in life, which they must accept."

"I accepted it for myself, Mother. I cannot accept it for my child."

"It's that runaway nun, putting pernicious ideas in your head," said Grandmama.

"Leave her out of it," snapped Mama.

Charl had never heard her snap like that. He burrowed deeper under the covers.

And then his father, the earl, had come in—even older than his grandmother, and twice as ferocious—and the two of them had ganged up on Mama, as they often did. Charl hid all the way under the covers, and under his pillow, but he still heard them. It was his fault, somehow. He'd done something wrong—no, he *was* something wrong. They'd wanted a swan, and he was just a goose, but they could *make* a swan of him if only his mother would stop standing in their way.

Charl had started crying, which made them realize they'd been fighting too loudly. They took Mama away between them and finished the argument elsewhere.

The next morning, Mama came in very early and woke him by sitting quietly on the bed. She had circles under her eyes, and was wearing one of her "tall-neck dresses," as Charl thought of them. The morning after an argument, she often wore a tall-neck dress, or a veil if the earl had marred her face. She tried to smile, but that only made her look sadder and more tired.

"Listen, good heart, I don't have much time," she said, brushing hair off his forehead. "I'm going on pilgrimage with Sister Agnes, to the shrine of St. Abaster in Fnark, to ask forgiveness for my multitude of sins."

Charl was suddenly wide awake. "That's very far south."

Mama smiled. "You remember that from looking at maps with Agnes. She'll be pleased to hear it."

"But—" Charl tried to sit up, but Mama was leaning on the coverlet, obstructing him. "Can I go with you?"

"You cannot," said Mama. She leaned down close to his ear and whispered, "In a week or two, Sir Aris will come to your chamber at an odd hour. He will say, 'The moon has risen backward.' When this happens, you must go with him and do exactly as he says. Promise me you'll do that?"

"But Mama," Charl protested. His eyes were filling with tears. Something strange was going on. He didn't understand, and he didn't like it.

"Promise," she said again, her voice so low and serious that his heart trembled.

"I promise, Mama," said Charl.

She kissed his forehead, and then she was gone.

For days, Charl walked around like a ghost. It was that same feeling as before, of watching himself through a window. He watched his grandmother dress him up in more "suitable" courtly attire, and he watched himself learn to dance a bourrée with the music master. Only sometimes was he able to come back and haunt his own body, and then he managed to cover his silks in grass stains and shear off his hair with a paring knife so his grandmother couldn't curl it. He left himself again when spankings rained down, and hardly felt them.

Sir Aris—a former knight, even then, but the *Sir* still lingered—was the captain of the Earl of Ucht's personal guard, not someone Charl knew well at that time. When his mother left, Charl had started keeping an eye out for the man, but he wasn't around. Sir Aris had left on a wild boar hunt the same day she'd gone south with Sister Agnes.

It was two weeks before Charl was awakened around midnight by the sound of someone rummaging through his wardrobe. An enormous dark figure, like a bear, was filling a satchel with Charl's clothing. Charl, who had by this point forgotten what was supposed to happen, sprang out of bed, grabbed a candlestick, and tried to brain Sir Aris with it. The captain of the guard, who still had the reflexes of a dragon fighter, dodged the blow and grabbed the candlestick out of Charl's hand. Charl opened his mouth to scream and wake the house, but Aris managed to say in time, "The moon has risen backward."

The magic words! Charl could scarcely believe his ears.

Aris's brown face broke into a smile. "Come, child. Your mother is waiting for us."

They took Charl's clothes, and the blanket from his bed, and fled to the stables. Aris held Charl before him on the saddle, and they rode quietly out of Uchtburg. Aris let the horse gallop once they were out of earshot. They rode all night, hid and rested the next day, and set off again at dusk. Charl lost count of how many nights they rode through cold, mountainous terrain. It might have been four, or maybe five. They reached St. Muckle's in the middle of the night, in driving sleet. Mama and Agnes, wide awake still, ran out to meet them, laughing and crying and hugging them in the flagstone yard of the Fiddle.

"I know you remember your maps," said Mama later, when Charl was curled up on her lap in front of the fire. "Which way did you and Aris ride? Not south, toward Fnark."

"North," said Charl. It had worried him, but Mama had said to trust Aris, and so he had.

"So where do you suppose we've ended up?" said Mama.

Four or five days north . . . Charl didn't have a clear idea how far a horse could go in that time, over the mountains. But then they'd crossed a fairly wide river. He guessed: "Goredd?"

"Well done," said Mama, laughing. Her laugh was like bells; he hadn't heard those bells ring in a long time.

"But, Mama," said Charl, wriggling, trying to sit up straighter. "Goredd is still at war with the dragons, aren't they? They didn't have the good sense to make peace, like Samsam." That was how his father always put it.

"Well," said Mama, "that should tell you how badly we needed to leave, if I thought we would be safer here than in Uchtburg. But don't worry—dragons don't often come to this corner of Goredd. People don't, either. It is my sincerest hope that we shall be overlooked here, and left to ourselves."

The next day, and every day for a week, it snowed in the

mountains. Even if Earl Ucht had wanted to follow them, no one was getting over the mountains until spring.

But spring came, and no one came after them.

And then whole years passed, quick enough to take your breath away. Charl did his best to forget that there was any such person as the Earl of Ucht in the world, and hoped that his father had forgotten him as well.

Time passes differently during a plague. Each day seems like a week, each week like a month, and so Charl was hard-pressed to say how long it had been since the terrible day Wort and Hooey died, or since the harbor opening (and quick reclosing), or since Sister Agnes figured out that boiling would kill the beetle eggs. It seemed like a year since the upper floor of the Fiddle had been turned into a second infirmary, and Charl had moved into Mama's office along with Aris and the doctor—not that Dr. Caramus ever seemed to occupy his pallet, so busy did his laboratory and both infirmaries keep him. How long had it been since the starless night when a wagon had spirited Rafe away over the mountain toward Port Marti?

In hindsight, Rafe seemed luckier than anyone: he'd gotten out of St. Muckle's.

All the normal things that marked the passage of time were suspended. Sister Agnes's little school was closed until further notice while she nursed the sick and helped Caramus think. Fencing lessons with Aris were suspended while he led dangerous extermination expeditions into the sewers and storm drains.

Charl now filled his mornings boiling sheets—Agnes was extremely strict about clean sheets—and stirring ceaseless pots of stew with the cook. Afternoons, he pulled a wagon around town with his mother, delivering stew to families in need.

He had some vague notion that the year was progressing. The apple trees had bloomed. (Had they? He wasn't remembering last year, was he?) The turnips had been planted. The sun began poking its nose out occasionally, as the spring rains subsided.

Charl had grown a bit, too, somewhere in there. Mama had her suspicions when she administered his elixir (Caramus wasn't available to do it), and made him stand up against the wall in her office where she occasionally tallied his height with a notch.

"An entire inch!" she exclaimed joyfully. "Well, there's one nice thing."

One nice thing was one more than zero, but far fewer than the not-nice things that were rapidly accumulating. Whole families had been taken ill before they knew to boil the water; others, cleverly drinking beer instead of water, carelessly let themselves get bitten. People began dying in such numbers that the catacombs were full, and the graveyard was full, and even the potter's field (quickly consecrated for new burials by Father Donal) was very nearly full. The beetles found their way into the church crypt and began feasting like the nightmarish hellvermin they were. If you pressed your ear to one of the old tombs of the town founders, it was said, you could hear their clicking mandibles and scrabbling claws inside.

That last bit may have been some miscreant's embellishment, but it sounded plausible enough that anyone who heard it kissed a knuckle toward Heaven. And some folk, irrationally, began to whisper about ghosts.

It was a ghost's unhealthy miasma that caused disease, maybe. Any patch of cold, moist, or stenchy air might be of supernatural origin, and in a town prone to fogs and vapors, there were plenty to choose from. Even the soft morning mists rising from the Sowline were suspect. If you kissed your knuckle, recited St. Eustace's Call to All Souls, and walked backward through any questionable patch of air (which was most of it, when the weather was drizzly), you could keep the ghosts out of your lungs, and keep yourself well.

"Backward beliefs are now manifested in literal backward walking, and I don't even know how to argue with people anymore," Sister Agnes complained. But she did, in fact, find ways to argue, and it didn't make much difference.

One night, as Agnes and Mama and Charl were sitting wearily, staring into the hearth—so tired and disheartened that even Sister Agnes wasn't talking—the front door burst open and they heard Dr. Caramus shout, "Eileen! Help me get him up onto a table."

He was propping up Aris, whose head lolled forward alarmingly, as if he were very drunk.

The front of his shirt was wet and grimy, which was not unusual after one of his beetle hunts, but then Charl noticed blood trickling onto the floor behind him.

"No, no no," Mama cried, rushing to his other side and helping Caramus prop him up. "Agnes, get Charl out of here."

"Charl has seen blood before," said Sister Agnes grimly. "And he's likely to see worse before this is all over." She gestured toward the dining tables with her thumb; Charl leaped to his feet and helped her drag chairs out of Dr. Caramus's way.

They laid the big man face down on the table, and Dr. Caramus cut Aris's linen shirt open. Agnes sent Charl to the kitchen for hot water. He returned as quickly as he could, and then Mama was sponging blood off Aris's back, and Dr. Caramus was examining his wounds. Charl stood to the side, but did not look away. Agnes, not usually a hugger, stood behind Charl with her arms around him.

"Two wounds—two different weapons—likely improvised weapons," Dr. Caramus muttered out loud. "Something not very sharp jabbed him just *here*, and you see, Eileen, it hasn't gone deep at all. The other one looks like it was done with a shard of glass. That's the one that's bleeding so fiercely. He'll need stitches, but then he'll be fine. Unless he has beetle bites."

"Caramus, you morbid ghoul! How can you even think about plague at a time like this?" cried Sister Agnes, looking around for anything to throw at him. There was only Aris's ruined shirt. Undeterred, she wadded that up and threw it at Caramus's head.

"He's right—you should . . . check," mumbled Aris, still face down on the table. "I landed in a . . . puddle after they jumped me."

So Aris was stripped of the rest of his clothing, and while Dr. Caramus stitched him up, Mama, Charl, and Sister Agnes brought in oil lamps and examined his skin for bites. His skin was too dark for red dots to be very visible, so they looked carefully for raised welts. None were found, thank Allsaints.

Mama sent Charl to the office to fetch Aris some fresh clothes. When Aris was fully bandaged and dressed, Mama wrapped him in blankets and set him down before the hearth. Charl fetched him a cup of warm chamomile tea; Dr. Caramus plied him with humulus syrup. And Sister Agnes, of course, demanded, "How could you let these ruffians get the jump on you? You used to be a knight."

"I still have a knight's reflexes, even if I'm thicker in the middle than I once was," said Aris, patting his stomach. "But you never asked me how many of them there were."

Agnes rolled her eyes so hard Charl was afraid she might strain something. "Fine. How many?"

"I was coming back from killing bugs out by Tanner's Lane," said Aris. He couldn't lean back in his chair, for obvious reasons, so he braced his elbows on his knees. "I'd just parted ways with Zano Cooper and turned toward home when I saw a cluster of folk gathered in front of Allsaints Church. I thought that was odd, this time of night, but wasn't inclined to interfere until I heard anger in their tone. I thought maybe they were still blaming that Vasterich boy, or ghosts, or something, and I could calm their fears a bit. So I went closer and realized there was a man on the church steps, saying things to rile everyone up.

"'These bugs come down the Sowline every year,' he was saying, 'but we never had a problem until *she* got too clever and decided she knew better than our forefathers a hundred years ago. There's a reason they filled in the harbor: to prevent infestations and to stop this plague. It's her arrogance, ignorance, and ambition that's done this to us.'"

Mama looked stricken; even Charl could tell whose arrogance, ignorance, and ambition he'd meant.

"Oh dear," said Sister Agnes, reaching for Mama's hand and squeezing it.

"The harbor is a problem, but it's not the only problem," said Caramus, firelight glinting off his spectacles. "Some beetles crawl up the jetties—enough for a mild infestation, perhaps—but they can't climb the smooth stone steps, or the floodwall. The valves should have stopped them getting into the storm drains. It is rather a mystery how the valves seem to have failed, when they keep passing inspection."

"What are you implying?" snapped Mama. "That someone has sabotaged our drains?"

"We never did learn who hit Willie over the head," said Dr. Caramus, shrugging.

Aris dropped his head into his hands and groaned.

"The humulus should start working soon," said the doctor, helping Aris to his feet. "It may cause dizziness. You'll want to be in bed when it kicks in."

They'd taken three steps toward the office when Aris stopped short and turned back toward the fire, his face a mask of unhappiness. "Eileen, I didn't want to worry you, but in light of . . . drain sabotage . . ." He cut off, panting a little. "The man. On the church steps. I couldn't see him, but I thought I knew his . . . voice. It sounded like . . . like *Brus*."

Mama's nostrils flared. She shook her head—slightly at first and then harder. "No. You were mistaken. You must have been. The earl would not have sent Brus, after seven long years of nothing." Her voice had risen in pitch considerably. "He's given up on us. I refuse to believe anything else."

Aris's head bobbed as the sedative began to take effect. "We can talk . . . tomorrow. But he sicced the crowd on me, Eileen. He saw me . . . standing there . . . and . . ."

"All right," said Caramus evenly. "You need rest. There will be time to tell us in the morning." He nudged Aris along, off down the corridor.

Mama, visibly shaken, sat again and stared into the fire. Sister Agnes nodded at Charl, and then the two of them sat on either side of Mama, huddled close, as if to keep her warm. Mama closed her eyes and breathed slowly through her nose.

"I don't think I ever met this . . . Bruce?" Sister Agnes said.

"Jarlbrus," said Mama. "He was the earl's spymaster, and you may not have seen him, but I guarantee he watched everything you did in Uchtburg."

"Not close enough," said Sister Agnes. "I got you out of there."

Mama graced her with a wan smile. "Jarlbrus masterminded all of the earl's cruelest and most brutal campaigns against his neighbors, and then against the pagans. If we gave him the slip, it's because he was busy planning the massacre at Echstau, and because he didn't believe I'd trust Charl's welfare to anyone else, even Aris."

"So you outmaneuvered the mastermind," said Sister Agnes. "That sounds about right."

Charl's ears had pricked up at this talk of cruel and brutal campaigns. He'd been too young to really understand, but he'd had the impression that his father was always at war. Charl remembered watching columns of soldiers drilling on the parade grounds, and how gleeful his father had been when Samsam made its separate peace with the dragons—not because it was the *end* of a war, but because it opened the possibility of smaller, more winnable wars, which the earl promptly launched and then won.

But Charl had never heard of this massacre.

"What happened at Echstau?" he asked.

Mama and Sister Agnes exchanged an inscrutable look.

Mama spoke carefully: "It happened after we left, Charl, so we've only heard rumors. But they say—and I believe it—that Jarlbrus wished to make an example of a village, not merely to murder the pagans, but to destroy everything and everyone. He wanted villagers across the highlands to understand that helping or hiding pagans, or letting them live quietly among you, was also a crime punishable by death."

"That message wasn't just for villagers," said Sister Agnes darkly.

"We don't know what happened," said Mama, leaning her head against Agnes's. "And we can't always tell what we would choose, at a terrible moment like that, until we've faced it."

"I just wish I could ask," said Sister Agnes through clenched teeth. "Ten minutes alone with her, to make her tell me the truth."

Charl didn't know who they were talking about now, but he'd stopped listening a few sentences back. Jarlbrus sounded terrible, but surely he'd only been doing his master's will. If he'd destroyed an entire village, the earl must have approved. His own father.

Are you your father's son? Rafe had asked him, way back when. It made Charl feel sick to think of all the things that meant.

"A perverse, unscrupulous genius like Jarlbrus . . ." Mama's voice trailed off as she thought. "I could imagine him helping our beetle infestation along, to spoil everything I've accomplished and turn everyone against me. And, of course, I'd sound paranoid if I started blaming him."

Sister Agnes straightened up and stretched. "You don't know for certain that Jarlbrus is here. Aris could have been mistaken. I can hardly ever tell who someone is by their voice, and after seven years? I'd be hard-pressed."

"Maybe you're right," said Mama.

Sister Agnes started pacing before the fire. "We didn't come here to live in fear, Eileen. We came here to be free, to make a life exactly the way we wanted. And we've done it. The past can't touch us here."

Just then, there was a knock at the Fiddle's front door.

Charl, who had leaned his head against his mother's arm, felt her flinch.

Sister Agnes paused to listen. When the knock came again, she headed for the foyer.

"Don't!" Mama cried. It had been years since Charl had heard such panic in her voice.

"Seven years," Agnes called over her shoulder. "I refuse to be afraid in our own home."

Charl leaped to his feet, rushed to the fireplace, and grabbed the iron poker. It had a wooden handle and felt surprisingly well balanced in his hand. It wasn't a proper sword, but it would hit harder than his wooden practice sword. With Aris wounded, surely it was up to him—

"Charl, don't be foolish!" his mother stage-whispered at him. She had scurried over to the bar and ducked behind the counter. "Come and hide."

"No," said Charl.

"If your father has sent someone to fetch us back—"

"Then that someone will have a fight on his hands," said Charl, not at all sure where he got the nerve to speak to his mother this way, let alone stand up to whoever was on the other side of that door. But he stepped into the middle of the room and took a ready stance.

Agnes threw open the front door and cried, "Saints' bones—you?"

A quiet voice replied, and then footsteps approached the common room.

The woman who entered was plainly some sort of nun, dressed all in white; Sister Agnes, behind her, was white-faced, as if she'd seen a ghost. The older nun had a stern, creased face, and her hair was entirely hidden under a crisply folded wimple. She was not much taller than Charl, but the coolness of her gaze suggested that she was looking down on him from a great height indeed.

He lowered his poker apologetically. Behind the counter, Mama stood up.

The older woman took in the scene with a glance and sniffed disdainfully. "You left the convent for *this*?"

"I do a lot of good here," said Sister Agnes, her voice oddly hollow, as if she were in shock. She slapped her own cheek lightly. "Eileen, Charl . . . this is Mother Trude, my former prioress. At Our Lady of the Glacier."

"Once your prioress, always your prioress," snapped the prioress.

"If you've come to drag Agnes back to the convent, you can turn around and go," said Mama in a low voice, coming out from behind the counter. "She's happy here. And after a year and a day in this town—like all who come here—she became a free woman."

It was all true, but Sister Agnes nevertheless looked pale and mortified. Charl had never seen her cringe like this. She was the brashest, most fearless person he knew.

"Are all your friends this rude, Agnes?" said Mother Trude. "Or perhaps you have this plague so well in hand that you don't need any help. Tell me—have you eradicated the beetles that cause it? Have you learned to boil your water, or what you should do when a patient starts coughing gray? Do you even know the name and origin of this disease?"

Sister Agnes's eyes widened. "It's some type of blood fever—"

"Bog ague," said the prioress. "Highlanders catch it sometimes, digging peat. I've come to help you, child, bearing knowledge of highland remedies, but if you don't want me here . . ."

There was an eternity in which Sister Agnes seemed incapable of answering.

"Of course we want your help. And welcome," said Mama, breaking the stalemate. She stepped forward and took the prioress's ringed hand. "My deepest apologies, Your Grace, for my initial suspicion. But you see how essential Sister Agnes is to us. We would not last long without her. I let my fear get the better of me."

"Well spoken, Mistress Innkeeper, I forgive you," sniffed the old woman. Her sharp crow's eyes flitted to Charl. "And this is your child, one presumes?"

"Charl," said Mama, holding a hand toward him. "My son."

Charl, a little put off at being called a *child*, was leaning somewhat awkwardly on the fireplace poker as if it were a cane, as if he had harbored no intention of ever swinging it at anyone's head. He bowed to the prioress.

"Interesting company you keep, Agnes," said the old woman. "But we shall have time to catch up. First, I should like to see your patients."

"Now?" said Sister Agnes. "It's late. You're surely exhausted from the journey. We'll find you someplace suitable to sleep, and then you can visit the sickrooms in the morning."

Mother Trude laid a hand gently against Sister Agnes's cheek. "I'm fine. You're the one who needs sleep; I see it in your eyes. Show me where my help is needed now, and then you must take some rest, my dear."

Agnes, sputtering in confusion, led Mother Trude upstairs.

Mama sighed and seated herself before the fire again. Charl returned the poker to its rack and sat beside her on the high-backed bench. Her eyes were closed, but she spoke: "Charl, I never want to see you reach for a weapon in response to uncertainty again. There are times to fight, I acknowledge—however reluctantly—but violence must never be your first reaction."

Charl's face went hot. "It might have been that man, Jarlbrus, intending to force us back to Uchtburg!"

"Violence came so easily to your father it was like a reflex," she continued, as if he hadn't spoken. "It happened so fast I sometimes thought he couldn't choose. I am trying to give you every opportunity to grow up another way. Can you see that?"

Charl burned with shame. Of course he could see that, but . . . he was half his father. What if that part of him was too strong? What if he couldn't help himself?

Mama opened her eyes, studying him. "What good does violence do, ultimately? Can you force people to love you? Can you defeat this plague at sword's point?"

"No," said Charl sulkily, leaning into her.

She wrapped her arm around him and closed her eyes again. "All right. Let us put the ghosts of the past to bed. Maybe this is the moment our luck changes, Charl. If this Mother Trude knows as much as she seems to . . . I've heard Agnes praise her skill before. Maybe we will finally start to get ahead of this . . . illness."

Charl struggled against it, but his eyes finally closed. They dozed before the fire, mother and son, dreaming of better days ahead.

8

The Mothers

here was no time to tell Agnes anything that first night, but Mother Trude reasoned that she should take things slowly in any case. If she should spring the news all at once—*I'm your mother, surprise!*—that would surely shock Agnes, perhaps even anger her. The ground had to be prepared. *I wasn't always a nun* might be the place to start, followed by *Did you ever wonder why you were brought to Our Lady from the orphanage in Fnark? Did you notice, at the convent, how I helped and protected you, and all the sacrifices I made?*

Then, finally: *There are things in my life that I regret, but that I had no choice about.*

In the morning, they breakfasted with several others—Eileen and the boy, as well as Sir Aris (as the earl had called him, but he clearly wasn't a knight anymore). Mother Trude couldn't very well speak about personal things in front of strangers, so she waited patiently until she and Agnes were crossing town toward the Riverside Infirmary.

The sky was high and blue; the sun glittered off puddles on the street. Agnes, plump and vigorous as she'd always been, was a fast walker; Mother Trude had to scurry to keep up. She considered taking the younger nun's arm, to slow her down, but she recalled that Agnes was not fond of such contact.

"I'd hoped to have a chance to speak with you," Mother Trude began, a bit breathless from hustling along.

Agnes shot her a sharp glance. "If this is about why I ran away—"

"No, no," said Mother Trude, trying to sound reassuring. "Water under the bridge. You are forgiven. Don't let your heart be troubled on that count anymore."

"Don't worry," said Agnes. "I haven't spent one minute feeling bad about *that*."

Ouch. She might have felt a *little* bad. One minute's worth. That wasn't much to ask.

Agnes had pulled ahead again. Mother Trude stopped trying to stay caught up.

The Riverside Infirmary was as clean and tidy as they could keep it, but it still had that familiar sickroom smell, of bodies and their fluids, and something unnervingly sweet.

Death.

Her students at Our Lady always used to ask why something sad and frightening should smell sweet. And she'd never been able to answer the way her own mother used to: *Because it's not sad, or frightening, to depart this world for the Blue Country.* Mother Trude, as an old nun who knew better, had answered instead, "It's St. Eustace's perfume." A silly answer and not theologically sound, but it satisfied the novices.

Agnes showed her around, the way the patients were sorted—mild to severe cases, with a curtain hung to separate those who were coughing gray—and then the clean sheets, the medicinal tinctures, the teakettle. "Empty the bedpans and change the sheets. Hygiene first," she said.

"So you did listen to your old teacher," said Mother Trude, trying to restart the conversation, to remind Agnes what they had once been to each other.

"I'll send Charl down around noon, to pick up the soiled sheets and deliver fresh ones," Agnes continued, as if she hadn't spoken. "He'll bring lunch for you and Dr. Caramus."

"No turnips," called a voice from the other room, which Agnes had identified as the laboratory. "I won't eat another turnip."

"You will eat what there is," Agnes called back. "And what there *is* is turnips, mostly."

Mother Trude had traded her snow-white habit for a brown homespun kirtle—as close as she could get to the lay habit Agnes wore these days—and she began rolling up her sleeves. "Let's get to it. You lift the—"

"Ah, no," said Agnes. "I'll be up at the Fiddle, giving those patients my full attention for a change. You'll work with Dr. Caramus." She pointed at a furtive-looking man in a black apron who now stood in the laboratory doorway. His slender hands crawled restlessly all over each other, like two spiders.

Mother Trude's heart sank. She'd only caught a glimpse of Dr. Caramus last night, shuffling down the hall after he'd settled Sir Aris, but in the light of day he was clearly a dragon.

Not as obvious as some saarantrai, due to years of practice, presumably, but she'd known what to look for since childhood, and she was hard to fool. The doctor's hands, each of which seemed to have a mind of its own, were one clue; dragons never quite got used to their sensitivity and dexterity. That alone was not definitive, however.

What clinched it was the way he surreptitiously sniffed Agnes as she spun on her heel to leave, and then licked his lips as if he were also tasting the smell.

Other than that, he was quite good. Mother Trude studied him out of the corner of her eye while she changed the sheets. His bedside manner was overly formal, perhaps, considering that most of his patients were of plain peasant stock, but she could find no other fault with it. Where you'd expect a dragon to turn coldly away—when someone was in emotional distress as well as physical—he did not. He held hands and patted heads. He looked almost sad sometimes.

Still, she couldn't bear the thought of being stuck with him day after day, hardly seeing Agnes at all. She hadn't done what she'd done and promised what she'd promised for this.

(And it was not lost on her that if she fulfilled that promise and stole the earl's son away, the dragon doctor could track her by smell. She'd have to plan a way around that.)

Meanwhile, there had to be some way around her current circumstances. Perhaps she could alienate the doctor so thoroughly that he'd refuse to work with her. That wouldn't be easy, but no better idea had occurred to her immediately.

And so, after emptying bedpans and administering fever-reducing teas and making her patients comfortable, Mother Trude slipped into the little laboratory where Dr. Caramus had retreated. The shelves held jars of bog beetles in various stages of development, scrabbling horribly with serrated legs, trying to get out. There were herbs, fresh and dried, bottled concoctions, glassware in fanciful designs, and an elaborate array of lenses for looking at very tiny things. The doctor was perched upon a high stool, crushing something in a mortar.

"What do you need?" he asked without turning around.

Mother Trude pursed her lips, reviewing a phrase in her mind before saying it. "You're a dragon," she finally said in softmouth Mootya—that is to say, the language of dragons as spoken with a human mouth. She understood it perfectly well but was not accustomed to forming the sounds. Her pronunciation was surely off.

The doctor turned, however, and looked at her owlishly through his lenses. "That is correct," he answered in the same language.

"You don't trust me!" Mother Trude blurted out, and instantly regretted it. She'd meant to say *I don't trust you,* but had confused her grammar—as happens when you don't practice—and had said exactly the opposite of what she'd intended.

Dr. Caramus removed the magnifiers from his eyes, folded them slowly, and put them in the pocket of his apron. "Correct again," he said. "I don't trust you."

Mother Trude was taken aback. She had inadvertently stumbled upon a truth that she didn't know what to do with. She managed to stammer out, "Wh-why?"

"Because Sister Agnes doesn't trust you," said Dr. Caramus, still in his native language. "Even with this tiny, feeble human nose, I can smell it on her."

His nose was not tiny, by human standards, but Mother

Trude was too shocked to make any such rejoinder. All words had abandoned her, in every language she knew, and she could only stand there gaping incapably.

Agnes didn't trust her? *Agnes?*

Of course she didn't. The girl had run away from the convent, after all; something had been broken between them for years. And who knew what else she might have heard in the years since. Echstau? Prison? Even at this distance, news must have reached her, accurate or not.

Mother Trude had let herself be dazzled by hope. Her journey toward telling her daughter the truth now seemed not merely uphill, but up-mountain. Up to the heavens. Impossible.

"I smell deceit on you, as well as fear. So, no, I don't trust you," Dr. Caramus added. He turned toward his desk and took up pen and notebook, giving her to understand that the conversation was over.

It was just as well. Mother Trude had no idea how to respond. She did all she could think to do: she returned to the sickroom, rolled up her sleeves again, and got back to work.

She had done this so many times, gotten through pain and uncertainty by blocking it out with work, that she had it down to a fine art. She was tireless. She was a machine. Her presence made a tremendous difference right away, to her patients at least. She anticipated their needs and had no fear of those who were coughing gray, but tied a swath of filtering cloth over her face and kept working. They wept as she cleaned them and apologized for their condition. She held their hands, wept with them, prayed with them, and never lost sight that she, too, would someday be where they were. Toward death march we all, eventually.

As wrenching as the sickroom was, it was easy compared with other things she'd seen.

She had so much to atone for.

Before a week had passed, Dr. Caramus stood up after dinner and declared, in the bluntest, most draconic way imaginable, "Mother Trude is making a tremendous difference at the Riverside Infirmary, and you, Sister Agnes, of all people, ought to take that into consideration and feel a bit of gratitude for her presence."

Mother Trude flushed at this unexpected praise, but before she could take any joy in it, Agnes snapped, "A dragon is telling me how to feel. Thanks for that."

She flounced out. Mother Trude had never known a nun who could flounce like Agnes.

"You're welcome," said Dr. Caramus, absurdly, toward the space where Agnes had been.

"We *are* grateful, I hope you know," said Eileen, leaning across the table to gently touch Mother Trude's wrist. "We're seeing more recoveries under your care. It's very encouraging."

"A great boost to morale," Sir Aris agreed, and the boy, seated beside him, smiled at her.

(If Mother Trude kept thinking of Charl as *the boy*, it's because he was not quite what the earl had led her to expect. The name change should have been predictable. And of course he'd matured; he was fully teenaged now, not the child the earl still pictured. But . . . Mother Trude was having to adjust her brain, which took time because she was old, and she couldn't afford any missteps. Agnes already distrusted her; if the boy should conceive a distrust of her as well, then she had truly come here for nothing.)

If she hoped to spend time with Agnes, clearly she would have to create an opportunity. Waiting was a losing game: Who could say how much time was left before Miga lost patience and rained flame upon them all? Or before Brus began his endgame, whatever that might be? (Mother Trude hadn't seen him, but never doubted he was here, or that he knew *she* was here; he would have recruited a few faithful spies, even in a place like this.)

And so, one morning, Mother Trude simply stayed at the Fiddle and attended the patients there. She'd changed half the sheets before Agnes came up, which Agnes, alas, took as criticism.

"Am I not doing things to your satisfaction?" she cried, scowling at the laundry pile.

"I thought you might welcome company," said Mother Trude, biting back whatever else popped into her head. If Agnes wanted criticism, her old teacher could have provided some. It's not generally in a nun's nature to hold back.

Agnes grudgingly got to work alongside Mother Trude, and when the patients at the Fiddle were settled, she came along to Riverside and helped out there.

In silence, but still. It was better than nothing. Mother Trude felt her hope returning.

Because who had taught Agnes her devious nun trick in the first place? Mother Trude knew exactly how to learn what she wanted most to know.

"How fortunate that we have a dragon working on a cure," she mused one day while she and Agnes attended to the gray ward, protective linen over their mouths. "And how extraordinary that he chooses to live among Goreddis, when his people are still at war with Goredd."

"Oh, it was his own people who drove him into exile. They'd kill him if they found him again," said Agnes. And then she was off and running—or her mouth was, anyway, the linen notwithstanding. Dr. Caramus was considered a dangerous deviant, abhorred by other dragons for running controversial experiments. Eileen had found him living on the streets of Fnark when she was a girl, and had befriended him. She'd persuaded her mother to let him be her tutor, and he'd stayed on until Eileen married the earl, at which point . . .

The story went on and on, full of *Eileen* this and *Eileen* that. Saintly, wondrous Eileen, helping a poor, exiled dragon feel that he had a purpose and a place in this world.

Mother Trude was not entirely satisfied with this story. It made her squirm a little. But before she drew her conclusion, she tried again—this time on their way back to the Fiddle, upon seeing Sir Aris, mostly recovered from his attack, crossing the square to go beetle hunting in the crypt below Allsaints. He waved; Agnes waved back.

"How fortunate that we have an actual knight here to protect us," said Mother Trude. "But exterminating beetles seems like a step down, compared with fighting dragons."

"Oh, Aris gave up dragon fighting long ago," said Agnes, launching into another story, this time about a man who had grown disgusted and disillusioned with violence and war, whose conscience had weighed heavier with each passing year. Someone who'd felt like a fish out of water, until he'd met Eileen and saw that he had choices, that there was always another way to live.

It was a happy story—a hopeful story—but all Mother Trude heard was *Eileen, Eileen, Eileen.* What a remarkable person this Eileen seemed to be, showing everyone else the way.

Because, in fact, Mother Trude cared little for the details of Sir Aris's life or whatever bizarre thing Dr. Caramus had done. The question that had pressed upon her mind, and that Agnes had inadvertently answered with her enthusiasms, was why Agnes was here.

And why she had left.

Both stories pointed toward a distressingly clear answer: Agnes had felt like another fish out of water. Like an exile in her own home. And Eileen had shown her a place where she belonged.

Mother Trude, even though she knew she was being unfair and uncharitable, felt substantially soured on Eileen.

Then one evening, as Mother Trude helped with the washing up, Eileen—who was drying—said, "Agnes, there was something you wanted to ask Mother Trude."

"Not important," muttered Agnes, who was putting clean dishes away. She turned to put mugs on a shelf.

"Mother Trude," said Eileen, in a patient, explaining voice, "the night you arrived, we had been talking about you. And Sister Agnes said that she wished she could have ten minutes alone with you someday, because there was something she wanted to say."

Mother Trude, up to her elbows in dishwater, felt her heart lurch painfully as it once again filled with hope. She could think of only one thing Agnes might have wished to say: why she had left, what had gone wrong, that she hoped her old prioress would understand. Then it would be Mother Trude's turn to say something true, and she could finally tell Agnes the secret that had been burning a hole in her heart for decades. And while she resented Eileen's sticking herself in the middle of things, all would be forgiven once the truth was out and—

"How could you let it happen?" Agnes burst out, slamming a pan on the counter.

Mother Trude turned to face her, hands dripping all over the floor. "How . . . ? What?"

"You let the villagers of Echstau perish at our gates!" Agnes was red and shaking.

Mother Trude trembled, as before the judgment of Heaven. "Not a day goes by but that I think of them and pray for them," she said in a small voice. "They haunt me, I promise you."

"You used to *save* people, when I was there. You used to shelter pagans."

And yet you left anyway. This was not the time to say that.

"The earl sent his dragon. She would have killed us all," said Mother Trude, barely able to speak through chattering teeth. "I had no choice."

"There's always a choice!" Sister Agnes shouted back.

That was Eileen's credo, Eileen's philosophy coming out of Agnes's mouth. And then Eileen was at Agnes's side, wrapping her in a supportive hug and whispering in her ear.

It was too much. Agnes didn't like to be touched, but Eileen could get away with it, apparently. And Mother Trude couldn't very well say *I'm your mother, and the earl found out somehow and was threatening you,* not now, not when Agnes was so angry. That would only make everything worse.

"I need some air," said Mother Trude.

"Yes, let's all take a minute," said Eileen.

Mother Trude walked out of the kitchen, into the flagstone yard behind the inn, where she sat on the steps with her elbows on her knees and her head in her wet hands. She hadn't even dried them. The prioress sat there a long time, breathing heavily, trying not to weep.

Hating Eileen, even though she knew full well that hate diminished the hater.

The nerve of that ex-earlina, meddling in other people's affairs. Trying to facilitate a painful conversation that could not possibly have ended happily. Convincing Agnes that there's always a choice, when sometimes there wasn't.

Sometimes there absolutely wasn't.

Mother Trude looked up at the sunset sky—pink, orange, purple—and saw the first tiny stars beginning to wink into existence, as they did every night, whatever dreadful things the people of Earth had been up to that day.

A sound began to penetrate her awareness, across the yard, where laundry had been hung to dry. Someone was out there, moving among the billowing sheets; she could hear feet scuffling against the flagstones. Probably not Brus, or if it was, she couldn't imagine what he was up to. It could almost have been a dog, tussling with rats. She rose silently, crept over to the laundry lines, and peered around the end to see who was there.

It was the boy, Charl, lunging with a wooden sword, practicing his fencing footwork where his mother wouldn't see him.

Something seemed to cool and condense in Mother Trude's chest. She had not failed to notice the boy brandishing a fire poker when she'd first arrived; neither had she missed Eileen's horrified and angry reaction to it.

Here was another self-inflicted exile. A fish out of water.

Eileen was not the only person who knew how to pick up a lonely soul, gently, delicately, and find it a new pond to swim in.

The boy whirled around—not because he'd heard her, but because it was part of his sword drill. He saw Mother Trude then and froze, eyes wide, practice sword pointed at her stomach. Hastily, he tucked the sword behind his back.

"Don't stop on my account," she said. "I didn't mean to startle you. You're quite good. Have you been learning long?"

"Seven years, almost," he mumbled, looking at his feet.

"That's good exercise," she said. "And a useful skill to have, in these uncertain times. Anyway, I won't detain you."

She turned to go. The boy rushed up and laid a hand on her sleeve.

"Don't tell my mother?" he whispered.

Mother Trude smiled beatifically. "What would I tell her? That her son is taking care of himself? Someday she'll appreciate that you did this, but for now, your secret's safe with me."

The boy nodded shyly and went back to it. Mother Trude passed through the curtain of sheets and walked toward the house, looking up at the cold moon.

As cold as Mother Trude's calculations now turned.

She'd been given a task, and she'd made no progress on it, choosing instead to break her heart over Agnes. That had been a fool's errand from the start. Eileen had taken her child from her—well and truly, no getting her back—and so she would have Eileen's child, and she'd return him to that . . . that monster, his father. There was no point mincing words; that monster had given her no choice.

But Eileen, at least, was human and would grieve. And then she would know how it felt.

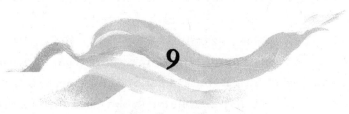

9

The Last Day

"I have good news," Dr. Caramus said one morning, bursting into the kitchen where Mama, Aris, and Charl were hastily shoveling down their oatmeal before the day's chores began. "One of my colleagues in Porphyry has finally come through with a research paper on the efficaciousness of certain northern herbs and resins on another ague—*hydroernica*, in Porphyrian, or 'marsh fever'—with a prognosis of—"

"Can you put it more plainly?" Mama interrupted gently, passing him a bowl of porridge.

"There may be a cure," said Dr. Caramus, accepting the bowl and tapping his spoon thoughtfully on the rim. "It requires some foreign herbs, but I was able to reach my contact at House Falerno and order them. I don't know how soon they will arrive, however."

"Good," said Mama. "Perfect. We just have to hang on until then."

Her voice sounded light and cheerful, but Charl could hear the strain.

Hanging on was only getting harder.

Aris's extermination crews were dwindling as one by one his men fell ill. The upstairs of the Fiddle had filled up, so patients were also laid out on pallets in the public room, the hallways, and the office. Every able-bodied resident now had to sleep in the kitchen. Mama still refused to believe Jarlbrus was the one spreading anger among the townsfolk—and indeed, there'd been no sightings since the day Aris got stabbed—but whoever was doing it kept the embers hot. The front door of the Fiddle was defaced more than once, and filth thrown at the windows. The stable roof was set on fire, although (this being St. Muckle's) it had started to rain before the blaze could do much damage.

Aris began looking for Jarlbrus, instead of hunting bugs. Mama, though she would not have admitted it, stopped speaking to him.

Charl began bringing stew around town by himself, in part because the infirmaries were so busy that his mother was needed there, and in part because things had begun to get ugly when she took the cart around. People would jeer or even throw things—and then get angry if she didn't give them any stew. They were better behaved with Charl, usually.

The work was more taxing than he'd realized when Mama was doing it with him. It wasn't the strain of hauling the cart, but of dealing with the people on his route. They all had frightened and grieving eyes. Gorlich Smith, whose Nancy had come down sick, looked ashamed to be taking food, but he had six children to feed. He could hardly meet Charl's eye as he accepted his share, and the next day he sent out Mellie and Gert.

This should have been easier, but somehow it was worse. Charl had hardly seen the twins since the plague began, a whole season, the longest they'd ever been apart, and yet it felt like years had passed. They had always been taller than him, but now they were at least six inches taller. They looked like strangers, almost. Like grown women, with their hair up and their kirtles cinched at the waist. Mellie was quiet—he'd never known her to be quiet—and Gert's eyes were swollen, because, plainly, she'd been crying.

"Stew for yew," said Charl, emphasizing the rhyme, returning their pot with a flourish. They didn't crack a smile, and he couldn't blame them. It had been a feeble attempt at cheer.

"Our mother has come down sick," said Gert dully.

"I heard," said Charl. "I'm so sorry."

"It's a bit strange, some say, that no one in your household ever gets bitten," said Gert. There was an edge to her voice that he'd never heard before, like she was angry but trying not to show it.

It *was* strange, truth be told, and it wasn't just residents of the Fiddle who seemed to lead a beetle-free existence, but also the Vasteriches, in Vasterich Hall, and their servants. Charl himself had noticed this and asked Sister Agnes about it. She'd had a theory, of course, which Charl now shared with the twins:

"The Fiddle was built on a little rise, and is solidly made of stone—same as Vasterich Hall. So the beetles don't get in easily. And anyway, they prefer the muck that accumulates down in the low—"

"In the *low* parts of town, is that what you were about to say?" burst in Mellie.

"I didn't mean it like that," said Charl, in some confusion. "Not the way Rafe used to."

"If the Fiddle is so safe, maybe you should have been sheltering healthy people there," said Gert, "so they could stay healthy."

The girls turned their backs on him and went inside. Charl could only gape foolishly, and then get on with his rounds. He came up with several snappy replies then, too late to do any good: *We've been tending the sick, killing bugs, and feeding people. What have the Vasteriches done for anybody? Go demand shelter from them.*

Maybe it was for the best that that reply had come too slow. He didn't want to fight with the twins. Everything was already upside down and wrong without adding an argument to it. On days like this, they should have been chasing each other around the square and netting eels at the millrace, not delivering charity or caring for sick parents.

Still, things stayed awkward after that. The twins accepted their stew quietly and wouldn't meet his eye.

One day, after Charl had been making the rounds on his own for a couple of weeks, one neighbor, clutching her full tureen, asked nastily, "How does your mother have the money to give away so much food?"

Charl was tempted to answer *If you don't want it, I'll take it back.* But he said nothing.

"Don't you know?" cried someone from a window across the street. "His thieving mother stole it from his noble father when she ran off with his captain of the guard."

It wasn't true. She'd taken nothing but her own dowry,

which belonged to her, and she'd done nothing with it but work to improve this town. Still Charl said nothing.

"Did she run off with old Aris, though, or with that backsliding nun?" called someone else, from two doorways down. "It's hard to tell. Which was it, Charleen?"

That got a cackle out of all of them—*ha-ha, good one, turn Charl into a girl's name, that'll teach the little blighter.* Charl hunched his shoulders, wheeled his cart around, and headed home. He hadn't made half his deliveries yet; cries of dismay, and a few threats, rose up behind him, but no one followed.

He hauled the cart into the flagstone yard, hardly able to see through angry tears, and flung himself down beside the kitchen door, curled with his head upon his knees. They'd cut him deeper than they knew, making fun of the name he chose. It wasn't like "Eileen," which was meant to be unmemorable; he'd put a lot of thought into it. And he knew he was overreacting, but why were people cruel when you tried to help them? It made no sense. He spent several minutes trying not to cry too loudly, then trying to stop crying, before he was able to focus on the voices wafting out of the kitchen. Four voices, speaking seriously together.

"I am never one to give up," Mother Trude was saying, "but we have to be realistic. We may have to evacuate the town."

"She's right," said Dr. Caramus. "Leave the sick behind, and send everyone else over the mountain to Fort Lambeth."

"I don't like it," said Mama.

"The beetles are too many," Sister Agnes said, almost pleading. "It would be easier to clear them out if the town were empt—"

"I don't like leaving the sick behind," Mama interjected.

"Most of them wouldn't make it to Fort Lambeth," said Dr. Caramus.

"What about the Old Abbey?" asked Mama. Charl could see her, in his mind's eye, folding her arms stubbornly.

There was a long pause. Charl stood up, wiped his eyes, and brushed off his backside.

"It is *dryer* up the mountain," Caramus conceded as Charl stepped into the kitchen.

"It might feel less like abandoning their homes," said Sister Agnes. "Less like defeat."

"It's not a bad idea. But let's discuss it more later," said Mama, her eyes flicking in warning toward the doorway. The others turned to look at Charl standing there.

For a moment, he didn't see why they would stop the discussion when he came inside, but then he realized. They'd been talking about evacuating to the Old Abbey. His mother didn't want to remind him of what he'd seen there. For some reason, this made him angry.

"I think the Old Abbey would be a sensible place to go," he said, glaring at his mother. "There's a well, and an orchard, and some of the buildings still have most of their roofs intact."

Mama opened her mouth as if to say something, then closed it again.

"At the very least, evacuate the children there," said Mother Trude, utterly misreading the situation. "It can't be healthy for them to see so much death so young."

Nothing was normal, and it felt like nothing would ever be normal again.

The church bell, always part of the background of life, had

taken on a new and sinister meaning: someone had died. It began to feel like a blow, every time it rang. Charl would hear the deep, resounding chime and know that another life had ended. Then, as if he were haunted by their ghosts, he'd see Wort and Hooey again, right in front of him, burning. They'd died before the plague, but they were the first people he'd ever seen die, and so each death knell brought them back. His heart would pound, his hands would shake, and he couldn't get enough air. When that happened, he hid, which didn't stop him hearing it—the bell of Allsaints Church was so large that no part of town escaped its sound—but kept him out of sight until the spell passed, so no one saw him like that.

The only thing he could do, the only thing that made him feel anything like he'd felt before Wort and Hooey died and before the beetles came, was to do drills with his practice sword, and there was no time for that—officially. Unofficially, he sometimes found time. If he could hang the laundry quickly enough, he could make himself a little fortress of billowing sheets, a screen behind which no one could see him lunging and parrying.

It focused his mind. Even ten stolen minutes helped.

Mother Trude had caught him at it once, but she'd apparently been good to her word and not told Mama. Maybe he shouldn't have been surprised; Sister Agnes wouldn't have told on him, either, and Mother Trude had been her teacher. The old nun had been tirelessly tending the sick, but this had made him appreciate her all the more.

Upon an overcast day near midsummer—a day he would later think of as the Last Day—he finally got caught. Mama, a whirl of red hair and sharp elbows, stormed into his sheet fort and snatched the practice sword out of his hand.

"Hey!" he cried, aware of sounding shrill and petulant, like a much-younger child.

"Don't you 'Hey' me," Mama said. She never shouted; she didn't have to, to sound perfectly angry. "I have been calling you and calling you to bring in the sheets and haul supplies down to Riverside. And I need water fetched and soup ladled, but here you are, flailing about with this violent nonsense."

Charl opened his mouth, but he knew anything he said now would come out with either a shout or a sniveling whine. Neither of those would get his sword back. Before he could come up with anything sensible to say, however, Mama broke the wooden blade across her knee with a thunderous crack. She dropped the pieces at his feet.

Charl could only stare.

"Mama, I needed that!" he burst out at last, dropping to his knees to pick up the pieces. He was working very hard not to cry.

"Our need is in the sickroom, Charl," said his mother. "The world is saved through diligence, care, and practical, thankless things, not flashy heroics. That's what I always hoped Aris would teach you—but now he's haring off after imaginary Jarlbruses, so maybe he isn't the role model I hoped he would be."

"Don't put this on Aris," said Charl. "Sword fighting is what I love and what I'm good at, Mama, whether you approve of it or not. That's just who I am."

"A swordfighter who sasses his mother."

She seemed to be deliberately misconstruing everything he said. "You're the one who always says we came here so we could be ourselves."

"There is a difference between being yourself and being selfish," said Mama solemnly.

"I wish we had never come here!" he cried, his voice echoing all around the courtyard. The sheets seemed to tremble with it, although that was probably just the breeze.

It was just then that Gorlich Smith peered around the end of the clothesline. "There you are," he said glumly, nodding at Mama. "Beg your pardon, young fellow, but I need to borrow your mother a moment."

"Oh no," she said, her face falling. "Is it Nancy?"

"She's taken a grave turn for the worse, Lady Eileen. She would appreciate being able to thank you one last time before she goes."

Mama got a funny look whenever anyone called her *Lady*, but she was able to rise to the solemnity of the occasion and not answer in her usual way (by throwing a title back at whoever was talking to her—in this case, Lord Gorlich). She said simply, "Tell her I'm coming. I have but one thing more to say to my son."

Gorlich bobbed his head and departed. Mama turned to Charl, eyes flashing, and said, "I don't ever want to hear you say such a thing again."

"It's true whether I say it out loud or not," he cried. "I could have been a prince in Uchtburg, and nobody would care if I practiced swords all day. Or we could have fled to someplace nice, like Segosh or Mundegal. But, no, you had to drag me here—"

"You would never have been a *prince*," Mama said, correcting his exaggeration, as if that were the point.

"To your muddy peasants' paradise," Charl continued doggedly, "where you think you know what's best for everyone. It's so much more satisfying than being an earlina, I guess, because you get to meddle in everybody's business directly. If that's not selfish, I don't know what is."

He regretted the words at once, but that just made him angrier at how mean he'd been.

The expression on her face told him he had sorely tested her resolve to stay calm. He could almost see that resolve, underneath the surface of her skin, stretching to the breaking point. She brushed her hands against her apron, like she was dusting herself off, and said in a tight voice, "I am too angry to speak to you just now, Charl. Finish getting the laundry in and then go help Agnes. She's at the Riverside Infirmary. You and I will have words later."

She turned her back on him and returned to the Fiddle to see Nancy. Charl dragged dry sheets off the line and shoved them into the basket without folding them.

And that was the last time he spoke to his mother, the last thing they each said to each other, for a long time. A stupid, pointless fight. Just the kind of thing to haunt a person later.

Charl dragged his feet all the way to Riverside, and he dragged the little handcart carrying food supplies. It would have been wrong to describe the cart as full. It held two sacks, filled mostly with oatmeal and turnips. At some point, when your town is under quarantine and ravenous beetles are eating everything, even money can't buy you better food.

The bugs seemed not to like turnips and oatmeal. Charl, by this point, didn't like them much, either.

At the infirmary, Sister Agnes and Mother Trude were

carefully turning a patient onto his stomach so they could clean his bedsores. Agnes spotted Charl in the doorway and came running over, a strip of fabric in her hand. She had a similar one tied around her own face.

"Tie this on," she said in a muffled voice. "We've got five coughing gray. They're at the back, behind the partition, but there may be spores floating about. Dr. Caramus has been pretty vague about how long they last and how far they float."

Charl did as she instructed and then pulled his handcart through the doorway. As he was hauling the wheels over the sill, a shadow seemed to cross the sun. He looked up, but the sky was overcast; either a bird had flown by or . . . he wasn't sure what. He was still staring upward when it happened again, a distinct moment of darkness, gone almost as soon as it began.

A shadow had crossed the sun *on the other side of the clouds*.

There was only one thing that could be.

He'd never seen a full-sized dragon, but that didn't stop his blood from freezing in his veins.

"Charl!" Sister Agnes called impatiently. "Come inside."

He turned to tell her what he'd seen and what he feared, but before he could say a word there was a terrible crash. The ground shook.

"What the devil was that?" cried Sister Agnes, rushing for the door. She pushed past Charl's cart and stepped out into the street. Charl went after her, followed by Mother Trude.

At the end of the street, the facade of a rooming house had collapsed into a pile of broken bricks. You could see into all the rooms, as if it were a dollhouse; the little people inside—those who weren't sick in bed—were running around screaming.

A dragon, rusty brown against the blue-gray slate roof,

clung to the roof with wicked-looking talons. It arched its sinuous, spiny neck, looking into all the rooms, neither flinching nor reacting as frantic, panicking people threw cast-iron pans and other heavy objects at its face. It knocked tables and other furniture over with its snout, and then it raised its head upright again. It seemed to shrug.

And then it unhinged its jaw and let loose a fountain of fire.

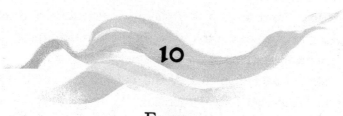

10

Escape

harl stared at the gargantuan creature, paralyzed, until he was yanked back indoors by Sister Agnes. She pulled Mother Trude inside as well, and barred the door behind them, as if that would do any good against a determined dragon.

"We're out of time," Mother Trude was muttering. "All the things I meant to tell you . . ."

Charl felt like the room was swaying. He couldn't focus his eyes.

"Charl!" barked Sister Agnes. She grabbed one of the sacks from his cart and thrust it toward him. He closed his hands around it uncertainly, in a daze.

"Run for the Old Abbey," Agnes was saying. "Take Mother Trude and keep her safe. Wait there for the rest of us. Can you do that?"

Everything snapped back into focus. "I can."

Sister Agnes shoved the second sack into Mother Trude's arms and hustled them both toward the back of the clinic—reminding Charl to raise his scarf against the gray. At the alley door, they heard screams and thudding feet outside. Someone began pounding on the front door of the infirmary, then multiple someones, crying and pleading, desperate to get in.

"Shall we let them in? Would that do any good?" said Mother Trude, her voice oddly acidic.

Sister Agnes ignored the sarcasm, lowered her face to Charl's level, and put her hands on his cheeks. "I'll find Eileen and Aris, and we'll come up after you, as soon as we're able."

Charl's heart quailed. If they weren't all going together, any number of terrible things might happen. What if . . . What if . . . ?

Sister Agnes was having the same fears—he could see it in her eyes—but she held herself together and said, "Courage, Charl. Be quick. Be quiet. Don't look back."

She flung open the alley door. Charl grabbed Mother Trude's hand, and the two of them plunged out into chaos.

The alley was full of people running in every direction—mostly away from the dragon, but some toward the dragon refuge under the town hall, as they'd been taught to do since they were young. But wasn't it full of beetles? Maybe beetles didn't seem as terrifying as a dragon.

The winged shadow passed overhead again. Everyone instinctively ducked, screaming.

Be quick. Be quiet. Charl did his best not to scream, weaving through the cowering crowd. Mother Trude did not stop, either, but gritted her teeth and followed on his heels. He knew this town like the back of his hand, so he led her up alleys, through shops and workshops (deserted—everyone had rushed off without locking up). They cut through a stable where the horses were shrieking and bucking, wild-eyed in their stalls.

Shouts came from all directions, and tall buildings blocked Charl's view of the sky, making it hard to tell where the dragon was at any given moment. There were ample signs of where it had passed—collapsed rooftops, roads blocked by rubble, gobbets of flaming dragon spittle.

He glimpsed Mellie and Gert looking sooty, terrified, and very small amidst a crowd. He cupped his hands and called their names, but they didn't seem to hear. He was about to go after them, bring them along to the Old Abbey, when Mother Trude's hand clamped on to his shoulder.

"We have enough food for *us*," she hissed in his ear. "We can't bring everyone along. If we all started running for the mountain at the same time, the dragon would torch us as we fled across the fields. We'd only be making it easier for her to kill us."

Her? How could one tell with dragons? Mother Trude was right about making themselves a target, though, even if it made Charl hurt inside to admit it.

A few more turns brought them to the northwestern edge of town, which opened directly into a turnip field. The northern road came out farther east, but that was a fool's route, with no cover. But they couldn't simply run across the turnip fields, because the foliage barely came up to their knees. Only the dense, brambly hedgerows, dividing one field from another, offered any concealment.

"Follow me," Charl said to Mother Trude. He slid down an embankment, scuttled over to the hedgerow, and began creeping along in its shadow.

He'd half expected her to complain, but she did not. He glanced back, and she was right behind him, furiously duck-walking.

Through gaps in the hedge, he could see people fleeing along the open road. Then he saw a swift shadow overtake them and a jet of flame from on high. They were incinerated in their tracks.

In his mind's eye, Hooey and Wort burst into flames again. Charl wrapped his arms around his head and curled into a ball.

Firm hands grasped his shoulders—Mother Trude, shaking him. "Boy," she said. "*Boy*. We have to keep moving or that will be our fate as well. Understand?"

He did. He wiped his cheeks with a muddy hand and somehow resumed crawling. On and on they went, past the hamlet (not yet on fire), and onward, endlessly.

The mountain was forested, but before they could reach the trees, the hedgerows ended. There was one last field to cross, with no concealment but the turnips themselves. Sister Agnes had told him not to look back, but he had to now, to see where the dragon was and what it was doing. Maybe some people were putting up a fight. Surely, Aris—though he'd sworn he would never fight dragons again—couldn't stand idly by and let the town be destroyed.

If ever there was a time for violence, surely this was it.

No one was engaging the dragon directly, however. The beast had curled itself around the spire of Allsaints and was looking around, its gaze like a lighthouse beam.

Dragons, famously, had such good eyes they could spy a mouse in a field of wheat. If he and Mother Trude tried to run across this last field, this dragon would certainly see them. But they couldn't sit here in the hedgerow forever. It might be days before it left, and they had nothing to eat but turnips and oats, which were barely edible uncooked. They had no water, except turnip-ditch water, which surely wasn't drinkable.

And might there be beetles in it? Charl didn't even want to consider that, not when that water might be their only way across. The turnips were planted in raised rows, with deep, muddy furrows between them. If you crawled along a furrow on your belly, snakelike, letting the dirty water cover your body, the broad, spreading turnip leaves might conceal your head just enough.

Possibly.

He told Mother Trude his plan. All she said was, "At least I'm already dressed in brown."

Charl slung his sack across his back and dove headlong into the nearest furrow. The nun followed suit. It was a long crawl; Charl paused frequently to let Mother Trude catch her breath, but he was getting tired as well. Crawling through wet mud was not like crawling on solid ground. The mud soaked through your clothes, and was so soft that any movement took twice as long, and twice again as much effort.

Suddenly, Mother Trude grabbed Charl's foot and hissed loudly, "Hold still!"

He stopped moving, and then, to his surprise, the nun threw her sack of turnips on top of him, so he looked like two sacks of turnips. He peeked over his shoulder, through the spreading leaves, and saw the dragon approaching. Its flapping wings created a powerful sulfurous wind, nearly flattening the foliage as it landed in the field perhaps fifty yards away.

She stood up and faced the dragon. Charl began to wriggle, thinking he should do the same, but she kicked him in the ankle and he understood to stay still beneath the turnip sacks.

The dragon screamed unintelligibly—to Charl, at least—but Mother Trude folded her arms and answered: "What do you *think* I'm doing? Hiding from you, of course. You were bringing the whole town down around my ears."

The creature screamed again.

"How should I know?" Mother Trude fussed. "I haven't been here long, and I have never met any such person."

The dragon roared so loudly the whole field shook.

And then, to Charl's infinite astonishment, Mother Trude roared back.

At least, that's what it sounded like she was doing. It took Charl a minute to hear that her roar was made of strange, gargled sounds, that in fact she was speaking to the dragon in its own language, or as nearly as she could manage without a dragon's tongue and teeth and . . . lips? Did those sharp, beaky parts count as lips?

The dragon made a curious gurgling sound, and Charl wondered whether it was laughing. But, no, it was preparing a mouthful of fire, which it spat in a targeted, precise stream, right at Mother Trude's feet. She flung herself backward, landing on the supply sacks—and Charl, squishing him deeper into the mud. For a moment, his face went under, and he felt panic rising again, but he managed to push himself up and take a breath without gasping too loudly.

And he managed, somehow, not to scream.

The dragon launched itself back into the air; Mother Trude flopped over into the turnip greens as if she'd gone boneless. For a while, she and Charl both lay there quietly panting.

"Is it really gone?" Charl whispered at last.

"Yes," said Mother Trude.

"Why didn't it kill you?" he asked, still not quite believing what had happened. "What did you say?"

Mother Trude was struggling to her feet. "I told her I was an old woman, alone, and not worth her time."

Charl shook his head incredulously. "And that persuaded her?"

"I learned a few things about dragons, long ago, that have served me well," said Mother Trude. "If you understand their language and speak to them without flinching, some dragons will be impressed enough that they won't kill you. It doesn't always work. We got lucky."

"Well, then, you saved my life," said Charl.

"Not if we don't get moving," said Mother Trude, lifting her sack again. "I am probably safe to walk, since she knows I'm here, but you should keep crawling until we reach the trees."

And that was what they did.

The passage across the turnip fields may have been the most perilous, but it wasn't the hardest part of their flight. They still had half a mountain to climb, and because they were avoiding the road, that meant picking their way through the undergrowth, their muddy clothes slowly stiffening, their sacks of provisions getting heavier with every step.

Charl had not previously appreciated the road and all it did. Its pleasant, efficient switchbacks and utter lack of brambles, its potholes and bumps—all seemed delightful to him, compared with the sinkholes and boulders he encountered going straight up the mountainside. At one point, he and Mother Trude hit a cliff, rising like a wall to block them, and had to find their way around it. They went right, until they encountered the road and decided that wouldn't do. So they turned back and went left, an extra mile, until they found a passable way up.

A way up that Mother Trude could scale, that is. She'd surprised Charl by gamely waddling and crawling across the valley plain, but the mountain was proving much harder.

The good news was: He remembered this cliff. There was an easy way around, if they just went far enough, and then the Old Abbey stood at the top.

It finally came into view, its hulking battlement walls glazed red by the setting sun. Charl picked up the pace, sprinting ahead of Mother Trude while calling over his shoulder, "I'm going to check whether the sally door is still open!" It wasn't so much that he was eager to get there as that he was worried: If the sally door *was* open, he might have one of his spells. Shaking, dizziness, a pounding heart. Reliving the last time he'd looked through that door.

He'd been worried for nothing, though. The big double gates were padlocked, as before, and the sally door barred from inside.

"Don't tell me we came all this way only to be locked out," said Mother Trude behind him. She sounded exhausted.

"There's another way in," said Charl. There had to be. Rafe, Wort, and Hooey had gotten in somehow. "Sit on this boulder, Mother Trude, and I'll find it."

The old nun didn't need to be told twice. She plopped herself down, and a cloud of dust—the mud that had dried all over her habit—billowed around her.

Charl started circling to the left, but it soon became clear there wasn't going to be a way through, unless a tree had fallen somewhere and knocked the wall in. He could circle the whole enclosure, hoping, or he could do what Rafe, Wort, and Hooey had almost certainly done—climb the ivy and open the sally door from inside.

Charl shivered. This was it, then. He was not merely back where Wort and Hooey had died, but following in their footsteps. He grasped the thickest ivy vine that he could find and began to pull himself up.

11

The Old Abbey, Revisited

At the top of the battlement wall, Charl paused to catch his breath and wipe ivy sap off his hands. He'd already disregarded Sister Agnes's instructions and looked back once, but somehow it was even harder the second time. Now he had some idea what he might see.

He braced himself and looked anyway.

The valley below was illuminated three ways. In the west, the sun was setting in a puddle of orange and gold. In the east, a lumpy pale moon was rising. And in the south, St. Muckle's was on fire.

The flames blurred. He wiped his eyes.

How many people were still there, in the midst of all that chaos? How many couldn't or wouldn't flee? All the plague patients. Neighbors protecting their homes. Was Aris there, leading the charge against the dragon? Was Mama there, leading people into the refuge, packing up more sacks of turnips, doing whatever she could to keep everyone safe?

Sister Agnes had promised to find Mama and send her up the mountain to him, but Mama wouldn't want to abandon anyone she could save. He felt sure of that.

And what about Dr. Caramus? Wasn't he a dragon? Couldn't he change back into his original form and fight that dragon as an equal? Why was there only one dragon in the sky?

"Boy!" called Mother Trude in her sharp Samsamese accent. She had apparently rested enough that she had energy to be cranky; she was frowning up at him, arms folded. "Stop gaping, and get that little door open."

Charl waved and nodded. It was his turn to feel bone-weary, and to do the thing he'd apparently been dreading even more than looking back at his home—facing the courtyard of the Old Abbey again.

When he turned and looked down at it, he was shocked by what he saw. He'd expected everything to be all burnt and blasted, a Hooey-shaped silhouette on the flagstones, smoke still rising from the smoldering birch trees. But time had passed, even if it had been hard to feel it in St. Muckle's, with a plague on, but he'd last been up here in very early spring, and now it was . . . late summer? The courtyard was overgrown with grasses and, shockingly, wildflowers. Some birch trees, those nearest the well, still had sooty bark, but other than that, there was no sign that two boys had died here and another had lost his mind.

For some reason, this made Charl ineffably sad.

"Boy!" Mother Trude's voice seemed to rattle the gates, or

maybe she was yanking on the padlock. "Let me in, quickly now. I hear wolves out here."

Wolves—if there were any—were going to hear *her*, certainly.

Charl hurried down the stone steps and across the courtyard toward the front gates, as fast as the tangle of weeds would allow. He slid the splintery bar of the sally door, and Mother Trude hustled in, a sack in each hand.

She dropped the bags, leaned against the stone wall, and clutched at her heart. She seemed to be trying to take deeper, slower breaths. Her face was almost as pale as her wimple.

"Are you all right?" said Charl.

"I'm fine," she snapped. "I'm not accustomed to running up a mountain, is all. And I am dismayed to find that this place is such a ruin. When your mother suggested evacuating people here, I'd envisioned something less . . . overgrown with thickets."

"That makes it a good place to hide," said Charl, feeling defensive on Mama's behalf. "Because it looks abandoned."

Mother Trude straightened up and stretched her back. "Well, we're here now. Is there any structure suitable for sleeping in?"

Charl barred the sally door, and then hastened after Mother Trude, who was already halfway across the courtyard. "At least there's water," she said, thumping the lid of the well. "I suppose we shall have to boil it, to be safe."

She meant safe from beetle eggs, obviously, but Charl knew what else had been in that well not long ago. He swallowed hard, and wondered how he was going to get himself to drink it, even boiled. If he was thirsty enough, maybe . . .

Mother Trude grabbed the edge of the lid. "Help me with the other side," she said.

"Now?" asked Charl, his voice going very high.

The old woman looked at him like he was being ridiculous. And she was right: he was. Wort wasn't still in there; his body had been fished out quickly by his family and returned to St. Muckle's for burial, back when there had still been room in the cemetery.

Charl helped her lift the lid and set it to one side. Mother Trude located the bucket and rope, cast it down, and drew up some water. Charl stood back so he couldn't see down the well. Not that there would be anything to see, but . . . some part of him feared that if he looked down the well again, he would be transported in his mind back to that night, standing at the edge, watching the water boil below him, futilely throwing the bucket down as if that would help.

At least the bucket had been replaced. This one wasn't even scorched. He carried it, so that Mother Trude wouldn't have to, and they went in search of a place to rest their heads.

The monastery consisted of more than a dozen buildings in varying stages of tumbledown, encircled by a stout wall. The monks' dormitory, which might have seemed like a logical place to stay, had experienced a cave-in at the front door. Charl could have climbed to one of the upper windows, he thought, but Mother Trude could not—and how would they bring up the water? Other buildings were in even worse shape. The stables had no roof. The cider house was full up with rotting casks and an enormous rusty apple press. The threshing floor was so unstable Charl's foot went through it.

With each rejected building, Charl's heart sank. He did not want to sleep in the courtyard, with his bad memories.

At the far end of the abbey stood the best-preserved building in the whole compound. The ivy that covered everything else had shunned its walls. The roof and spire were intact, and even the stained-glass windows looked unbroken. Charl wondered why Mother Trude didn't go straight toward it—it was the obvious place to shelter—but she seemed not to notice it.

"What about that building?" asked Charl, tugging on her sleeve and pointing at it.

The old nun stared where he pointed, looking confused. "The sanctuary? No."

Maybe it was considered disrespectful to sleep in the holiest part of the complex. Charl was about to ask, but Mother Trude stepped into another building and declared, "This will do."

He followed her into a spacious hall with small, high windows, mostly intact, and only one hole in the roof. The floor was littered with wood, the decaying remains of tables and benches. This had once been the monks' refectory—their dining hall. Mother Trude began shifting boards and ordering Charl about—haul this here, drag that there—until they'd cleared space in the middle, revealing a stone-lined pit. Together, they moved two tabletops to serve as benches or beds, and then the old nun began stacking small splints of wood in the stone pit.

"This abbey dates back to a time when chimneys were considered a decadent luxury," Mother Trude said, taking firestarter tools from her apron pocket. "The brothers would have built a fire right here, in the middle of the room." She rapped flint and steel together, making sparks.

"Won't it get smoky?" asked Charl warily.

"Originally, I'm sure it did," said Mother Trude as the tinder caught fire. "But you see, Heaven has thoughtfully provided a large hole in the roof."

The hall connected to a few smaller rooms, formerly kitchens and larders, where they were fortunate enough to find a large cooking pot that was rusty only on the outside, some cracked cups, a couple smaller pans, a bucket with holes in it, and some straw that was not too moldy. Charl spread the straw on the tabletops for bedding and then ran to fetch more water while Mother Trude began sorting through the supply sacks, figuring out what they might cook.

It was dark out. The moon was fully risen, but the sun had set and the monastery walls blocked the glow from St. Muckle's. Charl wondered how long it would take a town as damp as St. Muckle's to burn itself out. As far as he knew, in all the centuries of dragon war, St. Muckle's had never been burned to the ground. The joke among St. Mucklites had always been that they sort of wished a dragon *would* come and dry the place out a bit.

It didn't seem like such a funny joke now. And yet . . . was it possible the dragon might burn the beetles away? Could something good come of this, after all?

He could imagine Mama making that exact comment to other townspeople clustered in the dragon refuge, valiantly crushing beetles under her heel at the same time. She would not have lost hope. Neither would he.

Taking great care not to look down into the well—never mind that it was almost too dark so see where the well *was,* let alone see into it—Charl drew another bucket of water and sniffed it. It didn't smell bad, for whatever that was worth.

Charl was strong, considering how small he was, but water is heavy and he'd filled the bucket fuller than Mother Trude had. His arms began to tire as he carried it back. He set it down a moment, and saw that he was near an unruly orchard, where the monks had grown the apples for their cider press. Maybe there were apples. Charl took a few steps in among the ancient trees, but it was too dark to see. The trees thinned out toward the middle of the grove, where moonlight broke through the branches. Charl stepped in that direction and barked his shin on a large rock.

At first, he feared it was a tombstone, but it was just a flat, mossy boulder, nested among the tangled weeds to no apparent purpose.

In the moonlight, he could make out a second one, standing upright, and then a third. They were older than the orchard, by all appearances, boulders that had been too large to move, so the monks had planted the trees around them.

Suddenly, the air stilled. The crickets stopped chirping, and the light seemed to take on a slow, viscous quality, like honey. Charl felt like he had stepped into a puddle of pure cold; his breath frosted in the moonlight. And then his mind abruptly flashed to a memory—a terrible memory, but not the one he'd been dreading all day.

He was in the flagstone yard behind the inn, among billowing sheets, and he was incandescently angry. He was shouting at his mother, who had just snapped his sword in two.

Sword fighting is what I love . . . That's just who I am.

A swordfighter who sasses his mother.

You said we came here to be ourselves.

There is a difference between being yourself and being selfish.

Selfish? Hadn't he been helping every day for months? That had made him even angrier.

I wish we'd never come here!

I don't ever want to hear you say such a thing again.

I could have been a prince in Uchtburg—

You would never have been a prince.

Instead of coming to your muddy peasants' paradise, where you get to meddle in everybody's business. You're the one who's selfish.

I am too angry to speak now, Charl, but you and I will have words later.

Charl gasped as the memory ended, as if he hadn't been breathing the entire time. Maybe he hadn't. He was shaking all over, with leftover rage but also . . . with something quite different than rage.

With terror.

"You and I will have words later," she'd said, but what if they didn't? What if he never saw his mother again? What if the dragon had gotten her? He'd been so *mean*. That couldn't be the last thing he ever said to her. It would haunt him forever.

Please, let her be all right.

A breath of wind, rustling the branches, seemed to whisper the words Charl wished he could say to Mama right now: *I'm sorry.*

He scrambled through the twisted trees, retrieved the bucket, and hurried back to Mother Trude.

12

Something Stirs

In the depths of the orchard, among the standing stones, a wisp of mist lingered regretfully in the moonlight. It was joined by another. The wisps sighed, and the branches gently bobbed.

You touched him, Vilna, said a soft, accusatory voice. *You broke your own rule.*

He walked through me before I could react!

You didn't move out of the way, the accuser huffed. *I know what you'd say if it had been me who didn't move. "Maeve,"* you'd say, *"don't pretend you didn't see him."*

A chittering sound caught the attention of the misty wisps, and a pale, translucent squirrel appeared on top of the tallest standing stone, followed by an ethereal bird. A beam of moonlight shone directly down on them, like a silver spotlight.

Your elders are here to chide you, said the wisp called Maeve.

Go on, then, Iphi. Tell her off. Ognielle? You're surely disgusted by Vilna's hypocrisy. I'll tell her for you, if you like.

Will you stop? cried Vilna. *They can't understand you. You're making fun of them.*

I'm making fun of you, said Maeve. *You bossy little thing. "Let us nevermore feed on mortal memories," you said. "Let us fade gently, like dear Iphi and Ognielle, into blissful mindlessness." But now you won't. You'll still be here after we've gone. Does that seem fair to anyone else?*

Those last words were spoken loudly enough that a mortal passerby might have overheard, had any mortal been passing by.

If Maeve was expecting a chorus of agreement, however, she was disappointed. The only answer she got was some grumbling from the back of the orchard. *Do stop whining, Maeve,* said an imperious voice. *Some of us are diligently trying to practice being gone forever.*

For the merest moment, if anyone had been there to see, a girl seemed to materialize near the mossy stone where the squirrel and bird were perched. She was tall, plump and sturdy, wrapped in a checkered cloth. Transparent curls wreathed her transparent head. She reached out to the almost-invisible squirrel, and it climbed onto her immaterial hand.

Then girl, squirrel, and bird disappeared, like a candle winking out.

13

Stuck with the Old Nun

Charl heard none of the whispers from the orchard, but he did see something strange. He had almost reached the refectory when he chanced to glance toward the sanctuary.

Behind one of its stained-glass windows, a candle burned.

Charl almost didn't think about it. He was at the threshold of the refectory, hurrying because Mother Trude was waiting for him, when it finally hit him that what he'd just glimpsed was extremely odd. He stopped and looked toward the sanctuary again.

The candle guttered and went out.

A shiver traveled all the way up Charl's spine, from parts unmentionable. How could there possibly have been a candle in the window? Was someone else here?

Come to mention it, who had locked the gates? Who had built the cover for the well—or replaced the charred bucket, for that matter? Nobody from town would have done those things, would they? Did someone own this place, or was someone hiding out here?

His imagination, primed and overactive after the spookiness in the orchard, made a suggestion: *Smugglers.*

That would be bad. Smugglers were notoriously secretive and territorial; they assuredly wouldn't want an old woman and a young boy squatting in their hideout. If only he had a sword—a proper sword, something he could protect an old nun with.

Like . . . What was it Rafe had been planning to show him up here, supposedly?

The Battle Bishop's sword.

No sooner had he thought those words than the sanctuary lit up again. Multiple candles, from the look of it. Every stained-glass window gleamed, blood-red and poisonous yellow, as if they each had a dozen candles behind them.

Impossible. How was this happening?

Come closer and find out, the light whispered.

Charl set down his bucket, never taking his eyes from the lights. He took a step forward into darkness.

He took another.

"Boy!" cried Mother Trude, and Charl nearly jumped out of his skin. She had stuck her head out of the doorway behind him. "What's taking you so long?"

Charl stared at her, bug-eyed, his mouth moving uselessly. He pointed toward the sanctuary, but when he looked, the windows had gone dark again.

Mother Trude rolled her eyes. "Come inside. I've sorted the food. The situation is less dire than I'd anticipated."

Buried in a sack of oats had been some goose eggs—miraculously undamaged—several squashed rolls, a cheese, and some tack biscuits. Mother Trude had already boiled the eggs. "The cheese will keep longer," she said, handing Charl a roll. "We must eat everything from most to least perishable. I wish there were some tea, but I suppose we're lucky to have any variety at all.

"Tomorrow, we must see if there's any wild mint to be found," she continued. She sipped a cup of boiled water so daintily that Charl wondered whether she was pretending it was tea. "And I thought I saw green apples in that feral orchard. They'll give you a bellyache straight off the tree, but we can boil them until they're edible."

Charl, peeling an egg, tried to smile, to cover up the dread in the pit of his stomach. That bad, vivid memory had rather put him off the orchard.

Which was silly, now that he thought about it. The orchard wasn't responsible, surely.

"How are you holding up, boy?" said the old nun, shifting her weight and looking at him shrewdly. "It's a grim thing to have your village burn down around you."

"*Town*," Charl corrected under his breath. But then he added, "I'm all right."

Mother Trude stared at him hard. The starched linen of her wimple was folded with architectural precision around her head. Even after she'd crawled through turnip fields and climbed a mountain, not a fold was out of place.

"I realize St. Muckle's is a town," she said at last, peeling her second goose egg. "I said 'village' because I was speaking from my own experience, long ago. Samsam wasn't always at peace with dragons, you know."

Charl squirmed, uncertain whether he owed her an apology.

"You're worried about your family, I'm sure," said the old woman. "Take heart that Sister Agnes is there, helping. I was her teacher before I was her prioress, and I never had a smarter, more resourceful student. If anyone can find your mother in all that chaos, not to mention that Porphyrian horseman . . ."

She meant Aris, apparently. "He's Samsamese, not Porphyrian," said Charl.

"He looks Porphyrian," said Mother Trude.

"People don't always look like what they really are," said Charl. "He was a knight in Samsam until he gave it up."

"Oh, yes, I think I heard something about that. Well, he gave up a noble calling, one that could have saved your *town* today," said the old nun tartly. "I suppose he left the knighthood for your mother's sake."

"I don't think so," said Charl. "He was my father's captain of the guard before we came here. He hadn't been a knight for years."

"But he loves your mother," Mother Trude pressed.

"*Everyone* loves my mother," said Charl, but only when he said it out loud did it occur to him what she was probably trying to find out, in her devious nun way. "They're not married, if that's what you're asking."

"Because she's . . . That is, because Agnes—"

"Because Mama was married already and decided she didn't like it," said Charl wearily. He'd been answering questions about Aris and Agnes and his mother his whole life, from adults and children alike. There was another set of questions they usually asked next—uncomfortable, personal questions about Charl himself. He hoped that wasn't where this conversation was going.

However, the old woman merely smiled wistfully and set down her rough clay mug. "I'm glad we finally have time to talk, child. Sister Agnes and your mother had asked me to speak with you, but the sickroom kept me so busy that I've hardly had time to say two words. Now, I suppose, we shall have more time together than we could possibly want."

How long would they be stuck here, in fact? Charl didn't like to consider that, so he asked the more obvious question: "Why did my mother want you to speak with me?"

It would be about the sword practice and the fire poker. Some lesson about the evils of violence. It had to be.

Mother Trude's mouth drew up into an earnest rosebud; her brows arced piously, like the buttresses of a cathedral. "She's considering your future, as any mother should. She asked me to assess whether you would be suited for the priesthood."

Charl's mouth fell open. Mama had never mentioned any such thing to him.

"Why would she be wondering *that*?" he said, picking a piece of straw out of his bedding, splitting it lengthwise, and tossing it into the fire.

"Good question," said Mother Trude. "I suppose you're pious, or have shown interest?"

"I'm not, and I haven't," said Charl sulkily.

"Perhaps you have an aptitude for reading, writing, and reciting scripture?"

Charl shrugged. He didn't mind reading, if there was anything interesting to read. Scripture was not, in his experience, interesting.

"Well," said Mother Trude, unfastening her cloak and spreading it over her bedding. "I can tell you what Sister Agnes told me, but you won't like it." She lay down, not removing her wimple, and wriggled a bit, trying to get comfortable. "She said you'd rather be a knight's squire, but you're small, and your mother is concerned that the other squires will pick on you."

Charl's face went hot. "I'm already quite good at swords. They'd only pick on me once, before learning that."

"I know you're good, and that you've been keeping up your practice," the old nun assured him, "but I couldn't very well bring that up with your mother. You'd asked me not to."

He had, at that. Still, he felt like arguing. "Anyway," he said, "the other *priests* might try to bully me, and that would be even harder to resolve. I couldn't challenge them to a . . . a *book* duel."

He imagined two priests swatting each other with books, which was almost funny.

"They'd be seminarians, not priests," said Mother Trude, closing her eyes. "You would be sent to a seminary first, to learn all you need to learn before you take orders."

"I don't want to do any of that," cried Charl.

"I'm surprised Agnes and your mother don't understand that," said Mother Trude. "But you may still be better suited to it than you think. It doesn't hurt to explore the question. Can you recite some scripture for me?"

Charl scowled, squirmed, hemmed and hawed. He had never been diligent about memorizing scripture, although he did have a good memory for the exemplar tales Father Donal sometimes told—stories meant to instruct you in living correctly. "Would you accept an exemplar tale, instead?"

She sighed. "Go on, then."

Charl told the first one that came to mind:

"Once, under the eye of Heaven, there was a young scholar who grew tired of memorizing scripture. 'What good is scripture,' he lamented to his teacher, 'except for putting people to sleep?'

"His teacher, who was a great sage of the order of St. Abaster, told him to wander the world until he found the answer.

"One day, on his travels, he saw a hundred villagers gathered together upon their knees, lamenting and wailing. He approached cautiously, trying to work out what was wrong, but could see nothing threatening them—no dragon in the sky, no marauders invading their village.

"'Why are you kneeling here, wailing?' the scholar said to one of the villagers.

"'The devil is here,' she cried, 'and he's eating our sheep. When he has finished them, he'll eat us next. He said that if we move from this spot, it will be the worse for us. He'll pursue us to the ends of the earth, and torment us before he devours us.'

"The scholar knew his teacher had ways of dealing with the devil, but he also knew that if he went to get the sage, the devil would eat every sheep in the village before he could return, and that would leave the villagers destitute. He had to take care of the devil himself, somehow, although he knew not how.

"Then he heard the voice of St. Abaster in his ear, as sometimes happens even to doubters in times of direst need. And then the scholar knew what to do.

"He went to the barn, where the devil sat on a large pile of sheep's bones, picking wool out of his teeth. The fiend had eaten only half the sheep so far. The others cowered in the corner of the barn, trying to keep out of reach. The scholar stepped up, cleared his throat, and began reciting every line of scripture he knew—many, many lines. He was not a bad scholar, just a dispirited and discouraged one.

"Some claim that a few stanzas of holy verse will make the devil melt down, explode, or run away screaming, but it is not necessarily so. It depends *how* the verse is recited, and on the heart of the one reciting. So in this case, because our scholar found the scriptures dull, they came out of his mouth in a tedious monotone. Because he'd memorized so many verses, the monotone droned on for hours.

"Until, finally, the devil fell asleep.

"'Well done,' said a voice behind him, and he turned to see his teacher, the great sage, approaching. St. Abaster had whispered in the old man's ear also, so he knew his arts were needed here. He dispelled the devil once and for all, using his manifest holiness, and then he said to his student, 'Now you have learned what you needed to learn: The scriptures are useful in accordance with the measure of your heart. Even the weary heart, longing for rest, can still wield scripture well enough to beat the devil.'"

Charl paused, listening. Mother Trude's breath was slow and even; when she exhaled, there was a faint whistling through her nose, like a light snore. The story had put her to sleep, just like the devil.

There was one way to make sure. Charl had thought of an additional ending for the story.

"Was that really the lesson, though?" Charl continued in the same tone as before. "The scholar had his doubts. He said, 'Couldn't I have put the devil to sleep with anything boring? What about shipping lists or tax rolls? I think you're making excuses, and trying to prove that you haven't spent your life learning something useless.' And with that, he walked away, never to return to his studies. In fact, he became a juggler, and whenever he saw the devil, he would drive him away by throwing balls at his head."

Charl had to clamp his mouth shut then, because he was about to laugh.

Mother Trude was quiet a long time. Charl felt his shoulders relax. Maybe he would enjoy telling the old nun religious stories if he was allowed to end them any way he—

"Who taught you to tell that story so disrespectfully?" The old woman's unexpected voice made him jump. "Not my Agnes. It can only have been that . . . *mother* of yours."

There was a word missing before *mother*. Charl could hear the hole where it was supposed to be, even if Mother Trude had thought better of saying it aloud. He couldn't guess what the word might have been, only that the nun had considered it rude.

Impious might have been it. *Arrogant. Uppity.*

Strong-willed.

Wonderful.

Charl felt a lump form in his throat. He missed his mother so much. *She* would have appreciated the new ending for the story—or if she hadn't, she would at least have said, "Now Charl, let's think this through and understand why you said what you said, and how it might strike other people." She was always trying to get him to understand other points of view.

Maybe that's why she thought he should become a priest. Maybe she thought he would learn to listen that way.

It still didn't make sense. It just didn't seem like something Mama would do. Whatever her point of view was on the matter, he couldn't find a way to understand it.

Charl flopped back onto his pile of straw and tossed and turned, trying to get comfortable. He was never going to fall asleep, he thought, but then miraculously, he did.

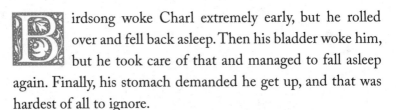

14

The Martin

Birdsong woke Charl extremely early, but he rolled over and fell back asleep. Then his bladder woke him, but he took care of that and managed to fall asleep again. Finally, his stomach demanded he get up, and that was hardest of all to ignore.

The old nun had removed her wimple sometime in the night and draped it over her face to keep the light out of her eyes. Charl stoked the fire, then went out to fetch more water (cautiously avoiding eye contact with the well). When he got back, Mother Trude was still sleeping, so he made a passable porridge and helped himself to a bowl. She still did not stir, so he had another. Only when he'd finished the second bowl did he begin to worry.

"Mother Trude," he said, nudging her shoulder. "Would you like some porridge, while it's still warm?"

"Nnm," she said, an ambiguous sound. "Go out and play, boy.

Yesterday's mountain sprint quite wore me out. I'm sore all over. I believe I will lie here awhile."

Charl was a little sore himself, truth be told. He left her a bowl of oatmeal, which had gone rather gluey, and a cup of boiled water, and then took himself outside.

Not to play, mind. Charl had serious questions that needed answering.

Everything outside was damp—not with rain but with a heavy dew. First things first, Charl climbed the steps back to the top of the wall. He had to know what was left of St. Muckle's, if anything. He rushed to the parapet and looked down upon the valley.

And saw nothing. The valley bottom was covered by a low-hanging cloud, or a very thick fog—just another cheerful St. Muckle's summer day. It had never occurred to Charl that one might look down at the *top* of fog. It was eerily beautiful, a wide, soft landscape gently gilded by the morning sun. He could almost believe the town was perfectly all right underneath, safely wrapped in fluffy wool.

Until the dragon burst up out of the mists.

The creature made a wide arc through the open sky, flaming and shrieking. Charl ducked behind the parapet and held his breath. Were its eyes keen enough to spot him on a distant wall? He didn't know, and he didn't want to find out.

With a feral scream, the dragon dove, and Charl felt safe to exhale. He stood up again, and saw a swirl in the mist where the dragon had plunged back under.

Where had it come from? And why had it attacked? St. Muckle's had never been of interest to dragons, but this one was clearly interested in something.

He'd seen its shadow above the clouds when it had first arrived, but which way had it been flying? He wanted to say from the south, but that didn't make any sense. Dragons wouldn't fly into Goredd from Samsam. Their homeland was far to the north. Anyway, it might have circled around before he noticed it. It might have come from anywhere.

Even from inside St. Muckle's.

Dragons could take human form, after all. It had never happened here, that anyone could prove for certain, but in principle, a dragon could take human form and walk into town without anyone noticing.

Well, Dr. Caramus would have noticed. "If there were another saarantras here, I would smell them," he'd once told Charl, in an attempt to be reassuring. But the doctor had been busy with the plague lately. It was possible that this dragon had been hiding in town without Dr. Caramus being aware.

And where was Dr. Caramus now?

That was the question that bothered Charl the most. Surely the most effective way to fight a dragon was with another dragon. Whatever Dr. Caramus was doing down there—treating injuries? working on his cure?—it had to be less useful than getting rid of the monster that was causing all the injuries in the first place.

Monster was the wrong word, he knew. Aris had told him so, many times. Charl could almost hear his deep voice now, saying, "I gave up dragon slaying because they aren't monsters, Charl. They think, they speak—they're *people.* That's the tragedy of Goredd's endless war. We refuse to believe that about them, and they refuse to believe that about us."

It was hard to believe any such thing, however, when a

ferocious, winged . . . *person* was burning your town to the ground. Was Aris so determined to stick to his principles that he was doing nothing? The marauding dragon was still flying around, after all, apparently uninjured and unopposed.

How frustrating to be stuck up here, on the mountainside, unable to do a thing about it.

A soft chirp near his left hand drew Charl's attention. Not far along the parapet, a small bird hopped toward him—a house martin, with a white underside and a slate-gray top, overlaid with dark blue upon its head and shoulders. It tilted its head, regarding him. Charl regarded it back, and was perplexed to realize he could see through it. At first, he wasn't sure, but then it hopped in front of a frilly lichen. Charl could see the lichen right through the martin's pale belly.

Charl blinked so hard it made his eyes water. The last transparent being he'd seen had been that weeping woman just before Hooey exploded. Sister Agnes had assured him that that vision had been his imagination, but also a harbinger of terrible things to come. Is that what this was? What on earth could a ghostly bird portend? If his imagination was trying to tell him something, it was doing a very confusing job.

The martin hopped closer. Charl held very still.

It hopped onto the back of his hand. Its tiny feet felt intensely cold.

And then Charl began to fly.

At least, his mind did. His body—he glimpsed it far below—stood like a statue on top of the battlement wall.

Deep down, he knew he should have found this worrisome, but he didn't feel worried at all. He felt . . . joyous.

Because he *was* a martin, or was merged with one, somehow. He was fast. He hurtled down the mountain like a comet, zipped over the fluffy face of the fog, and then dove down into the gray. There was St. Muckle's below him, spread out like an enormous maze. Parts of it glowed crimson with fire; parts were burned-out black. It saddened his boy heart to see these things, but his bird heart replied, *Look how the big is made small. Look how the beautiful is also fearsome. From here, we can see the ins and outs of things. The ups and downs. From here, it's all the smallest piece of the puzzle. Be still, and I'll show you.*

Big talk from a small bird, but Charl did as he was told. Indeed, he didn't see what else he could do, if he ever hoped to have his mind returned to his body.

When you're fast, everything else looks slow. With his martin's-eye view, Charl could see flies flying, each wing in motion, compound eyes sparkling. He circled a burning building, and each jet of flame seemed to flutter like a flag in a gentle wind. The ground was covered with burning beetles, their legs grinding slowly, pincers grasping futilely, carapaces iridescent with a color he couldn't name. The whole world seemed brighter, and slower, and wholly new.

Little by little, he began to recognize places as they flew by: the church, the town square, the river, the square again, the Fiddle. He seemed to fall toward it and then reel around, caught in its gravity, before shooting through the stratosphere toward someplace else.

Can we slow down? he tried to ask the martin. But he was not in charge here, and the bird had its own purposes, apparently.

To his surprise, a picture did begin to emerge. An impression. A story of a sort. If he relaxed his mind, he could begin to piece it together.

The dragon was nowhere to be seen—not in the sky, not on the rooftops, neither snaking through the streets nor swimming in the river. There were a few buildings on fire, others burned hollow, and a couple more collapsed, but fewer altogether than he would've guessed.

The martin made several large circles until Charl saw what it saw: Buildings had not collapsed at random. They blocked the road out of town and the bridge across the Sowline. People could still attempt to flee St. Muckle's—there was no wall around the northern part of town, the side facing the turnip fields—but it would be difficult to leave with wagons or horses or many supplies.

And, to gauge by the dazed and terrified citizens beginning to stumble out into the streets, not many people had fled. Most had hidden. Charl could hear the word spreading as he raced overhead—*Is it gone? Is it over? I don't see it anywhere*—and he could see expressions of hope and disbelief.

But the dragon wasn't gone. Charl had finally glimpsed it.

The martin passed in front of the church, where a small crowd had begun gathering. Atop the steps stood a pale-haired woman, wiry and fierce-looking. Charl noticed the two swords strapped to her back; the martin noticed that her skin glowed differently than other people's.

It was a color Charl couldn't normally see. He had no name for it. But that woman on the steps positively glittered with it. The martin, at least, understood why: the pale-haired woman was a saarantras.

Go back inside! Stay away! he wanted to cry to the crowds as he dartled overhead.

The woman on the steps began to speak. It was hard for Charl to focus on her voice (although he did notice every moth and mosquito and gnat in her vicinity). Her words finally broke through his understanding.

"I'm here for Eileen," she was saying, "and for her hatchling—I forget its name. But the absurd child is the offspring of Earl Ucht, and as such, worth money to me. Bring them quickly, and no further harm will befall your stupid town. In fact, I may even help you. The crypt beneath the church is full of noxious insects—I could burn them all away."

Mutterings arose from the crowd. Charl couldn't tell whether they meant to do what the dragon demanded or rise up against her. He hoped for the latter, but the martin, ever restless, took off for the Fiddle now. It circled the building twice, as if looking for an open window or door, then seemed to remember it was a ghost bird, and flew right through the wall.

Charl flinched as if his heart might stop, but felt nothing as they passed through.

What he saw in the public room almost stopped his heart, though. His mother stood before the hearth with her hands on her head, facing a burly man with a scar through his left eyebrow. He held a sword pointed directly at Mama's heart.

There were no gnats in here to chase. The martin fluttered into the rafters and perched.

"I'm not going anywhere, Brus, until you tell your comrade to stop destroying our town," Mama was saying, chin raised defiantly.

"We're not together," said the man. "She's my rival, not my co-conspirator."

"What is the earl paying you?" Mama asked. "I can pay more."

"I doubt that," said Brus. "And you certainly can't pay off Miga—or all the others who may attempt this. Every motivated mercenary in Samsam will take up the challenge if we fail."

"To kidnap me?"

"To bring back his child. *You* aren't worth nearly as much, unless we destroy everything you've built here. He wants you to see it and suffer."

"Well, you'll have to split your bounty, then. Miga has done a better job than you of wrecking everything—and accomplished it much more quickly as well," Mama sneered.

Charl was shocked at how unafraid she seemed.

"Miga?" the man sputtered. "Miga doesn't have the brains she was born with. *Who* painstakingly researched a way to slowly, miserably destroy this town and make it look natural? Who has lived here on and off for months, helping sell these dullards on your newfangled harbor idea? You think the Vastericles just relented and accepted it finally? I paid them off. I made everyone hate you. Any blunt instrument can break buildings; it takes finesse to break your heart."

There was a long pause before Mama said, "What a mind you have, Brus, and what a shame to have wasted it all these years in an evil man's service. What might you have become with better friends, under someone else's gentle guidance?"

Charl wanted to encourage her, wanted to send her strength from the rafters, but the martin had held still as long as it could stand to, apparently, and they were off again, launched up through the roof into the clouded sky.

A group of angry-looking citizens had broken off from the crowd in front of Allsaints and was heading for the Fiddle.

Other townsfolk, more subtly, had slipped away from Miga and were silently making their way in ones and twos up alleys and byways, toward Vasterich Hall. It was the most fortified building in St. Muckle's, after the Fiddle, and Charl was fascinated to see it from above for the first time. All that wealth, over centuries, spent on stone walls and reinforced roofs—more for fear of peasant uprising than dragon attack—and now former peasants were sneaking in the back. The original designers of the place were surely spinning in their catacomb graves.

The martin dove through the layered house, top to bottom, giving Charl glimpses of tapestries and fine furnishings like he hadn't seen since Uchtburg. The ghost bird plunged into the sub-basement, a torchlit vault with a coffered ceiling supported by columns—a private dragon refuge. Of course the Vasteriches would have one. The martin darted in and out of the columns before alighting atop a storage trunk.

Charl could finally focus on the people. In the center of the room, Aris and Lord Vasterich stood with their heads together over a map table, consulting; Aris was using a nub of charcoal to mark certain buildings. Collapsed? Safe? Charl couldn't tell. Sister Agnes paced behind them like a caged bear; Dr. Caramus, his skin shining with that new color, leaned against a pillar; other people Charl recognized but didn't really know clustered around and spoke in low voices.

"We might lay a trap *here*"—Aris's voice trickled into Charl's consciousness—"and pin the dragon down. The trick is to move quickly, as one, and to muzzle her so she can't spit fire. We'll need whatever heavy chains we can scavenge from the harbor and from your old drawbridge, if you still have them."

"They're yours," said Lord Vasterich. "Whatever my wife may say, Sir Aris, I trust to your judgment in this matter. I don't see us surviving this without a knight's expertise."

This was new, to see a Vasterich groveling and cooperative. The dragon must have truly terrified him.

A clattering upon the stairs was two townsfolk come from Miga's speech in the square. "Sir Aris! It was the dragon—you were right. She told us what she wants."

"Which is . . . ?"

The pair looked at each other, suddenly shy. "Lady Eileen and young Charl," the second one said in a squeaky voice. "Earl Ucht has put a bounty on their heads."

Something almost imperceptible changed in Lord Vasterich's face, as if it had just occurred to him that maybe a knight's expertise *wasn't* the only way out of this. Aris didn't seem to notice the change; Charl wished he could have screamed out *Don't trust that man!*

But now Dr. Caramus was saying, "I told you I smelled Miga."

"Damn it!" cried Sister Agnes, increasing the pace of her pacing. "I should never have let Eileen go back to the inn alone."

"She's resourceful, Agnes. She'll be back soon," said Aris.

Sister Agnes paused by the trunk where Charl and the martin were perched, her shoulders tensed nearly to her ears. Aris's words seemed not to reassure her at all, but to fill her with frustration. She pounded her fist on the trunk, apparently not seeing the ghostly bird sitting there.

The martin hopped away, but not before Sister Agnes's fist intersected with it.

Instantaneously, Charl seemed to feel all of Agnes's feelings: her terror and her sorrow for all the people of St. Muckle's had endured, her anger at the dragon, her love and worry for his mother, her mistrust of the Vasteriches, and too many others, too tangled to discern.

And in that same instant, her face contorted into an expression of horror. She turned back toward the others and said, "Aris . . . you never found any trace of Jarlbrus in town, did you?"

"Nothing definitive," said Aris.

"And you never sniffed him out, Doctor?"

"I've never met the man, and don't know what he smells like," said Caramus.

"I've never met him, either, but based on what Eileen said . . . don't you think he'd be the *first* person to come looking for her and Charl?" Sister Agnes was fidgeting.

"Dragons are fast; a dragon would surely have beaten him here," offered Dr. Caramus.

"But Jarlbrus has been Earl Ucht's right hand for years," said Aris. His dark eyes stared intently into Agnes's. "He might have known about the bounty before it was even offered."

"All I'm saying," said Agnes, "is that I got strange feeling just now. A . . . a premonition, almost. Jarlbrus is here, and he's taking advantage of the terror and confusion that Miga has sown to snatch Eileen from under her very claws. I don't know how I know, but I know."

"Sorry," one of the folks who'd come from the church piped

up, "you're not talking about *Brus,* are you? Fellow with a scar? Always calling Lady Eileen a fraud?"

There was a long silence. Aris clutched at his heart; he moved his mouth, but no sound came out.

"Charl is safe with Mother Trude, at least," said Sister Agnes. "Breathe, Aris."

"We'll solve this," said Dr. Caramus. "We could use Miga and Jarlbrus against each other. A way will present itself."

Aris nodded dumbly, and that was the last Charl saw of their secret meeting, because the martin wouldn't or couldn't stay any longer. It shot straight upward, warbling a song no one could hear.

And then Charl stood on the battlements of the Old Abbey again, not entirely sure how he got there but half breathless with panic himself.

He sank down with his back to the parapet, curled in a ball, trying to breathe slowly. None of his nearest and dearest were dead or injured, although Mama was certainly in peril. But a knight, a dragon, and a very clever nun were making plans to rescue her, and to stop the town from being destroyed any further. If ever there was a group to have confidence in, it was them.

Unless Lord Vasterich decided it would be better to stab them in the back. How Charl wished he'd been able to warn them to keep a close eye on that man!

But he hadn't been completely useless. When Sister Agnes had touched the ghost bird, and he'd glimpsed her feelings, she had somehow, miraculously, gotten a glimpse of something in his mind as well. Without that, they would not have realized Jarlbrus was there, and Mama was in danger.

It wasn't enough. He squirmed with impatience. How could he sit here, hoping everything went well? It was infinitely frustrating.

Charl felt sorely tempted to rush back to town and offer his services. Aris could surely use another skilled swordsman, even a short one.

What I need, said the Aris in his head, *is for you to stay safe and hidden.*

Charl ignored this. He'd already thought of something better. He could sneak into the Fiddle and take this Jarlbrus by surprise. He'd enter through the kitchen, creep behind the bar in the public room, sneak from table to table, press the tip of his sword to the man's spine, and say, "Drop your weapon, sirrah."

It was a beautiful plan.

It's a foolish plan, and you're going to get yourself killed, said the Agnes in his head. She was harder to ignore.

Mama in his head just gave him a sorrowful look, and that was hardest of all.

Fine. He couldn't have done it anyway. That plan required a sword.

It also required Jarlbrus and his mother not to move from the spot where he'd seen them for however many hours it took to arm himself (somehow) and get back to the Fiddle. Acquiring a sword (or a big knife) might have been possible, but time wouldn't freeze for him, no matter what he did. So much for that.

Charl glared across the broken rooftops of the abbey compound. Only one roof was completely intact, its slate clear of vines and moss—the sanctuary, at the far end. The place where he'd seen candlelight last night.

That's where the Battle Bishop was buried, and where his long-lost sword would be, if Rafe hadn't been lying.

If you could trust a Vasterich.

It really was strange how pristine and intact the building was. Uncanny, even, as if someone—or something—had protected it from the ravages of time.

That night, the night Wort and Hooey had died, the night that was emblazoned upon his memory forever, Rafe had wandered away from the courtyard in a daze. Charl's memory had a gap in it after he'd looked in the well, but . . . Rafe had staggered off in the direction of the sanctuary, visibly shaken, but not screaming and crying, not yet.

He hadn't lost his mind seeing Wort and Hooey die; he'd lost it later, somewhere deeper in the ruins.

What if death wasn't the only terrible thing that had happened that night? What if Rafe had gone to the sanctuary and run into something even worse?

Sister Agnes had told Charl a million times that there were no such things as ghosts, but hadn't he just seen a transparent bird, of all things? And hadn't it carried him down to St. Muckle's somehow? He had a good imagination—but that wasn't his imagination.

If the ghost bird was real, maybe the weeping woman had been real. When she had passed through Hooey's body, Hooey had frozen in place, just like Charl had done upon the battlements. (That had been the creepiest part of touching the bird.) Hooey had failed to catch the pyria because he couldn't move. A figment of Charl's imagination could not have petrified him.

It didn't take much imagination to suppose that there were more ghosts than just the bird and the weeping woman here, or that whatever had broken Rafe was still here somewhere and best avoided.

Still . . . Charl glanced toward the sanctuary again. If the Battle Bishop's sword was here—if it even existed—he'd feel a lot better with it in his hand. Maybe he couldn't charge down the mountain and save everyone on his own, but the dragon might yet figure out where he had gone and come after him. Surely it was prudent to be prepared. Even the Aris and the Agnes in his head couldn't argue with that.

Rafe had probably been lying, anyway.

Charl scrambled to his feet, went down the stairs, and returned to the refectory, giving the well wide berth as he passed it.

15

Vilna

Mother Trude was still abed, one arm flung over her head.

"Would you stir the fire a bit?" she muttered when Charl came in.

He dutifully poked at it and added a couple sticks. She'd drunk the water in her cup, he noticed, so he dipped some more for her out of the big pot. She hadn't touched her porridge; it had solidified into an unappetizing lump.

"What have you been up to?" asked the old woman.

"Exploring," said Charl, which was what he had intended to do, until he'd been unexpectedly whisked away by a ghost martin. "There might be supplies here we can use."

"Good thinking," she said. "Don't forget to gather apples."

He'd forgotten all about the apples, in fact, possibly because he dreaded going back to that spooky orchard—

He'd felt cold last night, right before getting swept up into that bad memory. Intensely, unaccountably cold. Just like when the ghost martin had landed on his hand.

"Mother Trude," he said, "do you think there might be ghosts here?"

He felt foolish asking the question. He felt more foolish when she moved her arm off her face and glared at him. "What did Sister Agnes teach you?" she asked sharply.

"That they don't exist," he said, chagrined. "That it's all just pagan superstition."

"There, you've answered your own question. Now let me sleep." The old woman rolled onto her side, away from him.

Charl took up both buckets—the sturdy one for water and the leaky one for apples—and went outside, his mind racing. He knew she was right. Everything he'd ever been taught said ghosts weren't real. It was his imagination or . . . or the guilt he still felt from the last time he was here. He could almost dismiss feeling cold as the crawly feeling Sister Agnes had talked about.

But then how could he explain what he'd seen happening in St. Muckle's? Had it been a dream? Was any of it true? Did he really have any idea what was happening down there?

His mind in a whirl, he went to the well for water.

He was so preoccupied that he forgot to be careful. He hooked the bucket to the rope, tossed it in, and looked down to watch it fill.

Flames roared under the water. Wort, burning, thrashed and screamed. His eyes rolled, showing only the whites; his mouth was a terrible dark chasm.

Charl screamed, too, and fell back.

Everything went quiet. He crawled to the edge and peeked down again.

Nothing. The bucket was bobbing quietly. He hauled it up hand over hand, although it was only half full, and his heart was going a thousand beats a minute, pounding so hard he could feel it knock against his windpipe.

It couldn't be a ghost. It was just his imagination, or a flashback to that terrible night.

His heart didn't slow. He felt like he was choking.

He staggered back toward the refectory with his buckets, but he didn't make it. He couldn't breathe properly; his knees buckled beneath him. He was near the orchard, and so he flung himself down under one of the gnarled trees, half convinced he was going to die.

Eventually, the cool shade, or the touch of damp earth on his back, or the light filtering through the leaves calmed him down. He could see apples clustered up in the branches, hard and green. A little transparent bird perched among them, chirped, and flitted off.

That was two ghosts within ten minutes.

What if Mother Trude and Sister Agnes were *wrong*?

"You taught me to think for myself, Sister Agnes," he said aloud, to no one in particular. "When Grandmama and the earl claimed I was one sort of person but I knew myself to be another, you and Mama told me to trust myself. These look like ghosts to me. I'm going to believe my own eyes until I have a better explanation."

Charl sat up and then stood up, feeling a bit better for having gotten that off his chest.

He figured he may as well pick some apples while he was here; Mother Trude needed to eat, and she'd asked for apples specifically. Most of the trees branched low enough that they were easy to climb, but the fruit was out at the ends of the branches.

Charl shimmied onto a branch. Small though he was, the branch bobbed and careened wildly under his weight, and finally cracked. He fell onto a patch of thick moss, fortunately, nothing but his dignity hurt. He plucked the apples off the broken limb—five hard green nuggets—but he didn't like harming the trees to get at the fruit. There must be a better way.

He could see almost a dozen boulders among the trees now. Charl clambered up one of the large rocks to see if he could reach the apples from there. He was surrounded by several large clusters, more apples than he could carry at once. He'd left his bucket on the ground, so he tossed the apples down into it. They hit the water with a splash.

Oops, wrong bucket.

"Oh," went the wind, sounding more surprised than was usual for a light breeze. Still, Charl might not have taken any notice had it not also added, "You spilled some."

That was not the wind. The hairs rose on the back of Charl's neck.

He squinted at the ground around his boulder, trying to see who had spoken. At first, he thought there was no one.

Then he saw the girl.

She was almost invisible among the gnarled trees, because she was nearly transparent.

Another ghost. Sister Agnes was going to hear all about this, if he ever saw her again.

As gratifying as it was to be right, it was also slightly terrifying. Charl's stomach seemed to contract to the size of a walnut.

He feared it might become too small to hold its contents and that he might lose them at any moment. He shakily lowered himself so that he was sitting on the boulder.

The girl stepped toward him, her feet passing through the roots and weeds. She was wearing a cloth wrapped around herself, which Charl assumed was her shroud. It wasn't white like funeral cloths in St. Muckle's, but checkered, a sort of plaid, although he couldn't tell what colors it had originally been. The girl seemed to consist mostly of air, in shades of nebulous blue.

She stopped at the base of his boulder and looked up with impossibly wide eyes. She was very thin, her cheeks hollow. Her dark hair hung in two braids, also very thin. She gave him a watery smile.

"Who are you?" said Charl, sounding a bit like the wind himself. His voice wasn't working quite right.

"My name is Vilna," she said. "I won't hurt you."

Charl supposed that was reassuring. "I'm Charl," he said in a brave voice, although he was still not brave enough to come down from his perch.

"I know," she said. "I ran into you last night and glimpsed your memories without permission. It was an accident. You stumbled through me in the darkness."

The cold. That had been her.

But . . . *memories*?

"I relived one memory," said Charl. "A bad one."

"I saw more than that. Your insides. All of them—heart, mind, the thoughts you were trying not to think. Anyway, I'm sorry. It's a hazard of being . . . this."

She lifted her transparent hands apologetically.

"A ghost?" Charl thought it was high time the word was said aloud.

Vilna smiled sadly. "I have to give something back. I don't feel right, otherwise."

Whatever she was going to give him, Charl felt entirely certain he didn't want it.

"You don't owe me anything," he said. "It was a misunderstanding."

"But . . ." Her eyes were luminous in the shadow of the trees. "It's a story. I think you'd like it, and you could use a story, I expect."

In fact, he *could* use a story. Mother Trude was surely going to ask for some scripture or another exemplar tale before bed. A story would be more entertaining than either of those, and if she didn't like it, maybe she'd stop asking.

Charl climbed down from the standing stone and leaned back against it, arms crossed. "All right, then," he said. "Tell me your story."

"No, no," she said. "It takes a lot out of me to speak like this. There's a simpler way."

She held out her ghostly hand. Charl was evidently intended to take it.

Charl hesitated, not quite trusting her, but then curiosity got the best of him and he reached out. Her hand was bitterly, fiercely cold.

For a moment, nothing seemed to happen. Then there was a flash behind his eyes, and the feeling that he'd been punched right in the brain. He blinked, trying to undazzle his vision, and when he could finally see again, Vilna had disappeared.

She'd given him the whole story at once, complete and entire. Charl felt weirdly . . . full. And content. It was a lovely story, in fact—one that he'd never heard before.

"Thank you," he called, hoping she heard him. He hefted his buckets—one empty, one full of apples and water—and hauled them back to the refectory.

Mother Trude was still sleeping when he arrived. It was late afternoon by now, but he told himself not to worry. She was old—who could say how old, even?—and the climb yesterday had clearly sapped all the strength out of her.

Charl cut up the green apples, stoked the fire, and then put a potful of water and apples on to boil. In another pot, he started some oatmeal. (It was better than turnips; those turnips would last forever.) Apples and oatmeal simmered and grew fragrant, but still Mother Trude didn't stir.

As the shadows lengthened outside, Charl did begin to worry.

"Mother Trude," he said. "You should eat something. Keep up your strength? I'll mix some apples in with the oatmeal—how would you like that?"

She didn't answer. Something was very wrong.

He touched her shoulder gently, to wake her, and could feel heat coming off her skin even through the fabric of her habit.

She turned to face him at last, and Charl gasped. She had dark purple rings under her eyes, as if she'd been punched, and her skin was deathly pale. Her cheeks glistened with sweat, and her eyes held a feverish light.

Charl had seen symptoms like this too many times to be in any doubt: Mother Trude was in the first stages of the ague. She must have been bitten before they came up, or in the turnip fields—or inhaled the gray, even through her kerchief—and the disease had been lurking in her blood ever since, waiting to reveal itself.

Charl snapped into action. He was his mother's son, after all.

He spread the old nun's cloak more neatly over her, put fresh straw beneath her head, and refilled her cup. He began a mental list of things he should look for in the ruins tomorrow—blankets, a proper pillow, some rags to make a cool compress. He vigorously stirred the apples in their pot until they grew encouragingly mushy.

"I'm sorry, boy," croaked Mother Trude. "I feel a fool. I'm supposed to be watching you, and keeping you safe, and I . . . I know how this disease goes. I'm going to need your help."

"You shall have it," said Charl stoutly. He knew how the disease went, too. It would go all the worse without Sister Agnes or Dr. Caramus to help him.

Medicinal herbs, he added to his mental list. Those, he would need tonight, although he didn't see how he was going to find them in the dark.

He was about to ask Mother Trude what sort of plants to look for when, to his shock, he realized she was crying.

"Let it out, let it out," said Charl, patting her hand. That was what his mother would have said, even if he sounded somewhat more frantic than she ever did. He dished mushy apples into a wooden bowl and noticed his own hand quaking slightly.

This was no good; they were both panicking. They weren't going to last long if they couldn't calm down.

"I . . . I just learned a story," said Charl. "Would you like to hear it?"

Mother Trude wiped her eyes with her wimple, inhaled shudderingly, and nodded.

Charl sat beside her, stirring the steaming apples until they were sauce, until they were cool enough that they wouldn't burn her mouth.

"This is the story of the Wise Girl, the King of the Wolves, and the stone circle," Charl began.

"No," said Mother Trude, so softly Charl wasn't quite sure what he'd heard her say.

"Once upon a time," he said, "an elderly couple had a baby long after they had believed they could. They called in the village's holy woman—the corna—to bless it and examine its spirit (for they half believed the child might be a mischievous sprite). The holy woman examined the child all over, taking the measure of its mind, heart, and soul, and finally said, 'This girl is going to grow up unusually wise. She may be the girl I have been looking for, to take my place. Since you are old, and were not looking for a child, let me raise her for you, and teach her the way.'

"So the elderly couple, somewhat relieved, gave their daughter over to the holy woman to raise. And indeed, the girl proved to be as wise and insightful as the holy woman had predicted. By the age of five, she could read the entrails of chickens; by the age of seven, she could read portents in the stars. When she turned nine, she was able—if she concentrated very hard—to see the Blue Lands—"

"Stop," said Mother Trude, loudly this time.

Charl stopped speaking. She scowled at him through the fire.

"That is a thoroughly pagan story," she said. "I know Agnes would never tell you such things, so who did? That unconventional mother of yours?"

"No," said Charl. But he knew she wouldn't believe a ghost had told him.

"Well, don't let me hear such dangerous nonsense out of your mouth again," said Mother Trude. "Thank you for the apples. I think that I am comfortable enough to sleep now."

With that, she rolled over and fell asleep again.

Charl sat watching the fire, peevishly picking at his own portion of apples, annoyed that she wouldn't even let him finish the story. It was quite a good one. But that wasn't the only thing bothering him. Everything felt changed—everything *was* changed, honestly, by Mother Trude being sick. Even if he found the Battle Bishop's sword, how could he run off to St. Muckle's now and leave her here? She wouldn't last long without someone to help her.

It would be a lie to say resentment didn't creep up on him then and make him frown, but it was what it was. This was the hand he'd been given.

Do what you can—he heard his mother's voice. *Need is right in front of you.*

Right now what he needed was sleep. Surely the way forward would seem clearer in the morning.

15.5: Vilna's Story

This is the story of the Wise Girl, the King of the Wolves, and the stone circle.

Once upon a time, an elderly couple had a baby long after they had believed they could. They called in the village's holy woman—the corna—to bless it and examine its spirit (for they half believed the child might be a mischievous sprite). The holy woman examined the child all over, taking the measure of its mind, heart, and soul, and finally said, "This girl is going to grow up unusually wise. She may be the girl I have been looking for, to take my place. Since you are old, and were not looking for a child, let me raise her for you, and teach her the way."

So the elderly couple, somewhat relieved, gave their daughter over to the holy woman to raise. And indeed, the girl proved to be as wise and insightful as the holy woman had predicted. By the age of five, she could read the entrails of chickens; by the age of seven, she could read portents in the stars. When she turned nine, she was able—if she concentrated very hard—to see the Blue Lands, the glow of life, and the coming of death.

And that was how she knew her teacher was going to die, and soon.

The old holy woman crossed into the Blue when the girl was ten years old, and then she was the only corna in her village.

Ten was too young, though—or so some of the villagers thought. They tried to prove their point by creating more and more difficult problems for her, to demonstrate that she couldn't solve them. They brought her a lamb born with two heads, but she easily revealed this as a fake. The village children mysteriously disappeared, but she soon found them in a nearby cave. A blight of grasshoppers landed on their fields (this problem was real), and she called down the powers, as was her training and her gift, and sent them on their way.

One day, a gang of shepherds came running breathless to her hut, crying, "Woe, woe! The King of the Wolves is attacking our flock and killing our sheep!"

These were the same shepherds who had hidden the children away in the cave, so the Wise Girl felt disinclined to believe them. However, they insisted, and then other people took up the cry—that the King of the Wolves was on his way *here*, to the village—and finally the Wise Girl had no choice but to go out and have a look.

And indeed, who should she see coming down the mountain but a massive wolf, nearly as tall as a horse, the blood of a dozen sheep smeared on his muzzle. And the Wise Girl felt cold all the way down to her bones, because she knew how to deal with wolves, but she had never seen a wolf like this. She would never have guessed that there could be wolves like this; her mentor had said nothing.

Still, she was the corna. This was up to her.

She threw her shoulders back, raised her head high, and walked out to meet it.

"King of Wolves," she said, "how are you properly addressed?"

The king, surprised by her politeness, answered, "I am called Magla. I am come to destroy your village."

"You may not," said the Wise Girl. "Look elsewhere for your dinner."

One cannot become King of the Wolves by savagery alone; Magla was shrewd and clever and not entirely unwise himself. He knew that only someone very wise or very foolish could stand before him and speak to him this way. If this girl was merely a fool, the gods would not mind if he gobbled her up. But if she was wise, the gods were with her and would punish him for harming her or her people. Alas, he could not tell the answer just by looking.

But he knew of a test. A mile from the village was an ancient stone circle, the dwelling place of ghosts. Only the very wise could spend a night among ghosts and survive.

"I will leave this place and never return," Magla told the girl, "if you can spend one night in the stone circle, among ghosts."

Because she was wise, the girl quaked in her shoes. She believed she was wise enough to survive, but only a fool could imagine it would be easy.

The villagers accompanied her to the stone circle, singing songs of encouragement, but some of them were glad in their hearts. The King of the Wolves had devised a better test than any of them had been able to. Maybe this would end the young upstart once and for all.

The Wise Girl settled herself into the very center of the circle, and prepared for a long night. The villagers returned to their homes.

No one can describe the ordeal she endured—it is not for the rest of us to know—but one thing is certain. She suffered. She endured. And at first light, she took the trail back to her home, alone.

The King of the Wolves was waiting there for her, and when he saw her returning, he knew that the gods were against him, and he should turn back and look for his dinner elsewhere. And that is what he did.

The villagers cheered her coming, and even the doubters were now satisfied that this Wise Girl was sufficient unto herself, a true corna after all.

But the Wise Girl was wise enough to know that it is possible to be very wise *and* very foolish, together at the same time. The part of her that was wise had survived, but the part of her that was foolish had died painfully and now lurked as a ghost in her blood. She had saved her village from Magla, and she had brought on her own death, a cancer that would grow until it consumed her as surely as any wolf.

Let us never imagine ourselves to be just one thing.

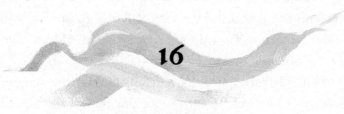

16

The Sanctuary

he old nun slept poorly, and Charl slept worse. Every time she moaned in her sleep, he was up, trying to figure out what he could do. She finally noticed, and said, "It's fever dreams, lad. Ignore me. I won't die of dreaming, and if I do, well, there's nothing you could have done."

Exhaustion finally got the upper hand and knocked Charl out until dawn.

He awoke determined to scour every inch of the abbey for useful items. Determined, even, to risk a peek into the sanctuary. There might be a kneeler pillow, or an altar cloth he could use as a blanket.

If the Battle Bishop's sword was really there, Charl wasn't even thinking about it.

First, he went to the orchard, though, to see what Vilna could tell him about medicinal herbs. If there was one thing Charl thought he knew about pagans (besides their being misguided, un-Saintly, and—apparently—the object of his father's many military campaigns), it's that they were all of them witches, and witches knew herbs. Vilna, however, was nowhere to be seen. This was probably to be expected in a ghost. Surely they couldn't be seen most of the time, or people would see them a lot more often.

"Vilna?" he called, stepping carefully through the overgrown underbrush. He circled the grove looking for her, and as he did, he noticed something. These boulders weren't simply random rocks that the monks had been too lazy to move. There were, perhaps, twenty in all; the largest was twice Charl's height. A few had toppled onto their sides, but most were still standing, deliberately arranged into a circle.

Like the stone circle where the ghosts had lived in Vilna's story.

That gave the whole orchard a different aspect. This circle had been here long before the monastery. He'd heard of such things. Legends abounded—the circles were tombs, or altars to unknown gods, or evil places—but Sister Agnes (who'd been his schoolteacher, more or less his whole life) had been adamant that they were calendars, lined up with the sun at solstice.

That they were pagan, though, was unquestionable. Charl wondered how long it had been since Vilna, with her very pagan stories, had died, and what she'd died of.

A chirp drew his attention—the martin, perched in a sunbeam on top of one of the taller stones. Charl picked his way toward it, holding out a finger in hopes it might perch there. "Hello, martin," he said. "Hello. My friend is ill. Are there supplies somewhere, or herbs I could gather? Do you know? Would you help me?"

"She can't understand you," said a voice near his ear, making him jump.

Charl whirled around to see a different transparent girl—not the one he'd been expecting, anyway—standing behind him with her hands on her hips. She looked older than Vilna, maybe fifteen or sixteen, and was quite a bit taller, although similarly swaddled in a checkered shroud. Vilna had looked underfed, but this girl was plump, with a heart-shaped face and curling hair that might have been as red as his mother's, if the green of orchard foliage hadn't been visible through it. She had a mischievous expression, and she waggled her eyebrows at him.

"That's Ognielle," the new girl explained, pointing at the martin. "She was human, originally, and used to look it, but she's faded now. A bird shape is all she can manage. She doesn't talk."

Charl was bursting with so many questions that he hardly knew where to start, but he felt he should introduce himself first. "I'm Charl."

"I know," said the girl, tilting her head coyly. "Vilna told me. I'm Maeve."

Now the questions could start tumbling out. "Are you two buried here, in this circle? Is it some sort of graveyard?"

Maeve put her hands behind her back and strolled partway around the circle. "We *are*, and it's *not*, but that's kind of a rude question to ask a ghost, don't you think?"

"Is it?" said Charl, suddenly mortified.

Maeve looked at him sternly, then burst out laughing, a soft, ghostly laugh, like falling snow. "You were asking Ognielle about useful supplies. I know where some might be, but—"

"And which herbs might help with a fever?" Charl burst in eagerly.

She gave him a skeptical look. "What do I look like to you?"

It was a trick question, and he could tell as he answered that he was getting it wrong: "A pagan?"

"And we're all herbalists. I see." Maeve snorted. "Anyway, your foolish assumptions aside, I can only go where the orchard goes."

"Meaning what?" asked Charl.

"I am bound to this stone circle, but the orchard has been growing here so long that it has become a part of the place. The binding has blurred. If you put an apple in your pocket, I can follow you a ways before I am pulled back."

Charl had had no apples in his pockets—or even in his stomach—when he'd encountered the ghost bird, Ognielle, on the battlements, but maybe the same rules didn't apply to a faded ghost. He'd already been rude once and was nervous, therefore, to ask. However, he climbed onto one of the toppled stones, plucked an apple for each pocket, and hopped down again. Maeve looked satisfied with this and began directing him which way to go.

She steered him toward the courtyard, but as they neared it, his feet began to slow. "Is there another way to get where we're going?" he asked. "I'm . . . avoiding the well."

"You were here that night, weren't you?" said Maeve, a bit too eagerly. "Vilna hinted at that. We all felt them die. It was terrible."

Charl's heart sank. "Are they *both* still here? Wort and Hooey?"

"Are those their names?" asked Maeve. It was harder to see her in direct sunlight, but Charl could tell she was wrinkling her nose. "And, no, the one who exploded departed with his body and has moved on. The other one was confused and is still in the well. We hear him thrashing about from time to time."

"Does he . . . Does he go where his water goes?" said Charl, barely able to do more than whisper at this point. The thought of Wort, all aflame, bursting out of the water bucket in the middle of the night was appalling.

"Oh, no, don't worry about that," said Maeve. "He isn't spiritually bound like we are. He's bound by his own ignorance. That is, he hasn't entirely realized he's dead."

She considerately led Charl in a different direction, though, around the dilapidated cider house, until she found some wagon tracks in the long grass. They looked well trodden.

"Who comes here?" asked Charl.

"Smugglers," said Maeve gleefully, waggling her eyebrows at him again. "Porphyrians, really. They're honest traders, for the most part, but they've stored a great load of something down in this cellar, and I suspect, from the way they whisper, that it's something they're not supposed to have."

She pointed to a pair of sloped cellar doors, made of the same wood as the well cover. Charl felt a tension release in himself, his half-formed worry about actual smugglers, which seemed silly now. Porphyrian traders would presumably be the same ones who visited St. Muckle's with goods; dragons would attack Goreddi supply wagons, but they weren't at war with Porphyry, so they let those merchants pass. The traders he'd met weren't frightening—one of them had stopped Rafe from beating him too badly, after all, before he'd learned to defend himself—and what was more, they might be storing all kinds of useful things. Eagerly, he flung open the doors and climbed down the steps on the other side.

There were a few useful items, like an oil lamp and a couple sacks of lentils (that most Porphyrian of legumes), as well as less useful things. Boxes of buttons and spools of ribbons. Most of the room, however, was taken up with stacked crates, all alike.

The nearest one was open. Charl looked inside, and his heart gave a painful lurch.

The crate held five ceramic jugs, each the size of a small cabbage; there was room for six, but one was missing. He'd been behind the bar at the Fiddle, and knew that alcohol might come in similar containers—cheap stuff, like pisky—but these looked exactly like the jug Rafe had been holding when he'd returned to the courtyard.

The one he had tried to toss to Hooey, and Hooey had failed to catch. Which had turned out to be full of pyria.

If these crates were all pyria, that was incredibly dangerous. Just jostling the jugs too hard could set them off, and there was surely enough here to blow the whole abbey sky-high. He gingerly uncorked one to make sure. If it was merely pisky, he'd recognize the smell.

He shouldn't have stuck his nose directly over the vessel's mouth. A piercing, painful odor seemed to stab him right in the sinuses. It burned his nose and made his eyes water. He clumsily recorked the jug, and then staggered back out into the sunlight, where he sneezed a dozen times and clawed at his nose between sneezes.

"What is that stuff?" said Maeve, seated almost invisibly on a pile of fallen stone. "Nothing we had in my day, I assure you."

"Pyria. Knights use it for fighting dragons," moaned Charl, his nose running. He rummaged for his handkerchief and was embarrassed to find it was completely brown. He'd crawled through the mud, after all, and he hadn't brought a change of clothes. The largest clumps had dried and flaked off, but every inch of his clothing, and probably his face as well, was still . . . dirty.

"Yes, you look like a walking smudge," said Maeve, noticing his anxiety. "Go ahead and wipe your nose, though. Can't make it worse."

It was mortifying to be spoken to in such a way by a rather pretty, somewhat older (or probably hundreds of years older, actually) girl: as if he were a child. Charl grumpily turned and wiped his nose on his way back into the cellar to fetch up the lentils and the lamp, which he'd left behind.

"What else is here?" he asked when he returned. "Any old monks' belongings? Trunks? Library?" He said the last one to make himself sound a bit less childish, but a book would have been most welcome, even scripture. Who knew how long he'd be tending Mother Trude?

"You're staying in the refectory, so you've found what dishes remain," said Maeve, rubbing her ethereal chin. "Anything else useful has been picked over by thieves or rained on."

"What about the sanctuary?" said Charl. "Its roof is intact, so that's kept the rain off."

"Intact, you say?" said Maeve, looking at him sidelong. "That's a bad sign."

"*Sign?*" said Charl. "It's always been like that, surely." He pointed toward the sanctuary, visible above the other buildings. Maeve did not look where he was pointing.

"It doesn't strike you as a bit odd that there should be one building still standing among all this mess?" said the ghost girl, making minute adjustments to her shroud. "And that it should be the building that houses Bishop Marcellus's tomb?"

The hairs rose on Charl's arms. "The Battle Bishop, you mean?"

Maeve rolled her ghostly eyes. "If you *must*."

"Is he . . . Is he still there?" whispered Charl. "In ghost form, I mean."

Maeve drew her mouth into a pouty rosebud. "If he is, that could only mean his so-called Heaven refused him entry, for his crimes."

And with that, she vanished.

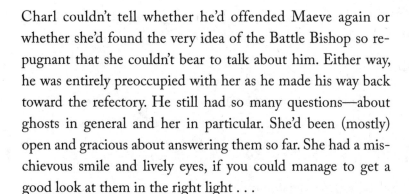

Charl couldn't tell whether he'd offended Maeve again or whether she'd found the very idea of the Battle Bishop so repugnant that she couldn't bear to talk about him. Either way, he was entirely preoccupied with her as he made his way back toward the refectory. He still had so many questions—about ghosts in general and her in particular. She'd been (mostly) open and gracious about answering them so far. She had a mischievous smile and lively eyes, if you could manage to get a good look at them in the right light . . .

And she was dead. It wouldn't do to lose sight of that.

Mother Trude was sitting up when he got in. She'd even cut up some turnips and set them simmering. She smiled wanly and said, "Ague patients sometimes feel better first thing and get worse again as the day goes on. I thought I should get some food in me, while I can stand to."

Charl helped out, starting some lentils in the other small pot. Mother Trude seemed exceedingly pleased by the lentils, which was nice. He'd found something useful, anyway. There was an old trunk by the wall of the refectory, its leather hinges decayed nearly to dust; Charl placed the leftover oatmeal, turnips, and lentils inside it. And the hard cheese. He'd forgotten there was cheese.

His mouth watered, thinking about cheese, but he knew he'd better save it. No one was coming for them—not until they'd rescued Mama and trapped the dragon—and who knew how long that might take?

He couldn't dwell on it. He had to stay strong for Mother Trude.

After lunch, he filled Mother Trude's cup and saw that she was comfortable, and then he went back outside and turned north, toward the part of the compound where the sanctuary stood.

There had to be something in there he could use.

Charl picked his way around shattered beams and crumbled walls. The closer he came, the quieter everything seemed to get. Birds stopped chirping; insects stopped chattering. When he climbed the sanctuary steps, even the breeze seemed to still.

He glanced up at the stained-glass windows. It was hard to tell, by day, whether any candles flickered inside.

Charl laid one hand on the bronze handle in the center of the imposing oaken door, half expecting it to be unnaturally cold, but the sun had been shining on it and it was warm. The limestone of the elaborate arched doorway had been carved into three tiers, like the bands of a rainbow. The outermost tier was evidently meant to represent Heaven, and depicted the Saints, their dogs, and other delights. The middle showed ordinary people doing ordinary things—being born, dying, working. The lowest tier, nearest the door, held all the devils and monsters of the Infernum.

Technically, the door itself might be considered a tier even lower than the Infernum. What was worse than the Infernum? Charl hoped he wasn't about to find out.

He gritted his teeth and pushed on the door, expecting it to be heavy and stuck. It glided silently open, as if on newly oiled hinges.

While his eyes adjusted, Charl could only tell that the air smelled oddly sweet, like incense. The wooden trim on the ceiling was lacquered black. Sunlight filtered through stained glass, turning the marble floors opulent gold and fiery red. Niche tombs lined the walls, topped with reclining statues of deceased clergymen, but the biggest grave monument, shaped like a stone table, dominated the center of the chapel. At the far end, a statue of St. Ogdo glowered down upon an altar draped with purple cloth.

Of all the things that thieves might have stolen from the Old Abbey, how had they overlooked the gold leaf and jeweled reliquaries? The plush, velvet draperies, untouched by time and decay? Even the lingering incense struck him as deeply odd. The abbey had been abandoned for two hundred years, at least. How had these treasures—to say nothing of that smell—lasted all that time?

Why, just the twinkling gold candlesticks by the altar must be worth . . .

They were twinkling because the candles were *lit*. Someone, or something, had lit them.

Charl shivered, and not merely from the spookiness. It had grown colder in here.

Did ghosts radiate cold the way fire radiated heat? Would he be able to sense the Battle Bishop drawing near, even if the ghost was invisible? Could he avoid walking through him? If a little slip of a girl like Vilna could wholly immerse him in painful memories, and a tiny bird—a ghost who had faded, so not even a full-strength spirit—could whisk his mind away from his body, Charl hated to guess what a ghost like the Battle Bishop might do to him.

Oh. Oh dear.

Could that be what had happened to Rafe? He'd left the courtyard, left his friends burning, and gone this direction. What if he'd followed the candlelight? What if he'd come in here, either to look for the bishop's sword or because he was in shock, and what if he'd walked through a powerful ghost?

Or the ghost had passed through him, on purpose.

Charl was trembling a bit now. He was scaring himself, thinking these things. Anyway, he didn't have to linger here. He could turn around right now and go back to Mother Trude and have a bowl of reassuring lentils like a sensible person.

And he would have. He really would have, except—

There was the Battle Bishop's sword. Right there, on top of the grand tomb in the middle of the chamber.

Charl had seen elaborate tombs before, but never like this. It consisted of a marble table with a bronze statue lying on top: a man in pleated robes wearing the tall, pointed hat of his office. His head rested upon two bronze pillows, and a cherub sat on each of his shoulders. Under his feet, absurdly, lay a little bronze dog, forever frozen in an attitude of loyal devotion.

The bishop's hands were folded piously around the hilt of a longsword that lay on top of his body, pointing toward his toes.

The longsword was not merely a part of the bronze statue, to be clear, but the real thing, with a jeweled hilt and an edge so sharp you could almost hear it sing.

Charl, it seemed to say.

He forgot his fear. He took a step toward the tomb, and then another. Crimson draperies hung between the legs of the stone table, but as Charl approached, he noticed a gap in the curtains, and that there was something concealed under the table. Something that glittered. Curiosity got the best of him. He drew back the drapes and gasped in horror at what he saw.

There was a second bronze statue, lying directly underneath the marble table that held the first. It clearly depicted the same man, in the same position, but in a state of skeletal decay. His fine robes lay in tatters around him. Bronze rats perched on his shoulders, bronze worms burrowed in and out of his scalp, and a bronze snake coiled in the pit of his hollow belly.

It was a memento mori—a reminder that all mortal things must die. Charl didn't feel that he needed a reminder just now. He let the drapes fall back in place, taking care to close the gap.

The tomb's inscription caught his eye: HERE LYETH HIS MOSTE REVEREND EXCELLENCYE, MARCELLUS, FIRST BISHOP OF ST. OGDO'S-ON-THE-MOUNTAIN, REST HE ON HEAVEN'S HEARTHSTONE. The letters were carved in stone and then illuminated with gold leaf. Charl traced the name Marcellus; his finger came back coated in tiny gold flakes.

A chill breeze blew, raising the hairs on his neck. The candles flickered. Charl held his breath until everything stilled.

Charl, the sword seemed to say again, and his eyes locked onto it.

Suddenly, he wanted that sword, wanted it more than anything. Wanted to rush down the mountain with it and drive it straight into the heart of that dragon, or Jarlbrus, or both of them—anyone who was threatening his mother or his people or his town.

Yes, said the breeze. *Yes.*

He reached his hand up, up and across, ready to slide the blade out from between the statue's lifeless fingers. Never mind that the sword was almost as long he was tall, or that he probably could not have lifted it above his head. Where there was a will, there was a way, and his will to wield it was mightier than the paltry laws of nature—

Yes.

Except . . . no. Charl pulled back his hand.

The candles guttered peevishly.

However much he longed to do it, he couldn't go haring off down the mountain to wreak vengeance on his enemies. Not while Mother Trude was so sick, with no one else to care for her.

In fact, his annoying conscience now reminded him, there were things he needed more urgently than that sword. Charl tore his eyes away from it and quickly spotted a kneeler cushion that didn't look too tattered. Maybe that could go under her head. He grabbed it. None of the draperies looked like they would make good blankets, except the purple altar cloth, which was of heavy felted wool. Candles might also be useful, if he could work up the nerve to blow them out.

Charl tiptoed toward the altar, one hand stretched before him, trying to detect anything invisible radiating cold. The air felt like it had near the tomb. There was another kneeler beside the altar, but its cushion didn't look as nice as the one he already had. It was smudged and dark.

Charl froze. The air above the cushion was also oddly darkened, as if a shadow had settled there. But what was casting that shadow? The candles should have dispelled it.

Keeping his eyes on the shadow, Charl reached for the purple altar cloth, slowly, slowly, grasped the corner, and tugged on it.

The shadow began to solidify into a shape. The shape of a kneeling man.

The candles went out.

The shadow man turned to face Charl, and all he saw were two unfathomable wells of darkness, eyes like bottomless pits. He felt shocked and frozen, all at once, as if he'd been struck by lightning made of ice.

Look deeper, a voice seemed to say. *Let yourself fall into my eyes, and see what happens.*

Charl wrenched his gaze away, dropped the altar cloth, and ran, ran, ran—past the tomb, out the great doors, into the restoring sunshine.

17

Refugees

hen Charl's feet finally slowed, he realized he'd sprinted past the refectory, all the way back to the orchard. He put his hands on his knees, his head down, panting, waiting for his heart to slow.

When he stood upright again, he saw two black-haired girls peeking out from the apple grove, hands over their mouths to hide their giggling. Charl blinked, and they were gone.

They'd looked like twins, almost, and he hadn't recognized them. Vilna and Maeve weren't the only orchard ghosts, it seemed.

Voices began intruding upon his thoughts—loud voices, accompanied by banging and rattling. He followed the sound toward the courtyard, cautiously, not quite convinced it wasn't Wort kicking up a racket in the well. But, no, there seemed to be several people outside, rattling the gates by yanking on the padlock.

Not the Porphyrian merchants, then, returned for their pryia. They'd have had the key to their own lock.

Were these people friendly? He couldn't tell. Charl grabbed a fist-sized rock in each hand, then crept into the courtyard as quietly as he could.

"Is anyone here? Let us in!" boomed a voice. A familiar voice. In fact, Charl knew it well—Gorlich Smith. Charl dropped his rocks and sprinted the rest of the way toward the gates.

"Can anyone climb that ivy?" someone else was asking.

"Maybe there's another door."

Charl drew back the bar, threw open the sally door, and flung himself at the nearest townsperson. It was Jenny Sugar, the pie maker. She emitted a prodigious shriek. A couple men drew daggers in alarm, but Gorlich boomed, "Charl! Sister Agnes said you would be here, but I was beginning to doubt you'd made it. It's good to see you in one piece."

It was such joy and relief to hear the name Agnes. Charl wanted to ask more, to ask after his mother and Aris, but a painful bubble seemed to rise in his chest, and he couldn't speak around it.

They were a bedraggled group of sixteen: Gorlich Smith, his six children, Jenny Sugar, and eight others who Charl didn't really know. Most carried sacks, although there were two wheelbarrows full of belongings and a third hauling Gorlich's youngest children. Everyone looked exhausted and a bit singed around the edges.

"Come in," Charl managed, holding the sally door wide. The townspeople bustled inside. Jenny Sugar tousled his hair as she passed. And then there were Mellie and Gert, flashing him a double smile, as if all were forgiven and forgotten. Charl found that his own smile came easily, though not without a pang. Only one man, a scrawny fellow with a ratty mustache—the one who'd drawn his dagger and not yet put it back—scowled and seemed reluctant to enter. Maybe he remembered what had happened to poor Rafe in this ruin.

Or he wasn't overly fond of Charl's mother. Charl gave him what he hoped was a reassuring nod, but the man brushed past him without speaking.

As soon as they saw the well, everyone rushed toward it; they hauled up bucket after bucket of water and took turns sticking their faces in it, drinking like thirsty cattle. "It's a parched time now in St. Muckle's," Gorlich explained, wiping his dripping beard on his sleeve. "We still can't risk the water, but it's hard to find the leisure to boil it properly, when there's a dragon about.

"But you're not all alone, are you?" the smith added, looking around at the crumbling buildings. "Sister Agnes said her old prioress—"

"She's here," said Charl. His heart dropped as he realized what he had to say next. There was no way to lie; he'd be found out as soon as they saw her. Anyway, he needed their help.

"She's got the blood fever," he said.

All around, faces fell. As if he sensed the dismay in the air, Gorlich's baby began to cry.

"She's not contagious," said Charl hastily, to reassure them.

"Not contagious *yet*," a smudge-faced young woman piped up, folding her arms over her sooty kirtle.

"The illness doesn't always run that way. Dr. Caramus says—"

"Is he here, too?" the woman shrilled, startling a flock of birds out of the birch trees.

"Rozzy, peace," said Gorlich. His brows beetled as he turned to Charl. "Is he, though?"

"N-no," said Charl.

"How could he have gotten here ahead of us?" someone else piped up. "He was at the forge when we left."

"He might have flown here," the skinny man burst out, his mustache quivering with rage. "I told you, he's a dragon, and we can't trust him."

"He's not a dragon, Geoffrey, you paranoid villain." Gorlich spoke quietly, as if he were trying to calm the man, but those words weren't likely to accomplish it, if so.

"He *is* a dragon. Don't tell me you've never suspected," cried Geoffrey, reddening as he raged. "And he refuses to take his dragon shape and fight that other dragon—which is how come I *know* he's a dragon, for certain. They won't fight for humans against their own kind."

All the adults started arguing. Finally, Gorlich bellowed louder than anyone, "We're here now, and we're all tired. We need to rest and recover a bit. I know some of you are uncertain, but you know what Lady Eileen would say: 'Let's put it to a vote.' All in favor of spending one night here before moving on, raise your hand."

Five adult hands went up, including Gorlich's. Mellie and Gert tried to vote, too, but their father shook them off; the vote was only for adults, apparently, never mind that they were both taller than Jenny Sugar.

"All in favor of moving on?" said Gorlich.

Five different hands went up.

"If we'll sleep outside, far from the sickbed, I'll change my vote," said Jenny Sugar.

"Agreed, and that settles it. We stay here tonight," said Gorlich.

They set about getting comfortable in the courtyard, beside the birches, unrolling blankets and pallets, clearing a place for a fire. Charl helped as best he could, but when dusk began to fall, he grew worried about having left Mother Trude alone so long. He excused himself to go check on her.

When the others heard where he was going, they scraped together some useful things for him to take with him: a couple blankets, a spare kettle and mug, and some powdered willow extract to make a fever-reducing tea.

Charl thanked them, then hurried back to the refectory, pausing only to pick up the kneeler pillow he had dropped near the orchard earlier. He kept his eyes down, trying not to notice whether there were lights in the sanctuary windows.

"What's happening out there?" asked Mother Trude when he came in. "I heard voices."

"Some people have arrived from town," said Charl. He raised one of the blankets to show her. "They've brought some things to make you more comfortable."

Charl tucked the kneeler pillow beneath her head. It was velvet and smelled of incense, and he worried that she'd realize he'd stolen it from the sanctuary. Mother Trude said nothing, however. Charl draped both blankets over her, and set the kettle to boil for the fever-reducing tea.

"It will be nice to have company," he said, trying to fill the silence. He was already missing the abundant chatter the townspeople had brought with them. "It will raise your spirits to see more people than just me, I think."

The nun sighed. "They won't be visiting *me*. You'll see."

Charl didn't want to believe that. He fed Mother Trude spoonfuls of applesauce between sips of tea, washed the bowl, and emptied the slop bucket (which was really a rusty pot, unsuited for anything else). That took half an hour, at least, and still nobody came from the courtyard to say hello. Maybe she was right.

There was a rustling noise, and Charl turned to see Gorlich standing awkwardly in the doorway, hat in hand. The smith was a large, well-muscled man; he took up almost the entire doorway.

"I only wanted to give the prioress my best wishes—and thanks," Gorlich muttered, drawing cautiously nearer. He took the nun's pale hand between his two ham hands. "You nursed my Nancy, Your Reverence, and although you could not save her, you eased her suffering, and I'm glad of it."

"I remember her," said Mother Trude. "She said she'll always love you."

Gorlich was crying now. Tears trickled through his thick beard. "Thank you, Mother. Did she have any words for the children?"

"That they must be good and obedient, for her sake, and never give you a day's worry."

"That will mean so much to them. Thank you, thank you," said the smith. He would normally have kissed her hand at this point, but he hesitated, for fear of the ague. He pressed her hand to his forehead instead, then dried his eyes and went back out to his people.

The distant sound of a fiddle could be heard, and laughter.

Charl opened and closed his fist on the handle of the water bucket, feeling guilty.

"Go ahead, boy," said the old nun without opening her eyes.

"Spend an evening with people who are lively and well. The tea is doing its job. I feel much relieved, and I think I could sleep. I'll be fine, as long as you look in on me once or twice."

"Th-thank you," he stammered, scrambling to his feet.

She opened one eye, and said, "I'm not a monster, boy." When her eye closed again, she began to snore.

Still, Charl hesitated. What if she took a turn for the worse? Most people lingered with this illness for weeks, but sometimes they died suddenly. If she needed him but he was outside, would he be able to hear her? Charl wished he had a bell to leave with her, something loud and clangy to call him back.

"Go on, Charl. I'll watch her," said a whispery voice from the doorway.

Charl turned and saw Maeve stepping over the threshold. Her transparent feet were bare.

"Have you been spying on me?" asked Charl, only half joking, not sure he wanted to know the answer.

"How am I supposed to resist, when you're leaving apples everywhere?" she said, gesturing at the refuse heap where he'd tossed all his cores. "We don't get out much these days. Sometimes a squirrel will carry off an apple, and we'll have a bit of an adventure, but that's it. When the monks lived here, we could haunt them in the kitchens, the cider press, and the latrine. And here." She put her hands on her hips and looked up at the ceiling. "I wouldn't say this place has aged well."

"How many of you are there?" asked Charl.

"In the orchard, you mean?" said Maeve, giving him a sidelong look.

"Yes?" said Charl. "It's just, I saw two new faces, earlier. Two dark-haired girls, who looked just alike."

"Ah," said Maeve, breaking into a smile. "Anya and Zedig. They look like sisters, but they're actually aunt and niece. They're shy, but they may speak to you eventually.

"Anyway, there are five of us who still have our wits about us," said Maeve. "And two who have faded and don't."

"But why are you all together in the orchard?" asked Charl. He remembered Vilna's story about the stone circle, which had had ghosts in it but no explanation as to why. "The monks didn't murder you, I hope."

That made Maeve laugh. "No, no. We were there long before the monks came." Her eyes twinkled; if they'd had a color, Charl would have guessed they were green.

They were still pretty, even if he could kind of see through them.

"But go on," she said. "Enjoy yourself while you can. I'll keep an eye on this one, and if she gets any worse, I'll come tell you. You still have that apple in your pocket?"

He did. He thanked her profusely and turned to go.

He took one last look back as he stepped outside. Maeve had settled herself close to Mother Trude's head and was looking down at the old woman with an odd expression on her face—so odd that it took Charl a moment to put a name to it.

Maeve looked fond and amused, the way one might look at a baby, but she also looked *hungry*.

Maeve seemed to notice that Charl's footsteps had stopped. She looked up at him and broke into a perfectly innocent smile. "Have fun, Charl. We'll be fine here."

Charl hurried out toward the yard, feeling confused and unexpectedly worried. Was it really all right to leave Mother Trude in the care of a ghost? What had that hungry look meant?

Maybe it had really been more like envy than hunger. Mother Trude was alive, after all, and Maeve was not. Ghosts didn't *eat* people, surely.

But then again, they weren't exactly safe, either, if Vilna's story about the Wise Girl proved anything. Charl's feet slowed. What had Bishop Marcellus done to Rafe, exactly? Something worse than making him relive a bad memory. A part of Rafe had been taken, if not eaten.

Could Charl really say it hadn't been eaten, though?

He would have turned back—he was right on the verge of it—but he could already see the fire. And then Mellie and Gert saw him and waved him over. Charl felt an ache in the very center of himself and realized he had been feeling terribly lonely and scared, even if he'd hardly dared to admit it to himself. He would spend a little time, just half an hour, in the company of other people, and then he would go back to Mother Trude.

With eager feet, he hastened toward the circle of warmth.

18

Irmentrude Remembers

Mother Trude stirred a little, at the edge of sleep. The fever tea was helping; she could already feel herself sweating out the fever heat. She'd been having terrible dreams, the kind a fevered mind vomits forth. Dreaming that she was a burning city. Dreaming that she was lost in the forest, wolves chasing her and trying to convince her that she was also a wolf.

She wasn't. She wouldn't be. She was here because she had no choice.

You're just a pawn, is that it?

Her eyes popped open. She thought she'd heard something. Or, no . . . she'd felt something. A fleeting breath of cold. Not fever chills, but a cold presence.

She knew exactly what it was.

"Begone," she muttered. "I am unwilling."

But when had a ghost ever cared if you were willing?

She had been a child once, called Irmentrude—and now she was again.

She awoke on her thirteenth birthday with the sheepdogs around her, and her big sister beside her under the sheepskins. Mama already had the cauldron boiling breakfast; she and the aunts were finishing Irmentrude's dedication robes. Irme's older brothers were out with the sheep. Today, Papa would have gone with the antler-priests to the bog, to read her portents in the rising mist.

Irmentrude sat up, remembering what day it was. She had a crawly feeling on the back of her neck, but maybe it didn't mean anything serious. Maybe it was just excitement.

Her robes, dyed blue with woad, had appliqué all over them, leaves and birds and flowers, meticulously outlined with glinting chips of mother-of-pearl. Her aunts helped dress her, brushed her pale hair, and placed the crown of hedgethorn flowers on her head. Mama fussed over her face, painting it as white as the moon. It would be dark when she met the ghost, after all, and it needed to be able to see her.

The day was a blur. Neighbors gave gifts and promises. The retiring Maiden, who was at least sixty, came by to give her advice about the Sage, and about dragons. Her father chose a sheep for sacrifice, which the antler-priests undertook with both Maidens—old and new—standing close by. The sheep's blood was poured out to the four corners of the world.

As the sun began to set, the whole village walked her to the top of the dolmen path, said goodbye, and cheered her on her way. She'd trodden this path before, upon every solstice since the Maiden had chosen her as her successor, carrying a wreath for the Sage. Today, she carried no wreath except the flowery, brambly crown on her head. Today, she was the gift.

The path was little more than a sheep track, winding through heather and around rocks. At last, the dolmen came into view on its hill, stark and unmissable. It consisted of two enormous pillars of stone with a third stone—flat, and yet even more massive than the others—balanced upon the pillars, like some impossible two-legged table. It was the work of giants, some said.

The three stones formed a doorway, where the Sage would appear.

Irmentrude stood in the doorway, trying not to fret about the massive stone overhead, precariously balanced on just two points. Trying not to think how easily it could crush her.

A ghost rose before her, a womanly figure with a gentle voice. "I have seen you here before, my child. Tell me why you have come."

"I am the Maiden," said Irmentrude, bowing her head dutifully. "And I have come for knowledge."

"All I have in my mind shall be yours," said the Sage, who had been a Maiden herself, centuries ago, and saved her village from destruction.

She grasped Irmentrude firmly in her ghostly hands, and the girl cried out at the cold and at the flood of memories that suddenly rushed through her. Every bad thing, every regret, every moment of pain, all came back in a torrent. But Irme had been taught how to bear it. She was a Wise Child; that was why she'd been chosen.

When the ghost had finished with her, Irme felt wrung out.

The Sage had made her relive everything, but she had given Irme a vast cache of knowledge in return. The newly minted Maiden sat between the stones, as she had been instructed, and meditated upon these things as the stars reeled overhead.

The Sage had taught her to understand the speech of dragons, and given her stories, parables, and memories of how to deal with them. *If you run from dragons, you are prey,* said the voice in her mind. *If you speak to them, they may yet eat you later, but you've bought your people some time . . .*

When morning came, Irmentrude left her crown for the Sage and began the long walk home. She felt changed, to her very bones. Now she could protect her village. If a dragon came, she would step up boldly and speak to it while her people got to safety.

As she walked, the crawly feeling returned. She walked faster.

A billow of smoke rose from behind the final ridge. A lot of smoke—someone's house was on fire. Surely a dragon could not have come while she was away. But what else could it be? She ran as fast as her legs would carry her.

Her whole village was on fire, but there was no dragon anywhere to be seen.

The village swarmed with soldiers, under the green-and-gold banner of some earl or other, whoever currently claimed this rocky corner of the highlands as his own. An overzealous earl who had decided it was time—again—to purge the pagans.

Irmentrude didn't stop to think. She kept running, straight into the fire and blood, convinced that if she could just *talk* to someone, the head dragon, whoever that was, she could buy her people some more time.

Mother Trude came back to herself, because there was a gap in that memory.

"Sorry, ghost," she muttered to herself. "I don't remember the worst of it, and you can't make me. It's gone."

But she had plenty of other nightmares to relive. Mother Trude was quickly sucked down into the vortex of memory again.

The next thing Irmentrude knew, she was lying in a muddy ditch, looking up at the sky. A dog was nudging her cheek, as if imploring her to wake, to move. Irmentrude got up, sore all over and caked with filth, and looked toward where her village had stood.

Everyone was gone. Only blackened stone walls were left. She hunted for human remains and buried whoever she could find, digging in the mud with her own two hands. She took stones from the ruined walls to make a cairn over them. Irmentrude haunted the ruins for days, but there was nothing to eat and no shelter. Finally, she had no choice but to leave if she wanted to live.

A day's walk east, across the bald hills, was another village. The sight of their thatched roofs felt like a miracle to Irme. She staggered across one last pasture, scattering the sheep, and the villagers saw her coming. They sent out a small delegation to meet her.

"Go away," cried the village's headwoman. "Don't bring your ill luck here."

Irmentrude, the Maiden, who could understand dragons, could not seem to understand what the woman was saying.

"We know what happened to your village," the broad-shouldered woman continued, glaring. "You brought it upon yourselves, refusing to convert to the faith of Allsaints. Look at you, still in your pagan robe."

Irme clutched her torn robe tighter around herself, ashamed. "What could I do in penance, for you to take me in?"

"Nothing," snapped the woman. "You are tainted. You will blight everything you touch. You should have died with the rest."

Irmentrude did not know what to say to this. Dumb with shock, she simply nodded, turned away, and walked off into the hills.

She lived rough for three-quarters of the year after that, with her village's last remaining dog for company. Finally, in the spring, she realized she was with child. She had never seen a human baby born—she was the youngest of her family—but she'd seen plenty of sheep. She dug a hole and filled it with soft grass and knelt on all fours above it, moaning and mooing until finally the baby was born, right there in the soft grass.

A traveling nun, passing by on the road, had heard Irmentrude's terrible groans and followed the sound, thinking it was an animal in distress. She arrived just as the baby dropped. The nun gave a cry and rushed over to help, throwing a woolen traveling cloak over Irme's shoulders. The cloak was blissfully warm; Irmentrude wept to receive it.

"My curse on your people," said the nun, "for letting you give birth in a field, like a beast. Come with me, and you will be cared for, as is your right under Heaven."

The nun removed the wimple from her own head and

swaddled the baby with it. Then she guided Irmentrude back to her mule, put girl and baby on top of it, and led them away toward her convent, Our Lady of the Glacier.

Irmentrude was glad to be led. She would have followed that nun to the end of the earth, for this was the first kindness she had received in months.

But it was the last she would see of her baby for a very long time.

The cold in Mother Trude's head began to dissipate, and the pressure of the memory eased. The ghost had taken what it wanted, apparently.

But it was still nearby. Mother Trude could feel the back of her neck prickling at its presence. She had known how to listen to ghosts, once, although she was decades out of practice. Still, it was said that one never forgets.

"Why are you lingering, fiend?" the old nun muttered.

You were born a pagan, came the sibilant whisper. *And yet you let pagans die.*

Ah, of course it knew. A ghost saw all, even if you only saw one memory at a time.

"I had no choice," said Mother Trude.

No choice? Are you dead? Are you a ghost? Let me tell you what it is to have no choice.

"A human may be bound, spirit, as surely as any ghost."

She was bound to her regrets, certainly. The past was a vulture, digging its talons into her neck, waiting for her to let down her guard so it could eat her.

That wasn't how vultures worked. The fever was making weird pictures in her mind.

You're a monster, hissed the ghost. *You're lying to Charl, every day. His mother never asked you to take him to a seminary to become a priest. You're just going to take him back to his horrible father.*

"Perhaps I *was*," said Mother Trude irritably, "but all plans are moot now, or had you not noticed? I might not be leaving this place alive."

I could see to it that you don't.

That there were spirits who could do such a thing, Mother Trude had no doubt. That this particular ghost could do it was less certain. She sounded like a teenage girl, even through her vicious whisper. Surely she did not have that kind of power.

"And how do you think Charl's going to feel about that?" said the nun, gathering her blankets more closely about her. "Do you think he'd forgive you for it? You'll have a nice long time to contemplate your regrets, anyway."

That shut the ghost up for the moment, even if it was still inexplicably sitting near her head. Mother Trude closed her eyes and tried to ignore it. Eventually, the past unclenched its talons just enough that she drifted off to sleep.

19

The Lady

here was actual stew, with actual ham in it (as well as turnips, but you don't last long in St. Muckle's if you can't stomach turnips). Mellie handed Charl a bowl, and Gert handed him a spoon. They led him over to a wide chunk of stone and sat on either side of him while he ate.

And ate. And ate. He'd had nothing so delicious in days.

"That's Jenny's ham, that she brought with her," Mellie told him. "She'd buried it in her yard. For a special occasion, she said."

"Or so she wouldn't have to share it with anyone," Gert whispered.

Ordinarily, Charl might have enjoyed a tidbit of gossip about a neighbor, but this reminded him, distressingly, of what the twins had said about his mother the last time he'd talked to them. They were acting friendly now, as if all were forgotten, but he still felt stung by what they'd said, and found himself struggling to pretend nothing had changed.

It was painful; he had to say something.

"Are we all right?" he began. That was too vague, but he didn't see how else to start.

Both girls seemed to stiffen. "What are you talking about?" asked Mellie.

"Just . . . you seemed mad before, and you hurt my feelings, and you haven't said three words to me in weeks," he blurted out. Now he was saying too much.

"Our mother was dying," snapped Gert.

"Could you *not* remind us of those days?" cried Mellie.

That was it, then. That was as far as they would let the conversation go, and he couldn't blame them. They were hurting, too, probably more than he was. He understood that, even if he didn't like it. The painful past stood between them like a wall; they could be friends up to that point, but no further. They could speak lightly and pleasantly, share stew and a gossip together, but even that much took effort and goodwill.

Maybe it was the best anyone could do right now.

The fiddle was still going; the tune struck Charl as a mournful one, a dirge for the home they had left and for the uncertain future. People hummed along dreamily.

Gert, smiling with apparent effort, said, "I hope you'll be coming with us, Charl."

"Coming where?" said Charl cautiously, thinking maybe she wanted to explore the monastery. Could he give the twins a ghost-free tour? As long as they avoided the orchard, the sanctuary, the refectory (because Maeve was there), and the well—

Mellie cut through his thoughts: "Fort Lambeth. The adults already voted where to go next. We're leaving in the morning."

"Wait, *all* of you?" cried Charl, louder than he meant to.

The music stopped.

Everyone stared into their bowls except Gorlich. He sighed, rubbed the back of his neck with one meaty hand, and said, "Girls, let the lad enjoy his evening. No need to alarm him."

"But he's welcome to come with us, Papa, is he not?" said Gert.

Gorlich made a kind of helpless gesture, as if to say *Of course he's welcome, but . . .*

Charl understood: He could come if he wished, but Mother Trude was not well enough to cross the mountain unless they hauled her in a wagon. And they didn't have a wagon.

Nobody wanted to stay?

"I can't leave Mother Trude by herself," said Charl. "She'd never make it."

No one would look at him. They passed a guilty glance around like a hot turnip.

"I don't mind staying," said Charl, as much to reassure himself as anyone else. "We've been all right so far, and my mother will surely get here before much longer."

The silence seemed to sharpen. What on earth was going on?

"Sister Agnes will be coming soon, I should think," said Gorlich, with all the enthusiasm of a man on the gallows.

"My *mother* will be coming, won't she?" said Charl, his voice rising.

Gorlich ran a hand down his face and then all the way down his beard, looking exasperated, but nobody else seemed willing to speak up and bail him out. "I don't know, lad. She was in a tight spot when we left."

Before the dragon attack, when Charl had been arguing with Mama about his sword, it was Gorlich who'd interrupted, asking Mama to say goodbye to his dying wife—who had been upstairs in one of the Fiddle's beds.

"Were you still at the Fiddle when the dragon attacked?" Charl asked. "Did you see what happened to my mother after that?"

Gorlich nodded, his eyes glinting. "When the dragon struck, we were upstairs, saying goodbye to my Nancy—rest she in the arms of Heaven. When we realized what was going on, Lady Eileen and I started helping the sick, whoever of them were strong enough to walk, down into the cellars of the Fiddle, where there's a secret tunnel to the catacombs."

"Catacombs full of beetles," spat the mustached man, Geoffrey. "Typical Eileen."

"Beetles are safer than a dragon," said Jenny Sugar.

"Not by much."

"And then," said Gorlich, looking cross at the interruption, "I carried the folk who couldn't stand . . . No, sorry, it all blurs together. First, my Nancy passed. I buried her that night, behind the forge."

Mellie and Gert were at their father's side in an instant, arms around him. He put a hand on each of their heads.

"Next morning, I'd had no sleep, but I staggered back to the Fiddle to see if I was needed. Your mother had stayed all night, I guess, tending the sickest of the sick. There was a knock at the door, and she ran to answer it. I'm not sure who she was expecting—everyone was in hiding by then—but in rushed some scar-faced brute who threatened her with a sword."

Jarlbrus. Gorlich had been there when he'd arrived.

"You . . . you couldn't stop him?" asked Charl in a small voice.

"She wouldn't let me try," said Gorlich, glowering. "She bargained with the man, and he agreed to take her captive and let the rest of us go. She ordered me to get the sick out of the inn, to safety. I didn't know where to take them, so I carried them one by one to the forge. It's squat, hard to knock over, and made mostly of fireproof brick. It seemed safe enough.

"When I had moved everyone, I rushed back, thinking to take on the swordsman at last, but again she wouldn't let me. 'Gorlich,' she said, 'do not fear for me. This man was sent by my husband. He'll be paid more for *not* killing me. There are two dozen sick people in your care now, and you've got to let Dr. Caramus or Sister Agnes know. Can you do that?'

"I did as I was told," said Gorlich miserably. "I got word to Caramus, who eventually arrived with Sister Agnes. She took me aside and whispered, 'Take your children and what neighbors you can gather, and flee to the Old Abbey. Mother Trude and Charl are already there.'

"So I got these good folks together, and now here we are." He shrugged his massive shoulders. "And we're leaving for Fort Lambeth in the morning. We've got to tell the knights what's happening. Only knights—real knights—can save our town from this dragon."

"Real knights" sounded like a dig at Aris—who hadn't been mentioned once in the story. In fact, the most recent events in Gorlich's account had happened yesterday. The situation had surely changed since then. "Nothing new happened overnight?" Charl asked.

Gorlich shrugged. "We traveled under cover of darkness, extremely slowly, so as not to draw attention. The dragon was active all night, flying, screaming, torching . . . certain buildings."

His vagueness gave Charl a bad feeling. "The Fiddle?"

"I don't know that it caught fire, much," said Gorlich. "But half the roof is gone now."

Charl felt cold all over. He'd wanted to know, and now he wished he didn't know.

"So we're just going to leave that boy here to care for a sick woman all alone?" said Geoffrey. "He's a child. It's irresponsible."

Charl bristled at this. "I'm almost fourteen."

Geoffrey raised his hands defensively, mouth crimped into a mirthless smile. "I was going to offer to stay and help, young master. But *almost fourteen* is clearly a much more advanced age than I'd realized, too competent and self-sufficient for—"

"Geoffrey, thank you," Gorlich interjected. "It would ease my heart if you would stay. I was not going to rest easy, worrying about Charl being all by himself."

Charl opened his mouth to object, but Gorlich flashed him a stern look, and he lost his nerve. Still, Charl had difficulty mustering much gratitude for Geoffrey and his ratty mustache.

Another bowl of stew was on offer, along with some stone slab–baked oatcakes. Soon Charl was stuffed to the gills and getting sleepy. He touched the apple in his pocket, wondering whether he should check on Maeve, but she'd said she would fetch him in an emergency, and he was so warm and sleepy, and Mellie and Gert were nodding off beside him, and—

Charl woke with a start, hours later, because he'd heard a

noise—a creaking sound. The fire had burned low, and everyone was scattered around the courtyard on blankets, sound asleep.

He heard it again. Charl looked toward the sound and saw that the sally door had come open, creaking on its hinges in the slight breeze. Apparently, no one had bolted it shut. That seemed unwise. A wolf could have crept in without anyone hearing. Charl was on the verge of sitting up when a movement at the corner of his vision made him freeze in place.

Across the courtyard, among the birches, a shimmering, semi-transparent lady came forth, her face buried in her hands.

It was *her*, the weeping woman! The first ghost he'd seen here, and he'd almost forgotten about her.

She wore an elegant, flowing gown with long trailing sleeves. Her pale hair wafted behind her as she moved, almost as if it were alive. If she noticed the people sleeping on the ground around her, she did not acknowledge them or change her course. Her feet passed through one sleeping woman's legs—the woman called Rozzy. Rozzy shuddered in her sleep as if she'd felt a sudden chill, pulled her blanket around herself, and rolled over. The ghostly woman's path took her toward Geoffrey next. She stepped into him, and the long train of her ethereal gown was dragged right through his head.

Charl watched in fascinated horror. What were those two feeling while this happened? Cold, sure, but would they also relive bad memories if they were asleep? Maybe it would seem like bad dreams.

The weeping woman disappeared.

Geoffrey slowly sat up.

He looked toward Charl. Charl quickly closed his eyes and pretended to be asleep.

Charl could hear Geoffrey stand up and brush himself off. Geoffrey began to slowly, carefully pick his way around and between his fellow travelers. He was so quiet and stealthy that Charl had to open one eye a crack to see which way the man was going. He was circling around the fire, plausibly making his way toward Charl.

Charl pretended harder to be asleep, but all his muscles were tensed and his heart hammered like it would choke him. Surely, Geoffrey was merely looking for the cessbucket or a drink from the well. Maybe he'd had a bad dream, in fact, when the ghost stepped on his head, and he needed to walk around and reassure himself that everything was all right. The man had offered to help him, after all. Charl had no reason to feel so alarmed.

Except for the crawly feeling on the back of his neck.

Charl heard nothing for several long moments. Cautiously, he opened one eye again.

Geoffrey's face hovered inches above his. The man's eyes were wild, his chin trembling.

Before Charl could so much as gasp, Geoffrey clamped a hand over his mouth. "Get up—quietly," the man hissed. "I've got a dagger, and I'll use it if you wake anyone else."

Charl couldn't see the dagger, with Geoffrey's hand immobilizing his head, so it was hard to gauge whether he might disarm the man. He could hear Aris's voice in his head saying, *Go slow, be sure. Your opening will come.* Charl stood slowly, taking care not to wake Mellie or Gert. No one else was stirring. Geoffrey gestured toward the sally door with his knife, finally bringing it into view. It was not a dagger, but more like a kitchen knife—which was no consolation. You could gut a pig with that, if you knew what you were doing. It was not yet clear how skilled Geoffrey might be. The man gestured again, and Charl pretended not to understand what he wanted; if Geoffrey to speak, maybe *he'd* be the one to wake someone up.

"Move!" Geoffrey hissed, giving Charl a shove.

Charl began picking his way toward the gates, keeping the knife in his peripheral vision, thinking hard. This made no sense. Geoffrey had offered to stay and help take care of Mother Trude. Maybe that had been a ruse, and he'd been plotting harm all along, but then why kidnap Charl now? It would have been simpler to do it after the others had left for Fort Lambeth.

Something had hurried him along: the weeping ghost, the Lady of the Birches. Geoffrey must have relived some terrible memory that had lit a fire under his feet.

If he could find out what it was, maybe he could reason with the man. As they neared the gates, Charl slowed. Surely he could whisper here, without waking anyone up. He had to try. "Where are we going?"

"*I'm* going to save my town," Geoffrey whispered back. "We don't need the knights to do it; Gorlich is a fool. I was there when that dragon spoke in front of the church. She's looking for *you*. If I hand you over, she'll go away and leave our town alone."

It was a sound plan, Charl realized, except for the part where his father wanted the town destroyed so Charl's mother would suffer. Charl didn't know how to explain how he knew that.

And he didn't have time to figure it out. A shadowy shape was materializing behind Geoffrey.

It was Maeve. She gave Charl a wink, and then she stepped right through the man.

Geoffrey gave a cry like a wounded animal and fell to his

knees. He waved his arms wildly, swinging his knife at something only he could see.

Maeve disappeared again.

Everyone woke up.

Gorlich, guessing that the adult with the knife was the dangerous one, even if he was on his knees, swooped in, hauled Geoffrey to his feet, and pinned his arms. Geoffrey was crying now, with tears rolling down his cheeks and snot glazing his mustache. Gorlich's big bear arms around the man looked almost like a hug. Charl hoped it was *partly* hug, anyway. Wailing Geoffrey reminded him, upsettingly, of Rafe.

What had Maeve done to him? Something worse than Vilna had done to Charl.

"What happened?" Gorlich was asking.

Geoffrey seemed in no state to answer, so Charl spoke for him: "He wanted to take me back to St. Muckle's and hand me over to the dragon."

"The knights will never get there in time!" Geoffrey burst out. "Everything will be ashes before they cross the mountain. Everyone will die. Our only hope is to give the dragon what it wants."

Gorlich gave the man a little shake. "Think what you're proposing, man. You'd give an innocent child over to that monster?"

"He's not so innocent. His mother brought the beetle plague upon us, and her ex-husband sent the dragon to destroy us. Let them all go back to Samsam and leave us alone!"

Gorlich didn't answer, but his mouth crimped down. He marched Geoffrey back toward the circle of firelight. "Ropes," he called to the others. "Bind his hands and feet, and then let's set a watch tonight. I don't trust him, even bound. Show of hands, who volunteers to stay up and watch?"

The townsfolk organized watch shifts as Gorlich walked Charl back toward the refectory. "All of Geoffrey's family has died these last two months," said the smith quietly, laying a big hand on Charl's shoulder. "The beetles took his parents and his sisters. Dragon fire killed his son. He's . . . he's suffering. I'm sorry he thought harming you would ease his pain."

Charl didn't know how to answer that, but now he was wondering: maybe the lady and Maeve had merely made Geoffrey relive terrible memories after all, only his memories were a lot worse than anything Charl had ever lived through.

Gorlich's mouth flattened and his beard bristled. "I'll ask once more, son," he said. "Won't you come with us to Fort Lambeth? You'd be safer there."

Charl hesitated. The doorway of the refectory was visible, illuminated by the low fire. He looked at it, then back at Gorlich. "I can't leave her to die here alone."

The smith bowed deeply, the sort of courtesy he'd have shown a young lord, and then he kissed the top of Charl's curly head, which was more like he'd have treated his own children. "An answer worthy of your worthy mother, lad," said the smith before turning to rejoin his people in the courtyard.

Worthy of your worthy mother. It took Charl a minute to collect himself.

Saints in Heaven, let her be all right.

Mother Trude was asleep when Charl entered. Maeve was sitting near the prioress's head again, as if she'd never left, as if nothing had happened. She gave Charl an impish smile. He tried to smile back, but his heart quavered. She was his friend—he believed that—but she wasn't exactly . . . safe.

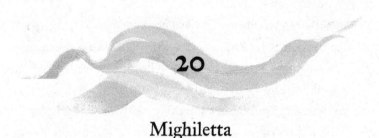

Mighiletta

The dragon Miga was itchy in her brain.

It was the worst kind of itch—the kind you can't scratch and yet everything seems to irritate it further. The weather vane atop the town hall, for example. Miga could see it from the steps of the church, where she'd given a speech to the sniveling townspeople. It creaked when the wind blew, and instead of depicting an ox and a plow (as was usual in Samsam), it had a seven-pointed star and a bird. Something small and beaky.

Every time it moved, Miga wanted to scream.

She had no reason to feel this bothered by a ridiculous weather vane, no reason even to have noticed it—the creaking wasn't that loud—and yet as she'd given her speech to the townspeople, every point of that star had seemed to jab her in the eye. The bird had seemed to leer and chirp like it was trying to talk. What was it trying to tell her? Argh, she itched.

If only she could have opened the top of her head and scratched her brain, like a dog scratching fleas. Surely that would have brought some relief.

Or oblivion, which would have been its own kind of relief.

The townsfolk had run off in various directions, presumably in search of the erstwhile earlina—Eileen, they called her, not Sylvina, like the earl did—and her offspring . . . Bah, how was one supposed to remember anything with an itchy brain, let alone the names of insignificant children? Anyway, the townsfolk could see reason. They would ferret Eileen out, wherever she was hiding, and bring her back to Miga. Then they could have their stupid, broken town back.

All Miga had to do was wait patiently—not her forte, admittedly—and not let the weather vane drive her to violence.

Miga tore her eyes away from it, looking for anything else to distract herself. She had offered to clear the beetles out of the catacombs if her quarry was brought quickly enough. She supposed she might go see what she was up against. She stepped into the cool, high-ceilinged church. The stairs to the crypt were at the far end, behind the altar.

That was going to be awkward. To exterminate the beetles, she had assumed she could take dragon form, stick her head into the crypt, and let loose a jet of flame. Roast those beetles crispy. But she wouldn't be able to squeeze all the way into this church in dragon form, not without knocking over columns or tearing half the roof off. Not that she cared about that, but she had sort of promised to stop wrecking the town if she got what she wanted.

Presumably there was another way into the catacombs.

She stepped back outside, itching again, but it was a more

directed feeling, somehow. *Turn around,* said a voice in her mind. *Go up the alley.*

Miga got goose bumps. She had no idea what she would find there.

At the end of the alley, in a wide green space between buildings, was a hidden garden full of carved memorial stones. A graveyard. Humans were so quaint; they couldn't just let themselves rot into dirt, like other creatures. They had to commemorate it. Miga walked across the graves and found, at the back, what looked like a small house. Behind its stone door there would be a stairway leading down into the catacombs.

Miga didn't know how she knew that, but she knew.

Carved into the door was a seven-pointed star. Miga traced the cold shape with her finger, shuddering.

We'll be ruined if they have their way! Understand? House Asterrink will be no more—

The fragment of memory felt like an electric shock through her body. Whose voice was that? What did it mean? She slammed her fist against the stone door.

Asterrink, though. That name was the most concrete fragment of memory yet.

"Miga!" someone was shouting from the square. "We found her!"

Miga hurried back up the alley.

A lone man stood in the square. He stared into the sky, as if Miga might come from that direction, but looked down again at the sound of Miga's clicking boots. His face was very pale; Miga could not read his expression. "Found her. At the Fiddle. He's got her tied up, and we couldn't . . . get her free . . ."

He was running out of air, and Miga soon realized why. He

was wounded, bleeding copiously and pressing a cloth against his chest. He seemed to have a punctured lung, which prevented him from taking a full breath. The man bent over, hands on his knees, and wheezed.

"The Fiddle is what, her inn?" said Miga, striding toward him, pulling her swords from their sheaths. "But how did you get hurt? Who's with her? Brus? Aris? What's-her-name, the wicked old nun?"

That wouldn't be it. The man had said "he."

"I don't know his name . . ." The man gasped. "But he killed everyone . . . who tried to free her . . . Danny and . . . Orpo . . . and Rod and . . . John Sun-Hat. . . ."

If the townspeople had been fighting Brus, the list might get long; Aris, from what Miga recalled, would have tried *not* to kill anyone. And he wouldn't have tied up the earlina, now that Miga thought about it. Still, she had to be sure. It would affect how she approached the situation. "Was he a dark-skinned human or a pale and pasty one, like yourself?"

"P-pale," said the man. Blood was dribbling down his chin now.

Brus, then.

"Good to know," said Miga, already plotting her moves.

She stalked past the injured man, and as she passed, she put him out of his misery with one sword blow. He fell to the flagstones, dead.

He smelled delicious. Well. He'd still be there later.

Miga had located this inn during one of her scouting trips to St. Muckle's. It was surely a little surprising that Brus had captured Eileen there. Why hadn't she tried to hide? That was what most people did when dragons started burning their towns down around them.

Brus must have been holed up near the inn, just waiting for his chance, and surprised Eileen before she could flee. That's why he was Earl Ucht's chief spy: he was always one step ahead. He'd been the brains at the court of Uchtburg, and Aris had been the muscle, and Miga had been . . . the other muscle? That wasn't right.

Aris had been the conscience, no—the heart. That's why he hadn't lasted. He'd felt too much for the enemies he was ordered to kill. And too much by half for the earl's earlina.

Miga took the front steps of the inn in a single leap, slipped through the door, and peered into the public room from the foyer.

There was Eileen, erstwhile earlina, tied up in front of the hearth. And there were, indeed, half a dozen dead townspeople who'd come in here trying to steal her away. For some reason—some inscrutable human reason—Brus had moved most of the bodies over behind the tables and covered them with tablecloths. Red trails of blood showed where he had dragged them. Brus was dragging the sixth one now, grasping the corpse's thick ankles and walking backward.

He looked up as Miga rushed him, his one and a half eyebrows shooting up in surprise. She kicked him in the head before he could dodge, and knocked him to the floor.

"Miga, wait," Brus shouted, rubbing his ear. He rolled away as her sword came down. "Don't do this. We former comrades should be working together, by rights."

"Can't," said Miga. "I need every coin of that bounty." Her

sword was stuck in the floorboards. She wrenched it free and came after him again.

Brus crab-walked under a table, then kicked upward and sent it flying toward her. Miga caught the edge before it could hit her, but it slowed her down. Brus scurried behind the bar.

"You can't buy your memories back," he said, peeking up briefly and then dodging as Miga's throwing knife whizzed past his ear. It shattered bottles on the shelves behind him. "They're not keeping what they took from you in a jar somewhere, ready to stick back into your head."

Miga leaped up onto the bar and stepped on Brus's hand. He howled.

"I know that," she said, grinding her foot. "It's reconstructive surgery. They can coax the memories into growing back from the bits and pieces left behind."

"Any doctor who promised you that is nothing but a black-market, back-alley charlatan," Brus whimpered. "They'll take your money and leave you with a head full of milkweed fluff."

That would be an improvement, Miga wanted to say. *Anything. As long as it doesn't itch.*

But before she could speak, someone grabbed her ankles from behind and yanked her feet out from under her. She landed hard on her stomach, across top of the bar. She rolled over quickly and sat up just in time to see Aris making a strategic withdrawal toward the hearth, his blade at the ready.

Brus took the opportunity to crack a bottle over the back of her head.

Miga shook it off. Then she leaped into the air, swung on the chandelier, and missed knocking Aris into the fire by inches.

She landed on her feet with a hollow thump and crouched, taking stock. Brus was coming around the far end of the bar; Aris had backed up among the tables.

"Well, isn't this just like old times," called Brus. "The chief spy and the captain of the guard, coming to the defense of the Earl and Earlina of Ucht—"

"Is all this your handiwork?" said Aris grimly, gesturing at the dead bodies. "Then it *is* like old times, you butcher."

"Aris is not your friend, Brus," Miga called. She had to keep them hating each other, or they'd gang up on her. "You and I should team up against that traitor."

"Oh, *now* you think so?" said Brus disgustedly. "Well, you lost your chance, Miga. You got greedy. Besides, I feel reasonably certain I can defeat Aris on my own—"

"In your dreams," said Aris.

"After the two of us defeat *you*," Brus continued, as if Aris hadn't spoken.

Miga snarled and held out her swords, holding the men at bay for the moment.

The thing was, Brus wasn't wrong. The three of them were like rock, paper, knife, each strong against one and vulnerable to the other. Earl Ucht had planned it that way, used them to keep each other obedient. Knight defeated dragon; dragon terrorized spy; spy outwitted knight.

But that wasn't even the game today. Today's winner was whoever took the lady.

Where was she?

She'd been by the hearth when Miga came in, but she was not here now. She'd been tied up, but she could have crawled away, perhaps, inching like an inchworm. She couldn't be behind the bar, or Brus would see her. A quick glance said she wasn't under the tables behind Aris.

Aris! How had *he* gotten in here?

Through the trapdoor, of course.

What trapdoor?

The floor had sounded hollow when Miga had landed. She glanced down now and saw that the hearth rug was crooked. There was a trapdoor underneath. Had to be. Aris had come up through it and sent Eileen down. There must be an escape tunnel out of the cellar. Aris was buying time for Eileen to get away.

"Brus?" Miga taunted. "Where's your captive, Brus?"

The spymaster looked around frantically, only now realizing that Eileen was gone. Miga kicked the rug aside, revealing a trapdoor. She bared her teeth at Brus—humans called this a grin, but Miga meant it as a threat—and braced herself for his onslaught.

Brus screamed an order at Aris—"Flank her!"—and then flung himself headlong at Miga. She put up her blades to meet his, parrying easily. He was no slouch as a swordsman, but he wasn't young anymore. He'd come in swinging wildly, frantically, trying to occupy both her swords and all of her attention so that Aris could stab her in the back.

But Aris wasn't coming. He had fled through the kitchen. Miga really did grin this time, because she had predicted correctly and Brus had not.

Aris had run off to meet Eileen wherever her escape tunnel had led her. And Miga knew where it led, because Miga—unaccountably, inexplicably—knew this town.

Brus was already realizing that he'd been betrayed. "Curse

you, Aris!" he shouted, but he should have saved his breath. Miga rained down blows one after the other, and it was all Brus could do to fend them off. Murdering so many townsfolk earlier had worn him out.

"And to think they once called you the Butcher of Bennburg," Miga sneered. "Scourge of Pagans. Destructor of a Thousand Villages. You're getting old, Brus."

"Don't I know it," he grunted, narrowly dodging a swing at his head. "Oh, to be a long-lived dragon—never mind that you can't remember half of it."

Miga swung at him again, and he just managed to bend out of the way. He taunted her again: "Are you sure you want to kill the one person who's thoroughly researched this town and might have a solid lead on who you once were?"

Miga paused and studied his face. She couldn't read him at all; even humans couldn't generally tell when Brus was bluffing.

"Does the name Amberfinch mean anything to you?" he said.

Miga raised a sword.

"How about Asterrink?" he added hastily.

That name again.

Miga didn't bring the sword down—yet. "Talk, Brus. Quickly."

"A hundred years ago, this valley was ruled by two noble houses—Asterrink and Amberfinch. The Asterrinks ran the town as wealthy traders; the Amberfinches owned all the farmland. They got hit by an infestation of blood beetles—a bad one—not just overrunning the town, but all across the farmers' fields as well. People were dying, crops were dying, everything was dying. Only the Asterrinks and the Amberfinches were untouched by the plague, wealthy enough to shut themselves up in their fortified houses and wait things out.

"However, the son of the Asterrinks and the daughter of the Amberfinches had fallen in love. Very tragic and star-crossed. They weren't allowed to see each other, so they passed messages using the one person, immune to the ague, who could cross town safely—a dragon in the employ of Lord Asterrink. A dragon called Mighiletta."

Miga felt as if she had turned to ice. "I saw that name in the town records. She was a pancake maker."

"A cover," said Brus. "Not all nobles have the guts to claim an assassin on the payroll."

Miga shook her head fiercely, as if to shake his suggestions out of her skull. "I don't believe you. You're trying to manipulate me."

"I *am* trying to manipulate you," said Brus. "And I'm telling the truth. How did you find that trapdoor so quickly?"

"I deduced it was there from the hollow sound when I landed."

"Nonsense," said Brus. "I didn't deduce it, and I'm the deductive genius here. You knew it was there. You know this house."

In fact, she had known it was there, and had reasoned backward from that knowledge. The realization gave Miga goose bumps again, which she hated. She wanted to claw them all off.

She couldn't let Brus know he was right; he'd use it against her. "I don't know what you're talking about," she insisted. "I don't recognize a thing."

"Look above the hearth," said Brus. "This was where the Amberfinches lived, back when there were Amberfinches. Back before you killed them all."

Miga didn't want to look, but her head seemed to twist around of its own accord. Above the hearth, set among the bricks, was a bas-relief carving of three plump, beaky birds, just like the one on the weather vane, next to the Asterrinks' seven-pointed star.

Don't! Wait, listen to me. Killing us won't change anything. You Asterrinks will still have to close the harbor. There's no way around it. Eldegarde has studied the problem from all angles, and—

Miga clapped her hands to her ears—her wrists, really, since her hands were clutching swords—as if she could block out the remembered voice.

"I'm not sure why it should bother you that you were a murderer in your forgotten past," said Brus. "You're a murderer now."

That wasn't the problem, but Miga was having a terrible time articulating what the problem actually was. She was feeling . . . something. Something more than just itchy.

Before she could speak, Brus struck a blow—an unfair, underhanded sneak attack—and cut her thigh above the knee. Miga howled in pain, and not just physical pain but *anguish*. That was what it was called, the feeling that came with these past memories, and it was worse than all the sword cuts in the world.

She could have borne the cut; she could have cut Brus back and harder; but she could not stand the *emotion* that accompanied all these fragmented memories, and so she did the only thing she could think of to get away from it. She transformed herself back into a dragon.

There wasn't space for a full-sized dragon in the Fiddle, even with the public room's high ceiling, but Miga didn't care. She unfolded herself, bursting through her clothing, like stretching after a long time confined. Her neck telescoped up, her tail extended back, the fragile membrane of smooth skin burst forth into glorious scales. Her teeth—can you imagine stretching your teeth? Feeling them pressing forward and reaching and growing? Feeling horns break through your smooth forehead, sprouting like young saplings? Her wings unfurled like sails. Everything felt the way it was supposed to.

Everything but her brain, which still itched. Her brain took up a much smaller proportion of her body when she was this large, however.

She'd knocked over all the tables, smashed the bar, sent the chandeliers swinging wildly on their chains. Brus was rooted to the spot, dumbfounded, staring up at her, his face drained of color. He'd apparently forgotten she could do this, or hadn't believed she would be mad enough to do it indoors.

Indoors wouldn't be indoors for long. The only way out was through the roof. It would be a minute before she solidified enough to break through it, however. She took that time to rumble a single word at Brus: "Run."

He staggered back, coughing, choking on her sulfuric breath. He tripped over the corpses he had made, ran into a jutting table leg, scurried like a mouse in search of the door, and finally escaped through the kitchen. Miga waited patiently. Brus only had short little legs, and she knew this town. He could run, but she would catch him; he could hide, but she would find him.

And then she would find the ones she'd come to find, and go home.

She smacked her lips, rolling a bit of flame around her mouth. It was ready.

A jet of flame blasted the roof off, and a thrust of her powerful legs catapulted her through the hole. She screamed, not in pain, but in greeting to the sky. As expected, Brus hadn't gotten far. Absurdly, he had taken off across the turnip fields. Maybe he'd thought she wouldn't look for him in that direction, since it was a ridiculous way to go. Even with night falling, he was still visible to her. There was really no place to hide.

If he was giving up his claim to any share of the bounty, fine. Miga accepted his resignation and felt no need to kill him. She did set him on fire, however, as she circled past. She heard his screams behind her as she flapped her wings and set her sights back on the town.

She knew where Eileen must have gone.

The Asterrinks and the Amberfinches had built this town for their own convenience. There were tunnels everywhere—from the inn to the town hall, from the town hall to the catacombs, from the catacombs to what was now Vasterich Hall (but hadn't always been, she now realized; it had been Asterrink Manor long ago). If Eileen had fled, she might be in the dragon refuge under the town hall, in which case she was going to be hard to reach, or she might have gone farther. If she meant to reach Vasterich Hall, which was well fortified, she would have to pass through the catacombs. That would be slow going. The catacombs were a maze, and they were full of beetles.

Miga circled slowly above the town square, trying to gauge how long it had been since Eileen had escaped, how far she could have gotten, and what she would have been trying to do in any case. The latter was the unfathomable part; humans could be unpredictable. It was their most effective defense, Miga sometimes thought.

The person to look for, she suddenly realized, was Aris. He'd left by the back door. He would have had to cross town on foot, so there should be scent traces of him somewhere.

Miga landed lightly in the square and sniffed the air. He'd been here, all right, and recently. His track began in the corner nearest the inn and led across to—

She turned in time to see the man himself, sticking his head out of the front of Allsaints Church as if to gauge whether it was safe to emerge. There was someone behind him. Miga held still, hoping they might not notice her across the square in the dark; no one had lit the streetlamps tonight, and there were no lights from windows to give her away. A dragon could hold very still.

Aris saw her, though. He held up a hand to stop his companion, waved her back into the shadows, and began backing cautiously into the church again. Now he was the one hoping not to be seen.

Miga sighed heavily, but there was no time to waste. She leaped across the square, heedlessly knocking over the statue of Pendergard Vasterich. Aris took off running, shouting at his companion to head for the crypt.

Miga's shoulders slammed into the columns on either side of the doorway, cracking them, but it wasn't hard enough to bring the stone arches down upon her own head. It was one thing to break through a timber roof, and quite another to withstand falling chunks of marble. She could see Aris in the darkness, running as hard as he could. She let fly a fist of fire.

Too late. Aris dove down the stairs out of range, just in time.

Well, the joke was on him.

Miga pulled her head out of the church and launched herself into the air, a simple arc, shooting up, gliding down. She landed in the graveyard at the back, leaving large claw prints in the grass and knocking down several tombstones. She grasped the little stone kiosk in her jaws, the Asterrink memorial, wrenched it out of the ground, and tossed it aside. It shattered.

Beneath it was a gaping hole. Steps led down into a buzzing, moving darkness—a vast swarm of beetles. Aris and Eileen would have to tread carefully to avoid being bitten.

Miga, however, had no fear of such creatures. She stuck her long neck down as far as she could, and let loose an enormous fireball.

21

The Princess

hen Charl woke up, a pile of supplies had materialized just inside the doorway of the refectory—spare food, more fever remedies, proper tea, and some odd items of clothing.

The refugees, however, had already left for Fort Lambeth.

"They dropped those off before dawn, and then they scarpered, the villains," said Mother Trude. She seemed a bit restored again after a night's sleep, her tongue sharp and her eyes bright.

Charl put the foodstuffs in the trunk with the turnips and oats, and then took stock of everything: two cheeses, two loaves, a bit of bacon, lots of turnips, two small sacks of oats. Someone—he suspected Jenny Sugar—had left a pot of jam and a lump of butter. Tea and fever tea, but those didn't count as food. And, of course, there were plenty of green apples in the orchard, still.

Who could predict how long they might have to survive here alone?

He assessed the contents of the trunk again, trying to guess how much they'd eat every day. Maybe Mother Trude wouldn't eat much—ague sometimes made people lose their appetite—but he included her in his estimates because she *should* eat. She needed to keep up her strength.

The food might last a week, or a little longer. He wasn't used to thinking this way, so he wasn't completely sure.

The scrap of parchment protecting one of the cheeses had come half unwrapped while Charl was moving things around. There was writing on the parchment. Charl pulled it out and saw that Gorlich had written him a note. The smith had attended Sister Agnes's night classes for years, and was one of her most devoted pupils, but he was still not the most precise speller:

> Sharl, sorry we must leeve you. We will send the knigts as soon as we ken. They will set things right. I got Geofferoy all tied up for it is not safe to let him go, he wood run back and tell the drgon where you are. We will take him to Fort Larmbith, Heaven oversee us all. All will be well. You are a brave boy. I am very sorry, still.
> —Gorlig

He was so worried about leaving Charl alone that he'd apologized twice. Charl, who had been teetering on the edge of worry himself, felt the man's concern like a push into a cold pond. *Was* Gorlich doing the wrong thing, in fact, by leaving

Charl to take care of the old nun? What if Charl couldn't do it? What if he wasn't capable or clever enough? What if she died?

Well, she'd be in good company, at least. Add one more to the tally of ghosts.

At that morbid thought, Charl emitted an odd, choked noise. It might have been a laugh or a sob. Even he was not certain which it was.

What he did know was that his heart was beating very fast, like it did sometimes. His hands shook. Next, his throat would get tight—he could feel it already—making it hard to pull breath into his lungs—

"Boy, are you all right over there?" called Mother Trude.

He wasn't. He really wasn't. He hated feeling like this. He looked over at her with eyes full of tears. She looked far away, like she was at the end of a long tunnel.

"Come here," she said, holding out a hand toward him.

Shakily, he staggered over and collapsed on the floor beside her pallet. She touched his cheek and then his forehead. "I don't *think* you're feverish. Give me your hand," she said. And then, "Oh my, you're as clammy as a fish. So tell me: How many fish do you know? What kind of fish swim in the Sowline River?"

"What?" gasped Charl, rather like a fish out of water. He had no idea why she would ask such an eccentric thing, although he could feel his racing thoughts starting to slow.

"Think, boy. And breathe. Take a very slow breath, counting to five. That's right. Now let it out just as slowly. Good. Now tell me a fish."

"Trout?" said Charl.

"Ah, my favorite. Now breathe again," said Mother Trude.

She had both his hands clasped in hers. Her hands were as hot as Charl's were cold, but at least his had stopped shaking. Now they felt all full of pins and needles.

When he had inhaled and exhaled five times, and named five fish—in fact, he said "eels" twice, because he was not such an expert on fish, but Mother Trude pretended not to notice—Charl could tell he was back to normal at last. The nun smiled tiredly at him.

"Well done," she said. "You're still quite pale. If I didn't know better, I'd say you'd seen a ghost."

"Oh. Um. No," said Charl. "Not today."

That made her chuckle, which turned into a cough. Charl ducked back, afraid she might be coughing gray, but it was an ordinary cough. Mother Trude looked at him wryly. "I have treated many patients, lad. I will warn you when you're not to come near me."

"Do you need anything?" asked Charl. "Applesauce? Fever tea? I could make porridge."

"Fever tea, yes, alas. I can feel my head growing hotter already. Even my eyes feel hot. And if you would mix some applesauce in with the porridge, that would be lovely."

Charl prepared everything as she'd asked. It was such a relief to be busy, puttering over the simmering oats, measuring out the willow powder, wrapping his sleeves around his hands so as not to burn himself on the kettle. He mixed a bowl of applesauce porridge for himself as well and found it to be a significant improvement over plain oats.

When the nun had eaten, and had drunk her tea, she lay back and closed her eyes. "Now I have one more request to make of you, lad," she said.

"Tell you another exemplar tale?" asked Charl. The question came out sounding strangely eager, not because he had another story in mind, but because he had no wish to be alone with his thoughts again.

"Absolutely not," said Mother Trude, opening one eye and looking at him shrewdly. "I want you to go take a bath. Warm the water first, and use your shirt as a washcloth. Then wash your shirt out and let it dry in the sun—and that's you clean *and* half your clothes."

"But," Charl began.

"Then you should go outside and play."

"But," he tried again.

"Charl," she said sharply. Charl could not remember her using his name before; she'd been calling him "boy" all this time. "I'm beginning to understand how you might make a decent priest after all," she continued, her voice gentler. "You have a good heart, lad, and a need to help people. That's what Sister Agnes and your mother see in you, isn't it?"

Charl felt his throat start tightening again, at the mention of those two. What if they never—

Stop it. Breathe.

"I'm the one who's meant to be taking care of *you*, though," Mother Trude was saying. "So please do as I ask, and take a bit of time to care for yourself. Get cleaned up—you'll feel more human, I promise—and then go out in the sunshine. You should not have to bear the burden of me every minute of the day."

He didn't need to be told thrice. Charl picked up the water bucket and went outside. The moment the sunshine hit his face, he felt a bit better. The morning was beautiful, not too warm or too cold. The sky was almost unbearably blue.

It was hard to imagine a dragon in that sky. Such blueness surely overcame everything.

He felt tempted to climb the battlements again and look down at St. Muckle's. It must be clear enough to see all the way to town today without the martin's help. But something quivered in the pit of Charl's stomach. He was desperate to know, and yet he wasn't sure he could bear to know.

Instead, he dutifully headed for the well, his feet slowing as he neared. The townsfolk had replaced the cover; he was going to have to remove it.

Knowing that Wort was possibly waiting for him on the other side.

Charl stared hard at the cover, half expecting it to jump and rattle on its own, but nothing happened. With trembling hands, he grasped the edge, counted to three, and hauled the cover off.

All was still.

He could do this. Wort was sleeping in, maybe.

Quietly, cautiously, Charl hooked the rope onto the bucket handle. Standing back a ways, Charl tossed the bucket toward the well. In it went, and down, trailing the rope behind it. He heard it splash and felt a weight on the rope as the bucket filled with water.

Charl pulled on the rope to haul the bucket back up, but it wouldn't budge. It was caught on something. He pulled harder, to no avail. He let the rope go slack and moved to the other side (still giving the well wide berth) and tried pulling from there. The bucket caught again.

Suddenly, the rope gave way. Charl fell on his backside, and the rope came flying at him—empty. The bucket had come unhooked and was still in the well.

The hook itself hadn't broken. He thought he might be able to use it to fish the bucket out, if it hadn't sunk, and if he could get the hook around its handle.

That meant looking down the well, to see what he was doing.

Charl shuddered. He could skip the bath (although Mother Trude would certainly fuss at him), but he couldn't leave the bucket down there. They were going to need water.

He got onto his belly and crawled toward the well. He paused, listening. No sound echoed in the depths. He took a deep breath, to brace himself, and peeked over the edge.

The scream hit him like a slap. The burning face of Wort glared up, eyes bulging, mouth twisted into an eternal grimace, flailing, splashing, roiling the waters with his agony.

Charl threw himself away from the edge, heart pounding, and tried to wrestle the cover back over the top. The screams intensified; gray, ghostly fingers scrabbled at the stone lip of the well but couldn't seem to get any purchase. Charl dropped the cover onto them, and they disappeared.

The ensuing silence was so intense it felt unnatural. Wort's screams still rang in his ears.

He couldn't . . . He couldn't . . . He couldn't look down there again, or get his bucket, or stop this from happening, or catch his breath.

What had Mother Trude said to do?

Fish. Breathe, and count fish. He came up with six this time, no repeats.

That quelled the panic, but it did nothing for the basic problem, which was that he and Mother Trude were going to die of thirst eventually if he couldn't get that bucket out of the well.

Maeve would know what to do, surely. She seemed to be

the friendliest ghost in this place, even if she was a little creepy. Maybe when you were a ghost, you had a right to be.

Charl made a beeline for the orchard, the summer sun beating down on his head. He was sweating by the time he got there and feeling self-conscious about it. Could ghosts smell? Maeve had called him a walking smudge before.

He wiped his forehead and tried to smooth down his curls, having no idea whether he was improving things or not. At least it was cooler in the shade. "Maeve?" he called, stepping into the grove. No one seemed to be home. Not even the ghostly martin appeared.

Where were they when they weren't here? Surely they *were* here, merely unseen.

But wait, that squirrel, sitting atop one of the mossy stones, didn't look entirely solid. Hadn't Maeve said there were two ghosts who had faded? Was this the other one?

"Hello, friend," whispered Charl, holding one hand out reassuringly. "And who might you be? Can you deliver a message to Maeve, or Vilna?"

"She can*not*," said an imperious voice behind him. "And Maeve and Vilna can hear you perfectly well from where they are."

Charl turned to see an entirely new ghost, one he'd never glimpsed before. The fifth and last of the unfaded orchard girls, he presumed. Unlike the others, who wore only their shrouds, this girl had a crescent-shaped gold necklace and jeweled earrings depicting dragons' heads. Her ethereal hair—which must have been quite pale in life—was pinned up in a twist, making her neck look long and graceful. She was no older than Maeve, but she studied Charl with the cool, unsurprised expression of one who had reached adulthood young.

"I've been sent to tell you—as if I were a mere errand wench—that Maeve is unavailable at the moment," she said.

"Unavailable as in . . . busy?" asked Charl, wondering what she could possibly be doing.

The haughty girl rolled her eyes. "Unavailable as in *grounded*. As in being punished for her naughty exuberance last night."

Last night?

"She saved me," cried Charl. "Geoffrey would have marched me back to town and—"

"I know that," snapped the girl, crossing her slender arms. Ethereal bangles tinkled on her wrists. "But we made a pact, all of us, to let ourselves fade away like Iphi and Ognielle. Maeve got greedy and broke it, and now she'll be the last to go."

"Vilna broke it first, though, by touching him," said another voice, one of two dark-haired girls who had materialized in the underbrush. Anya and Zedig, Maeve had called them. The slightly shorter one had spoken; the slightly taller one was pointing at Charl.

"That was an accident," said the blond girl crossly. "Maeve has been haunting people on purpose! She haunted the old nun while pretending to look after her."

Maeve had haunted Mother Trude? This was new information, and Charl was very curious about it, but he felt he needed to smooth things over with this irritated girl before asking more questions. "Forgive me, milady," he said, bowing. "I didn't catch your name."

"I didn't give it," said the girl, sniffing disdainfully. "I am Princess Luti, daughter of Queen Athquenti."

"Your Majesty," said Charl, giving full courtesy, as best he could recall now from when he'd been a small child in Uchtburg.

Courtesy had surely changed since Princess Luti's time, but she seemed to recognize what he was trying to convey. She looked momentarily placated.

"Why are there so many of you here?" asked Charl, when he felt safe to speak again.

"We were bound here," said Princess Luti, fingering her golden torque.

"But why were you bound here?" Charl suddenly wondered whether they were the very ghosts from Vilna's story, who were so terrifying that only the very wise could spend a night among them. None of these girls seemed particularly frightening, though, at least not compared with the Battle Bishop.

"Were you supposed to guard the stone circle by haunting people?" he pressed. "I guess that didn't work very well."

Princess Luti's expression suggested he ought not to have said that last thing out loud.

Charl tried to clarify: "I mean . . . it's just . . . the monks built a whole abbey around you, so they . . . maybe weren't *very* scared of you?"

He was merely digging himself in deeper, he could tell.

Anya and Zedig clapped their hands to their mouths in just the same way, their eyebrows raised in identical arcs, clearly shocked that he would dare to speak that way to Princess Luti.

"We are still here, and the monks are *not*," said Luti coldly. "Oh, they tried to get rid of us. They knocked over a couple of stones—we couldn't prevent it, alas—but we haunted them until they gave it up."

"Eventually. We weren't very good at haunting, at first," said Anya, or Zedig. "No one had explained how. We had to figure it out on our own."

"After they planted the orchard, it got easier," said Zedig, or Anya. "Anywhere an apple ended up, we could go. The kitchens. The cider press."

"The latrines," said Princess Luti, smiling again at last. "That was Maeve's specialty—sneaking up on the prelate when he was trying to poop."

The other two squealed with laughter. "Maeve scared the poop out of him, every time!"

Prelate was another title for a bishop. "You don't mean Bishop Marcellus, do you?" asked Charl. "The fellow with the fancy tomb in the sanctuary?"

Their laughter abruptly died, and even Luti looked a bit spooked. "Don't speak his name," said the princess. "He is here, and I don't know whether he can hear us, but he can certainly sense *you*, the living. He has to sustain himself, too, you realize."

Charl recalled the Battle Bishop's bottomless-pit eyes and shuddered.

And he wasn't even the ghost who scared Charl the most. That ghost was in the well.

"What happens when you haunt someone?" he asked quietly. "You touch them and then . . . you see everything in their mind?"

Princess Luti seemed to close in on herself. Her gaze turned inward, she chewed her lip, and a shadow seemed to cross her face. "Haunting sustains us. Without human contact—new knowledge, new memories—we grow less and less ourselves, until we fade. We have lived many years here alone, subsisting on lost hunters and the occasional bear. It is not a nice existence. There is nothing left to guard—not really—and so we were all going to . . . to disappear together, like Iphi and Ognielle. And now . . ."

And now they wouldn't, because Charl had stepped through Vilna by mistake and Maeve had taken matters into her own hands.

Luti looked distraught. Charl didn't know how to comfort her, but then he had an idea. He held out his hand. The princess looked like he was offering her a dead fish.

"Take it," he said. "Haunt me."

"If I do, it will *hurt* you. I'll see everything, but you will only see what gives you pain."

"I know," said Charl. "I went through it before. I can bear it."

She pressed her lips together, flattening them to a line. "No," she said at last. "Maybe Maeve has no self-discipline, but I made a promise. Some of us have *principles*."

And with that, she disappeared.

Charl was left holding his hand out, feeling foolish. He turned to Anya and Zedig, because it seemed rude not to make them the same offer.

The taller one shook her head firmly. The shorter one said, "Maeve saved you from one peril, but not the other. A wolf got in, Charl. Through the open door."

He remembered the sally door being open—remembered worrying about a wolf, in fact—but before he could ask anything more, Anya and Zedig averted their eyes, retreated into the undergrowth, and disappeared.

Charl was alone again, the bucket was still down the well, and he hadn't managed to ask the main question he had come here to ask: What could he do about Wort?

21.5: Luti's Story

Long ago, the River People fought the Mountain People for six generations, until neither side remembered how it began. Still, they fought back and forth across the plain. The blood of dead soldiers soaked into the dust, turning it to mud; the bones of dead soldiers were ground deeper and deeper into the mud by the thundering hooves of horses. And every night, the ghosts of dead soldiers rose up to terrorize the living and to spur them to more and more desperate acts of revenge.

Halfway up the mountain stood the Great Gate of Sages, a doorway to the Blue Country, where the living could converse with the dead—not the restless, vengeful dead, but the sorrowing dead. The ones who were at peace, or could have been, if they had never looked back at the doings of the earth.

They looked back and wept. Some of them, sometimes, those great merciful souls who were stirred to pity, stood in the doorway and reached out to help the living.

There was a princess among the River People who heard about the Great Gate and said to her mother, "My queen, let me go find the Great Gate of Sages and consult with the wise about how to end this war. For we cannot fight forever. Already the best of us are ghosts."

"My daughter," said the River Queen, "that gate is behind enemy lines, halfway up the mountain. You will be dead before you reach it if the Mountain People catch you, or mad if the ghosts do. I forbid you to attempt this."

"I understand and obey," said the princess, but she did not understand.

And she did not obey.

That night, she slipped away and crossed the field of battle on her own. All around her, angry ghosts rose up, swinging their ghostly swords and hurling their ghostly spears, just as they'd done in life. The princess squared her shoulders, gritted her teeth, and endured it, marching onward through bloody mud up to her knees. She was not afraid, as many are among ghosts, but she let her heart feel pity and let her eyes weep compassionate tears for the River and Mountain dead alike.

When she had crossed the killing field, there was still the mountain left to climb. And it was not long before a patrol of Mountain People captured her and led her before the Mountain Queen.

"You are a spy, and I should kill you," said the Mountain Queen.

"I am no spy, but the River Princess," said the girl. "And I have come to consult the Great Gate of Sages."

"That old place? Don't you know it's haunted?" said the Mountain Queen.

"We are all of us haunted," said the River Princess, and something in her voice made her enemy shiver and think that perhaps it would be foolish to kill this girl. The war burned hotly enough when no one could remember why they were fighting it, after all. The people didn't need another reason to fight.

So the Mountain Queen and a small retinue accompanied the River Princess to the Great Gate of Sages, to see what there was to see. And no sooner had they arrived than the River Queen arrived, along with her people, for a mother knows her daughter, and she had suspected she would find her daughter here.

"Stop!" cried the River Queen. "Think what you are doing, daughter. No good can come of speaking with the dead."

But the River Princess had already heard the Call of the Beyond. She stood in the open doorway, haloed by a luminous blue like none of them had ever seen before, and gave her mother an otherworldly smile. "I am not here to speak with the dead, my mother, but to live among them. You must join hands with your enemy now and swear before the Wise that I shall be the last casualty of this war."

The two queens, heartbroken, joined hands and swore this oath before the Wise: that the war would end and no one else would die. The princess stepped through the doorway and was embraced by the no-longer-sorrowing dead.

And it is true, by the Wise, that the peace lasted a hundred years from that day.

22

The Prelate Ponders

In the sanctuary, the Battle Bishop stirred.

The child had come right to him, and he had been too slow to react. He could still sense the bright, nourishing spark of life, though—*sparks,* really, more than one—glittering mockingly, well out of reach.

How he resented the living.

Death was forever, it turned out, and forever was a very long time. Time enough to revisit your life in excruciating detail, poring over each questionable decision and outright mistake, every cruel and thoughtless action, but with no power to fix any of it.

At first, he had felt betrayed. This was not Heaven, the reward he'd been promised and was certain he deserved. It wasn't even the Infernum. It was much, much worse. He was a *ghost*—a theological impossibility—and if that could be true . . .

He had been wrong about a great many things, just as Vilna had told him.

He'd spent a hundred years or so in torturous denial, raging bitterly against reality, not caring what he broke or who he hurt. He made the abbey a living hell for his brothers. It hadn't been the pagan ghosts who drove them off, ultimately, but their own bishop, who had not passed on to a better place, and refused to lie quietly in his grave.

They'd brought in an exorcist to get rid of him. Church doctrine claimed ghosts did not exist but allowed that devils might, and so they'd called him a devil (which was not wholly inaccurate), even though they knew perfectly well who was rattling the sanctuary's chandeliers and howling spitefully, leaving them all hollow-eyed and haunted.

The exorcist was an elderly priest with a talent for soothing spooked horses and treating apoplexy. He had never in his life faced anything so near to an actual devil as the ghost of Bishop Marcellus, but he did his best. After a night in the sanctuary, he emerged pale and trembling, and could give no sensible report. He just stared at his (spotless) hands and repeated over and over, "Look at this blood. I will never be clean."

Bishop Marcellus's beautiful sanctuary was off-limits after that, used only as a tomb for later prelates, none of whom ever seemed to live long. He'd been forced to prey upon callow novices, who might still be lured with murmurs and winking candles. He learned to follow his property, like the orchard girls followed their apples, and any monk who stole from him— a jeweled reliquary, his secret stash of brandy, even the smallest piece of incense—would live in agony until they brought it back.

The monks of St. Ogdo's-on-the-Mountain finally realized they would never be free of him while his sanctuary still stood, and so they called upon a dragon of their acquaintance—an ungrateful creature that he had raised from an egg—to demolish the stonework and set whatever she could on fire. Drawing upon every ounce of strength and will he still possessed, the bishop had roared back at the dragon until the ground buckled, walls cracked and roofs collapsed. Seven monks perished in the cataclysm, and that was the last straw. The rest of them left. He had ruined his own monastery, as peevishly as a tantruming child, and now he had eternity to think about what he'd done.

And it was painful.

He'd never had doubts, not one, until the twilight of his life.

At the age of seventy-five, after a lifetime spent in wholehearted, full-throated service to the Saints, Bishop Marcellus—Scourge of Pagans, Hammer of Dragons, Indomitable Monastic Marshal of South Goredd—was brought low by a tiny clot in a tinier blood vessel of his brain. An apoplexy, his physicians called it, though some people call it a stroke.

"When will I be on my feet again, ready to ride back into battle?" Bishop Marcellus asked, but no one could understand him. Half his face was paralyzed, and the things he believed himself to be saying bore little relation to the sounds coming out of his mouth.

After a month of diligent effort, he could talk a bit more intelligibly and he could walk to the sanctuary, but he would never again ride a horse or lead a service, kill a dragon or raze a village. He spent most of his time in his chambers, feeling reduced and rageful, and few of his brothers, though they still kissed his ring when he emerged, ever seemed to find time to come up and spend an afternoon with him.

Autumn came, mellowing the light through his window. A novice brought him three apples from the tree in the center of the orchard—his favorites, streaked crimson and gold—but fled before Bishop Marcellus could remind him to cut them up and bring them closer. They languished in their golden dish on a table across the room, and they were lovely to look at, but he would have liked to taste them one last time, so tart and sweet and intensely appley—

"So you do understand that you're going to die soon," said a not-entirely-unexpected voice near the head of his bed. "It's true. You are. And I fear for you, after that."

"Have you come to torment me, devil?" he cried. "You will not drag me down to the Infernum. I have loved the Saints and served them with every iota of my being. I pray to them now to fling you into the abyss from whence you came! O, St. Ogdo, hear my heartfelt plea—"

Here he failed to swallow his own spit and burst out coughing. The novice popped back in, whacked him on the back a few times, and asked, "Are you well now, Your Grace?"

"The devil!" Bishop Marcellus barked. "The devil is back, and he's trying to drag me down and cast me into the Furnaces of Oblivion!"

"That's all right," said the novice, wiping spittle from the old man's lips. He hadn't understood a word, it seemed, and wasn't taking the bishop's urgency the least bit seriously. "Here, now you're all tucked in again. Heaven soothe you." And out he went to the anteroom again, to whatever busywork he did to avoid keeping his prelate company.

The curtains wafted gently, and for a moment the devil did not speak.

"Are you not here to taunt me, devil?" said Bishop Marcellus. But he knew she wasn't. Vilna never mocked him; she left that to Maeve.

"I'm thinking how to approach this," said Vilna's disembodied voice. "Iphi and Ognielle said from the beginning that this was a hopeless task, that you have bound yourself so tightly that no one can untangle you. And I admit, if I could change your mind, to say nothing of your soul, surely I would have done it by now."

"I have resisted your foul machinations," said Bishop Marcellus, not without a certain pride. She and her horde of demons had infested this monastery since it was built—since before it had been built, even. Since the day he'd ordered his monks to pull down their infernal stones. The devils had fought back, using their terrible powers to reduce grown men, fierce warrior monks, to sobbing, gibbering wrecks.

Vilna's voice had come to him then, for the first time: *Plant an orchard*, she'd said, *and let us have peace.* He had taken her suggestion before realizing she was a devil, and that the apples would let her cohort infiltrate the entire abbey.

Their powers, or maybe just their wrath, diminished outside the circle, however. They might haunt a pie or pop up out of the latrine, but these seemed more like childish pranks than real attacks. The two most powerful devils (Saints spare the righteous from all harm) were the ones called Iphi and Ognielle, who never deigned to leave the shelter of their stones. The others grew almost familiar. The monks gave them nicknames: the Queen of Hell, who haunted the kitchens at night; the Perfidious Twins, who cornered you in the cider press; and the Tricksy Imp, terror of the latrines.

And then, of course, the Quiet One.

Ironically, it was the Quiet One who used to converse with him. If he set out a dish of apples (*Like a pagan offering,* no one had ever dared suggest within his hearing), Vilna would come to his chamber at the loneliest hour of the darkest autumn nights. He felt a wintry chill and heard her eerie, disembodied voice, but she never let him see her true, undoubtedly hideous form: her cloven hooves, her gnarled horns. She would argue with him—calmly, gently—about complicated and esoteric points of theology, ethics, and history, which he hated to admit that he enjoyed, and then try to convince him of the most diabolical heresies.

Those, he resisted with every ounce of his being.

We are ghosts, she'd say. *There is no Heaven, and no Infernum—at least not as you think of them. There is only the Blue Country. But you will not be going there.*

This would force him to recite St. Vitt's Invocation of Righteous Ire Against Heresy, which cast her back into the infernal ether, or possibly bored her until she left.

His mind had wandered; she had kept talking. "I want you to look at me, Marcellus."

"Do you dare to show your accursed face at last?" he cried, limbs flailing beneath the covers, trying to free his hands. There must be something he could get ahold of to throw at her.

"Over here," she said, as calmly as ever. "By the apples."

There was no one by the apples.

"Look harder," she said. "You are nearing the final door, the one that leads out of yourself. That is when people, even those most hardened against it, sometimes begin to perceive the ghosts all around them."

"There's no such thing as ghosts," sputtered the bishop, but even as he said the words, a form was taking shape beside the dish of apples. It looked like a pale vapor, at first, but then it condensed into a short, skinny girl with hollow cheeks, dark eyes, and two limp braids. The light from the open window shone through her checkered shroud.

She was a . . . a *child*. The devil he'd been having nuanced theological arguments with for years looked like she was about twelve years old.

Clearly, this was trickery. An illusion. Who knew what a devil might resort to?

"Begone, fiend," he said, rolling onto his side so he wouldn't have to see her.

"Friend," she corrected him. "I'm trying to help you understand what's going to happen, because maybe, even now, it doesn't have to happen. You will not cross into the other world, because you are monstrous in your soul. You will linger as a murderous, devouring ghost—"

"Lies," he muttered. "Heresy."

His left arm was still numb from the stroke, but he felt her diabolical touch there nonetheless, the burning, blistering cold, before his mind was swarmed by memories—village elders locked in a barn and burned alive; a young mother screaming as he ripped her child from her arms; novices burned at the stake for heresy; babies dashed onto the rocks.

These were plainly intended to torment him, and indeed,

such images had driven his brothers mad. Bishop Marcellus could withstand the onslaught because he knew that everything he'd done—every grandmother or child he'd killed—had been for a righteous cause: the glory of the Saints in Heaven.

He would have pulled the standing stones down with his own two hands if he'd had the strength. He alone, of all his brethren, apparently, had a clear conscience and no regrets.

"Get up," Vilna was saying—maybe this was why she'd touched him. "Get up. There's something I want you to see."

It wasn't easy for him to get out of bed. In fact, it was so difficult he wasn't sure why he took up his cane and complied. A devil should be resisted, even if she truly, inexplicably, seemed to be a *child* devil. But no one else was taking the time to talk to him these days. He could lie in bed and wait to die, or he could humor her. Let her do her worst. All she had to compel him with was her icy touch and his own memories.

Vilna was pointing out the open window at the courtyard. "Tell me what you see."

"The flagstones," he said, after a moment to catch his breath. "The front gates. The well."

Her dark eyes twinkled. She laid her small, ethereal hand upon his large, liver-spotted one. He flinched at the cold (but not the memory, the massacre of a hamlet, just one of many).

"Look again," she said.

He looked, and gasped.

There were girls in the yard now, girls as transparent as Vilna. Her sister devils, these must be, the ones his monks had named. She spoke of them so often he knew who must be who: Anya and Zedig played a counting game as if they were living children, slapping each other's hands faster and faster until they were giggling too hard to continue; Princess Luti, a haughty-looking girl with golden hair, sat demurely nearby, pretending to ignore them, until Maeve—the Tricksy Imp—grabbed her hand, pulled her to her feet, and spun her around.

Suddenly, the air of the courtyard seemed to burst into a swirl of glittering blue sparks. Anya and Zedig gave a squeal of amazement, and then all the girls were jumping up and down, trying to catch the twinkles in their hands, their laughter as sparkling as the air.

"What are those?" he asked in hushed tones. The horrors in his own head had left him unmoved, but beauty still had the power to shock him, apparently.

"Those are just gnats," said Vilna.

"Never!"

She smiled at his surprise. "When you're dead, everything alive looks so beautiful—even murderous, hateful old men."

How dare you, he wanted to say, but her eyes seemed suddenly infinitely deep, and he felt himself teetering on the verge of something, a revelation, or maybe just an admission: That she really might be a three-hundred-years-dead twelve-year-old. That all of them might be exactly what she said they were.

Ghosts.

No. No!

"I have always thought it a pity that we never get to see the world like this while we're alive," she was saying. "Maybe we would value each other more if we could see how we shine."

They weren't ghosts. They could not be ghosts. If he had been wrong about that all along, he could be wrong about *anything*.

"Look at the glittering moss between the flagstones," whispered Vilna. "Look at your sparkling brother monk, crossing the yard. How would we be different if we saw what really is? Could we kill each other, if we had even the tiniest inkling of what we're made of?"

He had killed people for believing in ghosts. Three novices, new converts who'd had opinions about what his monks were experiencing when they'd tried to uproot the standing stones. He had ordered those novices burned at the stake. He saw their agonized faces in his memory, heard their screams for mercy.

His chin trembled.

"Let yourself doubt," said Vilna. "Let yourself consider that maybe you were wrong."

"No!" he cried, jerking his hand out of her grasp, almost falling over with the force of it.

How had he let the devil get to him like this? He'd known better than to listen. A righteous rage arose in him, and with it a final burst of unexpected strength. With a roar, he struck the dish of apples with his cane and swept it to the floor. He pulled books off the shelves with his one good hand and threw them, tore down curtains, knocked over the candelabrum with a terrifying clatter.

Novices, physicians, senior monks, anyone within shouting distance came running to help. He was restrained. It was another apoplexy, they said. It had stolen his sanity, they said.

He was confined to a small cell, constrained with leather straps for his own safety, and made as comfortable as possible with sleeping draughts. The physicians came in and out, but no one else visited him in the last week of his life before he died.

No one living, that is. Vilna visited often and told him stories: Who she and her sisters had been, when they had lived.

What they had died for. All the truth he still refused to absorb. When she ran out of stories, she sat in a corner looking solemn, but she never left his side.

It had taken him a century to stop raging, settle down, and admit a few things to himself.

Ghosts existed. He should know. He was one, and he was stuck.

Those novices, the ones he'd burned for heresy, had died for no good reason. For nothing. He'd given the order to kill them; that had made him a murderer.

He had killed a lot of people, in fact, many with his own hands. He'd forgotten about half of them while he lived, so little did he think of all that life he'd squandered. Now that he was dead, he remembered everything with perfect clarity: every one of their faces, and every reason—bad, wrong, and, yes, even occasionally good—he'd had for killing them.

He'd had a lot of time to think about this from every angle. To count the people he had wronged. To realize he could never make it right. To wonder what it would take to unbind himself from this prison of his own devising. To admit that he would never find the way, not while his regrets were still intertwined with resentment.

Not until he stopped *missing* the murder, surely.

Because sometimes he had enjoyed it. He was monstrous, just as Vilna had said, and he did not see a way to change that.

Even now, two hundred years dead, he had enjoyed feasting

upon that Vasterich boy's sanity—a fellow murderer, as it happened, so maybe he deserved it—but it had reminded him of what he'd been, and all that he had lost, and it had rekindled his rage at everyone still living.

Because it was true: Life shone as brightly as the sun. It was indescribably beautiful, but it did not bring him joy. It filled him with a cold and enduring hatred.

He could sense every squirrel and finch that ventured inside the perimeter of his awareness, so he knew that there were people in his abbey right now, who might be lured into his lair. He'd almost had one on his hook—the smallest—but he had proven wise and slippery as an eel.

No matter. There were two others here, and both of them were murderers.

23

Wort

here comes a point when you cannot bear the weight of everything alone. You have to tell someone what's going on. Charl had reached that point.

He went back to the refectory, sat by Mother Trude's bed, and said, "I need to tell you something, and I need you to believe me."

The old woman stirred and opened one eye.

Charl took a deep breath. He could do this. He'd confessed to even more difficult things in his short life. When he'd realized, at age five, that he wasn't the person everyone else seemed to think he was, he'd chosen Sister Agnes as being most likely to listen and take him seriously. He'd whispered in her ear: *I'm a boy.* She'd hugged him close—she who hardly ever hugged anybody—and then she'd taken him to his mother and helped him tell her, too. And that was the first step along the road that had led them to St. Muckle's.

Mother Trude had been Sister Agnes's teacher; surely she knew how to listen.

"I know you said there's no such thing as ghosts," he said, pulling a piece of straw from her pallet. "But there are. I've seen several of them here. I've spoken with some of them. One, in particular, is a problem for me, and I don't know what to do."

Mother Trude closed her eye again. Charl feared she wouldn't speak, but finally she said, "Perhaps you should begin at the beginning."

Crimping the straw between his fingers, he told her about everything: the weeping ghost he'd glimpsed just before Wort and Hooey died; flying through the town with the martin; Vilna, Maeve, and the other orchard girls; the haunting of Geoffrey; all the way to losing the bucket in the well. The only ghost he omitted was Bishop Marcellus, but he had no intention of going back to the sanctuary again, and anyway he felt like he was already giving Mother Trude sufficient proof that he had possibly lost his mind.

The old nun smacked her lips and reached for her water mug. Charl helped her sit up and drink. When she lay back down, she said, "I am not supposed to know these things—this knowledge was to have died with me. But, Heaven forgive me, you need help, and I can give it.

"There are three kinds of ghosts, Charl. Most commonly, they're people who died violently and can't quite believe they're dead. We say St. Eustace leads everyone up the Golden Stair—that's our official doctrine—but sometimes he misses one. I don't know why. Those ghosts will stay where they died, doing the same thing over and over, as if it might turn out differently this time. Wort is one such. That weeping lady in the birches sounds like another."

What misery, to burn or weep forever! Charl couldn't help wondering who the Lady of the Birches had been when she was alive.

"The second kind," Mother Trude continued, "are bound to a place deliberately. Your orchard girls are of this kind."

"Why would anyone do that?" asked Charl. "And how?"

"I don't know how," said Mother Trude. "That ancient art was lost with a lot of other pagan things. As for why—usually they bound a great sage, someone wise, so their knowledge would not be lost forever. I don't know why anyone would make ghosts of young girls."

There was a long pause.

Charl broke the silence. "What's the third kind, then?"

"The third kind was someone so evil, willful, and monstrous that Heaven rejects them, and they refuse to go to the Infernum. If the first kind were the murdered, these are the murderers. They can hurt you, as well as haunt you. Pray to Allsaints you never meet one."

Charl, though, was picturing a pair of bottomless-pit eyes. He had already met one, there was no doubt in his mind. Maybe he'd been lucky to escape. He shivered all the way to his toes.

"The good news is, they are also stuck in place," said Mother Trude. "That's the worst part about being a ghost, I should think. You can't go anywhere else. Those orchard girls have found a lucky loophole—their apples. I'd never heard of something like that."

"But what about the martin?" asked Charl. "It flew all the way to town."

"Maybe fading frees them from their bond somewhat?" said Mother Trude. "I don't know anything about that. We never let our sages fade."

We? Who did she mean? Charl felt certain she hadn't meant to say it, that fever had loosened her tongue and she was hoping he hadn't noticed. Mother Trude seemed to be holding her breath. He wanted to ask, but was afraid that would end the conversation.

"Can I do anything for Wort?" he asked instead. "Or is he doomed to scream and burn until he fades?"

Mother Trude exhaled. "Possibly? He knows you. You might be able to distract him from his misery. Have you tried speaking to him, or letting him touch you?"

"No," said Charl, suddenly ashamed of slamming the well lid onto Wort's ghostly fingers. "Mostly I've been panicking and fleeing."

That made her smile faintly. Her eyes drifted shut again. "Well. Those are things to try. We need that bucket back, Charl. And you still need a bath." She pulled the blanket up over her nose unsubtly. "Now go. You've exhausted me."

Charl did as he was told.

All was quiet while the well was covered. Charl steeled himself and hauled the lid off.

Howls and screams rose to the sky. The blast of agony almost knocked Charl backward, but he righted himself, bent his knees as if bracing for a sword's blow, and edged forward again.

This time he could make out words. "Raaafe!" the ghost shrieked. "What did you dooo?"

"He killed you, Wort," said Charl through clenched teeth. He was at the edge now, ready to look down at the terrible figure in the water. He counted to three.

And looked.

Wort looked the same as he had in the last moments of his life, burning, writhing in torment, but this time Charl felt something different. Not terror, and not exactly guilt, but . . . pity? It might have been Charl down there, if things had gone differently. If Rafe had realized he'd found pyria, not pisky. If Charl had shown up when he was supposed to, instead of early. If Wort and Hooey hadn't been in the wrong place at the wrong time.

"Wort," he called to the thrashing, splashing ghost. "Can you hear me?"

Howls of pain, screams of agony, no sensible word that Charl could make out.

Charl lay on his stomach and squinted down into the darkness, trying to understand what he was seeing. It was hard to focus at first, but then he realized: he was seeing double. The water level in early spring, when it rained every day, had been much higher than it was now. Wort's ghost was thrashing, nonsensically, three or four feet above the current water level. If Charl concentrated hard enough, he could see his bucket underneath the transparent froth and flames, barely afloat.

He couldn't reach the bucket with his hand, but he could reach Wort, if Wort would reach back. He extended a hand into the well. The agonized ghost took no notice.

"Wort!" Charl called. No response.

"Rafe!" Charl shouted, thinking Wort might notice that name. Nothing.

"Hooey?"

At the mention of his friend, the ghost of Wort surged furiously upward. Charl shrieked but managed not to move as a wave of ferocious cold broke over his head.

It was worse than when he'd bumped into Vilna. Much, much worse. Instead of one bad memory, Charl seemed to experience all of them at once in an avalanche, no gaps or breaks between them. Every regret, every terror, every heartache. Even after the flood had receded, he lay there a moment, wrecked on the rocks of his own pain, unable to move.

What was happening down in St. Muckle's? What if the dragon had killed ev—

A voice cut through his misery: "Charl? Cack, what are you doing here? You should go."

With tremendous effort, Charl raised his tear-streaked face. Wort sat on the stone lip of the well, afternoon sun shimmering through him. His curly, sheepdog hair flopped over his eyes.

Charl emitted a sound that might have been a sob.

"You should go," the ghost repeated. "Rafe will be back any minute. I think he actually wants to kill you. Me an' Hooey were trying to talk him out of it, but you know how he gets. All *lordly*. Won't listen to anybody."

Well, this was something. This was better. Wort was talking, not screaming, and he didn't seem to be on fire anymore. Charl pushed himself up to sitting.

"We'll hold him back, if need be, but it'd be easier if you just left," said Wort. "No shame in it."

Oh, but there was shame; Charl felt it keenly. "I should have told you to leave when I had the chance," he half whispered. "We could have left together."

Ghost Wort pushed his hair out of his face. "What'd you say?"

"You could leave," said Charl, a bit louder now. "You *can* leave. You don't have to stay here."

"I can't go without Hooey," said Wort.

"Hooey already left," said Charl.

Wort looked deeply startled by this information. He glanced around the courtyard. "It's daytime," he said, an odd note in his voice. "You—I saw something when I touched you."

Charl's throat was so tight he could only nod.

"I saw what happened," Wort said, sounding dazed. "Or what will happen. Was that the future, Charl?"

"No," Charl squeaked. "The past. It happened already."

"And Hooey went on, without me?"

"He . . . He didn't want to. But he didn't have a choice."

Wort laughed mirthlessly. "He probably thinks I got lost."

"Did you?" asked Charl. "Is that why you're still here?"

"I was just trying to climb out of the well," said Wort, a faraway look in his eyes. "I was so angry at . . . at Rafe. I wanted to fight him. I knew he killed Hooey. But where is he? Got off without a scratch, I bet, and is lounging about in luxury at home. That would be just like him."

No one was lounging about at home—home was forever changed. So much had happened since Wort had died that for a moment Charl felt dizzy with the weight of it. But he couldn't explain. It was too much.

"Rafe was in a terrible state the last time I saw him," said

Charl. "He was . . . haunted. Permanently. I don't know if he'll ever be well."

"Y'know, I think I saw something about that. In your head," said Wort, appearing to perk up a bit. "I guess that's not nothing."

"So that's that, then?" said Charl hopefully. "You can go?"

"Go where?" said Wort.

Charl blinked at him. "To . . . To Heaven, I suppose. Where Hooey is waiting for you, in the Golden House, along with all the Saints."

Wort licked his ghostly lips, considering. "I'm not so sure there is an afterlife, Charl. Or Saints, for that matter. Or Hooey. He may have simply dissolved."

"Dissolved?" cried Charl. "Dissolved into what?"

"Into the blue," said Wort, almost dreamily. "There is an awful lot of blue, I'll grant you that."

"Wort," said Charl, "I'm trying to help you. You have to move on now. You can't sit in this well forever and—"

"Can't I?" said Wort, something snappish in his voice now. His expression softened again. "You did help me. I'm not on fire anymore. I know I'm dead. But I was just sixteen, Charl. Not much older than you. I haven't done anything here in the world, and I'm not convinced there's anything to do there." He pointed upward, frowning skeptically at the sky. "So you may go now, with good conscience, and leave me here to contemplate my well, and my navel, and whatever else seems right to me."

"You'll fade, eventually," said Charl. He was pleading now but could not have said why. "You won't be yourself anymore. You'll be an animal or a bird."

"Good," said Wort firmly. "Good. I've never been a bird before. I shall enjoy it."

With that, Wort blinked out of Charl's sight, although Charl had no doubt that he was still there, in the well. There was no convincing him to leave, apparently. Charl hated to admit it, but maybe this was the best he could do.

Anyway, there was still the bucket to retrieve. He looked into the well again, and his heart sank. While he'd been arguing with Wort, the bucket had finally grown so waterlogged that it had sunk to the bottom, however deep that was. Charl couldn't see it, anyway, and he didn't see how he was going to hook the handle and pull it back up.

Still, he had to try. He lowered the rope hook-first into the water and carefully let it slide through his hands, farther and farther in. He began to worry that he would run out of rope, but finally he felt a bump, as if the hook had hit something. The bottom, perhaps. Carefully, slowly, he began to drag the hook back and forth, trying to feel for the bucket.

This was such a fiddly task, requiring such concentration, that the voice behind him nearly scared him out of his skin.

"Fishing, friend?"

Charl whirled around, dropping the rope and almost losing it down the well. Luckily, the fellow behind him had quick enough reflexes to step on the end of the rope before it disappeared altogether.

It was the Porphyrian boy who'd saved him from Rafe many years ago. Hardly a boy anymore, with the beginnings of a beard in the Porphyrian style, like the one Aris wore—no mustache. His face, however, had been seared upon Charl's memory, and beard or no beard, Charl would have known him anywhere. He wore finely embroidered Porphyrian robes and had a sword at his hip. One hand rested cautiously on the hilt, but he was smiling, for all that.

It was a pretty smile. Charl, ridiculously, blushed.

Behind him, Charl now realized, the great wooden gates had been unlocked and a horse-drawn wagon was rolling into the courtyard. The traveling Porphyrian merchants—owners of the padlock, the well cover, and the pyria—had arrived.

The Porphyrians

"I lost your bucket," said Charl, feeling foolish.

"Is *that* what you're fishing for?" said the young man, coming closer to peer down the well. "I'm sure we have a spare."

They likely did. Four large wagons crowded the courtyard now, and at least twenty traders, men and women and others, were preparing to set up camp.

"Yustinus!" called a voice, followed by what sounded like a scolding. The lad looked back guiltily at an older man coming around the side of a wagon. His hair was braided close to his scalp, and his beard was shot through with gray. Charl recognized him—Brasidas Malou Techys. He came to the Fiddle sometimes; Mama bought wine from him.

And it turned out Techys recognized *him*.

"The innkeeper's offspring," said the man in light, pleasant

Goreddi. He smiled. "Remind me, young one, how shall I pronoun you?"

This was Porphyrian politeness. Charl had encountered it before. *"He,"* he said. "I recall you use the same one, Master Techys."

"You recall rightly," said the merchant. "My nephew takes it, as well."

The nephew gave a little wave. "I'm Yustinus."

"But come, sit," said Master Techys, ushering Charl toward a flat slab of stone. "And tell us what you're doing here—alone? not alone?—and what has happened to your fair city."

Charl swallowed hard and told them about the plague and the dragon. Techys listened quietly, stroking his beard.

"We thought it looked like a dragon attack," said Master Techys. "But you give me little hope that it will be over soon. If the dragon is after your mother, it won't leave until it finds her. *We* certainly can't stand against it."

"Gorlich Smith went to Fort Lambeth to notify the knights," said Charl. "Did you not pass refugees on the road?"

Master Techys sucked on his teeth, thinking. "We saw a camp near the summit, but we didn't stop to speak with them. But most of the knights were ordered north to Reneville last week. The skeleton crew that's left will be reluctant to come out for St. Muckle's, especially if it's already mostly destroyed. And they've hardly any pyria left, in any case."

"There's pyria *here*," said Charl. "I assumed it was yours."

Techys grinned sheepishly. "Ah. That. My cousin Aramou's folly. It's contraband—we aren't supposed to have it—but Aramou found a source and thought he'd found a buyer in St. Muckle's. He hauled it this far before I realized what he was carrying. Any bump in the road might have made dogmeat of all of us. I made him leave it here; if his buyer wanted it, his buyer would have to drag it the rest of the way down the valley. Then, of course, his buyer fell through. Said he'd changed his mind, decided to pursue some other path, something subtler."

"Subtler?" asked Charl. It was an odd choice of words, and it reminded him of something, but he couldn't put his finger on it.

"Anything would be subtler than pyria," said Yustinus. A twinkle in his eye belied his solemn tone.

Charl found himself smiling back.

"He can only have been contemplating mischief," said Techys with a wave. "There's no legitimate civilian use for the stuff. Aramou was not invited to travel with us again. We don't deal with criminals."

"But . . . could you take the pyria back to Fort Lambeth," said Charl, "so the knights could come kill this dragon for us?"

Master Techys frowned. "I must consult with my partners. It would be the height of folly to go into St. Muckle's right now, clearly, but we can't sell there ever again if the dragon burns it all to ash. On the other hand, Pyria might burn *us* to ash, if we're not careful . . ."

"Oh no," cried Charl, finally appreciating the danger. "Perhaps you could leave it here and tell the knights where to find it."

"That won't do," said Master Techys glumly. "You've never dealt with knights before, I take it. They tend not to give one the benefit of the doubt. We're going to be in trouble merely for having pyria, but we'd be in much worse trouble if they knew we'd left it where any villain might find it."

"If the knights need it," Yustinus interjected, "and we *give* it, rather than selling it—"

"Yes, my soft-hearted boy, they might overlook our indiscretions," said Techys, quirking a half smile at his nephew. "However, the decision is not ours alone. We must speak with the others. But first, more questions need answering. Would you intend to accompany us to Fort Lambeth, young Charl, if that's where we decide to go?"

Charl hadn't even considered that possibility, but now that Techys mentioned it—

He realized he was looking at Yustinus. He looked away.

"Because I'm really hoping you *won't*," Master Techys added.

"Oh!" said Charl, suddenly mortified. Of course they wouldn't want to transport him anywhere, as badly as he still needed that bath.

"Not that we wouldn't want to take you," Master Techys quickly added, seeming to notice Charl's confusion. "It's just that I have a difficulty that I hope you might help me with, an urgent delivery for Dr. Caramus—something expensive that was difficult to acquire quickly—and I don't see how to deliver it, with all that's going on, or how I'm going to get paid."

Charl nodded slowly; he saw where this was going.

Master Techys continued, "Maybe it's not so urgent anymore. He might be dead; his patients might be dead."

"Uncle!" cut in Yustinus, with a warning glance at Charl, who had gone very pale.

Master Techys shrugged. "That came out more callously than I intended. What I mean to say is, this blood fever will likely still be a problem after the dragon is defeated. And I presume, even if the worst has happened to Caramus, there are others who will know what to do with all this resin and dried herb . . ."

Charl nodded vigorously. Sister Agnes would know.

Master Techys snapped his fingers and called out something

in Porphyrian. Two of his companions, who seemed to be his employees, brought over two small chests and set them at Techys's feet. One box seemed light, the other heavy.

Yustinus pulled a silver necklace out of his shirt. A little key dangled from it, which he used to open the boxes. The light one held packets of dried herbs. The heavier one contained chunks of a crumbly, yellowish substance. Most of the chunks were cloudy, but some were nearly transparent. The sunlight made them glow like honey, and, to Charl's surprise, a beautiful smell wafted from them. He leaned over and inhaled deeply. It was floral, and a bit piney.

"That's resin from the chiromastic tree," said Yustinus. "Have you never smelled it before? It's used in perfumes. And this herb is called destultia."

Techys sighed heavily. "Close those up, Yustinus. They lose their potency with too much exposure, and I don't know how long it will be before we can deliver them—or before anyone can make use of them.

"But here's my hope, friend," he said, turning to Charl again. "Do you think you could you get these to Caramus? Don't worry about the money—he can pay me later. Desperate times call for extending credit."

Charl's first reaction was no—not because he thought he couldn't do it or was too afraid, but because he had a sick nun to look after. But then he realized two things: maybe these medicines could help Mother Trude, and if not, these traders had wagons! They could carry Mother Trude to the infirmary in Fort Lambeth, where she'd receive better nursing than Charl could ever hope to provide.

When Charl asked how the medicines worked, however—

explaining Mother Trude's situation and his obligation to her—Master Techys was at a loss. "I'm sorry, child, I . . . I'm not an apothecary. None of us are, alas. I wouldn't know where to begin with this stuff."

"All right, but could you take her to Fort Lambeth, then?" said Charl. "I can't run off in search of Dr. Caramus and leave her alone here. She might—"

He couldn't say it. He couldn't put that terrible thought into words.

Master Techys understood the words he hadn't said, however, and nodded solemnly. "Let me see her."

The merchant rose in a whirl of embroidered robes, summoned his people, and quietly gave instructions. Some began making space in the wagons, while others went to the storeroom to fetch what pyria they could carry.

"Now let's speak to this nun of yours," said Techys, smiling at Charl again.

Charl led him to the refectory. Yustinus tagged along, grinning sunnily.

When Charl nudged Mother Trude awake, she didn't seem to know who he was or where she was. Her eyes widened at the sight of the Porphyrians. "Oh no," she said in a hoarse whisper. "He can't take me. I'm not ready to go up the Stair. I'm not finished here."

"We haven't committed to taking her yet. I must still consult with my companions," said Master Techys, his brow crumpled in confusion.

Charl had caught a detail the trader had not. "She thinks she's dying, and that you're St. Eustace, come to lead her up the Golden Stair to Heaven."

He pressed a hand to her forehead. It felt appallingly hot.

"She needs her fever tea," said Charl, trying to keep the tremor out of his voice.

"She needs more than that," said Techys, frowning deeply.

"Whosoever sees need and has the power to give, must give," said Yustinus, with the air of someone reciting a proverb.

"Quote Darmidius the Stoic at me, will you?" said his uncle. His voice sounded stern, but his expression was fond.

"That was Epinou of Vribata, actually," said Yustinus cheekily.

Master Techys heaved a long-suffering sigh. "This is your Aunt Nilde's fault, letting you run wild in her library. You'd better fetch her, I suppose." Yustinus nodded and ducked out.

He returned several minutes later with a diminutive older woman—Aunt Nilde, Charl presumed—who seemed made entirely of authority, along with three younger women, bearing buckets of cool water. Upon Aunt Nilde's orders, one took over preparing the fever tea, one began soaking broadcloths in water, and the other began helping Mother Trude out of her clothing.

"Hey!" cried Charl, certain she wouldn't appreciate this indignity. She hardly ever took off her wimple, even.

But Mother Trude did not protest. "I should have stabbed Miga," she muttered, her head lolling onto her chest as the women sat her up. "I had one chance. She was right there . . . sleeping."

"Come," said Techys, laying a heavy hand on Charl's shoulder. "They will lower her fever with cold compresses and get her more comfortable, and then we'll see. No one's going anywhere until tomorrow, in any case. But come: as that pesky Yustinus reminded us, hers is not the only need I see. What do you need, that we can give?"

The question nearly brought Charl to tears. This was how people were meant to behave when someone needed help, or so

Mama had always taught him. This was how St. Muckle's had been in the early days of the plague, before fear and mistrust had ground them all down. And so Charl got a bath at last. Aunt Nilde arranged it all: a wooden tub set within a little cubicle of hanging shawls, blissfully hot water with actual soap. As Charl was drying off afterward, he heard raised voices from the other side of the privacy curtain. He dressed hurriedly in the fresh clothes Aunt Nilde had left him—nothing elegant, like Yustinus wore, but some shorter person's serviceable cast-offs—and then he peeked through a gap in the curtains to see what was going on. The merchants had gathered in a circle and were engaged in a spirited debate of some sort.

The words "pyria" and "Fort Lambeth" came through clearly, as the only words he understood. They were deciding whether to help him. Whether to help Mother Trude.

Yustinus, young though he was, seemed to have a great deal to say in this discussion, and Charl was struck by how everyone listened when he spoke, and seemed to take him seriously.

"That Yustinus is quite a dashing fellow, isn't he?" purred a voice at Charl's elbow, startling him so badly that he nearly fell through the curtains.

"Maeve, do you mind? I'm trying to listen," he whispered back. Was there an apple here somewhere? In the pocket of his dirty clothes? Had she been here the whole time he was bathing? He felt himself blushing furiously.

Maeve was eyeing him closely. "I can't tell whether you're mad at me for startling you or embarrassed because you were thinking the exact same thing."

"Maybe I'm annoyed to be reminded that I'm not as *dashing* as Yustinus," Charl offered, to get her off the scent.

Maeve snorted. "You aren't *yet*. But you've got a few years to grow into it."

"I'll never be as tall."

"Bah, that's not where 'dash' is located, Charl. It's in his shoulders, and how he walks."

Was Yustinus a fencer, too? Charl had noted the sword belt, but hadn't thought about whether the young man had had any training. He looked like he had, maybe, now that Charl watched him more closely, addressing the assembled merchants. There was a certain give-and-take to the cadence of his argument, even if you couldn't tell precisely what he was saying . . .

". . . and then there's that beard," Maeve added dreamily.

That made him laugh, not at the beard—which was rather splendid—but at Maeve's dramatic sighing. "You have clearly been cooped up in a stone circle too long, my friend."

"Are you talking to me?" said Aunt Nilde, who'd been standing not far from the curtain. She turned toward him, eyebrows raised. "Do you need something, lad?"

Maeve grinned impishly and disappeared.

"I . . . I just wanted to know what's been decided," said Charl, opening the curtain a little wider. Behind Aunt Nilde, the meeting seemed to be over. The merchants were dispersing.

"My nephew has done the impossible. He's made all the philosophers agree," said Aunt Nilde. "And the moral course of action seems to be this: We will take your pyria and your nun over the mountain, you will take the medicines down to Dr. Caramus, and we will settle up in the spring, if there's anyone left alive."

Charl's hand flew to his heart. "Thank you," he said, and then he said it again, loud enough for everyone to hear.

Charl stayed and ate lentil stew with Yustinus and his aunt

and uncle. They would have let him sleep out in the courtyard by the fire, but he was determined to keep watch over the old nun for one last night. He stopped by the orchard for an armful of apples and then returned to the refectory.

Mother Trude was awake, dressed in a clean linen shift and wrapped snugly in a blanket. Her short brown hair was damp and her cheeks were flushed, but her eyes shone in the firelight.

"Charl," she called, her voice stronger than before. "I need to tell you how sorry I am."

"No, you don't," he said. "You couldn't help getting sick. Anyway, you're going to get better in Fort Lambeth. I will see you again later, and you can tell me then."

His words seemed not to reach her. She was crying now. "I have . . . regrets," she said through tears. "If you're going back to St. Muckle's, I need you to take a message to Agnes."

"Of course," said Charl. "The traders surely have something to write with, and you can write it up in the morning. Or I can write it for you, if you're feeling weak."

Mother Trude just nodded, her hand over her eyes.

"Are you hungry?" said Charl, crossing toward the chest where their food was stored. He had to dump his armload of apples in there anyway. "Would you like some bread and butter?"

And jam. There was jam. He'd nearly forgotten. He could really do with some jam right about now.

The jar was not in evidence, however. He moved the apples and turnips around, shifted the sacks of oats, but the jam did not appear. Neither did the butter. A loaf was also missing, as well as the cheese that had been wrapped in parchment. Gorlich's note fluttered, empty, like a dry leaf.

Mother Trude couldn't have taken all that food. She could

hardly keep her head up, let alone cross the room. Maybe the Porphyrians had helped themselves. But that seemed unlikely; they had whole wagonloads of supplies. And there was no sign of rats.

"Would you like some *bread*?" he asked.

But Mother Trude had fallen asleep.

Far from the fires in the courtyard, deep in a brambly thicket where the cloister garden used to grow, something stirred. A ragged, filthy, desperate person peeled wax off the cheese with trembling hands and then wolfed it down in frantic, crumbling bites. Then he gobbled the lump of butter as if it were cheese, whimpering occasionally.

Two ghost girls sat together nearby, atop a cracked cloister arch, watching him gnaw the stolen food. Because of course he had taken an apple, too.

"The wolf is wounded," Anya whispered to Zedig. "See his leg? It's starting to fester."

"He's in bad shape," Zedig whispered back. "Should we mention him to Charl again?"

"Tomorrow," said Anya. "If he survives the night. Let us keep vigil, so he doesn't have to die alone."

And so they watched all night, and they sang a song from when they were young, a song to comfort the dying:

> *We disappear,*
> *Bud and leaf,*
> *Flower and fruit,*

Song and singer,
Mother and child.
And everyone around you brings you love.
And everyone around you sends you home.

But the wolf, as they thought of him, could not hear them singing, and felt no comfort. Through gritted teeth, he moaned and panted all night, but he did not die. Before dawn, he ate the apple—core, stem, and seeds—and then the ghost girls couldn't stay. The orchard called them back, and that was all they saw of him that night.

24.5: Anya and Zedig's Story

After many years of wandering, the People arrived in a long-abandoned valley where the soil was black and rich and many things grew. The Antler-Men proclaimed that it was a fine place to settle, out of sight of their enemies, and mostly it was. But they soon learned that there was an unruly River to the south, which would sometimes flood its banks and drive the people from their homes.

This was an unanticipated hardship, and the Antler-Men had to think how best to address it. The oldest of their number went up the nearby Mountain, to fast and pray and see if the gods would answer.

When he finally came back down, he said to the People: "I spoke to Father Mountain, and he replied. He will protect us from the River, if we take our most holy Maiden, the seventh daughter of a seventh daughter, and give her to him for his bride."

The People muttered at this. They did not like it. There was, indeed, a seventh daughter of a seventh daughter among them, but she was still a child.

"It's all right," the Antler-Man assured them. "I glimpsed the

Mountain's other brides while I was up there, and they were also just girls. She won't be alone. She'll be fine."

So they let the girl, festooned with garlands like a young heifer, go up the mountainside with the Antler-Men, who poured her life's blood out upon the mountainside. And none of the People ever climbed the Mountain, or dared to go and see where she had died, for they all felt miserable about it in their souls.

However, the unruly River quieted down after that. For years, it gave the People no trouble, and the valley was bounteous and beautiful and like a paradise.

Until the day it wasn't. One day, without warning, a torrent gushed into the valley and washed away the bridges and flooded the streets of their town. The People complained to the Antler-Men, who hastily conferred about what to do. Their eldest, who'd gone up the mountain before, was long dead, but they remembered what he had advised: the seventh daughter of a seventh daughter, sent to be Father Mountain's bride.

However, there was no such girl to be found among the People now, for they'd sacrificed the last one before she could have any daughters of her own. The closest they could find was the seventh daughter of a sixth daughter.

They couldn't wait a whole generation for a more suitable girl, however. The River was washing away everything the people had built. Soon it would be too late. And so the Antler-Men took the imperfect Maiden up the Mountain, sacrificed her in the same way as before, and hoped for the best.

Only to make the River rage until it brought the Mountain down upon their heads.

And those few of the People who survived have passed along this tale to remind us: We are very small, and this world is very big. And death comes for the foolish and the wise alike.

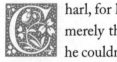

25

The Gray

Charl, for his part, hardly got a wink of sleep. It wasn't merely that Mother Trude snored like a dragon, but he couldn't stop himself from thinking, planning, picturing himself down among the wreckage of St. Muckle's. How much had the dragon destroyed? Which roads were impassible? Where would he be able to hide from the dragon's gaze? And which of Dr. Caramus's many haunts should he try first? Gorlich had seen him at the forge, but that was days ago now.

When the earliest birds began to sing and twilight illuminated the hole in the refectory roof, Charl gave up on sleep and got up. He went to relieve himself first, out of sight of the orchard. Then he heard stirrings from the courtyard. He went to see which Porphyrians were up, and found that they all were.

Yustinus was hauling water. He spotted Charl and waved him over. Charl hesitated, but he'd talked to Wort. Wort surely wasn't going to pop out at him again. Charl walked over, feigning nonchalance, and looked down into the well. Yustinus's bucket slopped water over the sides, perfectly normally.

"I couldn't retrieve that other bucket," said the older boy, apparently thinking that's what Charl was looking for.

"I . . . I thought I saw a ghost in this well, earlier," said Charl, as if he were joking.

"I don't doubt it," said Yustinus, bringing his bucket to ground at last. "There are ghosts everywhere in ruins like this."

"Do you Porphyrians believe in ghosts?" asked Charl.

Yustinus laughed warmly. "Have you never spent much time among our people? Half of us fancy ourselves philosophers; we don't *all* believe *anything*. But I've seen ghosts before. It's not a question of belief, when you've experienced it."

"Tell me about them." Charl just wanted to keep the boy talking. He'd been so hungry for company, and he was going to be alone again soon enough.

But did Yustinus have to go to Fort Lambeth? Charl imagined his staying on to help him look for Dr. Caramus. They would sneak down the mountain together, keeping watch for the dragon, and creep across the turnip fields by night—

"There's a famous ghost on the waterfront in Porphyry," Yustinus was saying. "A dockhand who was crushed by a falling crate. Lots of people have seen him."

They'd get Caramus his herbs, and help Aris and Agnes rescue Mama (if that still needed doing), and defeat the dragon. And having shared such dangers—

"And I saw my father," said Yustinus sadly.

That snapped Charl out of his daydream. "Did you speak to him?"

Yustinus looked searchingly at Charl. "Should I have?"

"He might have recognized you, and believed you that he was dead," said Charl.

Yustinus shook his head. "That's a job for a priest."

"I helped a friend of mine that way. It wasn't that hard," said Charl, omitting how terrified he'd been, or that Wort was still hanging around the well they'd just used.

Yustinus's solemn face broke into a grin. "Well, your vocation is clear, then. You would make an excellent priest."

Charl felt his face go red. "No, I wouldn't. I'm sure I wouldn't. Our priests don't even believe in ghosts!" he cried, following Yustinus toward the cook fire, yapping at his heels like an aggravated terrier. The last thing he wanted this elegant, tall boy to think was that he, Charl, would like to be stuck in a seminary. "I've been learning sword fighting, actually. Not a very priestly pastime."

"Indeed?" said Yustinus, his eyes brightening. "What's your weapon? Rapier? Saber?"

Charl racked his brains for a way to make "wooden short sword" sound more sophisticated.

Luckily, Master Techys showed up then, ahead of several people bearing pyria crates, and interrupted their conversation. He took Charl aside and said, "There are a couple crates of pyria missing, child. Did you move them? They're very dangerous."

It took Charl a moment to understand. "Uh . . . there was one jug missing when I was down there. I know who took that. I didn't move anything."

Techys frowned deeply. "Well, it's been months since we were here. I suppose the crates might have been missing for a while. Still, it's disturbing. This is not the sort of material you want to fall into unpracticed or malicious hands."

The old trader went to supervise the loading of his wagon. Charl followed him, and finally got up the nerve to say, "Master Techys, I've been thinking of what dangers I may face in St. Muckle's. There's something I want, if you have it—a sword."

Techys pursed his lips. "You aren't foolishly considering taking on the dragon, I hope."

"I'm not," said Charl. "But there are other, smaller people to fear in that town. And it would make me feel better if I could defend myself."

He didn't want to mention the man with the scar, the one who'd captured his mother. He felt reasonably sure Techys wouldn't like him taking on that fellow, either.

"Do you know how to use a sword?" said Techys, eyeing him skeptically.

"I won the town fencing tourney last year, against a boy four years older than me," said Charl, puffing out his chest. Trying to look a bit taller, anyway.

Techys nodded, although he still didn't look happy. "Very well. I can hardly ask you to go into danger undefended."

He whistled to one of his companions to fetch a sword from the back of a wagon, but Yustinus piped up: "He could have mine."

"He can *borrow* yours," said his uncle, not looking entirely pleased by his nephew's reflexive generosity.

Yustinus unbuckled his sword belt and rebuckled it around Charl's waist. With trembling hands, Charl carefully drew the weapon, a short sword with a well-worn grip. It was sharp, though. Sharper than any of the practice swords he'd ever used.

"How much?" said Charl. "I'll let my mother know, and she'll pay you when she's—"

"You heard my uncle," said Yustinus, raising his hands laughingly. "You're borrowing it. I'll be back to collect it someday, so see to it that you take good care—"

"By both gods, keep the damned thing," Techys said, cutting him off with a wave of his hand. "You're doing me a favor, delivering those crates to Dr. Caramus. The sword is an investment, to help ensure that *he* will eventually pay me. That's where I stand to lose real money, not on a secondhand sword."

They had breakfast next, including Charl, and then it was time for the convoy to depart. Techys, Yustinus, and Charl went to bring Mother Trude out and get her settled in the wagons. As they neared the old dining hall, however, Charl began to get a crawly feeling on the back of his neck. He walked a little faster.

Through the doorway, he could tell that Mother Trude's sleeping pallet was empty. Had she stumbled off to answer a call of nature? But her blanket was gone, too . . .

"Mother Trude?" Charl called.

"Not one step closer, boy," said a faint, phlegmy voice.

But Charl did come one step closer. Three steps, in fact—right up to the doorway so he could see the whole hall.

Mother Trude was at the far end, under the hole in the roof, where the floor there was littered with broken roof tiles, fetid puddles that never dried up, and sprouting weeds. Mother Trude had apparently crawled there, dragging her pillow and blankets with her. She now sat huddled beside a pile of debris, blankets wrapped tightly around herself. She shivered with fever; her face was the color of wet ashes.

Charl crossed the threshold. "What are you doing—"

"Stop right there!" Her voice echoed. "You promised to stay away when I said you must."

As if the shouting had been too much for her poor lungs, Mother Trude burst into a fit of uncontrollable coughing.

And with each cough came a puff of gray dust.

Master Techys clamped a hand onto Charl's shoulder, as if he were afraid the boy would foolishly run into the room, but it took every ounce of Charl's self-control not to run *away*.

Mother Trude had the dusty cough. They were all in danger if they got too close.

"I can't travel in this condition," she said through chattering teeth. "I would endanger your people, Master Techys."

"I don't want that to be true," said Master Techys, "but I fear it is, and I'm so sorry."

"What?" cried Charl. "What? No. There must be a way."

"Get Charl out of here," called Mother Trude. "And return with pen and paper. I have a final favor to ask."

A final favor. A *final* favor. This couldn't be happening. She was supposed to get to Fort Lambeth and be saved. Charl struggled with tears as Yustinus led him back to the wagons.

After many minutes, Master Techys approached, folding a piece of fine rag paper in half and in half again. He handed it to Charl. "For Sister Agnes, if you find her in town."

"I can't *go* to town," Charl cried, shoving the paper into his pocket. "You won't take Mother Trude with you, so I've got to stay and take care of her."

"Only for a day or two more, I suspect," said Techys. His mouth flattened grimly. "We have a tincture that will stop her from feeling any pain. I'll leave some with you."

"She's stronger than she seems," said Charl. "And people get better, even at this stage."

This wasn't true, but he couldn't face the alternative. He refused to.

Techys began giving orders to his fellow travelers. One pressed a vial of black liquid into Charl's hand. Another rushed to the top of the abbey wall with a flare and a smoldering taper. He lit the fuse. With a shrilling whistle, a streak of smoke raced into the air, high above the trees, high above the mountainside, and burst with a bang and a flash of yellow.

"I have signaled Dr. Caramus with flares before," said Techys, his low voice deepening even further. "If he saw or heard that, he'll know what it means."

And if the dragon had seen or heard it? Charl wished they had asked him before setting the thing off.

"Give Dr. Caramus three days to get here," Techys was saying, "and if he doesn't come, then you're going to have to go and find him yourself."

Only if Mother Trude was dead. Charl was so wrenched with grief that he couldn't speak.

"I know you don't want to leave her behind," said Techys. "This buys you some time."

"Uncle, what if I stayed?" said Yustinus, stepping nearer. "I could tend the old woman. Or I could sneak into town and—"

"You could *not*," said Techys, and Charl heard a new sharpness in his voice. "I have generously given a sword and two chests of valuable ingredients to help the people of St. Muckle's. I will not give my widowed sister's only child as well."

Yustinus bowed his head and did not try to argue.

Charl, for his part, hadn't even had time to get his hopes up.

The Porphyrians hitched up their horses and left in single file through the abbey gates. They locked the gates behind them. Charl stood on the battlement wall, watching them until they had rounded a bend in the road, out of sight.

"Welcome to a ghost's life," said a voice at his elbow, breaking his reverie. "Can't leave. Can't act. Stuck in one place for five hundred years."

It was Maeve, leaning back against the parapet, a faraway look on her faded face.

"It's very frustrating," Charl agreed.

"People aren't meant to be stuck," she said wistfully. "People are meant to grow and change. Being dead is the worst."

"What exactly binds you here?" said Charl. "The standing stones? Some sort of magic?"

He felt foolish saying "magic," but ghosts weren't supposed to exist, either, and here he was talking to one.

Maeve sighed and turned to face him. The morning sun made her glow all over. "I don't rightfully know. We were all killed in a certain way, and incantations spoken over us, but—"

"Wait—you were *killed*? On *purpose*?" Charl's voice hiked up an octave.

Maeve gave him a small, pitying smile. "We were sacrificed. Did you really not know? Not Iphi and Ognielle. They were sages, wise women bound on their deathbeds to preserve their wisdom. And Vilna, really, was something of a sage as well— a Wise Child—who was already at death's door."

Like the girl in her story, with a cancer in the blood. It had been *her* story, for true. Charl felt foolish for not having understood until now.

"But the rest of us were killed to appease the gods, or for the greater good, or *something*." She turned her gaze outward toward St. Muckle's and rested her chin on her hand. "I was the last. By that point, they'd kind of forgotten why they were doing it."

"They never *told* you why?" That seemed unbelievably cruel.

"Oh, they told me. It was supposed to end a drought," said Maeve. "And, to be fair, the drought did eventually end. I'm not sure my death had much to do with it, though."

"And there's no way to release you from this bond?"

"Fading was supposed to do it," said Maeve. "That's what Iphi and Ognielle thought, in their wisdom. Of course, they're still here. They may be having a better time than the rest of us, though."

She was giving Charl a great deal to think about. "So . . ." he said, "what about Wort?"

"Who's Wort?"

"The fellow in the well."

"Ah." She smiled at this, unexpectedly. "The Thrashing Splasher. What about him?"

"Is he bound to this place?" asked Charl. "Could he leave if he wanted to?"

"He could go," said Maeve, "now that you've talked to him and he understands that he's dead. But he might not feel like it yet." She looked toward the well and squinted, as if trying to see properly. "He's down in the water, humming contentedly. Probably counting animalcules."

"Animal*cules*?"

"Tiny little specks in every droplet. They're alive. When you're dead, you can see everything alive, all glowy and beautiful.

Everything you'll never be again and can't have . . ." Her voice trailed off, her gaze gone sad and distant, but then she looked at Charl and smiled. "He'll go to the Blue Lands when he's ready. I know that's not what you call it, but that's what my mother used to call it. The Beyond. The Far-Distant Unknowable. Now he can choose. That's surely all a person could want."

She sounded like his mother. It made him happy and sad at once.

"It was actually terribly lucky that he knew you, and would listen," she said. "Poor Eldegarde has been here a hundred years at least, so she wouldn't know anyone still living. I suspect she's stuck until she fades."

"Who's Eldegarde?" asked Charl, confused by the change of subject.

"The Lady of the Birches," said Maeve, gesturing toward the trees. "She's there right now, weeping under the roots. I forget you can't see inside of things. Hmm. One point in favor of being dead."

"What happened to her?"

"Murdered," said Maeve, with perhaps a bit too much relish. "I didn't see it, but Princess Luti did. Apparently, Eldegarde was an Amberfinch, in love with the son of the rival Asterrink family. He gave her an opal ring, which is still in the tall grass under the trees, somewhere."

"Is it?" said Charl, peering toward the grove with greater interest now.

"Don't even think of looking for it," said Maeve. "It's the most tragic, haunted object in this entire abbey, you may be sure, and that's saying something. Anyway, Eldegarde was supposed to meet her Asterrink lover here and run off, but someone else was waiting, someone who killed her. But I imagine you know the story, having grown up in St. Muckle's."

"I don't recall anything like that," said Charl, racking his brains for Amberfinches or Asterrinks. The name Vasterich sounded a bit like Asterrink, but that was not much to go on.

Maeve heaved a sigh. "You see, the world forgets. Only a century out, and their great rivalry is dust. Two centuries have crumbled this abbey into a ruin. Almost a thousand years passed between Iphi's death and mine, enough time to degrade us from sages to guardians to sacrificial victims. Whatever we died for is gone. The people who bound us are gone. The way to unbind us is long past forgotten, if it ever existed at all."

"I'm so sorry," said Charl.

"Yes, well, sorry doesn't *help*." And with that, she disappeared.

As much as Charl had enjoyed seeing Maeve—she was his favorite, so lively it was hard to remember she was dead—he'd been secretly hoping Ognielle would come again and take him back to town, even if only in his mind. It was agony not knowing how his mother was doing, whether she was still held captive by that scar-faced lout, or whether Aris and Agnes had pulled off a rescue. It was nearly as bad not knowing what the dragon was up to. He didn't see her overhead anymore, and while a few buildings seemed to be smoldering, the town was barely half destroyed—maybe she'd given up.

But Ognielle wasn't coming, and the sun had fully risen now. He'd left Mother Trude alone too long. Just because she was dying didn't mean she should be alone. The new clothes the Porphyrians had given him included a colorful sash; he could tie that around his mouth and nose to keep the gray out. He would do what he could for her, even if it was only keeping vigil from across the room.

As he crossed the birch grove, he remembered the folded note Techys had given him. He'd shoved it into his pocket with the vial of medicine. He pulled them both out now and looked at them. The liquid in the vial was dark, viscous, and evil-looking, more like what he would have guessed poison looked like than painkiller. He supposed grimly that death would end most pain, although not necessarily all of it. Wort had taught him that.

As for the note . . . Charl wrestled with his conscience a moment. It was private—he knew that—but a lot of things might happen before he saw Agnes again. If he knew what it said, he could tell her about it, even if the note were to be lost or destroyed. He didn't want to risk Mother Trude's final words just disappearing.

He unfolded it and read. Sunlight through the birch leaves dappled the page.

> My dear Agnes—I had only one thing I still wanted in this world, but my courage failed, and I spoiled my chance. Let it not fail me now. Please read to the end, however hard it might be, and try not to despise your mother—yes, mother—who has loved you since the day you were born in that sheep pasture long ago . . .

Charl, at least, had no trouble reading to the end, his eyes growing wider and wider.

And then he had to sit down, because he was shaking all over.

Not at the news that Sister Agnes was Mother Trude's daughter, although that was surprising, nor at learning that Mother Trude had been a pagan originally—he had almost worked that piece out himself. But there were other revelations, upsetting revelations that pertained directly to him.

He had guessed some of this previously, but learning names and details made it so much worse. They made it real. His father, the Earl of Ucht, had destroyed the village of Echstau and forbidden Mother Trude from helping the villagers. Then—it was less clear how, and yet he didn't doubt it because he knew his father—the earl had had her thrown in prison for failing to help the villagers.

And then, he had let her out of prison on condition that she kidnap Charl.

That was the part that had set his mind awhirl.

It couldn't be true. Could it?

But why would she confess to it in her last letter to Agnes if it wasn't true? And she hadn't . . . She *hadn't* kidnapped him. They were here together, but it had been Agnes's idea. Was that merely a lucky (or unlucky) coincidence? Then why had she brought him here and not taken him, kicking and screaming, back to Uchtburg?

Well, he had brought her, actually. And then she'd gotten sick, and they'd gone nowhere.

Odd things began coming back to him now. All her talk about what a good priest he'd make—his mother and Agnes had surely never discussed this with her; he had always thought that was far-fetched. So, then, had Mother Trude merely been trying to lure him to somewhere his father could more easily reach him?

He remembered now how Mother Trude had spoken to the dragon in the turnip field, saving Charl's life. But that dragon, who had burned half the town trying to get at him, was also working for his father. Same with the man with the scar, who'd captured his mother and helped the plague destroy St. Muckle's.

They were all three working for his monstrous father, ultimately.

He felt a bit sick, thinking about it.

He wished he'd never read the letter, but he forced himself to look at it again, to scour it for some sign of regret. There was plenty of that, in fact. He could count the times she said she was sorry: four. Strangely, the word seemed to lose power the more she said it.

What he really wanted, though, and what he didn't find, was proof that she had thought of Charl as a friend, because that was how he had thought of her.

But if she was his friend, then he should ask her about these things, give her a chance to explain. And he should do it soon, because he might not get another chance.

She was dying. Nobody deserved to die alone.

He made his way back to the refectory. As he approached, suddenly Anya and Zedig appeared in his path, frantic energy swirling around them like a corona.

"Turn back," they cried together. "Don't go in there, Charl!"

Oh no. No.

He could only think of one thing that could have happened. With shaking hands, he shoved the letter into his pocket. Then he wrapped his sash around his mouth and nose, tied it tightly, and rushed past the two ghosts, convinced the worst had already come to pass.

26

Brus

ut Mother Trude wasn't dead.

She lay in the same place as before, along the back wall, but her hands and feet had been bound together. A swath of fabric was tied over her mouth and nose. When she saw Charl, she began to whimper.

Twenty feet away from her sat a rough-looking man with a scar through his left eyebrow. The man Charl had seen while flying with Ognielle. The man his mother had called Jarlbrus.

Jarlbrus did not look as well as he had looked three days ago. His hair was lank and dirty; a patchy growth of beard shadowed his face. His clothes had mud and ash ground into them. One sleeve was torn in jagged slashes, like he'd run heedlessly through the forest—or like the dragon had clawed him. Dark circles under his eyes suggested that he hadn't slept in days.

The worst part, which made Charl hurt when he saw it, was the man's right thigh. The fabric of his breeches had been burned away, revealing a large patch of blackened skin, which had begun to peel away from the angry, red flesh beneath. The wound oozed yellow, and stank.

The man looked up as Charl approached; his haunted, feverish gaze suggested that he had seen terrible things.

Sympathy was Charl's first reaction. He had to remind himself that this ragged, desperate-looking person—however pitiable he seemed now—had held Mama at sword's point. And there was the not-insignificant matter of Mother Trude, tied up and gagged. Jarlbrus was surely the one who'd stolen their food—who else could it have been?—and it seemed likely he'd moved the crates of pyria as well.

Anya and Zedig's warnings came back to Charl, and he realized what they'd been trying to tell him before. Jarlbrus was the wolf who'd sneaked through the sally door when everyone was sleeping.

Charl drew his short sword and pointed it at the man's face.

"Put your weapon away, little master," said Jarlbrus, looking at Charl with narrowed eyes. "I'm not here to hurt *you*."

"You've tied up my friend," said Charl, keeping the sword raised. "Let her go."

"Your *friend*? Oh, well done, Irmentrude. You've gotten him to trust you, without any inkling that he shouldn't," said Jarlbrus, smirking. "It would be extremely unwise to untie her, little master. She's coughing up gray, as you are clearly aware."

The man waited expectantly. When Charl didn't put the sword away, Jarlbrus sighed heavily. "We've gotten off on the wrong foot, clearly. My name is Jarlbrus—"

"I know your name," snapped Charl. "And I know you're a lackey of my father's, sent to destroy everything we've worked for and drag us back against our wills. I know you captured my mother already. What have you done with her? I want to see her."

Jarlbrus's eyes seemed to harden into two diamonds. "You know a startling amount—I am most curious as to *how*—but you seem not to have heard that your mother was taken from me."

Charl felt his throat closing. "B-by the dragon?"

"By that other notorious lackey of your father's, Sir Aris."

The weight lifting off of Charl's heart nearly staggered him. He could almost laugh at the insult to Aris.

"It remains to be seen whether he can keep the dragon from snatching her back," Jarlbrus continued peevishly. "But that's all right. Let them distract Miga as long as they can; I've found you, and you are worth more than any other part of this job. It would have been nicer to have the entire bounty to myself, I admit, but some is better than none, and foiling Miga is its own reward."

"How much is my father paying you?" said Charl. There had been gold in the sanctuary—gold leaf, anyway, which would have to be painstakingly scraped off. He couldn't imagine the ghost of Bishop Marcellus standing idly by and letting him take it.

Jarlbrus rolled his eyes. "Your mother asked the same thing. What a pair of connivers you are! You can't afford it—let me put it that way—even if you found a hidden monastic treasure hoard. Your father wants you back, you must understand. He loves you."

Before Jarlbrus could say another word, Charl had pressed the sword to his throat, to a soft little spot just below his jawline.

Jarlbrus did not flinch. A smile crept slowly across his face.

"You seem to have doubts," he said. "I guess 'loves' was laying it on a bit thick. But he's prepared to tolerate you. Attempts to produce another heir, in the years since your mother left, have failed dismally. He's come round to the idea that you are the only son he's ever going to have, and he's prepared to behave accordingly. You'll have a good life at the court of Ucht. You'll be treated like a prince, I assure you. You can practice swords all day, and no one will care."

His words were a mocking echo of the last argument Charl had had with his mother before the dragon attacked, and they seemed to stab him right in the heart.

Oh, please let that not be the last thing he ever said to her.

The pain must have shown on Charl's face, because Jarlbrus's grin sharpened into something wolflike. "You're not the only one good at spying, *prince*."

"What if I killed you?" Charl snarled through clenched teeth. His heart was beating so rapidly that his entire body seemed to vibrate.

Jarlbrus only seemed to grow colder and calmer. "What if you did? Let's think that through. How old are you, lad?"

"Th-thirteen," said Charl. His teeth were chattering, and his hand was shaking.

"And how old would you *like* to be someday?" said Jarlbrus, still perfectly calm.

Charl thought of the oldest person he knew: His maternal grandmother . . . No! His father. How old would he be, after all these years? Doing the arithmetic seemed to slow his pulse.

"Sixty-eight," said Charl.

Jarlbrus gave a low whistle. "Wisely chosen. Venerable, indeed. Older than I'll ever be, if I die today. However, consider that if you kill me now . . . Let's see, how much longer would you live on after that? . . . Can I work this in my head?"

"Fifty-five years," said Charl. His throat felt raw, as if he'd been screaming.

"Fifty-five," Jarlbrus agreed. "That's a long time to live as a murderer. You will carry me everywhere you go, a weight crushing your heart. I will be with you, haunting you, always."

Maybe he didn't mean it literally. Maybe he meant Charl would carry the *guilt* forever, but Charl had seen enough of the dead to know that Jarlbrus's oozing, unwashed ghost might really follow him the rest of his life. Charl's arm drooped; his sword lowered.

And in one swift movement, Jarlbrus grabbed the blade with his left hand and struck Charl's forearm roughly with his right, disarming him. Jarlbrus aimed the sword back toward Charl's chest.

Charl sputtered indignantly; Jarlbrus shrugged. "You didn't ask me how I knew what it was like to be a murderer."

"I didn't have to ask," said Charl bitterly. "It was always clear."

In the corner, Mother Trude moaned, struggling against her bonds again.

"Don't forget it," said Jarlbrus, withdrawing the sword and leaning his head back against the wall. "Of course, you're clever enough to have already deduced that I mustn't harm a hair of your curly head. I can't say the same for old Irmentrude here. She is utterly dispensable and, inconveniently, in my way."

Mother Trude began weeping. Charl could not let this continue. He stepped between Jarlbrus and the old nun with his hands raised. "Leave her alone. She's sick."

"Oh, relax," Jarlbrus snapped. A grimace of pain crossed his face, as if he had overtaxed himself. "Why should I do what nature will accomplish on its own in a few days? I won't harm her, unless you make me." Jarlbrus leaned over, stretching an arm toward Mother Trude, grabbed the corner of her blanket, which she'd kicked off in all her thrashing, and pulled it away. He tucked it around himself, except for his burnt leg, which he left out in the open air.

"Here's what's going to happen," said Jarlbrus, leaning back again and closing his eyes. "We'll lie low here for a few more days, until I'm well enough to walk again. That means no signaling for help, no letting the dragon know we're here, no running off or trying to kill me." He opened one eye again. "Try anything funny, and your Dr. Caramus won't get the supplies he needs to cure the good people of St. Muckle's."

Oh no. Charl looked around frantically, but his eyes only confirmed what Jarlbrus had said. The crates of herbs and resin were gone.

"You won't find them without me," said Jarlbrus. "So you're going to do as I say, and help get me on my feet again."

"Never," said Charl, folding his arms.

Jarlbrus sighed. "You are exhausting. You don't seem to appreciate, child, that your father is determined to have you home, by hook or by crook, and I am your best option. You can't go back to St. Muckle's: It's in ruins, and everyone blames your mother. I saw to that. This nun is going to die. Miga is . . . well, a *dragon,* and every unfeeling and untrustworthy thing that goes with it. You won't be safe with her, no matter what she says. You can cooperate with me, or the dragon can take you—those are your only real choices. Now help me make a bread poultice."

Under Jarlbrus's exacting instruction (and watchful eye), Charl made a poultice for the man's burnt leg. Jarlbrus, the rat, had stolen a loaf of bread for precisely this purpose, to let several slices grow damp and moldy with a particular blue-green mold. (The rest he'd eaten, along with all the jam and butter. And an entire cheese.)

The poultice turned out to be a kind of paste, which Jarlbrus insisted on applying himself. He spread it on his burnt flesh—wincing and cursing as he did so—and then wrapped it up in old linen he'd found somewhere. Charl didn't mind not being entrusted with this particular task; he felt faint just looking at the oozing wound.

When Jarlbrus had finished, he took a swig from a silver flask tucked into the front of his doublet. Pisky, was Charl's guess, to kill the pain. Charl went over to the fire and started some lentils.

The sun had set by the time the lentils were cooked. Charl picked at his, but Jarlbrus wolfed down two full bowls as if all the food he'd stolen had done little to fill his belly. Charl washed their bowls and then refilled one of them.

"Hey, what are you doing?" called Jarlbrus as Charl picked his way from the fire pit to Mother Trude's corner. "Don't waste food on her. She'll be dead by tomorrow."

"Not dead of neglect," muttered Charl. Not if he could help it.

Jarlbrus made a move, like he was going for the sword. Then he acted like he was going to get up and come after Charl.

However, he did neither thing, too hurt or too afraid of the gray to come any nearer to the old nun's corner.

Charl retied his sash over his face and knelt beside her. "I'm not going to let you starve," he whispered to Mother Trude, bending over to uncover her face.

Her skin was red and blotchy where the cloth had been; her lips were dry and cracked.

"Charl," said the old nun tremulously as he brought the spoon to her mouth, "Charl, I'm so sorry. Please let me explain—"

"Explain what? What a greedy hag you are?" drawled Jarlbrus from the other corner. "It's deplorable enough when a dissolute goat like myself will do anything for money, but you're supposed to be a woman of faith. Aren't you ashamed?"

"Don't answer him. Just eat," Charl murmured. "You don't need to explain. I read your note to Sister Agnes."

Tears welled up in Mother Trude's eyes; she could barely hold up her head. It was all Charl could do to coax three bites into her and a couple swallows of water. He left a full cup of water beside her and didn't replace the swath of fabric around her face.

"You're not going to leave her like that?" cried Jarlbrus.

"You're safe over there," said Charl. "Probably."

Jarlbrus, looking disgusted, rose unsteadily and staggered farther away from Mother Trude's corner. He dragged his pilfered blanket toward the fire pit and flopped onto one of the straw pallets—Charl's bed, of course. Charl sighed and started washing the dishes.

He had to get rid of this man. Maybe when Jarlbrus fell asleep, he could steal the sword back. He'd have to tie Jarlbrus up, first, to be sure. Charl could easily imagine that going wrong. He scrubbed and fretted.

"Little *prince*," said Jarlbrus, cutting across Charl's thoughts. He'd pulled the flask back out of his jacket. "Take a swig of this, since you insist on foolishly tending the dying."

"What is it?" asked Charl warily, but Jarlbrus didn't answer.

Charl sniffed at it. It smelled . . . perfumed. Floral and piney. Unforgettable.

Like chiromastic, that sweet-smelling resin the Porphyrians had brought for Dr. Caramus.

Jarlbrus was carrying around a cure for the plague.

The man gestured with his chin. "Drink. I get nothing for bringing you home dead."

And with that, Charl took a swig and swallowed it down.

27

The Plan

"I need to go outside," said Charl.

"What for?" said Jarlbrus, narrowing his eyes. When Charl didn't answer right away, the brigand seemed to guess. "Fine," he conceded. "I wouldn't want to pee in front of a nun, either. I know you won't go far. I've got Dr. Caramus's herbs, after all, and you've got your mother's overdeveloped conscience."

"Better than none at all," croaked Mother Trude from afar.

Jarlbrus picked up a stick of firewood and threw it at her.

Charl dashed off before Jarlbrus could change his mind—or before Mother Trude could goad the man into changing it. Charl needed air and space to think.

Jarlbrus seemed to hold all the cards. He had the cure, a sword, Caramus's herbs, and possibly pyria stashed somewhere. And he had Mother Trude's life in his hands.

And what did Charl have?

Ghosts.

He walked toward the entrance yard. He had an apple in his pocket, as he always did now. (He had a fleeting vision of himself as an old man, still with an apple in his pocket.) He grasped it firmly and thought of Maeve.

"I'm not supposed to talk to you," said her voice in his ear.

"That didn't stop you before," said Charl, turning toward the sound.

The yard was empty. The pale birches swayed in the breeze.

"Anyway, I need your help," said Charl. "You've seen that man? Jarlbrus?"

"I haven't," said disembodied Maeve. "But Anya and Zedig saw him arrive the other night, while you and the townsfolk were sleeping. And they saw him eating your food."

"Well, did they see where he hid those boxes the Porphyrians left?"

There was a pause. "They did not," said Maeve. "But there are places we can't go, and places we dare not go. He'd have a lot of hiding places to choose from, really."

Charl's heart sank, but no matter—he would search on his own. Jarlbrus couldn't keep an eye on him every minute.

If he lingered here too long, though, Jarlbrus would get suspicious. Charl turned to head back, but Anya and Zedig popped into existence in front of him, looking fretful. "He wants to take you back to your father," said the smaller of the two. "We can't let that happen!"

"How do you know what that villain wants?" Now Maeve appeared, hands on her hips. "Did you haunt him? Vilna, are you hearing this?"

"We didn't! We were eavesdropping, that's all."

Vilna appeared, then the squirrel and the martin, and then even Princess Luti was there, a swarm of ghosts all around Charl.

Vilna had a worried look on her narrow face; her big black eyes looked searchingly at Charl. "Is this true?" she said. She spoke so softly that the others quieted all around, trying to hear what she was saying. "I saw your memories. Your father . . . loomed rather large."

That was a polite way of putting it. Charl was suddenly struck by an arrow of grief that made his eyes well up. He couldn't find his voice.

"All right. Plan: haunt the living daylights out of this Jarlbrus," said Maeve grimly.

"Absolutely not," said Princess Luti, putting her arms around Anya and Zedig and drawing them closer to her. "We swore an oath. Some of us take that seriously."

Vilna's brows drew together fretfully. "Charl is our friend."

"No!" cried Luti. "He's *not*. You ran into him accidentally and saw his insides—that doesn't make you friends. You got a taste of life and are looking for any excuse to have another."

Vilna looked abashed, but Maeve puffed up her chest indignantly and snapped, "Ye gods, Luti, will you stop with the self-righteous—"

"You have no right to say anything," Princess Luti barked back. "You haunted two people the other night and came home practically drunk with it!"

"Did someone say 'drunk'?" said a voice from the well. "Because I had an idea, if anybody wants to hear it."

Charl and the girls all turned to see the ghost of Wort,

elbows propped on the rim of the well, grinning at them. He gave a little wave and tossed his transparent sheepdog curls out of his eyes. "Hello, ladies," he said, nodding. "As I was saying, Charl—here's my idea. Get the man drunk, and when he's sound asleep, tie him up. I don't know where it's hidden, but Rafe found some pisky up here somewhere. That'd do the trick, if he likes pisky."

Charl felt a stab in his heart. "It wasn't pisky, Wort. Rafe was mistaken. It was pyria."

Wort got a distant look in his eyes. "Well, cack. That makes more sense, I guess." He slipped back down into the well.

Princess Luti made a disgusted noise and disappeared; Anya and Zedig, ever bashful, faded into the birches. The squirrel capered off, and the martin fluttered. Only Vilna and Maeve were still visible, and they were staring at each other, hard.

"It's too dangerous," said Vilna.

"He was already in there once, and he survived," said Maeve.

"That won't happen twice."

"What are we talking about?" asked Charl, dread creeping up his spine.

Maeve's face grew a bit more pointed, like a fox's, so sly was her expression. "In a cupboard, behind the altar of the sanctuary, the bishops always kept a stash of brandy."

"Do you think it's still there?" said Charl.

"Mm-hmm," said Maeve, looking pleased with herself.

"And you think I can steal from the Battle Bishop without getting caught and losing my mind?" asked Charl.

Maeve looked less certain now. She flicked her gaze toward Vilna. Vilna sighed.

"If he catches you, it will be a hundred times worse than when I touched you," said Vilna. "I was trying *not* to touch you, and released you as quickly as possible. He will have no such qualms. He will grasp you as tightly as he can and not let go."

"So how do I escape his notice?" asked Charl.

"No one escapes his notice. If he didn't grab you the first time you went in there, it's because you took him by surprise. He'll be ready this time."

"So then . . . what can I do?" Charl's heart seemed to be sinking into the ground.

"First, remember that everything you're experiencing is merely a memory," said Vilna firmly. "It's over, and in the past. Second, push back. He has memories of his own, which you can use against him. I've seen his mind, all the way down to the bottom, and it is a terrible place. He has the blood of thousands on his hands. He was not the first of his faith to declare that all pagans must convert, but he was the first to start killing those who would not."

"He razed one hundred sixty-one villages," said Maeve, her voice flat. "Over ten thousand people. Two hundred and eight he killed himself."

Charl couldn't fathom this. "There aren't ten thousand pagans in the whole world."

"Not anymore, there aren't," said Vilna. "Not who will admit to it, anyway. The village burning still happens, wherever a whole village can be found. Wherever people are careless about pretending to have converted."

"But are you listening to what she's telling you?" burst in Maeve. "When he makes you remember your pain, remind him of his. Call him a butcher and a monster. Fight back."

"He never used to have regrets, but he's had time to learn some," said Vilna. "Not enough, or he wouldn't still be here, but maybe enough to let you—"

"Boy, you have until the count of five!" Her plea had been cut short by Jarlbrus, shouting.

"Cack," said Maeve, who'd apparently picked that word up from Wort. "You'd better get back. Go fetch the brandy later, when you can."

They popped out of sight and hearing, into the ether, or wherever they went when they disappeared. Charl hurried back to the refectory.

"Looking for the herbs?" said Jarlbrus when Charl arrived.

"Of course," said Charl. Jarlbrus would not have believed him if he'd said no.

"I figured. Next time, I'm going to carve a slice off of Irmentrude here. You understand me? Poop at double speed, or she pays the price."

In the far corner, Mother Trude didn't even whimper, too sick to raise her head.

Charl realized then that he had one chance to save her life: he needed Jarlbrus's flask of chiromastic. The sword, important as it was, came second to that. And he couldn't put it off. He had to go after that brandy as soon as he could.

However difficult getting around the Battle Bishop would be, finding a way to give Jarlbrus the slip again was going to be nearly as hard.

Charl put another pot of lentils on the fire and sat stirring it, watching and waiting for his chance.

28

The Bishop's Gambit

That chance was a long time coming. Jarlbrus, although it clearly hurt him to do so, got up and followed every time Charl said he had to answer nature's call. When Charl complained, Jarlbrus said, "Get used to it. When we travel back to Uchtburg, I don't intend to let you out of my sight even for a moment."

Night fell, and even then Charl could not sneak out. Jarlbrus slept in the doorway, the sword clasped to his chest.

Charl climbed onto the food storage trunk and tried to climb out one of the broken windows, but he ended up knocking out a shard of glass. It shattered, waking Jarlbrus, who shouted: "Get back to bed this instant. Don't make me tie you up."

It was odd, Charl thought, as he crawled back under his blanket, that he wasn't tied up already. But he wasn't about to ask why. Jarlbrus would surely take it as a suggestion.

It became clearer the next morning: Somebody needed to

stoke the fire and make breakfast. And lunch. Whatever excuses Charl came up with—he needed more water, he needed apples—Jarlbrus hobbled after him, using the sword as a makeshift cane.

The more time passed, the worse Mother Trude got, and the more desperate Charl felt. He took one last gamble: he purposefully tripped over his own feet and sent a pot full of hot oatmeal flying toward Jarlbrus. Charl had been aiming for the man's face, but the projectile porridge fell short and hit his leg.

His bad leg.

Jarlbrus screamed, and flailed around for something, anything, to wipe it off with.

"Oh, cack, sorry!" cried Charl. "I'll fetch some wash water."

He snatched up the bucket and ran in the direction of the well. As soon as he was out of sight, however, he turned right and then right again to circle behind the refectory. He heard loud cursing and clumsy footsteps, but he pressed himself against the refectory wall until Jarlbrus had staggered past, moving quickly for a man in pain.

Charl moved quickly as well. He did not want to be here when Jarlbrus got back—not without a bottle of brandy in his hand. He hoped Maeve and Vilna were right and the brandy was still there, and still good after all these years.

If it wasn't there . . . well, he'd have a choice to make. He could come back, get tied up, and watch Mother Trude die, or he could take his chances running away.

Mother Trude still died in the second scenario. However complicated that letter had made things, her death was going to weigh on him if he ran off and let it happen.

The sanctuary gleamed in the afternoon sun, its limestone

walls polished to an unnatural sheen. How was it the only part of the Abbey still intact? Charl fretted that Jarlbrus would look for him here—it seemed the obvious place to go, the most obvious place in the whole complex.

Come, it seemed to say.

It *did* say. He'd been hearing a voice all along, he now realized. It wasn't his imagination.

He was expected, apparently.

He stepped up to the doors, but before he could open them, another voice said, "Charl."

Maeve stood behind him, barely visible, little more than a shimmer in the air. He was almost her height, standing one step up.

"Are you coming in with me?" he whispered, putting a hand on his pocket. The apple was still there.

"I dare not," said Maeve. "Ognielle used to say a ghost of that sort—a monstrous soul—can harm even other ghosts. So I wanted . . . I don't know what I wanted."

She looked away, clearly flustered, and Charl understood. She was worried about him.

"If Vilna thinks this could work, surely there's a chance," he said.

"I know," said Maeve. "I'm trying to remember that. But you don't know how long it's been since we had someone new and friendly to talk to, and I just . . . You're our friend, I hope you realize, whatever sour old Luti said."

"I didn't take that personally," said Charl, smiling a little at her now. "She's hungry."

Maeve nodded, with a shaky intake of breath that made Charl wonder. Ghosts didn't actually breathe, did they? It was a leftover habit from being alive, probably.

And then she swooped in and kissed him on the cheek, the lightest, coldest kiss imaginable. He experienced no sudden flash of memory, and so he suspected that she hadn't really touched him but had come as close as she could to it.

His cheek burned with cold; he put a hand to the spot.

"That's for luck," she said, before disappearing in a puff of embarrassment.

Charl smiled at the space where she'd been. "Thank you," he said, sure she would hear.

And then he turned back to the daunting task before him.

He pulled on the handles, and once again the sanctuary doors glided open easily. Soundlessly.

Everything inside was as Charl remembered—the cadaver tomb, the statuary, the altar. The candles had been relit; no speck of dust seemed to have fallen in the centuries since the place was abandoned. Only the missing kneeler cushion revealed that anyone had been here.

The opulence struck him differently, though, now that he had some inkling what the Battle Bishop had done while he was alive. Everything glowed blood-red in the light from the stained-glass windows. The dark wood took on a sinister aspect. How much of this treasure was stolen? Surely nobody razed villages to the ground before taking whatever there was to take.

Charl didn't spend too long wondering. He had to get in and out. If it was too much to ask that the murderous ghost not notice him, maybe he could outrun it. Vilna's plan had sounded vague and uncertain enough that he hoped he wouldn't have to try it.

He didn't see the ghost's shadow anywhere.

Charl tiptoed up the aisle, pausing at each gilded column (as if he could blend in) and looking around again. Nothing stirred; the candles didn't even flicker. His feet echoed on the tiles, so he tried to make them sound like the scurrying of mice, or the skittering of leaves.

He reached the altar. To get behind it, he had to take two steps up onto the dais.

The first step squeaked appallingly.

Charl froze. Nothing happened.

He let himself exhale.

The second step was silent. Charl could see the back side of the altar now, the cabinet Maeve had mentioned. A green door with a silver handle.

Charl knelt and reached for the handle.

Another hand appeared from nowhere—a large, rough hand, with hairy knuckles. It grabbed Charl's hand and wrapped its icy fingers tightly around.

Charl screamed as bad memories closed in over his head. It was like being plunged into cold, black water.

Rafe kicking him in the ribs behind the stables, until Lord Vasterich arrived. No time to feel grateful, however—his lordship slapped Rafe hard across the face "for beating up a girl."

Mama, her jaw swollen so she couldn't even smile. "Merely an infected tooth. Too many sweets," she said. But it was a broken tooth, and it was the earl who broke it.

Charl gasped for air. None of this was happening now. The ghost was making him relive it.

Mama, at the Fiddle, cleaning him up after a fight: "We came here for you. I put my own life in danger—for you. The least you could do is show a little gratitude."

"Not only for me. You weren't any safer than I was, in Uchtburg," Charl cried, but memory dragged him under again.

Charl, age six, standing before his father's throne. "You're no son of mine," said the earl, his sallow face contorted into a rictus of disgust. "I should have drowned you in the well at birth."

"At least I'm not a murderer," Charl wheezed into the empty sanctuary. His breath steamed in the cold. "Not a village burner or a baby killer."

Are you really not a murderer, though? a voice echoed in his head.

Hooey bursting into flames. Fire everywhere, body parts falling from the sky. Wort burning, screaming, his arms flailing. Charl ran toward Wort, but his legs seemed to move slowly, like running through honey. Wort only seemed to get farther and farther away, until he plunged himself into the well. Charl reached the well, after what seemed like an age, and the water was boiling and steaming. Wort had been cooked like a dumpling.

Charl sank to his knees, sobbing. It was too painful. He didn't have the strength to push back or strong enough weapons to push back with. Vilna had been wrong about—

Abruptly, the tempest in his mind stopped.

Charl was on all fours, panting, weeping. He was vaguely aware of a figure looming over him. Two feet appeared before him, and the transparent hem of a robe.

"Vilna, did you say?" said a voice, like the one he'd heard in his head, but rougher. Unused to speaking.

Charl looked up at the ghost—not the menacing shadow he'd encountered before, but man-shaped and only a little transparent. Bishop Marcellus resembled the alabaster statue on top of his tomb. A ghostly version of his great-sword was strapped across his back; his white tabard had St. Ogdo's ring emblazoned on the front. His tidy beard was pointed at the end, the tips of his mustache curled, and on his head he wore a chain-mail coif, a hood that draped over his shoulders. The two smoking pits had been replaced by ordinary eyes—pale and drooping, framed by shaggy brows.

"Vilna?" the ghost repeated. "You've seen her? How is she? And the others?"

Charl realized then that pushing back had succeeded—pushing back with Vilna's name, that is, not with vague accusations. He wiped his eyes on his sleeve and said, "You knew her. Back when you were alive."

"Of course I knew her," snapped the old ghost. "I knew all of them, in some fashion. Some better than others. They were hard to get away from. But tell me how they are. I can do little enough to make up for all I've done, after two centuries, but I might be able to do something for them."

"Vilna said you would have regrets," said Charl. It was such a relief not to be in pain anymore that his tongue seemed loosened in his mouth. "She said you were a monstrous murderer."

"I was," said the bishop wearily. "That is, I *am*. That's not something you ever stop being, once you are one. The stain doesn't wash away, and in my case, I have the special distinction of having inspired generations of murderers. Your own father still follows my heartless example, slaughtering pagans—I noticed that in your mind."

Charl felt a bloom of shame rising in his chest. "My father is cruel enough to have invented it himself."

"You worry about becoming like him," said the bishop, his eyes narrowing. "I could have tortured you with that. You're a monster's son, with a monster's blood in your veins."

Something was happening to his face as he considered this. His eyes blackened, and his head became wispy, like smoke.

"Vilna was your favorite, then?" said Charl hastily. Clearly, this ghost was still not entirely harmless. Mentioning Vilna was the only defense Charl had against him.

Bishop Marcellus snapped back into focus and leaned heavily against the altar, which propped him up as if he were solid. "Vilna was . . . special. That's why she was bound, even though she was only a child—she was already a sage, like the older two."

"Iphi and Ognielle," Charl offered.

The ghost smiled wryly. "Iphi could speak to dragons, and Ognielle could travel outside her body—but you surely know that, if you've been talking to them. Vilna was a Wise Child, wise beyond her years. She had a cancer in her blood, and would not have survived much longer, so rather than lose her insights, they bound her to the circle.

"Of course, that changed the nature of the circle. Seeing the ghost of a child there made later people believe that sacrificing little girls was what the circle was *for*. Princess Luti offered herself up to secure a peace treaty."

"With . . . with whom? Our people?" asked Charl.

Bishop Marcellus rolled his eyes at this. "Those girls lived well before the Age of Saints, boy. Princess Luti made peace between two pagan tribes; it lasted a hundred years. Anya was offered as a gift to the gods; Zedig was offered in the next generation, since Anya's death seemed to have brought such boons. Maeve was killed in an act of desperation, not long before we built the monastery."

"What did you do to them, though?" asked Charl. "They all seem to hate and fear you—Vilna included."

The bishop's shaggy brows drooped. "I tried to destroy their circle; I purposefully built this abbey on top of it. Those girls defended themselves admirably, however. They drove my monks mad, tormented them, until we planted the orchard and stopped trying to move their rocks around. I thought they were devils from the Infernum, and I kept devising ways to exorcise them. Even when Vilna tried to make me understand, I wouldn't listen. I, in my arrogance, refused to believe a dead girl when she spoke of the afterlife. But she was right.

"I killed thousands, thinking it was the will of Heaven. But Heaven is not what I thought it was, and whatever that is—the Blue Land, she used to call it—even that is forbidden to me."

Bishop Marcellus stared mournfully, tragically, as if he were peering into the void of his own heart.

Charl had so many questions about all of this, but he couldn't ask right now. He'd come here for a reason; there was something he needed. Every passing moment was a moment Jarlbrus might be hurting Mother Trude.

"I'm here because Mother Trude is dying," he began.

"That nun? I saw her in your mind," said the bishop. "You feel terribly guilty about that. You feel guilty about a lot of things you shouldn't. That boy in the well. Even Rafe could not have predicted he would die."

So he *had* encountered Rafe. That confirmed it.

"You even feel guilty about Rafe," continued the ghost, a bit of vapor rising from his head. "You wanted him to be hurt. You rejoiced in it."

Cack. The bishop's monstrous nature was reasserting itself, but Charl couldn't stay here chatting about Vilna. Time was wasting. He said, "Is there still brandy?"

"There is," said Bishop Marcellus, his outline sharpening again. "And you may take it, perhaps—if you deign to answer the question I asked you."

Charl couldn't remember any question.

"How *are* they?" the ghost cried impatiently. "They don't visit. Not that I blame them."

Apparently, Bishop Marcellus couldn't see all Charl's memories, just the terrible ones.

Charl puffed air through his cheeks, considering. On the one hand, he didn't like giving the bishop information about the girls, since they didn't like him; on the other hand, the angry ghost couldn't seem to leave the sanctuary. "They're mostly fine. Iphi and Ognielle have . . . faded?"

The bishop's face fell. "Oh no. That's your idea of *fine*?"

"Fading is the goal for all of them now," said Charl defensively, "although some are keener on it than others. Won't they be free of their bond when they finally—"

"No, they will not be free, just blissfully unaware of their bondage," snapped the bishop. "Believe me, I've been tempted myself. No more regrets. No more burning ego. But that's not how they reach the Blue Lands. They must be released from their bonds—*all* of them. I have spent a century meditating upon this, and I may know a way. This is what I meant; the one thing I can still do for them—"

Bishop Marcellus cut off midsentence and turned even paler, if such a thing were possible. "You need to leave," he said. "My soul is fragmented into three parts: the Man Who Reasons has been ascendant this half hour, but the Monster Who Rages is always roiling just below the surface."

Charl waited a moment, thinking the bishop was about to name the third part of his soul, but the ghost snapped, "Take your brandy—now!—and promise you'll return, for I have . . ."

His face blurred and his eyes darkened before coming into focus again.

"I have instructions for you . . . how to help them . . ." He sounded like he was in pain.

"I'll come back, I promise," said Charl.

"I know you will. You are your mother's son, whatever your fears may tell you," said the bishop, melting into something that looked like a storm cloud.

Charl quickly opened the cabinet door. There were several bottles, but their contents had evaporated over the centuries, right through the corks. Only a crystal decanter with a glass stopper still had amber liquid in it. Charl grabbed the vessel and stood up . . .

In a ruin. The walls were rubble, the ceiling long gone. No trace of gold or candles or incense remained.

Charl felt utterly discombobulated, as if he had awoken from a dream. But no—he was clearly in the Old Abbey. The sun was setting, painting the tops of the crumbling buildings purple and orange. Only the sanctuary had changed: what had been pristine and intact was now decayed and overgrown by ivy.

He wondered whether it had been all along.

"Charl!" called a voice from some distance off.

Brus, and he sounded really angry.

The cheek Maeve had kissed felt unexpectedly cold. Charl hoped that meant his luck still held.

29

Luck

Jarlbrus stood outside the refectory, bellowing Charl's name and various outrageous threats. Charl circled around so that he seemed to be returning from the direction of the well.

"Where have you been?" shouted Jarlbrus.

"I spotted this earlier," said Charl, holding up the crystal bottle. "I thought it might help dull your pain."

"Liar! You were looking for the crates, after I told you not to," cried the old spymaster, swinging the short sword at Charl. It was a clumsy, unbalanced swing—the best he could manage with his injured leg—and Charl dodged it easily.

"Careful," said Charl, shaking the brandy bottle. "You know how prone I am to tripping and spilling things."

Now that he was closer, Jarlbrus could see exactly what he had in his hand. The older man's eyes locked onto the bottle. "Where the devil did you find that?"

"In the old dormitory," said Charl, thrusting the bottle at him.

"Liar," said Jarlbrus again, but he was too busy grabbing the bottle to grab at Charl.

Charl slipped past into the refectory. He quickly looked to the far end, to see how Mother Trude was doing. She was curled up in a ball; he couldn't even tell if she was breathing.

"I haven't touched a hair of her miserable head," said Jarlbrus. "No thanks to you. I should have sliced her to ribbons you've been gone so long."

A groan arose from the blanket, followed by more dusty coughing. She was hanging on.

Charl turned toward Jarlbrus again, to invite him to have some brandy, but the man had already plopped himself down and pulled the stopper out with his teeth. He spat it out onto the ground, took a swig of the amber liquid, and burst out coughing.

"Saints' farts, that's strong!" he wheezed, but he looked delighted.

Charl sat warily on the other side of the fire, never taking his eyes off Jarlbrus. He wasn't sure how much brandy it would take to put the man into a sound, careless sleep. The fact that it was strong might be encouraging, unless that meant he'd drink less of it as a result.

Jarlbrus turned the bottle this way and that, examining it against the firelight. "This is too good to waste on pain relief, but beggars can't be choosers." He took another swallow and didn't cough this time. "I should save some for later."

No, no no. "I saw another bottle," Charl lied.

"Did you? That's good news," said Jarlbrus, smiling slightly. He took another sip.

Charl had to keep the conversation going, keep Jarlbrus

talking so he'd stay thirsty. "How long have you worked for my father?" asked Charl, reaching for any plausible subject.

"Since I was not much older than you," said Jarlbrus. "So . . . forty years? Forty-four."

"What do you do for him?" said Charl. "I assume you'll be in my service when I'm earl."

Jarlbrus burst out laughing. "Not if I can help it," he said, stretching his legs out on the straw pallet and leaning back. "This is my last job, and then I mean to retire. Take up sheep farming, or eel fishing, or some innocuous thing. A wee cottage where I can drink good brandy and never worry about court intrigue or military maneuvers or—"

"Or burning villages to the ground!" cried Mother Trude, raising her head from her deathbed just to shout that at him.

"For the last time, woman," Jarlbrus shouted back, "I wasn't there at the destruction of Piss-Puddle, or whatever cesspit you grew up in. If our troops destroyed it, it must've been crawling with pagans. Maybe you were too young to realize. They probably didn't practice their sordid rites openly."

Mother Trude said nothing, but she wept hoarsely in her corner.

Jarlbrus had reclined again, the bottle tucked into the crook of his arm like a baby. Charl watched for signs of drowsiness, trying not to look like he was looking. But he couldn't help puckering his mouth in disgust.

"So was it good practice, destroying villages?" said Charl softly. "Is that what made you so efficient at destroying St. Muckle's?"

"There's a big difference—night and day," said Jarlbrus. "When I was a soldier, razing villages, I used whatever crude weapons were at my disposal. Only later, as your father's spymaster, did I perfect the art of letting a town destroy itself. Most towns will, with the right sort of nudge. I study the history, find the cracks, whisper in the right ears, and then watch things fall apart. St. Muckle's required more entomology than usual, but I appreciated the novelty.

"I leave brute force to the likes of Miga and Sir Aris." Jarlbrus was watching Charl carefully while he said this, and apparently he liked what he saw, because the wolfish look returned. "Maybe you don't realize what a cruel past your Aris has. After he gave up killing dragons, he became the scourge of pagans for a while. We could have eradicated them from the highlands altogether, if he hadn't gone lily-livered and soft on me. Or if he hadn't been lured by your mother into committing the greatest heist of all time: stealing you and her dowry from under my very nose."

Charl did a quick calculation in his head and decided Aris couldn't have burned down Mother Trude's village—he was two years older than Agnes, and Agnes was her daughter. It was still disturbing to learn of Aris's violent past, but then hadn't Aris always insisted that Mama had saved him? And wasn't he now the most peaceable man Charl knew?

Maybe murder was a stain that could never be washed away—and Charl was inclined to believe that Bishop Marcellus knew what he was talking about—but it seemed like Aris had kept washing, nonetheless. And he never stopped.

Jarlbrus gave a low chuckle, his eyes half shut now, his whole body loose. "Sweet mercy, that's better. You don't know what it is to feel a wound throbbing constantly, for days, all the way to the bone. Pray to the Saints you never do."

"The brandy numbs the pain?" asked Charl, trying to sound younger than he was, like he had only been trying to help.

"I don't know whether it makes the pain go away or whether it makes you just not care. Maybe both." His eyes fluttered closed, but his mouth did not stop talking. "Your harlot mother got away—and I don't care about that, either, see? Good brandy. At least I got *you* back. Your father shall have his heir. You shall have your pick of earlinas to marry, ha ha."

"Ha ha," said Charl, fed up with his taunts. "You are a horrible person."

Jarlbrus's haggard face split into a grin. "Whatever. Your father will be appeased, and then . . . it will be . . . out of his hands . . . by then . . ."

Charl held his breath, listening, as Jarlbrus's breathing slowed and deepened. The hand holding the brandy bottle twitched, and then abruptly relaxed. Charl dove forward and caught the bottle before it spilled everywhere, pulling it from Jarlbrus's unresisting fingers. The man muttered incoherently and seemed to try to stir himself to wakefulness, but sleep pulled him under again. Charl held up the bottle and saw that it was only half gone.

Good. More for later, if needed. He found the stopper and set the bottle out of the way.

Jarlbrus had flopped down in such a way that his flask was poking its silver nose out of his jacket front, almost begging to be plucked. Charl slid it out gently; Jarlbrus's deep breathing never altered.

Tying his sash around his mouth once more, Charl crept over to Mother Trude's corner. For a brief, horrifying minute, she seemed not to be breathing, but then she took a rattling, rasping breath. Charl shook her shoulder.

She opened her crusty eyes and blinked as if she didn't know who he was.

"Here," he whispered. "Drink this. It's a remedy."

Mother Trude struggled to sit up. Charl sat beside her, propped her head on his knees, and put the flask to her lips. A little trickle of liquid ran out of the corner of her mouth, but she got most of a mouthful down.

How much should he give her? How often? How fast would it work? *Would* it work?

Too many questions, and not enough answers. *A cure is sometimes also a poison,* Dr. Caramus had once told him, and that was the only thing that stopped Charl from making her drink every drop in one go.

Charl leaned back against the wall and prepared for another long night.

He dosed her every hour, by his best estimate. It was almost morning before she felt strong enough to speak, and then she mumbled as if talking in her sleep: "You should've grabbed the sword, too."

It hadn't occurred to him. That is, he'd longed to have the sword back, but when the time had come, he'd done nothing to get it. And that was odd, if he thought about it. Rafe had lured him up here by offering him a sword. He'd been a keen study of swordplay for years; he'd been sneaking in some sword practice before the dragon attacked. A sword was the one thing he'd asked of the Porphyrians.

And yet he'd made no attempt to take the sword back from Jarlbrus. He'd forgotten all about it.

"That sword won't get you well," he said quietly, unstoppering the flask one more time. "And it might make a murderer of me, and I don't think I can live with that."

"Plenty of other people do," said Mother Trude when she'd swallowed her medicine. "But I suspect you are choosing the wiser course."

Charl gingerly moved her head off of his knees; both his legs had fallen asleep, and he needed to stretch them. Mother Trude resettled herself without complaint. When he made as if to remove the sash from his face, however, she stopped him.

"Wait," she said. "I feel stronger, but I still have the burn in my lungs. I can't promise I don't have more gray to cough up. Would you bring me some water?"

He brought water and a pillow, and got her tucked in again and nicely comfortable.

Jarlbrus was still snoring. There were things Charl needed to know, an important conversation he'd had to put off, and he didn't know how much longer he had before Jarlbrus woke up.

"Were you really planning to take me back to my father?" asked Charl.

Mother Trude coughed, and as she'd feared, it was a dusty cough.

She lay silent a long while, thinking, before she spoke. "I owe you my life, Charl, so I owe you the truth. I would have taken you, yes. I know what it is to miss a child, to search for them unto the ends of the earth, to have them reject you without ever understanding the beating heart inside you. And I did not know the entire story, because it wasn't told to me." She coughed again. "And maybe . . . when I finally learned it, I didn't care, because I envied your mother."

"Envied her? For what?"

"Because she could hold her child, and I could not. Because my child loved her better than she loved me. Because I was hurting, so I wanted to hurt someone."

That, he understood. He felt a pang of empathy, but he could not let that distract him. He wasn't finished. She'd done wrong, and there were more hard questions that needed answers.

"So then all your talk about what a good priest I would make," said Charl, "was a ruse to convince me to go back with you?"

The silence seemed to lengthen interminably, until she finally whispered, "Yes."

"I see."

"But then I got to *know* you," she said, almost pleading. "I wouldn't force you to go to Uchtburg against your will *now*."

Charl stood up, his legs wobbly and sore, his feet full of pins and needles. "But you knew what my father was, all along. You knew he was the kind of man who hires dragon assassins and ruthless spymasters. The kind of man who would strong-arm you into letting a whole village be slaughtered and then let you go to prison for it, while he and his cronies went free. *That* is the parent you pitied, the monster you were willing to return me to."

"Yes." It was almost inaudible.

Charl still wasn't finished. "Sister Agnes was a nun of your order. Did she never ask you, her prioress, how to help a friend in need? The wife of an earl, who was in danger from him every day? And didn't she *leave* your convent to go help her friend, because she thought that would be a more effective way to do good in the world? You, on the other hand, chose the horrible earl, every time, over his terrorized family."

"I had no choice!"

Mother Trude was weeping now, interrupted occasionally by coughs. The coughs were growing less dusty, but Charl was too upset to feel properly glad about this.

"You did choose, though, and you chose wrong," said Charl, and—he couldn't help it—his voice was getting loud. "I thought we were friends. I don't know what to think now."

Charl's raised voice had awakened Jarlbrus, who now propped himself on an elbow and cried, "Stop screaming, boy! My head feels like it might burst."

Charl set the flask down quickly, where Mother Trude could reach it—Jarlbrus was bound to notice it missing soon—and then he grabbed the water bucket and rushed out before Jarlbrus could say anything else. He needed air, and space, and time to think.

He was angry with Mother Trude, angrier than he'd been when he'd first read the letter. He'd been too shocked to really feel it then, and also, she'd been at death's door. Now maybe she was going to live, and if she was going to live, she was going to have to live with what she'd done. She'd needed to know that he knew.

And that he'd considered her a friend. It looked like that was over now.

He kicked a rock across the courtyard as hard as he could. It ricocheted off one of the birch trees.

The last stars were fading. One very bright star—a planet, Dr. Caramus had once told him—lingered in the lightening sky above St. Muckle's.

It had been two days since Techys sent up that flare. He'd said to give Caramus three days to respond. Of course, he'd also assumed Mother Trude would be dead, that the boxes would be findable, and that Charl could start making the journey to town then.

If there was any town left.

Charl climbed the stone steps to the top of the wall and looked over the valley, as if he might see Dr. Caramus crossing the turnip fields.

Unsurprisingly, he did not see Dr. Caramus.

He did see the dragon Miga, however. She had wound herself around the spire of Allsaints, like a snake, and was keeping perfectly still.

Looking directly at him.

He had been preoccupied, and had forgotten to be careful.

The dragon launched herself into the sky. Her wings were a black silhouette against the dawn.

She flew directly toward the Old Abbey.

30

The Lady of the Birches

Maybe the dragon had seen the flare the Porphyrians had sent up and had been waiting ever since for someone to stir upon these walls. Dragons were famously patient. Could she tell who Charl was at that distance? She had definitely noticed that there was *someone* here.

And now she was coming. How quickly would she be here?

Charl rushed back down the stairs, his heart racing and his thoughts a jumble. *I should look for the pyria. I don't know how to use pyria. Anyway, Jarlbrus has hidden it somewhere, maybe with the herbs. And Jarlbrus has the sword.*

There was no time for any of that. The dragon was already arriving—a dark, terrible shadow across the sky. Charl ducked in among the spindly birch trees, the nearest cover. A sulfurous wind nearly pushed him to the ground as the dragon flew low overhead, trying to get a look at him or a sniff. His father had surely given her some old article of clothing to smell. She'd identified him already, in all likelihood.

Her scaly belly grazed the tops of the birches, bending them as she came in to land. Charl dropped to his knees and curled up, trying to be as small as possible.

Something winked on the ground in front of him. An opal ring. Hadn't Maeve mentioned such a thing, called it tragic and haunted? She'd told him not to look for it, and so he'd forgotten it existed until now. Charl grabbed the ring, not sure what he meant to do with it. It was not much of a treasure to distract a dragon with.

The dragon landed in the courtyard, flattening the weeds. She was a large specimen, her neck arching above the abbey walls, which suggested that she was very old. Her scales looked dark and rusty in the early light; in full sun they would've shown more iridescence. She folded her wings fastidiously, lifted her head, and sent a screaming shower of sparks skyward.

Charl wrapped his arms around his head and quaked, keeping his eyes on the ground. A pair of feet stepped into his field of vision. Translucent feet wearing translucent silk slippers.

Charl looked up, into the cool, blue gaze of the Lady of the Birches.

"Is that my ring?" she said, her voice tremulous. "But I'm wearing my ring. Look." She held out her hand, and Charl saw a ghostly ring on her finger, identical to the one in his hand.

"I have had strange dreams lately. Or . . . maybe not dreams. Why am I here?" she asked.

Behind her, the dragon roared again.

Charl tried to look only at the ghost; he could see the dragon right through her if he relaxed his focus even for an instant. "I believe you are dead, lady," he said.

The dragon screamed and sent out another jet of fire—skyward again. Clearly, she knew she'd get no bounty for bringing Charl back burnt. She edged closer, turning her head this way and that, as if trying to gauge the best way to stretch her neck in among the birches and snatch Charl in her jaws.

The Lady of the Birches seemed not to have noticed the dragon at all; indeed, it was surprising that she'd noticed Charl. A ghost of her type was not supposed to have that much awareness of her surroundings, but she'd not only seen him; she'd understood what he'd said. She looked sad and bewildered now, like someone who'd just learned that they're dead.

"I walked through a boy, and then a man, and I saw things," mused the lady. "Is it true that a century has passed, and we Amberfinches are no more? I'd hoped those were dreams."

"That happened. I saw you. And it's true," said Charl, edging backward, trying to keep the ghost between himself and the dragon. If the dragon tried to grab him, she'd have to pass through the ghost to do it, and maybe that would freeze her for a moment.

The dragon tensed, her neck coiled like a snake ready to strike. Charl stepped behind a cluster of birch trunks. Each one was too slender to conceal his whole body, but together they were like prison bars, and the dragon couldn't get through. At least, he hoped not.

The dragon darted her head into the birch grove and snapped a small sapling between her jaws. She spat out the broken tree and then snapped off another.

She might snap off every tree in this grove to get at him.

The Lady of the Birches, who'd been caught up in her own sorrow, noticed the desecration of her trees. The dragon darted in for another sapling—passing through the ghost's incorporeal form—and darted back out again, unhindered and unperturbed, as if nothing had happened.

Were dragons immune to haunting? That was unfortunate.

The Lady of the Birches, however, gave an anguished cry and threw herself at the dragon's head, flailing at it with her ethereal fists.

"Mighiletta," she wailed. "You traitor—we trusted you!"

"Mighiletta?" Charl repeated aloud. Jarlbrus had called this dragon Miga.

The lady's immaterial pummeling seemed not to register with the dragon at all, but when Charl said "Mighiletta," *that* got a reaction. The dragon stared at him, a birch trunk dangling from her mouth like an enormous white toothpick. She spat it out, her gaze still fixed on Charl, and then she did something extraordinary.

Charl had never seen a dragon fold itself into human form before, and therefore he had never appreciated how brain-breakingly incomprehensible it was. The entire towering mass of scales and spines and wings and fire collapsed in upon itself, shrinking and softening, until all that was left was a fragile, naked human body, no trace of horns, claws, or wings.

Her saarantras was slim and white, like the birches she'd been destroying, with short pale hair and black eyes. In dragon form, she had been wearing a sort of wristband, which did not shrink and now revealed itself to be a rucksack. This she opened—not bothering to turn her back or hide herself—and pulled out a linen shirt and trousers, a vest, and a pair of boots. She got dressed, neither distracted nor hindered by the lady, who continued to scream and fling herself at the saarantras, over and over.

Charl was beginning to feel sorry for this ghost.

"Now you'll understand me when I speak," said the dragon as she shrugged into her vest. "My *name* is Miga. Explain why you called me Mighiletta."

"Because that is the name you used to go by, when you were the Asterrinks' pet assassin!" cried the lady, apparently believing the dragon was speaking to her.

Miga, oblivious to the ghost, stared expectantly at Charl.

This felt like an opportunity to Charl, if only he could figure out how to use it. The fire-belching dragon that had come to abduct him was now human-sized and apparently distractible.

"I heard you used to go by Mighiletta," said Charl carefully. He looked at the ghost, trying to catch her eye. "I have a . . . an acquaintance who knew you long ago. One of the Amberfinches. I'm trying to remember her first name."

The Lady of the Birches, who had been preparing to fling herself at Miga again, paused and looked at Charl. He raised his eyebrows in what he hoped was encouragement. She deflated, seeming to understand her predicament at last. "I'm Eldegarde."

"Eldegarde," Charl repeated, nodding. "That's right."

"'Eldegarde' means nothing to me," said Miga.

This elicited further wailing from the ghost.

"Amberfinch," the dragon continued obliviously, "is a name

I keep hearing, but I don't remember why it's important. And that smell—" She breathed deeply through her nose. "Why is *that* so familiar?"

What could she possibly be smelling? Charl smelled only the sap of broken trees.

"Does she really not remember?" cried Eldegarde. "How convenient. I wish I could go around cutting people's throats and forget all about it."

"My friend said you may have been a . . . a knife-for-hire, back when she knew you," Charl said cautiously. It seemed a terrible thing to have to tell someone about themselves.

"Of course," snapped Miga. "I still am. It's why your father hired me to retrieve you."

"Oh," said Charl, shrinking back. He had not wanted to remind Miga of her mission.

Miga was kicking at the weeds between the birches, as if she'd lost something there. Eldegarde Amberfinch watched her, hands on hips, looking more sad than angry now.

"We were friends, once, before the plague years," said Eldegarde. "Even when the plague first began, Mighiletta used to bring me love letters from Dagoberto Asterrink. It wasn't until I learned what was causing the plague, and what had to be done to stop it, that things turned ugly."

"Was it bog beetles?" asked Charl quietly, so as not to draw Miga's attention. The saarantras was on her hands and knees now, pawing at the dirt.

Eldegarde nodded. "I studied the beetles, their habits and their origins, and I realized that to control them, both families—Amberfinch and Asterrink alike—were going to have to sacrifice. First, we needed to build strong walls and levees, to stop the fields from flooding. My family owned farmland across the valley bottom, so we took that on as our responsibility, and put all our resources toward it. The Asterrinks, who prevailed in town, had only to wall off their harbor. They wouldn't do it. Dagoberto could not persuade them.

"He told me I was in danger, and he would help me get away. I was supposed to meet him here, but Mighiletta got here first. She killed me, all so the harbor could stay open."

"Well, someone eventually saw sense," said Charl. "Because they filled in the harbor. St. Muckle's has had no beetles for a very long time."

Until his mother came and rebuilt the harbor. She'd never known the story, and the town had forgotten it. As painful as it was to remember, it could be much worse to forget.

Miga was so preoccupied with digging and sniffing that she seemed not to hear Charl talking to Eldegarde. With a cry of triumph, she stood upright again, brandishing a human femur.

"No!" screamed Eldegarde, swiping at it futilely. "That's mine, and not for you!"

"Put it back," said Charl.

He made a grab for the bone, but Miga easily held it out of reach.

Miga bugged her eyes at him. "This is a piece of the puzzle, maybe even the most crucial piece. It smells like the other bones in the crypt. I'm going to take it there and see whether I can determine exactly who it is related to—"

"I already told you. It's Eldegarde Amberfinch," cried Charl. "Leave it here, with the rest of her bones. You've done quite enough to her already."

Miga grabbed the front of his shirt and pulled him close.

She snarled, "You don't know what it's like, *almost* remembering. It's like an itch you can't scratch, and it never, ever stops. You can't sleep. You can't concentrate. You would pay anything—anything—to find the answers. Or failing that, to find oblivion."

"Put the bone back," said Charl, not sure where he was finding the bravery. "You came here to find me. The bone is a distraction."

"Oh, I won't forget you," said Miga, letting go of Charl so abruptly that he almost fell. "I'll be back before you know it. Don't try anything while I'm gone. If you run off, I will kill your mother, and then I will find you anyway."

"You have my mother?" cried Charl.

"I have everyone you care about. Your mischievous mother. Sir Aris. That squeaky person who keeps crying. Your whole stupid town full of stupid people. Everyone."

The "squeaky person" didn't sound like Agnes—it sounded like the opposite of Agnes, in fact—and surely Miga would have identified another dragon as a dragon if she'd captured Dr. Caramus. This gave Charl some hope that she hadn't captured *everyone*, but . . . he hated that she had his mother.

He might really never see Mama again if this all went wrong somehow.

That was unthinkable, unbearable. Better to be captured than that.

He raised his hands above his head. "I surrender. Take me to them."

Miga ignored him and went toward her rucksack, the femur slung over her shoulder.

Charl hurried after her. "Please. I won't fight. Just let me see my mother one more—"

"I will *not* take you back to town," said Miga, removing her vest and folding it neatly. "You'd catch the ague and die, with my luck. Two-thirds of the bounty is for you alone. Your mother is worth nothing without you."

Charl's eyes began to prickle. He rubbed them with the heel of his hand. "There are two others after me, you know. Before you get back, one of them will surely have spirited me away."

"Not likely," said Miga, squatting in the weeds to tuck her human-sized boots back into her wrist rucksack. "I smelled them when I arrived; they're incapacitated, but on the mend. They won't be well enough soon enough to take you from me. Even if they tried, I know where they plan to take you. I'd fly ahead and ambush them on the road to Uchtburg."

She packed the bone into her rucksack, along with her remaining clothes, and gave Charl one last look over her bare shoulder. "One thing I do remember, and that you'd do well not to forget, is that I am almost three hundred years old. You don't live as long as I have without a sense of which things are worth expending energy on and which things are not. I found you once, I can find you again. Keeping you always in sight, guarding you jealously, and fighting off all comers is not the most efficient use of my resources."

"Was it efficient to tear a whole town apart just to get at my mother?" Charl couldn't help bursting out bitterly.

With a swift kick of her leg, Miga swept Charl's feet out from under him. He landed hard on his back, all the wind knocked out of him.

"I earn a bonus for destroying that town," said Miga calmly, as if she hadn't just been terrifyingly violent. "It was dying anyway. And it was mocking me."

With that, she did what she'd done before, in reverse this time, unfurling into her draconic form. It was just as brain-breaking in reverse. Charl closed his eyes until she was finished, because it made him feel dizzy and sick to watch. It took a few minutes for her form to solidify before she could fly again. Charl stayed on the ground the whole time, and dared to stand only once she had flung herself at the sky.

The lady, Eldegarde, had evaporated into her own screams, it seemed, but now Charl thought he saw her, a faint shimmer at the top of the wall, standing alongside another odd shimmer, a plump girl with curly hair. He launched himself up the steps.

"It should work like our apples," Maeve was telling Eldegarde as he approached. "You should be able to visit your bone, wherever it ends up. Think of it as an opportunity. A chance to see what St. Muckle's is like nowadays."

"It doesn't look too wonderful from here," said Eldegarde dismally. "But do you think any of my family still . . . linger? As ghosts, I mean."

"There's only one way to find out," said Maeve.

The ghost of Eldegarde Amberfinch reached out an ethereal hand. Maeve took it in her own for a moment, then let it go. Eldegarde disappeared.

Maeve stood with her back to Charl, looking out over the valley. "At least she understands she's dead now," she said at last.

"How? She's not bound, like you. She's not willfully evil, like . . ." He gestured back toward the ruined sanctuary. "I thought a ghost like her was supposed to have no awareness."

Maeve opened her mouth and then closed it again. She shrugged. "I'm not sure. She was very clever in life. Maybe that makes a difference. Or maybe it's *you*."

"Me?" said Charl, and he felt himself blushing unaccountably.

"You got through to Wort. Eldegarde spoke to you. You escaped nasty old Marcellus."

"I was given some luck, there," said Charl, trying to remind her of the kiss.

It was her turn to glow prettily. "I'm just saying, maybe you have a gift for it. Back in the disreputable pagan past, maybe you would have been a corna."

"Isn't that a wise woman?" Charl asked, making a face.

"They weren't all women," said Maeve. "But they were all wise—which in those days meant you could see and talk to the dead. And while some were born to it, usually it meant you'd been through terrible things. It was a useful gift, but a miserable one, too."

Charl mulled this over.

Maeve cut through his reverie, saying, "Would you believe I know that dragon? She's the reason I'm dead."

"I thought you were killed to stop a drought?"

"A dragon-induced drought," said Maeve, "caused by a dragon setting everything on fire. She blew away the clouds and reduced the Sowline to a trickle."

Charl could hardly picture this valley being dry and not soggy.

"They put me on the altar and pushed a knife through my heart," said Maeve, almost dreamily. "The gods were supposed to take care of the rest, but the gods did nothing. Then the Brothers of St. Ogdo came and chased the dragon away. We were saved, and everyone converted to the faith of Allsaints, and we all lived happily ever after—oh, except for that dead girl. Pity about the dead girl."

Charl frowned. "Shouldn't the brothers have killed the dragon, not just chased her off?"

"If they'd cared about that sort of thing," said Maeve. "They were really here to convert the pagans. She was the monastery's pet, raised from an egg. I was killed for literally nothing."

Charl watched Maeve's profile, her quivering chin, the gleam in her eyes that might have been tears. "And now I must fade without complaint, alongside my sisters-in-death," she said in an almost whisper. "And I don't want to."

Bishop Marcellus had an idea about that. Charl opened his mouth, but before he could speak he heard a voice from below, outside the wall.

"Charl!" said the voice.

Maeve, clearly startled, disappeared.

"Who's there?" called Charl, leaning over the parapet.

Dr. Caramus stepped out of the undergrowth, brushing leaves off his doublet. He gave a tight little bow.

"Let me in," he said. "Miga will be back. We don't have much time."

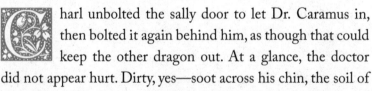

31

The Doctor

Charl unbolted the sally door to let Dr. Caramus in, then bolted it again behind him, as though that could keep the other dragon out. At a glance, the doctor did not appear hurt. Dirty, yes—soot across his chin, the soil of the turnip fields caked on his shoes. Tired, also yes, with much darker circles under his eyes than usual. His spectacles seemed to magnify them.

The doctor stared into space, fidgeting his fingers, muttering, "If she flies at a casual velocity, without pausing long in St. Muckle's, that should take . . . twenty minutes at most. If she hurries, it's over. Don't even contemplate that eventuality. The unknown factor is how long she will stop in St. Muckle's. Over the last several days, I have observed her to be very distractible."

That was how he began. Not with *Hello, Charl. I am relieved to see you well.* Not with *Don't worry. I've seen your mother and the others, and they're plotting a way to save the town.*

So Charl, too, got directly to business: "There's a problem about the herbs."

"I know there is," said Dr. Caramus. "My laboratory is a wreck. I'm not sure Miga left so much as a glass retort intact."

Charl was so taken aback by this response that he couldn't think how to respond.

Caramus continued: "It's lucky, in a way. She was so busy destroying my things that she didn't see the flare and instantly glean that you were here. I don't know how she suddenly worked it out, unless Lord Vasterich told her. He threatened to betray us to her more than once, but I managed to keep him quiet by promising him a hoard I don't actually possess. Maybe he finally figured it out—"

"Miga spotted me on the battlements," said Charl. "I forgot to be careful."

"Ah, that would do it."

"But I meant there's a *different* problem with the herbs," said Charl, finally finding his opening. "Jarlbrus, my father's spymaster, is here, and he's hidden the crates. I haven't been able to find them."

Caramus frowned at this news. "Is *this* where he went? He disappeared after Aris freed Eileen. We thought Miga had killed him, but your mother warned us not to underestimate his craftiness."

"Wait," said Charl, "my mother is free? Miga said—" His voice broke, and he could not finish.

"'Free' is not exactly the word for anyone pursued by a dragon," said Caramus. "But she is not confined or pinned down, or she wasn't when I left town. Your mother has been trying to keep Miga's attention away from you, in fact, like we all have. But how are you wandering around semi-free if the spymaster is here? And why haven't you run away?"

I was waiting for you, Charl almost said, but the truth was much more complicated. Before he could untangle it, Jarlbrus's voice rang out across the courtyard: "He didn't run because he knows, in his heart, that he'll be returning to his father one way or another."

Jarlbrus limped toward them, using the sword as a cane. "Perhaps you now appreciate, boy, that it should not be that dragon who takes you. She is a monstrous murderer, even if she doesn't remember the facts of the matter. She'll be more efficient and less distractible once she can afford to have her memories restored, and you can imagine what terrors she'll unleash upon the whole world then."

"Unlike you, I suppose," said Caramus.

"I intend to retire," said Jarlbrus tersely.

"From being a monstrous murderer," said Caramus, finishing the thought for him.

"Do you really want to criticize me?" snarled Jarlbrus. "Do you imagine that I failed to research you as thoroughly as everyone else, Dr. Deviant? A failed medical innovator who performed an experiment on himself and lived to regret it? Do you know why he hasn't taken dragon form to face Miga, boy? Because he can't. He literally cannot."

His bullying tone was like Rafe at his worst, and it made Charl furious. Charl stepped in front of Caramus, as if he could shield the doctor from insult with his body.

Jarlbrus laughed. "What a doomed mixture of loyalty and bravery you are, lad," said Jarlbrus. "Every stout-hearted, noble impulse, wrapped in a tiny, improbable package. You'd make a better earl right now than any half dozen grown men. Come back. The world could be yours."

"One world," said Dr. Caramus, his tone almost aggressively bland. "But, as your mother would say, Charl, is it the best world? Or can we make a better one?"

"What does that woman do to you all, to make you such incorrigible idealists?" said Jarlbrus. "No matter. What *is* must always trump what *might be*, here in the real world."

"Then maybe it's time for what *is* to become what *was*," said Caramus. "I came here for my herbs, but I will be returning the boy to his mother, as well."

Jarlbrus, with shocking speed for an injured man, flung himself at Charl and managed to grapple him, pinning the boy's arms to his sides. Jarlbrus swung Charl around, put the sword to his throat, and dragged him backward, away from Caramus.

"Here's my counteroffer," said Jarlbrus, his teeth gritted in pain. "You go home with nothing, Dr. Deviant."

Charl, feeling the cold steel against his throat, didn't dare cry out. He tried to calm himself by breathing deeply, and by reminding himself that one crucial thing kept him safe.

"If you hurt me, you won't get paid," said Charl.

"No money is worth the trouble you've put me to," said Jarlbrus. "You and your troublesome mother!"

Keep him talking, Charl, a disembodied voice whispered. *We'll take care of him.*

He glimpsed a form out of the corner of his eye—Anya. Or Zedig.

"I'm your . . . your *prince*," said Charl loudly. "And I command you to let me go."

Jarlbrus laughed and tightened his grip. "Accepted your

birthright at last, have you? That's all well and good, little prince, but you don't command me until you're back at court." He gave Charl a little shake. "I'm sure your father will throw you a great feast, and he'll give you your own horse, your own *princess*—"

As if the word *princess* had conjured her, suddenly Princess Luti stood before them, looking almost solid. She raised her chin imperiously, her golden hair shining with an unnatural light, her jewelry gleaming. She was regal and intimidating, but her face had a strained look, as if this manifestation had taken an extraordinary effort.

And it was extraordinary, because even Jarlbrus could see her.

"Release him, miscreant." Her voice boomed like thunder. "Or prepare to be haunted."

"Where did *she* come from?" muttered Jarlbrus, sounding more confused than frightened.

And then he screamed.

Anya and Zedig were on either side of Jarlbrus, reaching into his body—but he did not let go of Charl. He writhed and twitched, jerking Charl around with him, clearly in pain, but still somehow clinging to his prize and keeping the sword in place.

Princess Luti, apparently exhausted, collapsed into a heap of gleaming specks.

Jarlbrus, grunting like a wild pig now, hung on to Charl like a drowning man.

"Ye gods," cried Anya from the left. "I can hardly bear to look at his memories."

"He's too terrible. He's going to haunt *us*," sobbed Zedig, from the right. "Charl, I'm sorry. We can't hold him."

Charl couldn't see it happen, since Jarlbrus was holding him from behind, but he felt the change when the girls let go. The spymaster stopped shivering; his grip grew firmer, and he gave a dark, triumphant laugh.

And then he jerked and cried out as something else hit him from behind.

A turnip, having bounced off of Jarlbrus's head, rolled into the grass at Charl's feet.

A second turnip, launched with a recognizable grunt, came sailing out of the sky. This time, Jarlbrus dodged, releasing Charl in the process. That was all the time Mother Trude needed to rush in and whisk the boy away. Jarlbrus's previous lunge must have used up his strength, because he couldn't catch them. Mother Trude hustled Charl over to Dr. Caramus's side, then doubled over, panting and coughing.

Charl flinched at the sound, but the cough was normal, at long last. The herbs had worked. If only he could get them home.

It was Caramus's turn to step in front of Charl and shield him.

"I've figured out where you've hidden the herbs," said Dr. Caramus calmly, as if this had been the only matter under discussion all along. "You used pyria to mask the scent—a clever ploy, except that the scent only comes from two directions: from a cellar, faintly, and much more strongly from your hiding spot. You didn't think to set up any decoys."

"How can you still care about that?" cried Jarlbrus. "Who's left to cure?"

"He has a moral center, unlike you," cried Mother Trude.

"You're making unwarranted assumptions, woman. He's done monstrous things."

Those two kept yelling, but Charl had stopped listening. His attention was drawn to the spot where Princess Luti had been. Her ghostly sisters were silently gathering around—Anya and Zedig, Vilna and Maeve. Even Iphi and Ognielle. Luti had melted into a shining puddle in the tall weeds. Vilna knelt beside it, a hand over her mouth as if she were holding in a scream.

Little by little, the puddle condensed and coalesced, taking the form of a lithe, inquisitive mink, which scurried off into the grass.

The four remaining ghost girls all watched it go, looking haunted.

One more had faded. That was what they all had to look forward to. Maybe it would bring them peace and rest at last, but even Vilna had looked horrified to watch it happening.

Mother Trude was still haranguing Jarlbrus, harassing him like a crow, right up in his face. He staggered back a couple steps and raised the sword uncertainly. Mother Trude was yelling, waving her arms, almost daring him to stab her.

It was a diversion, Charl suddenly realized. She was trying to . . . to be a friend to him, for true, at the last.

He and Dr. Caramus might be able to slip away if they did it now. Charl tugged the doctor's sleeve and whispered, "Let's go."

"We wouldn't get far," Caramus whispered back. "Miga will be arriving soon."

"What?" cried Charl, cringing as he glanced at the sky. "How can you tell?"

Dr. Caramus shook his head. "Listen carefully, child, and remember everything I tell you: The herbs are behind the ruined sanctuary. You must get them to Sister Agnes. I have left her the formula for the cure. She will know how to make it."

"Even with your lab in ruins?" Charl burst out, but that wasn't what was upsetting him. Caramus seemed to be implying that he wouldn't be there to help.

"She's resourceful. She'll make do," said the doctor calmly. "Look for her under Vasterich Hall, in a strongroom where a previous lord kept his torture implements, apparently. Everyone was hiding there, but they may have moved while Miga was distracted."

Before Charl could ask who *they* included, Caramus drew a small box from his pocket. He opened it, revealing a dozen green pastilles, each one a slightly different size. "Your elixir. Dissolve one in a glass of water. One per month, in order. When you run out, there's a name in there, on a piece of paper." He closed the box. "My colleague. Find her, if I haven't found you again."

"Where will you be?" Charl asked in a tremulous voice. "Why won't you be with us?"

"It takes a dragon to stop a dragon, Charl," said Dr. Caramus. "And I think I know—"

Mother Trude screamed. Her fight with Jarlbrus had ended with him overpowering her, twisting her arms behind her back. Her face contorted in pain.

"Charl," said Jarlbrus with menacing calm, "come with me, or she will suffer. I know you won't allow that. You cared for her when all seemed lost, at risk to yourself. You won't let me do this." He wrenched the old nun's arm harder and she howled.

Charl opened his mouth to answer, but Dr. Caramus interrupted: "We need to deal with Miga first."

If Jarlbrus replied, it was drowned out by a fierce blast of brimstone wind as the dragon Miga touched down in the courtyard once again.

32

It Takes a Dragon

he came with ready flame in her mouth, which she spat into the birch trees, setting the branches alight. Smoldering leaves fluttered and dropped all around, like bright falling stars. Miga arched her neck and looked down superciliously, as if to say *Who's next, puny humans?*

The puny humans scattered: Jarlbrus scuttling toward the front gates, Mother Trude diving behind a pile of rubble, and Charl flattening himself behind the low wall of the well.

Dr. Caramus, the only person who was not human, stepped toward the monster and began to speak in soft-mouth Mootya. Miga focused the considerable weight of her attention on him.

Charl felt something cold wriggle across his back and up his shoulder, like a trickle of water in reverse. He half rolled over, swatting at it, then stilled when he saw a whiskered face with beady black eyes staring at him. Iphi, the ghostly squirrel. Her claws dug bright spots of cold into his arm. The contact didn't spark memories—just as Ognielle's hadn't—but soon, he realized what effect it did have.

"You'd recognize my draconic name, no doubt," Caramus was saying. "Kaska, the deviant doctor, fled from exile these fifty years. I know there's still a price on my head. I submit myself willingly. You may collect the bounty on me, provided you leave Charl alone."

Charl was used to understanding what Dr. Caramus said, so at first this didn't strike him as strange. Only when he also understood Miga's ferocious roar did he realize what Iphi was doing—she was letting him understand Mootya.

The bounty on you is not enough for my purposes, Miga screamed.

"Well, that's a bit insulting. But I can guess your purposes, and you may be right," said Caramus, his voice a calm counterpoint. "Memory restoration is expensive, because very few can do it properly. Who do you think can do this for you?"

Miga cocked her head, and Charl (no doubt with Iphi's help) recognized uncertainty in her body language. *Dr. Hrann, from the Ardakarn Institute. A reputable surgeon. He reverses excisions on the side.*

"Are you a mere hatchling?" said Caramus. "He will take your money and turn you over to the authorities. It's only your lack of funds that's stopped him from filing a report on you already. I suppose they removed your good sense when they removed your memories."

Miga looked stricken.

"And are you sure you want them back?" Dr. Caramus continued. "I remember your case. It was in all the journals, because it was rather extraordinary. You *asked* to have your memories removed. You wanted the procedure. Apparently, you were feeling something few dragons ever feel, and it was making you miserable."

What... What was it? If a dragon could whisper, that's what Miga was doing now.

"Remorse," said Caramus sternly.

Miga shook her head. She clawed at it, gnashing her teeth. *But this is surely worse, the itch of half memory. I need it to stop itching.*

"Well, then, I may have another way to help you, better than my bounty," said Caramus. "I was exiled for practicing deviant medicine. Enhancing draconic emotional capacity. Rendering the human form permanent. Aligning external anatomy with internal gender, or lack thereof. And, yes, restoring memories without a mind-pearl. I was the best at what I did. I will put my skills to your service—for free—if you will let the child go."

Miga inhaled deeply. *The child. I suppose the mother engaged your services for his sake?*

Dr. Caramus shrugged. "It is less accurate to say she engaged my services than to say she was a friend when I needed one, and I have striven to be the same. The loyalty I feel is not something I would expect most dragons to understand."

Miga straightened up. *I accept your offer. I will leave the child to these lesser bounty hunters in exchange for your services. Transform, and let us fly away together.*

"Ah," said Caramus. "That's the awkward part. My saarantras is permanent. I cannot take dragon form anymore without significant pharmacological intervention."

Only now did Miga look suspicious. Her eyes narrowed. *You can perform the necessary surgery on me with those tiny little hands?*

"Oh, yes," said Caramus. "Better than before. I used to need quigs for the finer details."

That seemed to satisfy her. She grasped Dr. Caramus in her front claws; he submitted without protestation.

Charl, who had leaped to his feet without realizing it, cried, "Caramus, no!"

"All will be well," said Dr. Caramus, speaking Goreddi now. "Convey my apologies and my esteem to your mother. I hate having to leave you with Brus and Mother Trude"—he paused while Miga hoisted him off the ground—"but Miga is too dangerous, and this is my only option. Those other two are merely human; you are their equal, even if outnumbered. Good—"

The final word—*luck*, possibly—was swallowed up by the whoosh of wings as Miga took off. Charl was flung to the ground, and found himself in the weeds again, face to face with Iphi.

The little ghost squirrel had translated Miga's words for him. Bishop Marcellus had said Iphi had once been a sage who understood draconic speech. She may have faded, might no longer look human, but some part of her was still herself. Vilna didn't seem to realize that.

Jarlbrus was tromping across the courtyard toward him, plants crunching underfoot. "Well, that was unexpected," said the man, a note of desperate laughter in his voice. "One hates to be in debt to a dragon, but I'd say we owe the doctor. Anyway, get up. We should be going."

Charl futilely pressed himself flatter into the dirt.

"You're not hidden," said Jarlbrus. "I can see your boots and your dusty curls."

Still, Charl didn't get up. Jarlbrus was going to have to drag him away. It would be slow going, with that bad leg.

Jarlbrus's shadow loomed, and Charl felt a cold sword tip pressing under his chin.

"Get up," said Jarlbrus, plainly not joking around anymore.

Mother Trude came barreling out of nowhere and tackled him. He landed hard in the weeds. "Run, Charl!" she shouted. "If he wants you, he's got to get through me first!"

They were tussling alarmingly close to the well, rolling over and over. Mother Trude had a rock in her fist and a wild look in her eye, but in the end it was the larger, stronger person—who also happened to have a sword—who prevailed. He sat on her chest, panting, pinning her arms with his knees, holding the blade to her throat.

"I should have stolen that sword from you myself!" cried the nun, hissing and spitting like a cat. "Charl didn't want to kill you, but I would have done it. I should have done it. Kill or be killed is sometimes the only choice we're given."

"And you shouldn't hesitate, when faced with a choice like that. It's almost always fatal," said Jarlbrus with a knowing nod.

"Why are you still here?" Mother Trude screamed at Charl, who'd gotten to his feet but seemed rooted to the spot.

If he ran, Jarlbrus would slit her throat—Agnes's mother's throat—and would come after him anyway. Maybe Charl could have escaped him, climbed up the side of the dormitory, found his way out of sight across the remaining rooftops and crumbling walls of the Old Abbey. But could he elude Jarlbrus forever? Did he really believe that a man who would destroy a whole town with plague just to get at him, would ever stop searching? Charl would never be safe, with this man around. Charl was too small, too tender-hearted, too merciful to stop him.

It takes a dragon to stop a dragon, Caramus had said.

And then he knew what to do.

"I'll go with you, Jarlbrus. Willingly, calmly," Charl said, raising his hands. "But only if you don't kill her."

"Little prince, you have yourself a deal," said Jarlbrus. He pulled the sword from Mother Trude's throat, took his weight off her, and got to his feet. As he stepped back, though, he flicked his sword and sliced off her left ear. Mother Trude screamed and clutched at her head.

"Hey!" shouted Charl, feeling furious and betrayed.

"Oops," said Jarlbrus, smirking. "You only said not to kill her."

"You'll wish you had, someday," snarled Mother Trude, scuttling into the shade of the smoking birches, pressing what had once been her wimple to the side of her head.

"Agnes is alive," said Charl, speaking loudly and clearly, since only one of her ears was available for hearing. "She's in town, under Vasterich Hall. You are free to go to her, Mother Trude."

The old woman looked hopeful and hurt all at once, but she nodded.

"Now," said Charl, turning to Jarlbrus, "it's a long way to my father's, and you don't have a horse. We should take provisions with us."

"Fair enough. No turnips, though," laughed Jarlbrus. He bowed slightly, gestured for Charl to take the lead, and followed him back to the refectory.

33

The Monstrous

"I was serious: leave the turnips," snapped Jarlbrus, packing some apples into a small sack of oats. "They take too long to cook. We'll just have to forage as we go. What we really want is water. There's none safe to drink until we're out of the valley."

Jarlbrus had a single waterskin, which Charl filled, submerging it in the bucket and squeezing bubbles out. It wouldn't last long. The bucket itself would be too heavy to bring along, and would slosh everywhere. The jam jar (which had reappeared among Jarlbrus's things, licked clean) had lost its lid and wouldn't have held more than a couple mouthfuls in any case. The only other vessel was the brandy bottle, which still had half an inch of liquor sloshing around the bottom.

"I suppose I can sacrifice for the greater good," said Jarlbrus. He drank it in three gulps. "Don't imagine for one instant that that was enough to put me to sleep."

"There's more in the sanctuary," said Charl, taking the empty bottle. Brandy might not be enough to tempt the man, so Charl added, "And there's gold, and jewels." That was an uninspiring description. "I think I saw a ruby on one of the reliquaries."

"Liar," said Jarlbrus. "I've been all around the sanctuary. It's a ruin, picked clean."

"Then where did I get this?" said Charl, waving the bottle at him. "This was real. You drank it. There were more bottles in a secret cupboard behind the altar, untouched by thieves. Shall I go fetch one for you?"

Jarlbrus stared skeptically. Then he licked his lips, and Charl knew he was thinking about the taste of brandy and feeling tempted.

"This is clearly some kind of trick," said Jarlbrus at last, "but I don't know what, exactly. I let you go by yourself and you run off? I go with you, bend over to get the 'brandy,' and you brain me with a rock?"

"Or it's no trick, and you get brandy," said Charl, trying to make his face blank.

Jarlbrus unsheathed the sword and gestured to Charl to lead the way. "I will humor you this once, little prince, and accompany you to find this 'brandy,' which I'm sure will turn out to be something horrible. Maybe a large snake or a pit for me to fall into. We shall all have a good laugh, and you will learn the futility of trying to outwit a spymaster who's seen every trick in the book. Who *wrote* the book of tricks, in fact."

Not every trick, Charl fervently hoped. Surely Bishop Marcellus had a trick or two up his miter.

Of course, the sanctuary had looked like a ruin the last time Charl saw it, too. But maybe the Battle Bishop had disguised the place, somehow, created an illusion of a ruin so that thieves would walk on by.

Unless the intact, perfectly preserved candlelit sanctuary had been the illusion?

As they walked toward the sanctuary, Charl's heart began to sink. The place still looked like a ruin. The roof was caved in, the walls collapsed. Everything was overgrown with vines. The great doors were falling off their hinges and wouldn't move; Charl had to squeeze through the gap. Jarlbrus squeezed through behind him and made a scoffing noise.

The cadaver tomb languished under moss and ivy. A big lump at the far end was probably the altar, but other than that, the ruined interior was unrecognizable. The woodwork had decayed. The golden statuary and jeweled reliquaries had long since disappeared. Sunlight fell harshly over the wreckage, no longer filtered through warmly colored glass. You could hardly tell there had ever been glass in the gaping window holes.

"You were saying?" sneered Jarlbrus, surveying the wreckage. "Where could that elusive brandy be?"

"Behind the altar," said Charl miserably.

The spymaster rolled his eyes. Charl couldn't blame him.

"So you tromped over here," said Jarlbrus, setting off for the altar, "through this thicket of weeds, and you pulled aside this . . . tenacious curtain of ivy . . ."

He bent over, pulling the clinging vines off the back of the altar. Charl bit his lip and leaned against the cadaver tomb to wait.

The tomb was ice cold, despite the sun shining on it.

Whatever else was true, Bishop Marcellus was at home.

"There was something you wanted me to do," Charl muttered to the unseen bishop out of the corner of his mouth. "To help the orchard girls. But you never got around to telling me what it was."

A chill breeze raised the hairs on the back of his neck.

"I came back, like I promised," Charl continued. "And I swear I'll do it, whatever it is, however difficult—if you would do one thing for me in return."

Cold burst over his body, like being hit by a wave of sea spray, and then it was gone. Bishop Marcellus had passed through him and moved on, toward the altar. In that fleeting moment, Charl knew what the bishop wanted him to do, and the bishop knew what Charl wanted, too. There had barely been time for one question.

And suddenly, the opulent sanctuary was back, in all its gleaming splendor. Sunlight filtered red and gold through the windows; candles twinkled, reflecting off the many-faceted jewels. The ghost of Bishop Marcellus took manlike form and soundlessly crossed the marble tiles toward the altar.

Jarlbrus stood upright, a bottle in his hand. His mouth opened and closed like a fish out of water; he gaped at the richness all around him. Not as if he were surprised or confused or disbelieving, but simply overawed by what he saw.

The Battle Bishop—the Monster Who Rages—stepped onto the dais.

Jarlbrus could only stare. Even as the ghost's eyes turned into two black pits, and his hands flickered like flames, Jarlbrus didn't move. The bishop smiled—a long, toothy smile that seemed to extend to his ears—and chortled so deeply the chandeliers shook.

Charl knew it was time to leave.

He rushed for the doors. Bits of stone and woodwork began

falling all around him. Only when he reached the doorway did he look back, just in time to see the Battle Bishop unhinge his jaw and take Jarlbrus's entire head into his mouth.

It was too grotesque. Charl wished he hadn't seen that.

But the bishop was merely doing what he'd asked.

There was only one ghost here evil enough to withstand the nightmares he would find among Jarlbrus's memories, only one who'd done anything in his life anywhere near as bad as the spymaster. The dragon who could defeat the dragon.

Can you hold him? was the one question Charl had had time to ask during that fleeting moment of contact.

Forever, the bishop had assured him.

Charl crossed the threshold, and there was crash like thunder and a blast of wind, gusting from all directions, blowing dust into his eyes and nose. He wrapped his arms around his head and ran toward the refectory. Only when he'd gone far enough to take shelter around the corner did he dare to look back one last time.

The sanctuary looked like a ruin again, but dust rose as if it had only just collapsed.

Charl wondered what remained of Jarlbrus, if one were to go looking for him. It was probably wiser not to.

34

The Apple

It took a minute to realize what this meant.

It was over. Miga and Mother Trude were gone; Jarlbrus might very well be dead. Nothing was holding him here any longer. His pace quickened until he was dashing toward the front gates, ready to pelt headlong down the mountain. He felt like he could run all the way home, or like joy might fly him back. Mama, Agnes, and Aris would be so glad to see him . . .

Wait, though. He skidded to a stop beside the orchard. There was still a plague on at home. He needed to find the crates of herbs and resin and a way to haul them down the mountain. *Everyone* was going to be glad to see him.

And there was something else that he had promised to do.

Bishop Marcellus had left a box of instructions in Charl's mind—not a literal box, of course, and yet Charl seemed to feel it sitting there, cold and hard. He closed his eyes and pictured a tiny jeweled casket, like one of the reliquaries in the sanctuary. He imagined himself opening it, and a whole memory popped out.

A memory of a conversation he hadn't even realized he'd had.

Bishop Marcellus loomed in front of him, tall and transparent. "To free a ghost, you must understand what binds it to the world," he said. "Many different things can do it. People. Places. An idea or a dream, even, can be powerful enough to hold you transfixed forever. These girls were bound to the stone circle at first, but they were bound there by someone else. It wasn't their doing—or even their choosing, in some cases. Over time, through shared hardship, they became bound to each other. You might break the bond to their stone prison if they chose to leave together, all at once."

"Then they'd no longer be ghosts?" asked Charl. "They'd fly off to the Blue Lands?"

"Not quite," said the bishop. "They'd still be bound to each other. That is a bond they must figure out how to break on their own—and whether they want to. But one fewer bond is one fewer bond, and being free to choose our own bondage is as close to free as even the living ever get, really."

Bishop Marcellus told Charl what he must do to free the girls from their stone circle. Charl nodded. It sounded straightforward enough.

"But what about you?" asked Charl. "Could I free you, too?"

Marcellus's eyes grew smoky and deep. "You are kind. Your parents, all four of them, would be proud of you. But I am bound to myself—my ego, my will, my rage—"

"The Monster Who Rages," said Charl, remembering what he'd said before about his soul. He'd said there were three parts to it, though . . .

"*The self is the hardest prison to escape,*" Bishop Marcellus was saying. "*This is my punishment; I must do my time. The day may come when I see the key to my release, shining in the palm of my hand, and it may not. For now, my work is here*"—he pressed a hand to his chest—"*and no one can do it but me.*"

Charl was turning to go, but there was one last thing he wanted to know. "*I've seen the Man Who Reasons and the Monster Who Rages, but you said there was a third part to your soul. What is it?*"

The Bishop looked at Charl and almost smiled. "*Do you really not know? I was a Wise Child, Charl. Like Vilna. Like Trude. Like you.*"

And then he was gone.

Charl opened his eyes and peered into the shadowed orchard. Nothing moved, or so it seemed, but then he saw a blur at the edge of his vision. Ognielle.

He entered the grove reverently, hands clasped, eyes searching among the branches. The ghostly martin flitted in and out, helping him look, finally alighting near an apple. The most perfect, ripe apple Charl had yet seen in this orchard, hanging by itself, as if waiting for him to find it. It was plump and round, wider than it was tall, streaked with red, darker red, and yellow. White flecks dotted it, like lingering stars at sunrise. Charl reached for it, and the tree seemed to bend to meet him. The apple came off easily, with barely a twist.

In the center of the grove, a single sunbeam warmed a stone, one of the toppled ones. Charl set the apple on the stone in the sunlight, and called, "Friends? Come here. I've had an insight."

This was what the bishop had said to say, warning him sternly that mentioning Bishop Marcellus would lose the girls' trust at once. *You must convince them it's your own idea.*

Of course, all this required Charl to trust that the bishop wasn't lying to *him*. He had a moment of vertigo, fretting about this. But only a moment, because suddenly there was Vilna, then Maeve, and Anya and Zedig. Their faces materialized out of shadows.

"What's this, then?" said Vilna, staring at the apple.

"I can take you away from here, as far as you want to go," said Charl. "And you won't be pulled back, if you leave together. You're bound more tightly to each other than to this place. At least, that's my theory."

"But what good would that do?" Vilna cried. "We need to fade—that should be our focus now. What does it matter if we do it here or somewhere else?"

"Maybe we don't all want to fade," said Maeve, seeming to solidify a bit as she spoke.

"And you didn't all choose to be here," added Charl. "If I took you somewhere else, together, it would release the bond that holds you *here*. And then—"

"We'd only have one bond left—a bond we chose, to each other—and we could choose to break it," said Maeve, apprehending the possibilities quickly.

Charl was considering the best way to phrase his hopes, so that Vilna would hear him and not reject the idea outright. "It's possible that fading would lose its appeal if you were somewhere else, someplace you've chosen. Or—if you were to break your bond to each other—it's possible you might find your way to the Blue Land at last."

"But some of us have already faded," said Vilna darkly. "What about them? It's too late for them to choose."

"I'm not sure it is," said Charl, and then he told her how

Ognielle had transported him to St. Muckle's, and how Iphi had helped him understand draconic speech. "They're not gone. Some part of themselves remains."

Vilna's mouth pursed, flattened, frowned, then pursed again, like she was chewing a piece of gristle extremely slowly. "But where would you take us?"

"Wherever you'd like to go," said Charl. "There's a whole world out there."

Vilna finally looked at Maeve, and Maeve looked at Vilna, and an understanding seemed to pass between them. Vilna gave a curt nod, and that was that. It was decided.

Grinning mischievously, Maeve stepped up to the apple first. She leaned over to touch it, and a bright swirl of light seemed to suck her into it. Anya and Zedig went next, holding hands and giggling nervously; they disappeared in one bright flash. Vilna turned away and, for a moment, seemed to have a change of heart. But, no, she was just holding her hand out to Ognielle, who flitted over and perched on her fingers. Vilna stroked her translucent feathers, making soothing noises, and then set her ever so gently upon the apple. Iphi was a little less cooperative, frolicking around and refusing to be herded, but her squirrel nature eventually got the better of her. She approached the apple curiously and disappeared.

Vilna, Charl realized, was doing what she always did—taking care of everyone. She was like him that way.

"Where is Princess Luti?" she said fretfully.

"I'll find her," said Charl.

Vilna took one last look at Charl, her dark eyes brimming. "I know this was *his* idea," she said at last. "But I trust you. This apple has seven seeds—is that why you chose it? Each one might be a new tree, a new home, a new chance, if you help us find the right places to grow. And you're right, it is better to choose. Maeve never wanted to be here. You should have heard her scream when they tied her down. We can do this much for her. I may still choose to fade, eventually, in my own place, on my own terms, without having to wait for the others."

Charl nodded solemnly. Vilna smiled, the weary smile of someone who's seen five hundred years already, and then she joined her sisters in the apple.

Charl glanced around the orchard and spied the sharp face of a mink, staring from the tall weeds, with bright, beady eyes.

"Princess Luti," said Charl, giving courtesy.

The mink bobbed its head in acknowledgment but came no closer.

"You *did* choose this, didn't you?" said Charl. "Your selfless sacrifice brought a hundred years of peace, I'm told. You have done your duty, but now your sisters need you. They can't leave without you. If you stay here, they'll be pulled back again. I hope you can find it in your magnanimous, generous heart to do them this kindness, and come with them."

The mink cocked its head, considering his words. Charl had no idea how much it had understood. Slowly, the little transparent creature climbed onto the flat stone. Charl stood back, giving it space. Inching along, it approached the apple obliquely, until suddenly a ghostly hand shot out of the apple, grabbed the mink around the middle, and pulled it inside.

Maeve's hand. Charl recognized it.

He wondered what it was like for the ghosts inside the apple, if they were aware of each other, and if they were still squabbling among themselves like the sisters they had become.

In any case, they were all aboard. Charl picked up the apple and stuck it in his pocket.

Charl went back behind the ruined sanctuary and found Dr. Caramus's crates easily enough, underneath some hastily strewn branches, surrounded by a few jugs of pyria. They weren't even that well hidden, but the sanctuary had always looked so alluringly perfect to him that it had been more tempting to go inside than to walk behind it.

He could drag the crates well enough, but he wouldn't get them down the mountain very quickly like that, and anyway, he should probably take the food supplies with him. Who knew what he was going to find in St. Muckle's? Charl took a minute to look for Yustinus's sword, but Brus must have had it with him when he disappeared. It had gone wherever he'd gone. There was an old—very old—handcart in the cider-press room, and it squeaked like the devil, but it rolled well enough. Charl loaded it up as best he could and pulled it toward the front gates.

His last stop was the well. He had less of a plan here, certainly no instructions in his head from Bishop Marcellus. But he couldn't leave without speaking to Wort one last time.

Wort was waiting for him, in fact, his hands folded under his chin on top of the well's low wall. "You're taking all my prospective girlfriends away," he said, cracking a wink, which Charl hoped meant he was kidding. "It's going to be lonely without them."

"You don't have to stay," said Charl, kneeling so they were more at a level. "Nothing is holding you here."

"Except my wish to not be dead!" cried Wort. "That's not nothing. But, listen, there's something you must do for me."

"All right," said Charl, "if it will bring you peace."

"Take a cup of my water with you," said Wort. "I will ride in it, like the girls are riding in that apple. I just want to see the dear old St. Muckle's once again. In the middle of the turnip fields, you can fling my water high in the air, and I'll fly away then."

"All right," said Charl slowly, trying to figure out how to carry a cup of water and pull the handcart. If he set it in the cart, it was going to slosh and splash all over everything.

"You must balance the cup on your head, the whole way down," said Wort earnestly.

Charl shot him an alarmed look, and Wort burst out laughing.

"Ah, never could keep a straight face," said the ghost. "You should have seen your expression, though."

"So you *don't* want me to—"

Wort waved him off. "Nah. Just . . . tell my mother I am well."

Charl almost laughed, but he realized in time that Wort wasn't trying to be funny. "I can do that," said Charl. As far as he knew, she was still alive. It was Hooey's mother who'd been so sick from drinking beetle eggs.

Wort looked sad then. "Thank you," he said. "That does give my heart some ease."

"Then are you ready?" asked Charl. "Can you move toward the Blue?"

Wort shrugged. "Stop fretting about that. I'll do it when I decide to do it. It's not up to you to make sure I go."

"But—"

"But nothing. It's the last choice I have. Let me have it."

Charl stood up and bowed cordially to the ghost. Wort, grinning again, bowed back, and then he was gone.

"That was well done," said a voice behind him, and Charl turned to see Mother Trude under the trees, scrabbling around in the dirt. She hadn't run off to Agnes, like he'd figured she would. Beside her was a small pile of bones. She was brushing soil off the top of a human skull.

"You're still here?" he asked, walking toward her.

"Where's Jarlbrus?" asked Mother Trude, craning her neck.

"Gone," said Charl. He wasn't sure how else to explain.

Her brows knit. "I won't ask whether he got what he deserved. That might tempt Fate to consider what *I* deserve, and how and when I am going to get it." She sat back on her haunches, the skull in her hand, and contemplated its empty eyes.

"Why are you digging up Eldegarde's bones?" said Charl.

"Was that her name?"

Charl tried to recall whether Mother Trude would have seen Miga dig up that femur or would have overheard their conversation about Eldegarde. But no—Mother Trude hadn't come out until later, when she'd thrown the turnip at Jarlbrus. How had she known these bones were here?

There was more to Mother Trude than she had ever let on. More, even, than she'd put in that letter to Agnes.

"Have you been seeing ghosts this whole time, all the while pretending you didn't?" said Charl quietly.

Mother Trude looked at him sidelong. "No, indeed. But the first night here, before I fell ill, I got a sleep cramp in my leg after climbing the mountain, and I was walking it off. I came out here and . . . I didn't see her. I can't usually see them anymore; it's been too long, and I did not keep in practice. But you never forget the feeling they give you when they are near. I felt her wandering restlessly, and I knew she had been murdered here."

"You were a Wise Child," said Charl. Just like Bishop Marcellus had claimed.

Mother Trude smiled bitterly. "I was indeed. The sort who'd spent a night under the standing stones, learning draconic speech so she could save her village, if need be. The sort who seemed to have been born old, into trying times. That story you told about Magla, the King of the Wolves? The pagan story I didn't let you finish telling? That might have been my story, in earlier days, insofar as I was the Wise Child destined to save my village."

Charl's eyes widened. "When I first met you, I thought you were the . . . the *nunliest* old nun I'd ever met."

"People don't always look like what they really are," said Mother Trude. "A Wise Child once told me that."

Charl fidgeted, torn between feeling flattered and feeling unsure whether *Wise Child* was really a compliment. "Someone else called me that, too. The ghost of Bishop Marcellus."

"The great evil in the sanctuary? I felt that, too," said Mother Trude. "You *have* been having adventures without me." She studied Charl's face a minute; she was still a devious nun, whatever her pagan past, and she could read him like a book. "You're wondering how a Wise Child like me ended up . . . like *me*."

"Or like Bishop Marcellus," said Charl miserably.

"Well, my corna used to say 'When courage curdles, wisdom

fails,'" said Mother Trude. "Or maybe I began believing that the *wise* must also be *good* and *right*, by definition. Alas, that's not how it works. One may be wise and wrong, just as one may be foolish and good. So don't put too much stock in your own wisdom, Charl. That is the wisest course to take."

She was speaking in riddles. "You're saying I should ignore what you both called me."

"I am, and you should. Anyway," she said, returning to her digging, "I am looking for this poor woman's bones, to return them to town for a proper burial. I know that doesn't seem like much, but I have penance to do for my betrayals, and it seemed like one good thing I could start with."

"I know her family name," said Charl. "We could put her with her people."

Mother Trude nodded. "Even better."

He helped her dig, pulling up clumps of weeds and scraping in the earth with a sharp chunk of rock. Whether he was wise in the sense she meant, and whether he should think of himself as such, the fact remained that things were going to be different when he got home. A lot of people—friends and neighbors—had died of the blood fever. Did any of them linger, like Wort? Would he be able to see them, and give them the choice to move on?

The apple in his pocket bumped against his leg as he worked. Of course he'd help the girls find a new home, too, separately or together. Maeve, in particular, might not want to put down roots right away. He smiled to himself, thinking of people, places, and things he could show her.

Thinking of home.

When they'd retrieved as many bones as they could (some having decayed, some having become irretrievably tangled in the birch roots, and one having been taken by a dragon), they wrapped them in an empty burlap oat sack and tied it with twine. Charl placed the bundle gently in the handcart.

Mother Trude balked at this. "I should carry my own bones. And I can wait until you're out of sight before setting off for town myself."

"Why?" asked Charl.

She stared at the ground, her cheeks hot with shame. "I just . . . I want to reassure you that I'm not going to try to take you to your father. You have no reason to trust me, I realize, so—"

"This cart is heavy, and the road is long, and we're going the same direction. I would appreciate the company," said Charl. "And this is yours and still needs to be delivered, I believe," he added, taking the folded letter from his pocket and returning it to Mother Trude's hands.

She turned it over and over, her mouth working as if she were trying not to weep. "She won't want to talk to me, Charl. She hates me."

Charl thought a minute.

"Hate is too simple for Sister Agnes," he said at last. "More likely she's dissecting everything she knows about you and examining it from every angle. She'll have theories—she always does—but they'll be incomplete. She needs more information. Give her that, at least, and let her choose. All you really wanted, coming here, was a chance to tell her the truth at last."

He understood that kind of wanting, how it might seem worth lying and betraying for.

There were people he might have done that for. It wouldn't be long until he saw them again.

Mother Trude, at a loss for words, just nodded.

"Well, then, come on," said Charl, hefting the handles of the cart. And they set off down the mountain, toward the people they called home.

Acknowledgments

The last few years left me feeling haunted. This book was an exorcism of sorts.

Thanks to my ~~ghostly~~ writing companions: Arushi Raina and Lindy Yang; Jen Larsen; Tom Goldstein; Terri Anderson, Katie Czenczek, and Micah Killjoy; and to the ~~spectral~~ students of my last, greatest class, Grammy's YA Attic—you know who you are.

~~Undead~~ Undying gratitude to the friends who wouldn't let me give up: Rebecca Sherman; Fran Wilde; Karen New; and my whole family, particularly Marvis.

Thanks to my agent, Dan Lazar, for finding the right ~~tomb~~ hands to place this in; to my ~~spooky~~ editorial team, Mallory Loehr, Emily Shapiro, and Lynne Missen; to all the folks at Penguin Random House, who always do a ~~scary~~ wonderful job; and to Eliot Baum for the gorgeous cover.

Thanks to John Wyatt Greenlee, Surprised Eel Historian, for the eel consult; to Casey and A.J. and everyone else we lost; and to VOLA, Devin Townsend, and Leprous for the ~~mortifying~~ inspiring soundtrack.

Finally, thanks and all my love to Scott, who held my hand through the most terrifying time of our life; thanks to all the good people at BCCH, CAPE Unit (a curiously monastic place), there when we needed them; thanks to Dr. N. S., to whom we surely owe a fruit basket; and thank you forever to B, who's still here.

Every day is a gift, friends. May we never lose sight of that.